ELFSORROW

ELFSORROW

LEGENDS OF THE RAVEN 1

JAMES BARCLAY

an imprint of **Prometheus Books**
Amherst, NY

Published 2010 by Pyr®, an imprint of Prometheus Books

Inquiries should be addressed to
Pyr
59 John Glenn Drive
Amherst, New York 14228–2119
VOICE: 716–691–0133
FAX: 716–691–0137
WWW.PYRSF.COM

14 13 12 11 10   5 4 3 2 1

Library of Congress Cataloging-in-Publication Data

Barclay, James, 1965–
    Elfsorrow / by James Barclay.
        p. cm. — (Legends of the raven ; 1)
    First published: London : Gollancz, 2002.
    ISBN 978–1–61614–248–3 (pbk.)
    I. Title.

PR6102.A76E44 2010
823'.92—dc22

2010029660

Printed in the United States of America on acid-free paper

For Michael, Nancy, and Virginia.
Finer siblings a brother could not wish to have.

BALAIA

NORTH BAY

Sunara's Teeth

TERENETSA

SetheRiver

TornWastes

PARVE

WESMEN
HEARTLANDS
(Uncharted)

Baravale Valley

Arch-Temple
of the
Wrethsires

EveLake

•LEIONU

SkyLake

N

W   E

Garan
Mountains

Southern Force

S

SOUTHERN OCEANS

The NORTHERN CONTINENT

Trivene Inlet
R. Tri
Trivene Mountains
JADEN
RACHE
BloodLake
JULATSA
DORDOVER
HAVERN
CORIN
Triverne Lake
Black Wings' Castle
LYSTERN
XETESK
Understone Pass
UNDERSTONE
Pontois Plains
PONTOIS
DENEBRE
Septern Manse
ERSKAN
HYLD
BLACKTHORNE
Yarhawk Crags
Grethern Forest
Tarnspike Castle
KORINA
Thornewood
GRESSE
The Butts
GREYTHORNE
Balan Mts.
ARLEN
ORYTTE
BLACKTHORNE
Bay of Gyernath
GYERNATH
Arlen Bay

Cast List

THE RAVEN

Hirad Coldheart   BARBARIAN WARRIOR
The Unknown Warrior   WARRIOR
Thraun   SHAPECHANGER
Ry Darrick   CAVALRY SWORDSMAN
Denser   XETESKIAN MAGE
Erienne   DORDOVAN MAGE
Ilkar   JULATSAN MAGE

THE COLLEGES

Dystran   LORD OF THE MOUNT, XETESK
Ranyl   CIRCLE SEVEN MASTER MAGE, XETESK
Aeb   A PROTECTOR
Vuldaroq   TOWER LORD, DORDOVER
Heryst   LORD ELDER MAGE, LYSTERN
Kayvel   MAGE MASTER, LYSTERN
Rusau   NEGOTIATOR, LYSTERN
Izack   GENERAL, LYSTERNAN CAVALRY

THE ELVES

Myriell   AL-DRECHAR
Cleress   AL-DRECHAR
Ren'erei   GUILD OF DRECH
Rebraal   LEADER OF THE AL-ARYNAAR
Mercuun   AL-ARYNAAR
Auum   LEADER OF THE TAIGETHEN
The ClawBound
Jevin   CAPTAIN OF THE *CALAIAN SUN*
Kayloor   A GUIDE
Kild'aar   VILLAGE ELDER

Note: The apostrophe in female elven names is an abbreviation. Traditionally, elven females took the name of their family or village as part of their name. Hence Ren'erei would be Ren-al-erei, with the "al" meaning "of the."

BARONS, SOLDIERS, AND BALAIANS	*Blackthorne* A BARON
	Gresse A BARON
	Erksan A LORD
	Selik CAPTAIN OF THE BLACK WINGS
	Devun SELIK'S DEPUTY
	Yron A CAPTAIN
	Ben-Foran A LIEUTENANT
	Erys A MAGE
	Stenys A MAGE
	Avesh A REFUGEE
	Ellin A REFUGEE
	Diera WIFE OF THE UNKNOWN WARRIOR
THE KAAN	*Sha-Kaan* GREAT KAAN
	Nos-Kaan

CHAPTER 1

The Unknown Warrior reined in on the crest of a rise overlooking the once tranquil lakeside port of Arlen. In the gathering gloom and encroaching mist, battle raged through its streets. Buildings were burning across the town, a heavy pall of smoke thickening the mist. The thud and crack of spells echoed against the mountains to the north, blue-edged for Xetesk, stark orange for Dordover. The shouts of men and the clash of weapons, muted by the mist, reached his ears.

In the last two seasons, he had seen and heard plenty of evidence of deteriorating relations between the two colleges but this was infinitely worse. This was war. He'd hoped to get them out before it started. Even thought his plan could bring peace. But here was proof of that folly.

"And you expect us to ride through all that to the dockside?" Diera was right beside him, her horse nuzzling at his.

He looked over to her and down to Jonas, his baby son, cradled in one huge arm. "I want to know you're both safe. And away from Balaia's the only way."

"Tomas didn't think so," said Diera, wisps of her light hair blowing outside the hood of her cloak.

"Tomas is more stubborn than any man I know," said The Unknown, smiling. How hard he had tried to get Tomas to bring his family too, to leave the Rookery, which they owned together. An inn now ruined by a hurricane. "Except one. He's never left Korina and he's blinded himself to the disease, the rats and the starvation. He thinks it'll get better now spring is here. I don't. I've seen Balaia. And it'll get worse not better. I won't leave you here. I can't."

Diera shivered, and as if sensing her unease from where he lay in the safety of his father's arm, Jonas started to whimper.

"Shh, shh," he said gently, rocking the child. "It's all right."

"It isn't all right," said Diera. "Just look down there. They're killing each other and you want us to ride through it."

"And this is just the start, believe me." He looked deep into her eyes. "Please, Diera. War is here. Nowhere on Balaia will be safe."

She nodded. "How do we get to the docks?"

"On one horse we can ride where ten or more could not but I need you close. Sit in front of me and hold Jonas. I'll keep you from falling. Try not to be afraid."

"Don't ask that," she said. "I'm terrified. You're used to the noise and blood."

"I won't let anyone hurt you."

"Better not." Her expression softened slightly.

"Just remember to do what I ask. It'll be difficult down there and there's no time for debate. You must trust me."

"Always."

She dismounted and he helped her up in front of him before handing her their baby son. He kicked his big stallion to a gentle trot down the slope toward Arlen.

Riding in from the northeast along a narrow, barely used trail, The Unknown could see the fires of a camp some miles off to the east and a Dordovan column under torchlight heading down the main track into the heart of the port. Xetesk had been in tacit control of Arlen when he put into port two seasons ago and he had no reason to believe anything had changed barring the fact that Dordover was now on open offensive.

Closer to, the sounds of buildings aflame and collapsing, of spells crashing into structure and soldier and the roar of close-quarter fighting were deafening. Jonas was crying and Diera was rigid in the saddle.

"We'll be all right," said The Unknown.

"Just get us there, Sol," she said, trying to comfort their bawling son.

Entering the town on a dark and shadowed street with the din a terrifying press on their ears, The Unknown snapped the reins.

"Hang on," he said. "It gets tricky from here."

He heeled his horse's flanks and the nervous animal sprang forward. In his ears the clash of metal and the shouts of warriors mixed uncomfortably with the wails from his boy. He fought to keep the horse in the middle of the street, galloping headlong for the docks. He aimed to ride down the eastern edge of the town past the Park of the Martyrs and through the Salt Quarter to emerge at the end of the docks where Captain Jevin had the *Calaian Sun* at berth.

But already he could see it would be difficult if not impossible to avoid the conflict around them. To their right, multiple FlameOrbs burned away the mist, their arcs of flight carrying them down to splatter into buildings and onto streets. The flat crack and orange flare of a ManaShield collapsing was succeeded immediately by the screams of those caught abruptly defenceless. Smoke billowed as mana fire gorged on wood and flesh, pouring out of a side street and billowing over rooftops, hemming them in still further.

Ahead of them, shapes ran, disordered and panicked; townsfolk trying to flee college blade and spell. There were dozens of them led by an uncertain trio of town militia. They were looking behind them more than ahead and all were weighed down by possessions or tiny human cargo. The Unknown cursed, the horse skittish beneath them and slowing automatically.

"Sit tight."

The townspeople ran on, all but one heedless of the lone horse as they raced out of town, fear stalking every face below streaks of mud and soot.

"Turn around, the way is blocked!" yelled one of the militia as he closed.

"The docks," shouted The Unknown. "Best way!"

"No way," came the reply. "That's what the bastards are fighting over. Run, it's your only chance." And then he was gone.

The Unknown pushed on, Jonas squealing and coughing in turn as the smoke thickened nearer the centre of the fighting. Diera's face was white and strained.

"Not far now."

More stragglers came by them as they rode quickly down the street, the park behind them. Ahead, the low warehousing and packed tenements of the Salt Quarter, once heavy with cargo and seafarers, now blazing in countless places and full of war. From the right, men ran in close form across their path, ignoring them. Dead ahead, fire blew up the side of a warehouse. Timbers creaked and collapsed. There was a roar and the renewed clash of weapons. They were on the fighting now.

The Unknown swung the horse left, down a narrow muddied lane between two lowering warehouses. Slightly muted for a moment, the tumult of the fighting was brought suddenly and horribly close. Cantering past a crosspath, The Unknown glanced right. The passage was full of men, blades catching the glare of the fires around them as they charged away toward an unseen enemy.

A heartbeat later, FlameOrbs surged from the gloom and smoke and into the front of the packed line. Fire scorched up walls, tore timbers from roofs, and the impact snatched soldiers from their feet and flung them backward, human firebrands shrieking as they died.

It was too much for The Unknown's horse. Already scared, the stallion jolted sideways and reared high. Caught by the double move, and already compensating to catch the slipping Diera, The Unknown lost his brief fight for balance. But as he fell left and back, he enclosed his wife and son in his embrace and took the weight of the fall for all of them, rolling across his shoulders.

He grunted, wind knocked from his lungs, pain stabbing through his upper back. The horse bolted back the way they had come. The Unknown carried on rolling, his broad back protecting his family from the wood and dirt firing from the passage. He dragged himself to his feet, bringing Diera with him, swinging her trembling body to face him and seeing Jonas too scared even to cry.

"Are you hurt?" he gasped, forcing air into his lungs, a sheet of pain washing across his rib cage.

Diera shook her head. "What will we do now?" she asked, pressing Jonas's head into her chest.

"Don't worry," he said. "I'll protect you." He stepped back and drew sword and dagger. "Do everything I say without question."

Diera flinched. His tone was hard, his eyes cold. He knew it worried her but there was no other way if they were to live. He assessed their position. Going on was their only option. Already, survivors were stumbling toward them from the crosspath, bloodied and angry.

"Back away," said The Unknown, pushing her gently in the right direction. "Don't run."

They'd been seen. Four men with swords ready. Brief guilt surged through The Unknown at the position he'd placed his family in. Others might have been ignored as Arlen townsfolk, but the shaven head, bull neck and sheer size of The Unknown Warrior made him instantly recognisable. And every Dordovan knew with whom he had fought on Herendeneth. Xetesk.

"Running to join your soul brothers?" sneered one. He was burned across his head but otherwise unhurt. "Just that little bit too far away, aren't they?"

"I'm just taking my family from here," said The Unknown. "I've no fight with you."

"You're Xeteskian."

"I'm Raven."

"But they aren't here."

"Keep clear, Diera," said The Unknown.

"Why?"

"And don't let Jonas see."

The Unknown tapped his blade once on the ground and ran at the Dordovans. They hesitated fractionally as he knew they would. It was their undoing. His blade sliced clean into the stomach of the first soldier but was blocked by the second. He fielded a wild swing from the third on the broad hilt of his dagger even as he dropped to his haunches, left leg sweeping out to knock the poorly balanced swordsman's legs from under him.

Bouncing up on his right leg, he stabbed straight forward into the neck of the second, his speed making a nonsense of the man's defence. Again he was moving as he struck. Left this time, dagger fending off a smart stab to his midriff from the fourth. He turned the strike aside, reversed his dagger and buried it in the soldier's eye.

Not stopping, he left the blade where it jutted from the dead man's skull, gripped his longsword in two hands, spun and chopped down through the shoulder of the last survivor as he tried to get up and defend at the same time, succeeding in neither.

The Unknown knelt to clean his gore-spattered blade on their clothes. He heard shouting close at hand. More Dordovans had witnessed his devastating attack. They were coming left and right, twenty yards distant. An arrow sang past him.

"Dammit."

He turned as he straightened, sheathing his blades. Diera was staring at him, her face white and eyes wide. She pointed behind him at the quartet of corpses.

"You—" she began.

"Not pretty, is it?" He grabbed her arm and swung her round, starting to run. "We've got to go. Now."

"They're dead. You killed them all."

"It's what I do. You know that. Now come on."

Almost lifting her from her feet, The Unknown set off down the narrow passageway. The fighting was concentrated to their right around the centre of the dockside, on the other side of the warehouse that loomed dark grey above them. He guessed they had two hundred yards to make it into the heart of the Salt Quarter. It would probably be no safer but they might find friendly blades.

The shouts of pursuit spilled into the passage behind them. A thud by his head and a skipping off a stone at his feet told him the bowmen had almost got their range. He pushed Diera in front of him, still trying to support her terrified stumbling run, Jonas whimpering again under her cloak.

"Keep running if I fall."

Another shaft whistled past his head, burying itself in the wall just beyond. Diera yelped. Ten yards ahead, a turning.

"Go left."

He saw her nod. Arrows clattered into the walls behind, another flew overhead. He ducked reflexively, arms coming up to protect Diera. They swung left. The Unknown sensed fighting very close. The passageway ended at a blank wall and went left and right.

"Right, go right," he said, pushing Diera ever faster. She half stumbled.

"Please," she said. "Jonas."

"Move!" he snapped. "Don't stop."

She started and ran on, taking the right turn.

Twenty yards and it opened out on to war. The street beyond was ablaze. Men ran everywhere, orders were barked over the deafening roar of battle. Spells fell at random, fire and lightning gouging rents in the ground and destroying unshielded soldiers. Corpses and the screaming wounded littered the ground.

"Ten yards and stop!" shouted The Unknown. "Take the doorway. Crouch small."

Not waiting to see her do it, he swung to face the opening, dragging out his sword, its point tapping rhythmically in the mud. Their pursuers were only moments away, their breath and words betraying them. First was a bowman, tearing blindly round the corner, an arrow nocked in his bow. The Unknown shifted his weight forward and drove his sword up between the archer's legs and out through his rib cage, the power of the blow launching him backward, dead before he hit the ground.

A couple of paces behind came a pair of swordsmen, one slightly in advance, both more wary than their erstwhile companion. The Unknown batted aside the first blade and straight punched the soldier in the face, feeling his nose break and sending him tumbling back. The second, quick and accurate, whipped a deep cut into The Unknown's left arm.

He swore at the sudden pain and brought his sword back one-handed low across his body, biting into his attacker's thigh. The man cried out and half fell forward. The Unknown took his chance, lashing out with a foot and catching the soldier on the point of his jaw. His head snapped back with a wet crack. He crumpled.

The Unknown advanced on the other swordsman, who looked at him through bloodied hands, turned and ran away, shouting for help. It would have to be enough. The Raven warrior hurried to Diera.

"Come on."

"Your arm." She reached out.

"It's fine," he said, glancing at the blood slicking over his hand.

"It's not."

"No time for bandages. We've got to go. Now." He leaned in and kissed her. "Stay close to me and you'll live."

"We're going out there?"

"It's the only way."

The Unknown knew what he had to do. Sword in right hand, Diera's trembling hand in his left, he moved quickly to the opening onto the main street, keeping as far into the shadows as he could.

Out on the street it was mayhem. To the left, Xetesk was defending the entrance to a small square but the line was fragmented. Dordovan forces were pouring down the street from the north, their mages bombarding the rear of the line with FlameOrbs and HotRain, filling the sky with orange radiance. Soldiers threw themselves on the wavering Xeteskians, pounding them, threatening to drive them back and turn their flanks. It had to be one of half a dozen key conflicts in the town but the defence he wanted wasn't there.

"Where are they?"

"Who?"

"You know," said The Unknown. A ForceCone tore out from the Xeteskian line, scattering unshielded Dordovans. There was an opening. "Let's go."

Diera's scream was lost in the storm of noise that assaulted them out in the street. The Unknown lashed to his right, a soldier fell clutching at his entrails. The big warrior hauled his wife and child behind him, running full tilt at the back of the Dordovan assault.

He ignored the voices raised against him as he passed, praying for the confusion of the fight to hide him for just long enough. He glanced down at Diera, so small and fragile, and fear grabbed his heart. That he might not get her through. That she and Jonas might fall under the swords of men who attacked them because of him and him alone. At the same moment, she glanced up, and through her terror, he saw determination. She clutched Jonas tighter under her cloak. The Unknown nodded.

Never letting her go but keeping her just behind him as he dodged through the chaos he hoped would shield them, he pushed men aside, sword hilt connecting roughly with shoulder, face and back.

"Move! Move!"

And they reacted like all conscripts to a voice of authority. For a few priceless heartbeats, a path opened to the fighting line but he knew it couldn't last. One of them turned and recognised him.

"What—?"

The Unknown's sword took out his throat. He tightened his grip on Diera's hand and surged on, soldiers on all sides alerted to the enemy in their midst. He drove his blade through the back of a man too slow to react and kicked him aside, swayed left to dodge a blow from his flank and clashed swords with a third who turned from the fight.

"Open the line!" he roared at the Xeteskians. "Open the line!"

But there were still Dordovans in the way. Just yards from relative safety and he was going to be trapped. He swung Diera round and backed toward the left-hand side of the street.

"Shout if anyone comes behind," he said.

FlameOrbs dropped into the centre of the street, flaring off SpellShields, the fire routed harmlessly into the ground. In the flash of light, The Unknown saw eight or ten Dordovans moving toward him, all wary of his reputation unlike the others before them, but all confident in their advance.

"Sol . . ."

"It'll be all right," said The Unknown.

But it wouldn't. He looked frantically at the line of Xeteskian warriors backed by archers and mages and hemmed in by the Dordovan aggressors.

"Push your right, damn you!" he shouted, not even sure now if they'd seen him at all.

A sword thrust came in. He blocked it easily. He squared up to the overwhelming numbers, letting go of Diera at last and gripping his sword two-handed. He weaved it slowly in front of him, fencing away the first feints. He identified first and second targets and wondered how many he could take with him.

"Take a dagger from my belt. When I fall, run. Hug the wall and try to get through. Find a Protector."

"I won't leave you."

"You'll do as I say. I got you into this and I'm getting you out."

He lunged forward, striking left to right, blade weight beating aside a weak defence and nicking through leather. The target fell back; The Unknown did likewise. The rest closed, scant feet from him now but unwilling to attack. They were a disparate group, not under command. Maybe. Just maybe.

Consternation rippled through the Dordovan line to his left. ForceCones flew out from the Xeteskian mages, scattering Dordovans behind the front. Two of his attackers fell. A heavy detonation sounded. The building next to him shook and tottered under an EarthHammer. More ForceCones. Very close. The edge of one caught him a glancing blow and he sprawled. Diera screamed.

The Unknown rolled onto his back. Dordovans ran at him, three at least fast on their feet.

We are come.

Panic spread in the Dordovan line. The trio running at The Unknown faltered then came on again. Halfway to his feet, The Unknown sheared aside a thrust to his chest and jumped back. A second came in but it didn't get close to its target, stopped by the flat blade of a massive axe.

Protectors sprinted in front of him. He drove to his feet as Diera yelped in surprise. He turned to see her lifted from the ground by one of the Xeteskian elite taking her to safety. He heard a voice by his ear.

"You go too."

He looked round into the blank mask of a Protector and nodded.

"Thank you."

"Go."

A backward glance told him the Protectors were holding the gap. The Unknown nodded again and ran after his wife down to the dockside where the *Calaian Sun* bobbed against the wharf.

With his wife and son safely below deck in their cabin, he came back to the wheel deck to shake hands with Jevin, the ship's captain, but could see instantly that all was not right. There were Protectors and Xeteskian mages everywhere on board and the ship was already under way.

"Thank you for waiting."

"It's what you pay me for," said Jevin curtly.

"What's all this about?" asked The Unknown. "I agreed half a dozen research mages. There must be twenty here."

"Thirty," corrected Jevin. "And a hundred Protectors."

"What?"

"Ask him." Jevin gestured at a tall young mage striding toward the wheel-deck ladder. "I've got a ship to sail."

The Unknown watched the mage quickly scale the ladder and smile as he approached.

"The Unknown Warrior," he said, extending a hand. "I'm glad you got through."

"Sytkan," said The Unknown, ignoring the hand. "Are you going to tell me what this small army is doing on board Jevin's ship?"

Sytkan at least had the good grace to look embarrassed. "It was felt at the highest level that Herendeneth should be secured from Dordovan invasion."

The Unknown cleared his throat and looked back to the dockside. It was ringed with fire but secured. Spell after spell crashed into the shields all around it and, high in the sky, he could just pick out the silhouettes of Xeteskian demon Familiars, watching the perimeter. He shuddered, imagining their maniacal laughs all too easily.

"This was to be a peaceful mission," he said. "You're sharing your findings with the other colleges. Or supposed to be."

Sytkan waved a hand at the ruins of Arlen. "Things change," he said. "The Dordovans wanted something we were not prepared to give."

"Which was?"

"Their mages in the research party."

"And this is the result?" The Unknown shook his head. "Gods burning, was it really worth going to war over?"

"If not this then something else." Sytkan shrugged.

The Unknown slapped the railing. "But this was supposed to help broker peace! What the hell went wrong?"

Sytkan didn't answer.

"Dystran and Vuldaroq," said The Unknown, answering for him. "You don't need this, you know—the colleges, that is. There's already unrest." He gestured back at Arlen. "This sort of thing will be the death of magic, ultimately."

Sytkan snorted. "I hardly think so."

The Unknown rounded on him and pushed his face in very close. "Don't underestimate Selik and the Black Wings. Now, if you'll excuse me, I have a family to attend to and a cut to stitch."

He nodded at Jevin as he descended the ladder, pain shooting through his left hip and lower back. Now the adrenaline was gone, the liberties he'd taken with his old wound were taking their toll. Before going below, he scanned the deck once more, seeing too many Xeteskians on it.

Ilkar wasn't going to like this. He wasn't going to like this at all.

Chapter 2

Two hours before dawn and the mood of the rain forest changed. Imperceptible to all but those whose lives were inextricably linked to the canopy but there just the same. Rebraal became utterly still, all but invisible against his background.

Behind him, the green-gold dome of Aryndeneth rose two hundred feet into the air, its apex on a level with the highest boughs of the canopy. The temple had stood for over five thousand years, its stone partially hidden beneath a tapestry of thick mosses, ivies and liana. It was periodically cleared but the voracious forest growth didn't lose its grip for long.

But whether cleared or not, the temple was barely visible more than fifty yards away.

It hadn't always been like this. In the centuries after its building, Aryndeneth had been a place of pilgrimage, revered by the elves as the centre of their faith. The Earth Home. A grand stone apron with a carved path between the massive slabs had greeted travellers, and the rain forest trail had been carefully cleared and maintained for a hundred miles north.

Now the trail was long gone, and though a portion of the apron and its path was still visible beneath the weeds and creepers the rain forest's march was relentless, and Rebraal and his people fought a constant battle against it.

Rebraal looked to his right across the great iron-bound wooden doors of the temple. Mercuun had sensed it too. His eyes were scanning the dark, his ears pricked gauging the forest mood. Further out, on the tree platforms, Skiriin, Rourke and Flynd'aar had bows ready. It was all the confirmation Rebraal needed.

He cocked an ear and listened hard, trying to gain a sense of the potential threat. The noise of the forest surrounded him, the heat stifling even in the hours before dawn. A dozen species of birds called mating or warning, monkeys screeched and greeted, their progress through the canopy marked by the rustle and crack of branches. Myriad insects buzzed, vibrated and rasped and the growl of a wildcat punctuated the predawn cacophony.

In every way but one, it was as every other night Rebraal could remember. This night though, the accent of the warnings was different. There was a change in the atmosphere and every creature in the forest felt it. Strangers. Close and dead ahead.

The clicking of a brown tree frog filtered down from one of the platforms. Rebraal looked up. Rourke signalled eight strangers approaching in single file; warriors and mages hacking a path to Aryndeneth. They were not pilgrims. No pilgrims were due until after the rainy season and that was fifty days away. Rebraal nodded, put fingers to his eyes and drew another across his throat. Whoever they were, they could not be allowed to escape with word of the location.

He snapped his fingers twice and heard Erin'heth and Sheth'erei move up on his left. SpellShields were deployed and he went forward, sensing Mercuun matching his pace. The two warriors made no sound, the mages behind them moving only to keep them within the shields. Glancing at the platforms suspended thirty feet into the trees bordering the apron, Rebraal saw the trio of archers tracking targets. From the angle of the bows, they were close, perhaps fifty yards away, no more. He stopped, hand up.

The blundering of the strangers was easily audible now and the forest around them was quietening. He waved behind him with his left arm, pointing up to send Erin'heth ahead to shield the platform. He drew his slender, quick blade, holding it in his right hand. With his left, he reached across and unclasped the pouch of jaqrui throwing crescents on his belt.

Now he paced forward again, acute eyes narrowing, seeing movement in the darkness ahead. The strangers were carrying no light but that wouldn't hide them. He could hear the regular hack of blades on vegetation, the cracking of twigs underfoot and the odd snatch of speech. No doubt they had been told that noise would deter predators in the rain forest. And so it was but with one particularly deadly exception.

The strangers would never set eyes on the temple. Rebraal called the peculiar wail of the tawny buzzard and began to run, footsteps ghosting over the edge of the apron and on into the forest.

Arrows whipped away from the platforms. Strangled cries came from the strangers and he heard the sound of bodies hitting the forest floor. Another volley thrummed into the dark. Orders and shouts snapped out and the surviving strangers scattered. Rebraal gripped a jaqrui and ducked low as he entered the thick growth, flicking it out backhand when he saw the face of a crouching warrior peering over a fallen log. Shaped like a miniature sickle with a two-fingered grip at one end, the razor-sharp double-edged crescent whispered as it flew, small enough to find gaps in the hanging vines.

The warrior might have heard it but he didn't see it coming, looking straight at its trajectory as it struck him in the forehead just above his eyebrows. He screamed and fell back. Rebraal tore on, flitting through gaps in the lush flora, circling the survivors with Mercuun appearing again in his vision to complete the pincer.

He could see a pair of mages, one crouched, one standing, staring blankly up into the canopy, searching for the platforms. One had prepared a spell, one had cast, his face creased in concentration. Presumably a HardShield to beat away more arrows.

Rebraal stormed in, the standing mage seeing him only when he was within five yards. He leapt the crouched mage and struck his companion with both feet in the chest, the man going down before he had a chance to cast. Rebraal landed astride him, stabbed down into his heart, turned and lashed his sword into the throat of the other, who had turned to stare at their assailant. Another arrow punched through the foliage and a man gurgled and fell close to Rebraal's right side. He heard the clash of steel, the thud of a sword on leather armour and a cry of pain, quickly cut off.

"That's all of them," came a voice from a platform.

"Keep watching, Rourke," acknowledged Rebraal. "Good shooting."

He checked for signs of life at his feet then moved away into the bush to retrieve his crescent. The warrior was still breathing but blood and brain oozed from the wound. Rebraal skewered his heart with his blade then placed a foot on the man's skull, leaning down to lever the crescent clear. He wiped it on his victim's shirt before returning it to the pouch, which he snapped shut.

He felt Mercuun at his shoulder.

"What shall we do with them?"

Rebraal looked into his friend's dark-skinned face, saw the brow above the angled oval eyes furrowed and his leaf-shaped, gently pointed ears pricking as he tried to come to terms with what had just happened.

"Get Skiriin and take them away from the path they made, over to the clearing north. Keep anything useful, shred their clothes and leave the bodies. The forest will take care of them."

"Rebraal?" There was an edge to Mercuun's voice.

"Yes, Meru?"

"Who were they and how did they know where to find us?"

Rebraal ran a hand through his long black hair. "Two very good questions," he said. "They're from Balaia certainly, but beyond that who can tell? I'm going to track back along their route in the morning, see if I can find anything. Meantime we have to keep vigilant."

"They won't be the last, will they?" said Mercuun.

"No," said Rebraal. "If I had my guess I'd say they were picking the path here. They were travelling too light for anything else. There will be more to come, and they might not be far away. We may not have much time."

Rebraal looked deep into Mercuun's face and saw the worry that he felt himself. It was bad enough that these men from the northern continent had managed to gain information no man should. But they had also evaded those that fed disinformation and the TaiGethen who killed those who persisted. It was an immense rain forest but the outer circle and town dwellers of his kind had kept the uninvited from Aryndeneth for more than four hundred years.

He clicked his tongue, a decision made. "Meru, I want you to get the word around. Start at sunrise. We can't wait for the relief. Every available Al-Arynaar must get here as quickly as they can. And the outer circles must press into the north. I want word as far north as Tolt-Anoor, west to Ysundeneth and east to Heri-Benaar. Take supplies for two days, start the message rolling and get back here."

Mercuun nodded.

Rebraal walked back toward the temple and took in its camouflaged majesty, a sight of which he would never tire. He knelt on the apron and offered a prayer to Yniss, the God of harmony, to protect them all. When he was done, he leant his hands on his thighs and listened again to the forest.

It at least was resting easy once again.

Hirad Coldheart shifted his back where he leant against Sha-Kaan's broad neck, feeling the scales chafing him through his wool shirt. He got a taste of the dragon's strong sour oil and wood smell as he did so and was glad they sat in the open air. The Great Kaan's enormous body, more than one hundred and twenty feet from snout to tail, was stretched out along a contour of the slope on which they rested, overlooking the tarnished idyll of Herendeneth.

The small island, no more than a mile and a half wide and two long, lay deep within the Ornouth Archipelago, which basked under the warm sun of the Southern Ocean off the northeastern tip of Calaius, the Southern Continent. It was a perfect mix of lush green slopes, waving beech groves and spectacular rock faces surrounding a shallow mountain peak on which stood a great stone needle, monument to the long dead of an ancient magic. But the perfection had been scarred forever by battle and the death of innocence.

Sha-Kaan had positioned his head so that he could see both Hirad and down the slopes to the groves, graveyard terraces and gardens. Beyond them were the ruins of the once proud house of the Al-Drechar, now devastated by a magic that had threatened the entire Balaian dimension. His left eye swivelled to fix the barbarian warrior with an unblinking stare.

"Are my scales an irritant to you?" he rumbled.

"Well they aren't the most ideal cushion," said Hirad.

"I'll have someone rub them smooth for you. Just point out those which require attention."

Hirad chuckled and turned to look into the Great Kaan's startling blue eye which was set into a head almost as tall as he was.

"Your sense of humour's coming on, I see," he said. "Still a long way to go, though."

Sha-Kaan's slitted black pupil narrowed. "One roll and I could snap your frail body like a twig."

Hirad felt the humour in his mind like tendrils of mist on the breeze. There was no doubt the dragon had mellowed during their enforced stay on Herendeneth. In times past, he might have made that comment with both sincerity and intent. Still, joke or not, it remained true.

"Just being honest," said Hirad.

"As am I."

They fell silent. It had been a long time coming, getting on for six years, but Hirad felt he could now describe Sha-Kaan as a friend. He had likened his relationship to the dragon to an apprenticeship. Ever since he'd agreed to become the Great Kaan's Dragonene, so giving the dragon a life-sustaining link to the Balaian dimension, he'd been the lesser partner in an unequal alliance. Although the benefits of direct contact and support from a dragon were obvious, throughout the time they'd known each other, the awesome creature, secure in his mastery and power, had felt he had nothing to prove to the human. Hirad had felt absolutely the reverse.

But the inequality had lessened during Sha-Kaan and his Brood brother Nos-Kaan's long exile in Balaia. Locked in a foreign dimension by a violent realignment of dimensional space and his home lost to his senses, Sha-Kaan had become aware of his mortality as his health slowly suffered. And Hirad believed that his unflinching loyalty to the Kaan dragons had proved that he was far more than a glorified servant but was a true friend. It seemed that at last Sha-Kaan concurred with that view.

Hirad's attention was caught by movement down on the terraces. A woman walked from behind a small tree-studded grotto and knelt by a beautiful array of flowers on a small mound of carefully tended earth. She was midheight, with a full figure, her auburn hair tied back with a black ribbon. She plucked some weeds from the bed and Hirad saw her nipping the deadheads from some of the taller fronds whose large yellow blooms blew in the gentle warm breeze.

As always when he saw her, Hirad's heart thudded a little harder and his mood dipped, sadness edging into his mind. To an untutored eye, the woman might have been simply enjoying the beauty she had created. But she was Erienne, who was enduring pain beyond comprehension, because beneath the bed lay the body of her daughter, Lyanna.

Lyanna, whom The Raven had come to save; whose five-year-old mind couldn't contain the power within it; and whose uncontrolled magic threatened to destroy Balaia. Lyanna, who had been allowed to die by the very people Erienne had trusted to train her and so allow her to live.

And that last was something Hirad found impossible to really understand; even though during his half year on Herendeneth he'd had plenty of opportunity to work it out. After all, two of the four Al-Drechar who had let Lyanna die were still alive and living in the habitable areas of their house here on the island. But their explanations about Lyanna's burgeoning power and her inability to ever control it, given her age and physical frailty, went straight over his head.

All he knew was that the nucleus of the One magic that Lyanna had hosted had been transferred to Erienne even as the little girl had died. And that Erienne hated it—felt it was a disease she couldn't cure—and that made her hate the surviving Al-Drechar even more. It made her head ache, she said, and though the Al-Drechar, both frail old elven women, said they could train her to control, use and develop it, she wouldn't as much as acknowledge their presence.

Hirad could understand that reaction. In fact he remained astounded she hadn't tried to kill the surviving pair. He knew what he'd want for those who murdered any child of his. But he was grateful nonetheless. Because, despite Sha-Kaan's current light mood, the dragon's exile in Balaia was slowly killing him; and the Al-Drechar with their understanding and expertise in dimensional theory were the Kaan's best chance of getting home.

It all added to the bowstring tension they had endured every day for their two seasons on Herendeneth. Hirad found himself needing the very people Erienne hated with a deep and abiding passion. Yet, even within that hatred, there was a part of her that needed the Al-Drechar too. Lyanna had been a child of the One, the ancient magical order that had dominated Balaia before the establishment of the four colleges over two thousand years ago. Erienne and Denser, her husband, still believed in it and the Al-Drechar were its last practitioners. What Erienne carried in her mind was the last hope for the order, but she would have to accept help from the Al-Drechar. That knowledge merely added to her misery.

"Her mind is clouded," said Sha-Kaan, looking down at Erienne. "Grief obscures rationality." There was no sense of any particular sympathy from the Great Kaan, who had been edging at the extremities of Erienne's mind with his own.

"That's only natural," said Hirad.

"For humans," returned Sha-Kaan. "It makes her dangerous."

Hirad sighed. "Sha-Kaan, she's seen all three of her children murdered; Lyanna by the Al-Drechar, her twin sons by the Black Wing witch hunters. I'm surprised she retains any sanity at all. Wouldn't you feel the same?"

"In truth, birthings are an increasingly rare event among the Kaan," said the dragon after a pause. "But when a young Kaan dies, we have to replace the infant. We don't have time to mourn."

"But you must have feelings for the mother and the youngster that dies," said Hirad.

"The Brood mourns and the Brood supports. The mother's mind is warmed by the Brood psyche and her pain is lessened by sharing. That is the way of dragons. For humans, grief is solitary and so is prolonged."

Hirad shook his head. "It's not solitary. We're all here to help Erienne."

"But because you can't get into her mind, you cannot help where she needs it the most."

A reptilian bark echoed across the island and Nos-Kaan flew around the thirty-foot-high stone needle, gliding in to land close to Sha and Hirad, his golden back scales glittering in the sunlight, the earth vibrating as his hind feet touched the ground. His mighty wings, a hundred feet and more tip to tip, beat once to steady him then swept back to fold along his long body, air whipping across Hirad's face. Nos-Kaan's neck half coiled to bring his head next to Sha-Kaan's and the two dragons touched muzzles briefly. Even now, so many years on, Hirad found the sight awe inspiring and felt a moment of pure insignificance in the face of such size and grace.

"Well met, Hirad," said Nos-Kaan, his voice pained.

"How did the flight go?"

"Do you wish the truth?" asked the dragon. Hirad nodded. "I must have the healing flows of interdimensional space or I will die. Before that I will be land bound."

Hirad was shaken. He had assumed the rest both Kaan had enjoyed these last two seasons in the warm climate on Herendeneth would cure them of the magical wounds they had suffered fighting the Dordovan mages.

"How long?"

"Another season, no more. I am weak, Hirad."

"And you, Great Kaan?"

"I am in better health," said Sha-Kaan. "But death is inevitable if I cannot get home before too long. Where are your Unknown Warrior and his researchers?"

"He'll be here. He said he would."

But Hirad had expected him before now. So long out of contact with the big man and he was beginning to fear something had happened to him. They had little news from Balaia—what they did get was through the incomplete knowledge of the Protectors—but none of it was good.

"Your loyalty is commendable," said Sha-Kaan.

"He's Raven," said Hirad, shrugging and standing. "Time to check the sea for ships anyway."

The truth was, he wanted to be alone for a moment. Only a season and Nos-Kaan would be dead. With the best will in the world, the research wouldn't have led to meaningful realignment spells by then. Nos-Kaan's grave was going to be Herendeneth.

He walked quickly down the slope, giving Erienne a wide berth and breaking into a trot as he passed the shored-up front doors of the house. The Protector, Aeb, stood at the entrance, unmoving, staring out northward. Hirad nodded to him as he passed.

The single path down to the island's only landable beach wove through waving beech groves to the small, reefed inlet. It was a peaceful walk. The warm breeze through the trees rustled leaves; the calls of birds on the wing filtered through the branches as did the distant sound of waves on the shore. Despite what he'd just heard, Hirad found himself smiling. He turned a corner and it dropped from his lips.

"Gods burning," he whispered, reaching instinctively for the blade he hadn't worn in a hundred days. He backed up the path.

Coming toward him were robed and cloaked men. Two dozen, maybe more. Mages. And where there were mages, there would be soldiers.

"Aeb!" he called over his shoulder. "Darrick! We're under attack!"

One of the mages held out his hands toward Hirad. Casting, surely. Caught unable to run and hopelessly outnumbered, Hirad did the only thing he could. He attacked. Yelling to clear his mind, he flew at the mage, fists bunched, braided hair streaming out behind him.

"Hirad! Gods' sake calm down!" came a voice from beyond the group of mages, who had stopped and were looking at him in some alarm.

Hirad slid to a stop a few yards from them, kicking up dust.

"Unknown?"

He looked harder. The unmistakable shaven head was approaching, a woman at his side, Protectors around him. Lots of them. Relief flooded through Hirad and he blew out his cheeks.

"Gods drowning, you had me scared," he said.

The mages parted and The Unknown walked through, his limp pronounced, a look of discomfort on his face.

"It's good to see you," said The Unknown, crushing Hirad in an embrace.

"And you, Unknown. You're looking pale though. Brought the family to pick up some colour, have you?"

The Unknown laughed as he released Hirad, stepping back. Diera, her long fair hair tied back and strong beautiful face pale, came up to his side,

Jonas squirming in her arms as he tried to see everything all at once. He fixed Hirad with a wary stare which the barbarian returned with a chuckle. The Unknown enveloped his family in one arm, pulling them close.

"Well, we've not had the luxury of relaxing in the sun these last two seasons," he said. "Unlike you, apparently."

"It's not been quite like that," said Hirad.

"I'm sure it hasn't," said The Unknown.

"I'm forgetting my manners," said Hirad. He leant forward and kissed Diera on the cheek then stroked Jonas's head. "Good to see you, Diera. I see Jonas has got his father's hair sense."

Diera smiled and looked down at her son's completely bald head. "Hirad, he's not a year old, poor little boy. He had plenty of hair a season ago."

Hirad nodded. "It'll grow back, young man," he said to Jonas. "Probably. And how are you, Lady Unknown? Looking a bit tired if I may say."

"Sea travel didn't agree with me," she said.

"You should talk to Ilkar then. He's our expert on shipboard vomiting."

"Hirad, you're disgusting," admonished Diera gently. "I just need a place to sleep that doesn't move about."

"I expect we can find you somewhere." Hirad looked back to The Unknown, tilting his head at the massed Protectors and Xeteskian mages.

"So what's going on?" he asked. "Bit more than a research party, isn't it?"

The Unknown's humour faded and he shook his head.

"Much more," he said. "Look, we can't stay here. There's work for The Raven on Balaia."

"Calaius first, I think." Hirad showed the way up the path with a last look at the Xeteskians. "Ilkar's not going to like this. Come on; let's get you up to the house."

CHAPTER 3

Dystran, Lord of the Mount of Xetesk, Balaia's Dark College of magic, sat back in his favourite chair, leather upholstered and deep. A fire warmed the chill late afternoon of early spring, filling his study with a yellow flickering light, augmenting the pale sun that shone through the window. A mug of herb tea steamed on a low table by his right hand.

He'd held Xetesk's highest office for more than six years now, a fact that truly astounded him. His ascension had been orchestrated by a powerful splinter group while the incumbent Lord, Styliann, had still been alive—an unprecedented series of events. Dystran had been aware that his tenure was intended to be brief and bloody, but circumstances and fortune had conspired in his favour.

Styliann had been killed, an invasion repelled and a period of calm demanded. It had left him alive but a puppet. The intervening years, though, had allowed him to build his own power base largely unopposed. The puppet master had become a subservient adviser and, while no Lord of the Mount was ever completely secure, Dystran had at least the respect of the Circle Seven, Xetesk's senior mages whose towers ringed the centre of the college.

And now, if Dystran was correct, Xetesk was on the verge of rightful dominion, though victory would be costly. The events leading to the unfortunate death of the Nightchild, Lyanna, had left a legacy of hatred and mistrust in the minds of nonmages. It was a disorganised threat and would be put down by aggressive magic when the time was right.

More positively, those same events had revealed the Al-Drechar. Dystran was determined to control them and the first steps were already in hand. A shame Dordover had chosen to fight him but, one way or another, war had been inevitable. As long as he could keep Lystern on the sidelines and Julatsa helpless, it was a war with only one possible winner.

Better even than the Al-Drechar, though, was a discovery his agents had made while studying texts on the complexities of natural elven links to the earth and magic. It had given him an idea, the successful fruition of which would very much hasten Xetesk's control over not just Balaia but Calaius too. He was impatient for progress but understood the need for care and secrecy, as did the former puppet master sitting across the fire from him.

The ageing Ranyl was not far from death yet retained a vitality and sharpness of mind that lit the eyes in his sagging face and belied his failing cancer-ravaged body.

"And when will we hear from the expedition?" asked Dystran.

"Not for some time, my Lord," said Ranyl. "Communion over such a distance is impossible. I have requested an interim report within thirty days but this could prove a long and difficult operation."

"We must have the writings, though," said Dystran. "I have to be sure. You have my permission to commit resources as necessary."

Ranyl inclined his head. "Thank you, my Lord."

Dystran picked up his mug and let the fresh, slightly sweet herb aroma fill his nostrils. He sipped the hot liquid, enjoying the taste.

"So, what of the food supplies?" he asked.

"We are fortunate to live within a walled city," said Ranyl by way of reply. "Our rationing has been effective and our people will survive until the new harvest. Not in comfort but none will starve. I cannot speak as confidently of the refugees at our gates, nor of the rest of Balaia. I understand conditions near Korina to be poor, also inland areas like Erskan and Pontois."

"Yet those refugees threaten us, Ranyl. They occupy our farm land and they practically surround our city. When the harvests start, they will demand food I am unwilling to give them. I need them moved by whatever means necessary."

"Be careful you do not drive them into Selik's greedy hands."

Dystran waved a hand. "There is a man and an organisation we can dispense with on a whim. And what would even he do with ten thousand starving Balaians, eh?"

"It's public opinion that should concern you," chided Ranyl.

Dystran chuckled. "I have no time for it. My concern is Dordover and the threat she poses. How are our forces holding out in Arlen? That route must be kept open."

"The situation is difficult but not disastrous," said Ranyl. "Dordover is a tenacious opponent."

"Keep me updated," said Dystran. "And you, my friend?"

"Difficult but not disastrous," said Ranyl, a hand automatically feeling across his stomach. "My spells keep the pain away and I will see the recovery of the writings you want. Beyond that, I am in the lap of the Gods."

"What will I do without you?"

"Prosper, young Dystran. You have the potential to be the tacit master of Balaia. The Seven will support you. You have time on your side and you must not hurry. I will school my successor to be as irritatingly cautious as I am."

Both men laughed.

"Do you think I'm doing the right thing?" asked Dystran, revealing his anxiety as he knew he must.

"As long as our people do not die needlessly in what may be to come, anything that is to the greater glory of the college and city of Xetesk is the right thing."

Dystran stared deep into Ranyl's eyes. He didn't think he'd ever seen them burn so fiercely.

Rebraal moved quickly along the path hacked into the rain forest by the Balaian intruders. It was crude and narrow, showing no regard for its effect on the forest, driving straight on, dripping sap onto the mulch underfoot. There were ways of making trails through the forest but they required understanding. Strangers never understood.

As he moved, apprehension began to descend on Rebraal. These men had had no business close to Aryndeneth. What they were was obvious: robbers. Why else would they come here uninvited and armed to fight? What Rebraal couldn't understand was where they had uncovered the information that had led them here and what exactly they had wanted. He assumed there were stories about hidden riches but these were very far from the truth. Nothing they could take would fetch a good price anywhere. Perhaps it was enough to prove they had been there. He didn't let himself consider desecration.

But it served to chasten the Al-Arynaar, too many of whom were sceptical of the need for such a numerous order guarding a temple whose location had been believed the best kept secret on Calaius. Reality was hard to accept and the elf had to quell a pang of anxiety while remaining proud that their vigilance had seen off at least the first attack. They had not let their guard drop. They had sworn that they never would. And depending on what he found at the end of the careless path, he felt they could maintain that pledge.

To Rebraal's knowledge, there had never been an attack on Aryndeneth. Of course the uninvited had come occasionally; those nonpilgrims who sought adventure rather than enlightenment. None had come seeking to harm or steal until now. But that possibility, however slight, was what had inspired the formation of the Al-Arynaar over three thousand years ago when the last priests had left the temple.

Rebraal sent a brief prayer to Orra, Appos and Shorth, the Gods of the earth, for the foresight of those that had gone before, a cold disgust replacing his brief anxiety. These men could not be allowed to disrupt the harmony. Aryndeneth, the Earth Home, was the centre of the elven race for so many reasons and the Al-Arynaar, the Keepers of the Earth, had a duty to elves that most would never even realise. They were not merely ceremonial guardians; that much was now unfortunately obvious. They were the guardians of the elven race itself.

With the sun climbing into the morning sky, humidity and temperature rose with the mist as it steamed from every leaf. Rebraal smiled grimly. Born and bred to the oppressive heat that built with every heartbeat, he moved easily, his breath even, his body sweating to keep him in balance.

At the end of this path however, any strangers would already be suffering as they had every day of their journey toward Aryndeneth. He understood what the conditions did to a man who was ill-prepared for them. Critical fluid loss, lethargy, heat sickness. The heat played tricks with the mind, made a man slow and irritable. And that was just the start of his problems.

Never mind the snakes, the big cats and the spiders; those you could see and fight. But the biting, crawling, burrowing insects and their all but invisible cousins, they could not be fought, only endured and cured. With herb and flower if you knew how, with magic if you didn't. No one was immune. Not the elves born here and certainly not strangers. Rebraal and the Al-Arynaar drank a crushed herb and petal drink morning and night. It kept the disease away, killed the eggs laid in the skin and lessened the itching. Nothing, though, would stop the barrage. The rain forest and everything that lived there were weapons for the Al-Arynaar. Rebraal determined to use them if he could.

From the rise in temperature, Rebraal guessed he'd travelled two hours before he smelled wood smoke. He'd heard nothing alien and the smell wasn't strong, just faint tendrils on the sluggish breeze. Even so, he slowed to listen harder. He had no clear idea what he faced and assuming the ineptitude of the vanguard would be repeated by those in the camp was dangerous.

He heard nothing out of place. The rain forest was awake. Birds screeched, boughs creaked as monkeys and lizards traversed overhead, the undergrowth was alive with rodent, arachnid, insect and reptile. The air buzzed and hummed. All was as it should be bar the acrid taint of char on the wind. He trotted on, footfalls silent on the path, ears straining for the sounds he knew would come.

It was another two hours before he heard them: voices filtering through the dense vegetation, the snap of a branch as it burned and the lazy flap of tent canvas. He pitied anyone who chose to sleep on the ground. Most of what crawled or slithered was poisonous to a greater or lesser degree. Too bad.

For the last three hundred yards, he left the path but kept close enough to study it. The strangers had posted two guards but they were scared men, eyes shifting toward every sound, real or imagined. Rebraal watched them for a time. From a distance of five yards they had no idea he was even there. He would have laughed but he didn't want to scare them into running. Instead, he left them scratching at their legs and swatting uselessly at the insects buzzing around their heads and moved on.

Closer to the camp, he slowed still further, frowning. The sound of voices, gruff and unhappy, was louder than he had anticipated, and the light from ahead brighter, as if they'd found or enlarged a clearing. The smell of wood smoke was stronger now and he could see its wisps edging through the shade under the canopy. The forest was quieter here, the presence of strangers scaring the wildlife and the smoke dampening the rampant enthusiasm of the insect swarms.

He edged through a waist-high sea of huge-leafed fronds, thick stalks tacky with sap, keeping crouched as he came, eyes fixed on the light ahead. Pushing aside a thatch of ivy hanging from the branches of a balsa tree, he leaned against its trunk and peered around it into the camp.

The breath caught in his throat. This wasn't a mere raiding party, it was more like an organised invasion. Eyes scanning the man-made clearing of something like three hundred feet a side, he counted them as they moved in and out of the cover of the tentage pitched in orderly form around a dozen campfires.

Warriors, mages and bowmen, there had to be one hundred and fifty of them. Maybe more.

Rebraal shrank back into the comforting embrace of the forest, his heart thrashing in his chest so loud he thought it might give him away, his mind churning with questions, options and nightmares. In no more than a day, these men would question the whereabouts of the dead trail-finders. Then they would come. Slowly maybe, but in force.

At Aryndeneth Rebraal had ten Al-Arynaar, and of them Meru was gone to spread the alarm. Too late. Whatever was to come, those at the temple would have to face it and beat it alone.

Before he inched forward to commit everything he could to memory, Rebraal offered a fervent prayer to Yniss for a miracle. Because sure as baking sun followed the rains, they were going to need one.

Erienne watched with detached disinterest the dragon swoop in to land on the upper slopes of the mountain, where the other Kaan sat with Hirad acting like masters of all they surveyed. They could have it. It was a traitor's kingdom.

All the while she hummed Lyanna's favourite song, her hands caressing the earth beneath which her daughter lay. She turned back. The bed was looking beautiful today, alive with vibrant reds and yellows, deep purples and lush greens. Lyanna was giving her energy to the earth; her inextinguishable life force would bless this place forever.

Erienne sat back on her haunches and looked left and right along the terraces cut into the gentle slope that led up to the mountain peak. She took in the arches, statues, pillars, grottoes, intricate rock gardens and perfectly formed trees. She opened her mind to the deep and ancient aura of magical power.

It was fitting that Lyanna lay here. Among the long dead of the Al-Drechar, the Keepers of the One magic. Lyanna should have been the first of a new generation, would have been had the memories of those past not been betrayed by the four that had still lived when she and Erienne had arrived on Herendeneth.

Erienne had come here with such hope. That Lyanna would be schooled to accept the power within her. That the colleges would understand that her little girl could be slave to none of them. That she must be left alone with her teachers to realise her potential and, more importantly, to live.

But the colleges were greedy for her power or, failing that, anxious she be killed. Erienne's own college of Dordover had allied with witch hunters to find her and Lyanna and see them both dead. Xetesk had pledged support but their motives had little to do with Erienne's desires and everything to do with lust for power and knowledge.

And then, at the very last, when victory had seemed within their grasp, when The Raven had seemed triumphant, the ultimate betrayal had taken her beautiful dancing child from her. *They*, the Al-Drechar, had decreed that Lyanna should die. *They* had decided her little body couldn't contain the One magic growing within her. And *they* had decided this entity, which Erienne had discovered to be independent of her daughter, should be transferred to her mind, killing the child in the process.

She glanced down at the ruins of the house. Two of them still lived. Elven witches who by rights should be dead but who The Raven now protected. She knew why and even sometimes confessed to herself they were right but she hated them all for it anyway.

A wave of guilt broke through her mind and her song faltered even as the tears threatened behind her eyes. But she hated no one more than herself. After all, everything that had happened was as a direct result of what she had wanted. Gods, she'd even slept with Denser that first time to conceive a child she felt might have the potential to develop the One magic.

Everything had gone according to her plan but the One had proved too strong, too chaotic. Impossible to control. In Dordover, they had made the mistake of awakening the magic in a mind too young to cope. That was why Erienne had run to Herendeneth. But Erienne's sin was far, far worse. For too long, she had ignored the fact that there was a child as well as an ancient magical talent awakening, so consumed was she by the potential of Lyanna.

She had only been a little girl. And no one, not even her mother, had given her either choice or chance.

Erienne broke and wept, head buried in her hands, her body rocking backward and forward as the grief, guilt, hate and love stormed through her, robbing her of any coherent thought. Images of Lyanna skipping in the orchard overlaid those of her tiny, still, blue-tinged body, lying on the kitchen floor. She heard Lyanna in her head, snatches of laughter and innocent questions. She could smell her body, clean after a bath, and sense the love in those beautiful eyes shining out, unconditional, trusting. Betrayed.

She heaved in a breath and sobbed out her sorrow, her lips moving, her voice choked. Nothing could bring her back. Nothing would ease the agony, the longing and the loss. And Erienne's only peace was that Lyanna would be with her murdered sons. Her wonderful twin boys, long gone but never forgotten. At least she wasn't alone.

Erienne felt a hand on her shoulder and heard Denser crouch by her, silent.

"Get away from me," she hissed.

"No, love," said Denser, his voice soft but determined. "Lean into me."

"You can't help me," she said. Every day the same. The words might be different but the sense never changed. "Leave us alone."

"No, I won't," said Denser, insistent. "I pledged that I would never leave you. Let me into you. Just try."

Erienne shook her head, too tired to argue. At least his appearance had stopped her tears for now. She wiped her face with the backs of her hands, accepting the clean cloth square Denser pushed into her left hand to wipe her eyes.

"Thank you," she said.

"Any time," he said. "I'll always be here, whenever you need me."

Denser moved a little closer, putting his arm around her shoulders. Erienne tensed, wanting to push him away but knowing she couldn't. She hated him for refusing to judge the Al-Drechar as she did but she loved him for his unswerving strength. So she sat with him in silence, both of them just staring at the bed of flowers as it ruffled gently in the warm breeze.

There was nothing to say. One day, perhaps, she would admit his grief. But right now she couldn't even begin to cope with her own.

Her head was throbbing. Like every day, the One entity was trying to assert itself. Trying to gain influence over her mind. But it was not strong enough and it gave her grim satisfaction that it could not rule her the way they had all let it rule and then destroy Lyanna.

Erienne knew it wasn't sentient, that it was just her subconscious mind interacting with a power that intrigued and disgusted her in equal measure. She imagined it as a disease, a cancer she couldn't destroy but could suppress and bend to her will. She knew that to let her defences fall would open her mind to power she wasn't sure she could control. And she knew that to do so would mean she had to talk to the Al-Drechar, because without them she would only hasten her own demise.

There had been times when that had seemed preferable to existence without Lyanna. But something inside her stopped her taking her own life. Deep down, she believed in the One. She just couldn't reconcile that she was now its last hope. She knew that some time she would have to accept what she was. But it would be on her terms alone. No elven witch or Xeteskian mage would pressure her.

Inside her was the power of the One, living. It shouldn't be there but it was. And it reminded her every moment of every day that Lyanna had been sacrificed for it to be within her. So, like so much, she both hated and craved it. But for now, and maybe forever, the hate held sway.

The confusion within her made her mind pound all the more.

She turned her head to look at Denser. His beard was trimmed, his black hair neat and short, his cheekbones and jaw angled and so attractive. He was looking down at the bed, tears rolling down his face either side of his sharp nose.

For a heartbeat, she thought about kissing his tears away. But in that moment, the grief deluged her again and she crumbled back into her nightmare.

CHAPTER 4

Rebraal arrived back at Aryndeneth after two sharp downpours, each followed by steaming heat as the sun forced its way through the cloud. He could imagine the strangers running for cover as an inch and more rain fell in drops the size of his thumbs, extinguishing fires and drumming on canvas, finding its way through every loose stitch and seam.

For his part, the leader of the Al-Arynaar had merely found the best shelter he could under the broad green leaves of trees, and had listened to the sounds the rain brought to the forest: the undergrowth alive with animals scurrying for holes and burrows; the spatter of water on leaf and branch; the shifting of vegetation at every level of the harmony.

Rain was something to be enjoyed, not endured. It brought a freshness to the air and drove the insects from the sky. It brought life to the environment. It was warm on his skin and cooled the extremes of temperature. Rebraal loved the rain.

Later, standing on the overgrown stone apron in front of the temple, Rebraal called the Al-Arynaar to him. It was a call to arms and one that struck a chord of fear and determination in all of them. He had wondered whether the call, a song that echoed out through the forest in an ancient and long-dead language, was really required. But in truth, the threat was so great even the Deneth-barine song couldn't communicate its magnitude.

With Mercuun gone to spread the alarm and light fading quickly with the close of day under a bank of thickening cloud, Rebraal faced just eight. Two mages and six warriors. Their faces told him they understood the gravity; he now had to explain the reality.

There was an expectant air, tinged with anxiety. The song had not been heard in the living memory of any of them or indeed the two generations before them. They gathered in a loose group around Rebraal as the evening birds began to call and the rasp of a thousand pairs of cicada legs sawed at the fading light.

"The strangers' camp is a half day standard march north. The path they made took me straight to it." He paused to take them all in. "The Al-Arynaar assembled here face a threat at least ten times our number. We will need all of our guile and the blessing of Yniss to survive."

Rebraal let his words sink in. He saw fear, which was right, but no desperation. He hadn't expected to.

"How long before they get here?" asked Caran'herc. Keen eyes and a fine archer even for an elf, Caran'herc had her hair close-cropped for convenience and a narrow face that robbed her of real beauty. Her eyes though, piercing and deep blue, shone from her face, bewitching.

"By the position of the sun, I left them four hours ago," said Rebraal, "and they were making no preparations then. They will miss their dead by dawn if not before and though the rain might slow them, they could be on us and wary before night falls tomorrow."

"Mercuun will be gone until the day after tomorrow at least," said Sheth'erei, a thoughtful, quiet mage. She chewed at her thin lips, the tips of her high cheeks pink, the hood of a lightweight cloak thrown over her head against the insects of the night.

Rebraal nodded. "Yes, Sheth. We have to assume we are on our own."

They took the situation in, each one weighing up the risks and possibilities. They knew the forest was their greatest ally, but that for all its strengths, overwhelming odds would ultimately be victorious. Unless the few were prepared.

"Sheth, Erin. Perimeter wards need to be laid and activated. So do the temple doors. When these are set, remember your distances all of you." He looked hard at the two mages. "It's up to you to tell us when we can no longer pray inside. Right. The rest of us. Check and unlock the stakes and pits. Re-lay the camouflage on the archer platforms, rub down the boards and check fastenings for silence. Check every arrow tip and shaft for imperfection, the toxin supply for age. Hone every edge of every blade. Clear your lines of sight, retie the netting. Leave no mark on the earth. That done we will talk of our positions.

"But first, we will pray."

Rebraal led them to the temple.

The Unknown Warrior walked through the entrance of the house, nodding at Aeb who stood just inside. The Protector inclined his head in return.

"The kitchen is still the most habitable area," he said in response to the question The Unknown had been framing.

The Raven warrior smiled. "And the rest of the house?"

"Safe from collapse. We have repaired roofing over some of the bedrooms but we lack tools."

"Not any more you don't. Nor do you lack muscle."

"A hundred of my brothers is a welcome addition," said Aeb.

"A hundred?" echoed Hirad.

"Later," said The Unknown. He turned back to Aeb. "We'll tour the house later, set some priorities. I'll be in the kitchen with my family."

Aeb inclined his head again. "I will have our brothers leave there."

"Thank you."

The Unknown pointed the way and led Diera toward the kitchen, which stood at the far end of the house. It was not a walk he enjoyed.

Directly opposite the shored-up frontage with its battered but repaired doors was the gaping space that had once been the wood and glass entrance to the orchard, the devastated centrepiece of the house. The Unknown paused and looked out, and the battle flickered back through his head with disturbing clarity.

He saw the orchard ablaze with mage fire from the bombardment of Dordovan FlameOrbs. The shapes of mages descending on ShadowWings into the blaze. The sound of spells drumming on the roof. The rush of cool air as the front doors were battered down. The spatter of blood on his face. Dear Gods, The Raven had fought so hard against such numbers.

The Unknown placed a hand on his forehead and felt the sweat sheen there. His hip ached in sympathy at the memory of the desperate run up the corridor to the ballroom and through to the kitchen. The ache intensified, jabbed pain at him.

The smells of ash and fear were in his nostrils once again. The deaths of Protectors blown apart by close-focused magic flashed in front of his eyes. He could hear Denser's frantic attempts to shield them from crossbows behind and Hirad's roar and the cut of his sword into Dordovan flesh. And, with sickening repetition, he saw a Protector sacrifice himself to save Lyanna from an IceWind, Ilkar's sword spinning end over end through the air and the blood that flowed from the mage's nose. There was Selik, too, standing over the prone body of Erienne, and Hirad charging toward him. And at the end, Darrick and Ren saving them all when they should have died.

All except Lyanna. And it was his abiding sorrow that everything had been reversed. Because she should have been the only one to live but ended up being the only one to die. For all their defence. For all the fight way beyond normal endurance. For all their belief, The Raven could not save her.

Nothing could have. He swayed against the door frame.

"Hey, lost in that head of yours, are you?" asked Diera, free arm linked through his.

They moved left to the long passageway which led up to the banqueting hall and overlooked the orchard all along its length. A long door-studded wall ran the other side.

"A little," he said. "You can't stop the memories coming back."

"You fought up here?" asked Diera.

The Unknown looked down at her as they walked. Hirad kept a respectful silent distance behind. She was glancing about as if trying to imagine the scene. Jonas had snuggled into her shoulder and looked asleep.

"All the way from front door to kitchen. When we weren't running, that is." He tried to smile but she shuddered.

"It must have been awful," she whispered.

"I thought we were all going to die," he said.

Diera leant a little further into him and he squeezed her shoulder.

"Gets to you, doesn't it?" said Hirad, coming to his side.

"You could say," he replied.

"It fades but it never goes away," said the barbarian.

"Come on," said The Unknown. "Let's get The Raven together. I'll worry about my mind later."

Rebraal led the Al-Arynaar into the dome of Aryndeneth and at once the majesty of the temple surged through his body and he felt, as they all did, the pulsing life of the harmony. Sweet and soothing, it swept away the threat that lay without and filled him with the surety of the everlasting. It stoked his belief and imbued his mind with the determination that set the Al-Arynaar apart.

He breathed deep and walked further into the cool of the great dome, toward its magnificent statue and glorious pool. Rebraal still found it hard to believe that Aryndeneth and all it contained had been built five millennia ago.

Beyond the threshold, marble and stone flags patterned the floor, the multicoloured slabs positioned exactly to catch the light of the sun at a dozen different times of the day, when prayers could be offered to the Gods of the forest and the land, of the air and mana, and of harmony. There were no seats in the main dome, although contemplation chambers at each corner of the temple provided rough benches and stands for candles. And further back, a corridor had other chambers on either side, the doors of which opened only at given times of the day or season. The dome itself was the place for silent reverence and hands touching the ground when praying brought the Gods closer.

Between the precisely set windows, the walls and domed ceiling were covered in intricate murals. They depicted the rise of Yniss and the trials of the elven peoples as they grew to longevity and earned the right to live with the land, vibrant colours tracing the history of Calaius. And, in the centre of the domed ceiling, was painted the only fully rendered impression of the Balaian dimension, with Calaius at its centre. Radiating out from the Southern Continent were the energy lines the elves believed linked the lands and the seas together. They were the lines that gave elves their innate sense of home anywhere in the world and originated from one place. Aryndeneth.

Beautiful though the murals, maps and line tracings were, they were as nothing in comparison to what dominated the temple. In the exact centre of Aryndeneth, a statue rose seventy feet into the dome.

It was of Yniss, the God the elves worshipped as the Father of their race and He who gave the elves the gift of living as one with the land and its denizens, the air and with mana. Rebraal's eyes tracked down the statue, which was carved from a single block of flint-veined, polished pale stone.

Yniss was sculpted kneeling on one leg, head looking down along the line of his right arm. The arm was extended below his bended knee, thumb and forefinger making a right angle with the rest of the fingers curled half fist. Every detail of the sculptors' vision had been intricately included. Yniss was depicted as an old elf, age lines around the eyes and across the forehead. His long full hair and beard were carved blowing back toward and over his right shoulder.

Romantic idealism had led the sculptors to depict the God's body as toned and muscled perfection. There was the odd age line but nothing to really divorce the body from that of a pure athlete. A single-shouldered robe covered little more than groin and stomach, leaving open the bunching shoulders, stunningly defined arms and powerful, sandal-shod legs.

Though there was no colour other than that of the marble itself, Rebraal always stared hard at the slanted oval eyes, their powerful lines and clever use of the temple's light and shadow making them all but sparkle with life.

The majesty of the statue, though, was all mere dressing for its purpose. The scriptures of Yniss spoke of him coming to this place to give life to the world and construct the harmony that made the elves, gave them long life and showed them the beauty of the forest and the earth. Yniss had channelled his life energy along forefinger and thumb into the harmonic pool, from where it spread throughout the land, bringing glory where it touched. The scriptures laid down the exact design of Yniss's hand for the sculptors who came after him, their precision ensuring the flow of life energy was forever unbroken. Pipes concealed within the statue's thumb and forefinger fed water from an underground spring into the pool beneath the statue's outstretched hand.

Rebraal believed the harmony was what kept him alive, though the scriptures were vague on the consequences of disruption, save that it would cause disaster. Perhaps the forests would wither or elves would die. It mattered little. While the Al-Arynaar lived, no one would damage the harmony, either by accident or design.

Rebraal knelt before the statue and in front of the thirty-foot-wide crescent-shaped and sweet-smelling pool into which the waters of life energy fed. He placed his hands firmly on the stone and bowed his forehead to touch its cool surface before lifting his head to look into Yniss's eyes and pray again for his miracle.

Selik, commander of the Black Wings, had travelled much of eastern Balaia since the death of Lyanna, Erienne's abomination of an offspring. He'd seen what the child's filthy magic had done to his country. He'd seen smashed towns and villages, ruined fields, and livestock corpses strewn across flattened pasture, rotting where they lay. He'd seen forests uprooted and levelled, rivers, flood plains, and lakes double their size, drowning all they touched. And he'd seen where the earth had opened to swallow the land, leaving great scars on the landscape that seeped death and disease.

And worse than the ravaged countryside was the suffering in those towns and cities where people still lived because they had nowhere else to go. In Korina, the extravagance of earlier years had come back to haunt the capital. With farm produce from outlying areas all but gone and no sensible provision for grain storage, the population was reliant on the remnants of the city's fishing fleet. But it was in a pitiful state. Less than thirty seaworthy vessels remained, the wreckage of the rest still lying among the smashed docks. But Korina's population exceeded a quarter of a million and even with the huge outflow of refugees to inland towns, they were fighting a losing battle.

The population had survived a harsh winter but were now close to starving, and though the storm and flood waters had receded, their legacy was disease and rats. He knew it was the same throughout Balaia. With four exceptions: Xetesk, Dordover, Lystern, and Julatsa.

Magic. Travers, his leader when the Black Wings he now led had been formed, had been right all along. Though magic did superficial good, it upset the natural balance. And where its hand had been then abandoned, people suffered and died. How fragile Balaia was and how blind so many had been to that fragility. But magic had always had the capacity to create disaster and now no eyes were closed to that fact. The evil child and her untamed magic had blighted a whole continent and left the innocent to struggle with the consequences.

And where were the mages now? Guilty by association, they had fled back to the safety of their college cities to hide, grow fat and prepare for war. And all the while those they purported to care for starved. Rightly, the populace was turning against them. Even where mages had stayed, the damage was too great for them to truly help and their efforts were born of guilt not concern.

They had shown their true colours. Magic was not strong; it was a force of opportunism turned on the helpless to force obedience. Well, now things were different. The helpless would learn to help themselves and would not see magic return to their lives. Once they could, they would live without it.

It would not be an easy path. Balaia would have to find a new strength and would need a new order. One that shunned and despised the wretches in their colleges. Never again could the users of magic be allowed to hold the balance of power.

Selik had seen all he needed to see. Already his followers were spreading dissent and rumour, preparing the ground. And already there was support for what he represented. The pure path. The righteous path. Once the majority of the population was behind him he could move to strike at the heart of the evil that had plagued Balaia for too long. He would smash them, their colleges and their towers, and liberate the people.

Selik smiled, the expression dragging his spell-ravaged face into a sick sneer. His time had come. The mages had struck the mortal blow against themselves and would not survive it. While they hid and licked their wounds, his power grew. What the great Travers had started as an exercise in control, Selik would finish as an example of extinction. And when magic was gone, his would be the dominant force; he would see to that.

He kicked his horse into a canter, fifty of his men behind him. Erskan and the villages nearby were next. He had heard that mages still worked their sick trade there. Some still had lessons to learn.

Rebraal waited in the temple long after the other Al-Arynaar had left to begin their tasks. His was the first sitting of contemplation and he had prayed fervently it would bring him new wisdom.

Aryndeneth was cool and quiet but for the waters of harmony falling precisely into the crescent pool before continuing their journey through the veins of the earth. It was a sound that he allowed to wash over him until he was conscious of nothing else but its sustaining beauty.

This evening was revered by the Al-Arynaar because of the conjunction of land, sun, and sky, and Rebraal was aware of the shifting of the light through his closed eyes. He opened them and watched, from his kneeling position, the amber glow of late sunlight through an exactly positioned tinted window set into the base of the dome.

Every point the light touched on the polished walls glistened, details of murals and mosaics picked out in glory then banished to relative shadow as it crawled by. He watched on, seeing the pool dancing and sparkling in the periphery of his vision. The light reached the statue; part of the diffuse beam pierced the crook of its left arm. In the back of the temple, stone grated on stone as a doorway to learning opened.

It would be brief. Once the light had passed the crook, the door would slide shut and twenty days would pass before it opened again. Some doors opened daily but here was a chance for rare study. This was the tome of Shorth, the fleet foot God. The Death Keeper. He was the balance at the end of life's cycle. He restored the living to the earth and their breath to the sky and their mana to the harmony. Rebraal had barely studied him. Perhaps he would learn enough to ensure this was not his last chance.

Offering a short prayer of thanks to Yniss, Rebraal rose to his feet and paced silently past the statue, his eyes easily piercing the gloom at the back of the temple. To his left, a doorway let into a small, mural-covered cell bathed in warm amber light from a large window above. A single desk and chair faced a double shelf full of texts, some almost too ancient to touch. Rebraal selected a heavy leather-bound book and began to read.

CHAPTER 5

The look on Ilkar's face when he strode into a kitchen filled with the delicious smells of soup and fresh bread that evening was just as The Unknown had expected. The elegant eyebrows were arrowed in, the lips thin, the high-boned cheeks reddened and leaf-shaped ears pricking furiously. His words stopped the desultory conversation around The Raven's table.

"I've had the most wonderful day," he said. "Clear blue skies, warm water, an island a short sail away just for me and the woman I love. Then, to cap off the perfection, I sail back here to find we've handed over control of Herendeneth to Xetesk. Anyone want to volunteer a reason?" He stared squarely at The Unknown. "Hello, Unknown. At least it's good to see you if not the rest of the passengers that came with you."

He sat down.

"Great entrance," said Hirad.

"Some performance," agreed Denser.

The briefest of smiles registered on Erienne's face, gone in a heartbeat.

"This isn't funny," snapped Ilkar. "Correct me if I'm wrong, but we agreed a research party of six. Now I'm not the world's greatest mathematician but I reckon I counted more than six Xeteskian mages on my way through the house. Oh, and I think there was the odd Protector in addition to the half-dozen who were here when I left this morning."

The Unknown would have laughed under other circumstances—Ilkar's sarcasm was always so perfectly delivered—but this wasn't the time.

"There are thirty mages and one hundred Protectors here. They are here because they fear invasion of this island by Dordover." The silence around the table was total. "That is because Xetesk and Dordover are now at war. It is open conflict and it will soon consume Balaia, our country, which is already starving and broken.

"They are here to research dimensional magics across the spectrum and we can't stop them or make demands of them. But we can do something about Balaia. There's a tide early tomorrow afternoon. We have to be on it."

Soup spoons were forgotten, bread hung from fingers. The Unknown Warrior could hear them all breathing—The Raven, less one notable absentee, the people in whom he had unshakeable faith. They would be tested now, for sure.

"We've fought for Balaia for so long. For peace and for somewhere we can grow old in safety and security. But I've brought my wife and son here because I fear for their lives from starvation, disease or the sword if I leave them there. We can't let it go on. Or everything else we've done will be for nothing."

"But I thought peace was being brokered," said Hirad.

"You thought wrong," said The Unknown. "We all did. This was just a matter of time."

In his chair to The Unknown's left, Ry Darrick shifted uncomfortably. The former Lysternan general had been accused of desertion back on Balaia to fight with The Raven but that didn't change the way he felt about his home.

"Lystern?" he said as if fearing the answer.

"Peace brokers with no peace to broker," said The Unknown. "They're out of it for now but . . ." He shrugged. They all understood. He turned his attention to Ilkar. The elf had not been mollified by his answer. "But there is a chance. We have to restore the balance. Raise the Heart of Julatsa."

"I agree." Ilkar nodded. "Assuming we can find a couple of hundred mages to help."

"Jevin's going to Calaius next for cargo. We should be with him. Plenty of mages there."

"Yes, Unknown, and they all returned there for a good reason," said Ilkar.

"Then you'll have to persuade them to go back," said The Unknown. "They'll listen to you." He stared at Ilkar until the Julatsan nodded.

"And meanwhile we let Xetesk have the run of this place?"

"What else can we do, Ilkar?" asked The Unknown. "We can't force them to leave and, more important, their research could free the Protectors and send the dragons home."

"But what about the other results, eh?"

"I know," said The Unknown. "And that's why we have to get Julatsa working as a college again. It's the only way to stop the war. I don't see we have any choice. Even if Lystern and Dordover allied, they wouldn't be strong enough. With Julatsa, they just might. But Julatsa needs its Heart. We all need to say our goodbyes and get going. Balaia can't wait. And what Erienne is carrying needs to be taken away from here. I'm sure you all understand."

Erienne pushed back her chair and stood up slowly, shaking off Denser's protective arm.

"I'm so pleased you've got it all worked out," she said. "Ilkar can go and find his mages to rebuild Balaia and, by the by, you can look after poor little me and take me away from those nasty Xeteskians."

She stopped and glared around the table, daring any of them to speak. The Unknown felt suddenly cold, knew he'd made an error and cursed himself silently. He knew what she was going to say before she said it.

"But any of you who thinks I will leave my daughter here to the tender mercies of her killers and the Dark College deserves nothing but my contempt. I'm sure you all understand."

She strode from the kitchen.

"That wasn't your cleverest speech," said Ilkar.

"No," agreed The Unknown. He'd misjudged the state of her grief and her mind; and though he felt empty for her, he couldn't fathom why she hadn't moved on a day since he'd left. "But she'll come round."

"By tomorrow? No chance," said Denser. "Her mind isn't rational one heartbeat to the next."

"Well, you've got to make it so. She isn't safe here. And we need her. She's Raven."

Ilkar shifted in his seat and narrowed his startling slanted oval eyes.

"There's something else, isn't there? Something's got you spooked because this isn't like you. You're too careful. What is it?"

The Unknown shook his head. "You weren't there; you didn't feel it. Balaia's dying."

"What are you talking about?" asked Hirad.

"I can't make you understand. But every Protector here will tell you the same thing. It's like the air itself doesn't taste right. There are forces trying to impose things on Balaia and its peoples that go against the natural order. Not just Selik and the Black Wings; the colleges too. They have stood for two thousand years as deterrents against one another. But now they've turned on each other and they'll murder Balaia too. I will not let that happen.

"Now, where's Thraun?"

Hirad sighed and looked at Ilkar. The elf was staring down at his food, Ren's arm around his shoulders. The Unknown wasn't about to like what he'd hear, he was sure of that.

The Unknown didn't find Thraun until well past midnight, and even then he all but tripped over the feral man. The dark of the night, the deep shadows under the beech trees and bushes and Thraun's utter stillness had made The Unknown's lantern-lit search fruitless for hours. He'd rejected all offers of help. For reasons he wasn't prepared to put into words, he felt he'd have more joy if he found the shapechanger alone.

When at last he came across the sleeping form, he stood and looked down at him for a time. Thraun's face was creased by a frown and his teeth ground together as he dreamed, memories and anxieties surfacing to torture his rest. He lay in a close fetal position, with his hands balled into fists and his legs tucked right up to his body. He'd made a bed from blankets taken from the house, and scattered about him was the detritus of a confused mind trying desperately to find itself but not knowing where it was lost. There was an empty bottle, a book, a square of torn tapestry, a knife from the kitchen, an empty bowl and an arrow. A curious mix.

The Unknown knelt next to Thraun, the shapechanger's eyes opening as he did so.

"Not too much wrong with your senses, I see," he said, setting the lantern down.

Thraun's eyes showed no fear, just tired puzzlement and then dawning recognition. His face relaxed.

"That's better," said The Unknown. "Good to see you again. Now, Hirad tells me you can understand most of what I'm saying but that you can't speak right now. Can you indicate that you've understood me?"

Thraun nodded, making an affirmative grunting noise. The Unknown stared at the ground briefly before looking back up.

"Sorry. I guess I shouldn't talk to you like you're a child, eh?"

A shake of the head.

"What's in there, Thraun? What is it that's stopping you? Part of your wolven self must be obstructing your human mind, mustn't it? What can we do?"

Thraun's face collapsed and he hunched up, eyes moistening, pleading at The Unknown. The big man reached out a hand and clasped Thraun's shoulder for a moment.

"Gods, but I understand like no one else can. Let me tell you something I've not told anyone before." He moved to a seated position, his back against a tree. The night was quiet but for the warm breeze rustling the leaves above their heads.

"My time as a Protector was mercifully short and a brave mage gave his life to free me and return my soul to me. But in the time I was one, I felt a bond the like of which I didn't think could ever be replaced. It went beyond kinship and love. It was deeper than either though based on both, I suppose. It was something hard to express except to say that it was an utterly binding sense of belonging. No one, I thought, who had not experienced it could understand. And when I was freed, though that was what I wanted desperately, I lost something I assumed was irreplaceable. You might remember how I was in the days after I was released; I don't know."

The Unknown stopped to gauge Thraun's reaction. The shapechanger was staring at him, eyes wide. Whether it was comprehension, remembrance or just plain incredulity that someone was talking to him this way was unfortunately not clear. At least he had Thraun's attention.

"The point is that I think you're in a similar position to me but the effects are keener because you spent five years as a wolf, not just a few days. The wolf pack gave you a similar bond; they laid their trust in you and you in them. You blame yourself for what happened to them both during the hurricane in Thornewood and on the docks in Arlen.

"And now you've reverted to human form you feel like you're running away. It isn't so. Like me and the Protectors, part of you will always be with the pack that still runs. Hang on to that, but don't let it cloud your mind. Remember it and use it.

"But what I want you to really understand, and I don't know whether you will, is that there is something that gives what you feel you have lost. It took me an age to realise it but it's undeniable. The Raven have that bond. Together we are stronger than we could ever be as a mere group of individuals. We make a difference to each other and in whatever we do. And if you look inside yourself, you know that to be true. Do you understand me?"

For a time Thraun did nothing, just continued to stare. There was a single tear on his left cheek and the frown was back, stamped hard on his forehead. But like a trickle of water finding its way gradually down a window, his face cleared and he sat up. He sucked his top lip and breathed in deeply. He made no move to nod or hint that he knew what The Unknown was talking about but it was there in his expression just the same. The Unknown felt he was struggling to communicate in another way.

"Go on," he said. "Try to make the words."

Thraun opened his mouth, his eyes still searching The Unknown's face, but nothing came save a dry rasp and he snapped his jaws shut angrily.

"It's all right. It'll come. Now listen, because there's something very important I have to tell you. All right?"

Thraun shrugged and exercised his jaws again.

"I know you're frustrated but you'll get there as long as you have faith. The Raven will be with you. We're your family always, and we're your strength any time you need us. And we want you to be with us in whatever comes next, but for that you will have to leave this island."

Thraun stopped moving.

"The Raven have to leave here to go back home and help with things there that are badly wrong. We can talk about what's happening another day, but for now I want you to think about what you're going to do. To make The Raven complete, we want you to be with us. We are stronger with you and you with us.

"Do you understand that?"

Thraun was staring at the ground and now drew his legs up to his chest, locking them there with his arms. He rocked backward and forward gently.

"Thraun?"

He didn't look up but The Unknown thought he saw a fractional nod of the head. It was enough.

"Good, good. I'll leave you now to sleep if you want. Think about what I've said and let me know in whatever way you can what it is you want to do."

The Unknown pushed himself to his feet, picked up the lantern and limped back toward the house, suddenly dog-tired and craving the arms of Diera.

CHAPTER 6

The rain forest was quiet. A sharp downpour had thrashed across the temple an hour before, sending the Al-Arynaar to cover under the broad leaves of a master banyan tree at the southern edge of the temple. Water still fell from the upper canopy to puddle on the ground before soaking away. Rebraal walked across the rain-slick apron with the mage, Erin'heth. It was the night following his time of contemplation in the cell of Shorth and preparations were now complete.

They couldn't afford to worry about the strangers themselves, who had to be approaching by now. All that really taxed Rebraal was whether their defence would delay the strangers long enough for Mercuun to return. An elf of his ability could make a great deal of difference.

"We can't rely on him, Rebraal," said Erin'heth. "Your plan is sound. We can only do what we can do. If Mercuun arrives, it's a bonus."

Rebraal tried to smile but couldn't help but be irritated that it was Meru that had left them. But then, who else but himself commanded the elves' respect? He'd really had no choice.

"Talk me through the grid," he said to concentrate his mind.

"We've laid as many wards as we could in the time," said Erin. "We have to be fresh for the fight and Sheth is already sleeping. There's no linkage but we've positioned the strike zones to herd them to the central position you want. Then it's up to you and the archers because if they move to leave the apron, the outer ring isn't going to hold them forever even though they're FlameWalls."

"And the temple doors?"

"It'll be carnage. Sheth spent a lot of energy on that ward. It's big. If we should die in the fight, don't touch it until you get a replacement mage."

"Didn't you tune elves out of the triggers?" Rebraal frowned.

"In the apron wards yes, but we can't risk a smart stranger circumventing the ward by forcing an elf to open the temple doors, so anything bigger than a panther will trigger it."

Rebraal nodded, stopped and turned a slow circle on the slippery stone apron. He could see the archer positions, he knew the ward trigger points. They'd done all they could. Yniss would see them safe or let them die for a greater purpose. He had to believe that, though it sat harsh in his mind.

The Al-Arynaar shouldn't rely on any God. They were placed here by Yniss to succeed.

"Come on. You need to get your head down," he said, ushering Erin away to the hammocks they'd slung under the archer positions. "I need to relieve Rourke on the path."

But the strangers didn't delay long enough. Rebraal ran into Rourke, who was chasing back up the path, slightly out of breath and very scared. They were coming slowly, travelling by lantern light in the relative cool of nighttime. Their pace would bring them to the temple apron an hour before dawn and well before the elves could expect Mercuun. The nine would take on, according to Rourke's count as he had watched them pass below him from the sanctuary of a palm tree, one hundred and thirty-two. Mainly warriors but with ten who were obviously mages.

Tension replaced quiet calm as the reality of the attack overtook the hope that somehow the strangers would be deflected; or that perhaps they were not here to find the temple at all. All the Al-Arynaar had had these thoughts but they seemed foolish now. There was nothing else of interest here for hundreds of square miles and Rebraal doubted they had come to map the mangrove swamps, the volcanic region to the south or the course of the three huge, sluggish rivers that wound their way through the vast rain forest from the northern coastal ports to the southern deltas where desert gave way to lush vegetation again after a thousand miles.

But why had the TaiGethen not found them and dealt with them? And why had the ClawBound not warned him days before?

The leader of the Al-Arynaar visited the platforms for the last time, reminding the archers to pick their targets and not to begin until the wards had caused maximum confusion. And when their stocks of arrows were exhausted, they were to wait for the signal, the threat call of the grey monkey, before moving to attack from the rear with swords, hoping to force whoever remained into the doors of the temple. To the mages, he had given the task of occupying their enemy counterparts, using spells that demanded magical shielding.

Everything else was in the lap of Yniss.

And so they waited and listened, pairs of elves in three of the four platforms that overlooked the apron, and Rebraal himself with the fourth pair, Sheth'erei and Skiriin. They took it in turn to rest in the hammocks below, while all around the forest hummed with anticipation. The denizens of the rain forest and their God, Tual, knew that evil stalked the ground and the calls were of warning and of danger.

As the very first vestiges of light were edging across the top of the canopy and filtering dimly through to the forest floor, the humidity increased dramatically, the darkness of night was abruptly restored to the sky and the rain came. It was harder than Rebraal had ever remembered; it fell in drops that tore weaker leaves apart, exploded on the ground and crashed among the broad boughs of the trees above to trigger miniature waterfalls as leaves sagged and dropped their loads of water.

On the archer platforms, with skins pulled across to deflect the worst of the deluge which was unrelenting for approaching an hour, the Al-Arynaar peered out at the wall of water falling all around them.

"Gyal is angry," said Skiriin.

Rebraal nodded. The capricious God of the rain who could withhold her life-growing nectar at a whim was venting her fury on the strangers now. Rebraal gave a silent prayer of thanks but knew they would need much more than that.

"Rebraal, look," hissed Sheth.

She pointed through the murk of the rain, which was now beginning to ease. Soon it would stop altogether and the sky would clear. Such was the way of the forest. There was lantern light out there. Blurred and dim but unmistakable. No torch would have stood up to the rain and Rebraal was surprised that lanterns had. Presumably, they'd been sheltered.

The call of the brown tree frog filtered across the apron. Rourke had seen them too.

"Sheth, be ready," said Rebraal.

"I will."

The mage sat cross-legged on the platform and closed her eyes. Through her mind she would now be seeing the mana shapes that made up the wards. So would Erin'heth. On the front of the apron, the wards would be activated only when enough of the strangers had crossed them. Every other spell was already active and waiting for the ignorant step of men who shouldn't be there and would learn that fact only in death.

Rebraal watched almost hypnotised as the bobbing lights approached. The sky was clearing quickly as the clouds dispersed, their cargo discharged. The strangers appeared as shadows within shadows, a hulking darkness in the forest growing larger with every pace. But soon he could pick out features, a growth of beard, a low forehead, the glint of weapons and mail, chains on a pair of boots.

Quickly he checked at his feet, saw his bow wrapped in leathers and his quiver of arrows, similarly protected. He stooped to remove the coverings, testing the tension in the string as he did and upending the arrows to stand their tips in a dish of blood poison. All they had to do was hit their targets. Nature would do the rest before the Al-Arynaar had to draw their swords and attack one to one.

"Now it starts," he said.

Next to him, Skiriin, first arrow nocked and ready, nodded nervously. The first strangers broke cover and stepped tentatively onto the flags of the apron. They spread into a loose line twenty men wide, all with weapons drawn, all moving with the cautious assurance of experienced soldiers, eyes everywhere as they advanced toward the temple.

Around them the forest was hushed, but the quiet was broken by a sharp warning from one of the strangers. One of the mages. A quick exchange followed and the attackers began to scatter.

"They've divined the wards," said Rebraal. "Now, Flynd. It's got to be now."

Upward of fifty men were on the apron when the southern perimeter wards were activated and tripped in the same heartbeat. Simultaneously, the scattering force ran into areas covered by wards already set and the apron became a furnace.

Explosions ripped along the length of the stone, hurling bodies into the air, showering others with lethal flame and rippling the stone itself. A wall of flame grasped at the sky, climbing fifty feet into the air, cutting off those on the apron from any help and forcing them toward the temple. Rebraal could see figures wreathed in flame staggering blind, dying and confused, and their wails and desperate shouts echoed against the blank unsympathetic walls of the surrounding forest.

The trapped tried to flee but more explosions held them in. Bodies were littering the apron now as steam hissed in great clouds into the sky. Around the edges of the apron, the rest of the strangers were running, looking for ways to save their comrades, shouts and cries lost in the roar of another FlameWall carving at the dawn. But for those on the apron, there would be no salvation and Shorth would see them to torment in death.

"Wait, Skiriin, wait," whispered Rebraal, hearing the elf's bow tense.

The wards hadn't worked as Rebraal had planned. Not enough men had been on the apron, and though the effects had been devastating and perhaps forty were dead, the elves still faced enormous odds.

The first FlameWall died away and, heedless of further danger, dozens of the strangers ran onto the apron. Anger had replaced helplessness and orders rang back and forth. While some men picked up comrades, dead and alive, three mages knelt in the centre of the stones while others moved toward the door again.

The call of the motmot rang across the apron, and before any of the strangers had paused to look up the trio of mages were dead and the Al-Arynaar were checking their next targets.

All semblance of order disintegrated as panic gripped the attackers. Some injured were dropped, others dragged unceremoniously over the apron to apparent safety in the forest where the stake traps claimed more screaming victims. A few crossbows were brought to bear and bolts fizzed harmlessly into the trees.

Rebraal watched one of the leaders. He was a tall and powerful man, large axe held in one hand, a heavy growth of beard covering cheeks, neck and chin. He was striding toward the doors of the temple bellowing commands to follow him.

"Excellent," said Rebraal under his breath. "Let's hurry you all up."

He tracked right and saw a terrified man debating a run back into the forest. He drew back his arm and let fly his arrow, the tip skewering the man's leg at the top of the thigh. The intruder fell to the ground, staring blindly into the trees, a shout of pain and fear bubbling from his mouth. Another man stooped to help him up. A shaft from across the apron took him clear through the eye. The arrows had the desired effect. The injured man struggled to his feet and joined his comrades fleeing toward the temple.

Faintly, almost inaudibly, Sheth'erei cursed. Rebraal tensed.

"Spell," she muttered.

And so it was. Droplets of pure fire swept from the cloudless sky, lashing into the trees either side of the apron. The soaked leaves of the banyan and fig trees at the edge of the clearing began to smoulder as the strangers' mage flame struck and bit. Across the apron, fire had already taken hold fifty feet up in the canopy, but still the arrows flew and still the strangers fell. A drop struck the platform on which Rebraal stood, where it hissed at the wood, blackening the area around it and sending new smoke into the sky.

"Sheth, your turn," whispered Rebraal.

She nodded and cast. Sweeping in from the north came a horizontal storm of hail, razor sharp and as fast as if driven by a gale. It slivered flesh from unprotected faces and hands, buried itself deep in leather armour and packed the strangers ever faster toward the temple doors. The cacophony was suddenly deafening. The crackle of flame from burning wood mixed with shrieks from deep within the forest as creatures fled what they feared the most, while on the apron the strangers yelled at each other and the blank face of the forest around them as they tried desperately to defend themselves against the DeathHail.

The hail was mercifully short. But the mercy, also, was short lived. Arrows flew unhindered, flashing out from the platforms, most finding their targets but the odd one skipping away off the stone or burying itself in the bole of a tree or lost in the undergrowth. Already, those struck first were feeling the effects of the poison. Their balance betrayed them and they staggered or fell. Their vision tunnelled then disappeared altogether and finally, before death took them, blood streamed from ears, nose and mouth, the poison rupturing vein and artery.

Over half of the strangers were now dead or dying. They had bunched ten yards from the doors to the temple. Ten yards from their goal. Their bearded leader had organised a rough shield defence, and once again crossbow bolts whipped out, chancing to find an enemy.

"They'll try to divine the ward on the doors," warned Sheth'erei.

Rebraal loosed another arrow. He was running short, as was Skiriin. "Can you stop them?"

"We need to distract them," she said, but paused and drew in a sharp breath. "Oh no. Erin, no."

For the first time, fear edged Rebraal's heart. "What is it?"

But he could see. The HotRain still fell but across the apron; it didn't reach the trees any more. Erin'heth was shielding it and the arc of cover was like a beacon to an enemy mage.

"We've got to break silence," said Sheth'erei. "They'll be killed."

Rebraal nodded. "Let's do it."

As one, they set up the staccato call of a water eagle. It was the flight warning and sounded too human. Immediately they'd finished, Rebraal, bow slung over his shoulder, led them down the ladder off the platform. Already he could hear the strangers reacting and the sound of running feet.

But it wasn't himself he was scared for. Turning at the bottom of the ladder, he saw four columns of fire streak down from the sky to plunge into the forest right above the two platforms. It was a spell he'd heard about but never seen, the one that sought souls and took them to hell. And Erin'heth's shield crumbled under its power.

Wood planks and splinters flew from the forest, carrying with them the tattered remains of protective leathers. The flash of the impact threw the temple and its surrounding into sharp relief, revealing them to their attackers for a vital instant. Rebraal saw a flaming body plunge from a platform to land in the undergrowth in a hail of sparks and cinders, the heat setting the vegetation smouldering and pouring out smoke. He heard an awful cry, cut off abruptly. The nine became five at a single stroke.

"Sheth, we have to trip that ward!" he shouted, all thought of stealth gone.

"I'll deal with it," said the mage, her voice thick with anger.

She dropped to her knees and began to cast, her fingers weaving intricate patterns in the air, her eyes closed against the fire that consumed the corpses of her friends. Beside her, Skiriin's bow thrummed and another stranger died.

Rebraal unclipped his jaqrui pouch and grasped one of the throwing crescents, sending it skimming head high into the half dozen strangers coming at them, not thirty yards away. It caught one on the side of the neck, slicing deep. The man cried out, dropped his weapon and clutched at the wound which jetted his life's blood to the earth.

Rebraal drew his sword. In the same instant Sheth'erei cast with devastating effect. Standing to give herself a clear view of the group by the temple doors, she pushed her hands outward, palms up. The ForceCone spread away, invisible, a battering ram of mana crashing into the front rank of shield-bearers who, completely unprepared, were hurled backward into their comrades. The Cone pushed on, and while some scrambled clear of its influence, others were driven back, helpless, tossed head over heels. The result was inevitable. One of them fell into the temple doors.

The flash seared into Rebraal's eyes and he half turned away. The detonation shook the ground under his feet and the branches of the great banyans overhead. The temple doors exploded and a beam of fire scoured outward like the breath of a great dragon, deluging everything in its path with super-heated flame. It reached halfway down the apron and the wall of air following it knocked the surviving Al-Arynaar from their feet.

Rebraal was bowled over but stopped himself quickly and drove back onto his feet, his bow snapped and useless. Nearby, Skiriin was up and had drawn his own slender blade. Sheth'erei was still down but moving, and from the other surviving platform Rourke and Dereneer were running to join them.

"Let's finish this," said Rebraal.

He broke into a sprint, the three other swordsmen hard on his heels, forcing himself not to stop when he caught sight of the apron. The ward had wreaked appalling damage. Fires licked at stone where they had set under-growth alight, bodies and parts of bodies, scorched and burning, lay scattered and twisted, and where a stranger had survived, he begged for death.

Of the group by the door, two were conscious and coming at them. One fired a crossbow, the bolt whipping by Rebraal to bury itself in Dereneer's stomach. The elf sprawled to the ground, sword skittering away. Rebraal leaped a fire and slashed his blade into the crossbowman's arm. The stranger dropped his weapon and staggered back and had no defence against the next strike, which tore across his throat.

Rebraal turned to see Rourke and Skiriin kill the other but behind them, away toward the path, more figures moved. Many more.

"Oh dear Yniss, save us," he said. "Sheth'erei, behind you!"

But the groggy mage couldn't react in time. Half turning in her crouched position she took a sword point through the neck, her scream turning to a gurgle before it and she died.

"No!" Rebraal ran at the enemy, sword raised in one hand, his other seeking a jaqrui. It howled across the closing space, bouncing harmlessly off a metal shoulder guard. A second followed it, this one whispering its danger, connecting with the sword hand of the same man, slicing through his thumb.

But still they came from the forest path. Ten, twenty and maybe more. Rebraal, Skiriin and Rourke took the fight to them, the elves' ferocity keeping them back from the apron and tight to the trees where they couldn't spread out. Rourke dragged his blade through the stomach of one man but the next was quick, jabbing into the elf's chest, and blood welled from the wound. Skiriin backed up, defending furiously, blade licking out at great speed, slashing and nicking. He downed one man with a rip across the neck but it couldn't go on forever. There were too many of them and a blade split his skull.

Rebraal pressed an attack and prayed to Yniss for forgiveness and to Shorth for vengeance. He opened up the defence of his opponent and raised his sword to strike. . . .

But his strike never came. He felt a violent impact in his left shoulder like someone had hit him in the back with a hammer. The pain was excruciating and he pitched forward, the dreadful orange glare of the fires greying to black.

CHAPTER 7

B aron Blackthorne was holding the latest report on the state of his lands handed to him by a trusted aide. He'd ushered the young man to a seat opposite him while he cast his eye down the summary sheet. It was a mild spring evening outside, though in the cool drawing room at Blackthorne Castle a fire roared in the grate between the fifty-one-year-old baron and his aide.

"Have a glass of wine, Luke," he said, indicating the decanter of young Blackthorne red on the table in front of him. "It's ageing well. We'll get a good price for it in a couple of years."

"Thank you, my Lord," said Luke.

He reached forward and grabbed the decanter, topping up Blackthorne's glass before filling his own. Blackthorne watched Luke sit back down on the hard armchair and a smile crossed his lips. The transformation in Luke had been remarkable. Blackthorne had encountered him first in the midst of the Wesmen wars as a scared sixteen-year-old who had lost all his family. He'd been struck then with the youth's pragmatism and straight talking and had made good on a promise to develop him. Luke's farming days were behind him but his experience on the land and his remarkable head for figures and organisation had made him absolutely indispensable.

Blackthorne was used to making people nervous. He was aware of his stature and the stern air lent him by his black hair, beard and hard angular face, and he exploited his advantages. Luke, though, had no fears and was one of the few who would challenge him. Blackthorne respected and admired him for it.

He took a sip of wine and looked down the page. "Am I going to like this?" he asked.

"Yes, Baron," said Luke. "Very much. Mostly."

"Quick précis then," he said. "I'll read the detail later."

Luke ordered his analytical mind before speaking. Blackthorne relaxed into his chair to listen, a finger idly scratching at his beard, which contained an irritating amount of grey these days. But then it had been a hard winter, even in Blackthorne.

"Grain supplies are holding up well and will see us through to first harvest at current population levels. We're still monitoring two bakeries for possible black market sell-on but the others are clear. The scurvy outbreak has been contained. The mages are confident of no further spread and our shipment of oranges began to offload in the bay yesterday.

"We've taken in two hundred more refugees, all families with children, and have now closed the town to more. Out in the fields, the planting is almost complete and spring crops should be ready for harvest in ten days or so. That'll help vegetable supplies. By your order, mounted militia are patrolling the ripening fields, but since the first theft we've had no trouble and the refugee areas are being closely watched.

"Livestock isn't so good, though it's not awful. The dairy herds are fine but we saw a marked depletion in breeding stock during the last two seasons, as you know. New calves, piglets and lambs are all down by up to seventy percent. You'll see I've made a recommendation in the report that we sell off all excess at the premium it'll command and use the money to buy whatever surplus breeding stock we can find and start aggressively rebuilding our herds. If we play it right, we can establish a very strong market position when this thing blows over."

"But eat bread and vegetable stew in the meantime, eh?" Blackthorne grimaced.

"Not entirely, my Lord. We've had some success with the rabbits of late." Luke smiled.

"Ah yes," said Blackthorne. "Those."

It had seemed a grand idea at the time. Capture a few rabbits and breed them. Quick and easy meat, so they thought. Minimal effort and the children of the town had been excited at the prospect of helping. But they had proved susceptible to disease, and they dug. My, how they dug, forcing the fencing to be hammered ever deeper. Blackhorne had been about to abandon the whole project.

"What's different?"

"Well, the mages have isolated the most common disease and devised a treatment for their drinking water that keeps them healthy. And they've also placed a border ward around the fence to a depth of twenty feet. Apparently, it's a low drain spell and is harmless. Just undiggable."

"Good. Excellent." Blackthorne smiled. Where would they be without mages?

"The figures are all inside. Shall I wait while you read them?"

"No, no. Thank you, Luke, that's excellent. I'll come to you with any questions." Luke made to rise. "Take your time. Finish your wine."

"Thank you, my Lord."

"And think on this, as I am. Now the colleges are at war, will the conflict spread here? And if it does, how many refugees will be pushed ahead of it? And when you've made that guess, tell me how you think our defences should be aligned and how our stores would be best protected."

"That possibility hadn't occurred to me," said Luke. "We seem so far away."

"My job to think ahead, yours to tell me how we deal with it. Take your time."

Luke stared into his wine.

Denser walked with his head bowed despite the beauty of the morning. Time was short and The Unknown didn't really appreciate what he'd asked him to do: try and get Erienne to see reason beyond her grief. There was seldom an instant when he wasn't pained by memories of their daughter, but he had chosen not to torture himself with the type of guilt with which Erienne had become so familiar. He didn't want her to stop grieving; he just wanted her to understand that Lyanna's death had been beyond their control. But today wasn't quite like every other day. Today he had to persuade her to leave Herendeneth.

He knew where he'd find her; it was where she spent most of her time. Either tending the grave or lying by it, perhaps singing Lyanna a song or crying into the grass. Sometimes, mercifully, she slipped into sleep.

This morning, Erienne was watering the flowers as Denser approached from slightly behind and to her left. She had a bucket and a cup and was gently pouring water on to the vibrant blooms and into the earth around them, occasionally reaching in to pull up a weed or pick out a dead leaf. Finishing her task, she filled the cup again and poured the contents over her head and face, the water splashing onto her light-weave clothes and running in rivulets down her face. Three times she refilled the cup, then shook her head to send a fine spray of water into the air. She pushed her hands over her face and through her hair.

Gods falling, but she was beautiful. The water had soaked her shirt; the material clinging to the curve of her breasts and the wet hair hanging down her back were bewitching. Denser sighed. For now, he consigned such thoughts to his dreams. He knew Erienne felt desire too but it was up to her to come to him; she knew he would be waiting.

As always, she heard him approach and half turned, the corners of her mouth turned up just slightly.

"I'm sorry I closed the door last night," she said.

Denser smiled and shook his head. It hadn't been the first time he'd slept elsewhere. "Don't worry, love."

"I missed your breathing."

"Did you?" Denser sat beside her, surprised at her willingness to talk. So often, this was the hardest thing for her. Seeing the grave brought everything back so clearly.

"Everyone has to have something real," she said, pushing a strand of hair away from her mouth. "Something that's there the next time you want it."

"And I'll always be there."

"But I know why you're here now. Right now."

"I assumed you would. You know he's right, don't you?" asked Denser, looking for the flash of anger in her eyes. It wasn't there. At least, not yet.

"But no one asked me, did they? You all just assumed I'd go along. That I'd leave her here alone." She reached out a hand to pat the ground and the tears were there so suddenly. "How can you ask that of me? She's my daughter."

Denser put out an arm but Erienne shied away, wiping at her face with her fingers.

"She'll never be alone. She'll be safe until you return, I'll see to that."

Erienne made a derisory sound in her throat. "Going to have one of the Protectors look after this bed, are you? It'll be ruined in a day."

Denser wasn't sure if she was joking or not. "There are the Guild elves."

"If I'm not here, those witches will meddle. Spoil what I've done." There was the flash and it saddened Denser's heart.

"Erienne, they haven't even the strength to walk here. Nerane can do it. She has the right touch, don't you think?"

Erienne shrugged but said nothing, just stared down at the grave.

"Erienne?" She looked up at him. "Please? We need you. The Raven isn't complete without you."

"You'd leave me, would you? If I said no?"

"I'm Raven," said Denser.

"You're my husband first, you bastard!" she snapped out. "But The Unknown snaps his fingers and you go running. Fine."

"When I asked for his help, he was there. For both of us," said Denser quietly. "And he left his family to do it. Balaia needs what we can give it."

"I've lost everything," said Erienne as if engaged in another conversation.

"Not quite. There's me, there's The Raven and there's Balaia. You'll never lose me but we have to fight for our country."

Erienne looked hard at him then, trying to discern any insincerity. "You really think The Raven can help, don't you?"

"Don't you?" replied Denser, and shrugged.

"We don't always win, do we?" said Erienne, her voice threatening to break again.

"No we don't. But we're there nonetheless."

"And you will go whether I do or not?"

"Oh, love, it's not a choice I want to make. But we've our lives together forever and I want us to have a country to live in that's worthy of you."

"Denser, you're so honourable sometimes," she chided gently, a smile brief as a blink on her lips. "But you're asking me to leave her and I don't know that I can do that."

"You'll be among your most trusted friends," said Denser, and this time she didn't shy away from his arm but allowed him to draw her close. Denser felt a thrill at her beautiful wet hair smell so close to him. "Here, you'll be alone. With us, you'll never be so."

"I'll be a burden. Hardly the Raven mage you all remember. I haven't got concentration enough to heal a cut."

"You'll be fine." Denser felt he was edging the argument. "And if you're not with me, I'll fear for you here."

Erienne tensed and pulled away. "Another lever to get me off the island and away from my daughter. Convenient indeed."

Denser cursed silently. "Don't be angry, please. I don't think The Unknown had much choice. They'd have come here sooner or later anyway. At least now they'll do some good too."

"Like forcing me from here, you mean."

"Like freeing Protectors and helping dragons," said Denser more sharply than he'd intended. He took a breath and softened his tone. "Look, right now, no one but we and the Al-Drechar know what you carry. And one day I'm sure you'll be open to the hope it offers. But if Xetesk finds out you have the spirit of the One within you, they'll stop at nothing to exploit you. You know that."

"You've got all the cards, haven't you?" Erienne stood up and brushed herself down, her stare cold. "Bet you all think you're being very clever, don't you?"

"Erienne, this isn't about forcing you from Lyanna, surely you see that? It's about—"

"Fighting for bloody Balaia again. Yes, I know." Denser all but flinched at the hardness in her tone. "Well look where helping other people has got me. Three dead children. When's someone going to help me for a change? When's someone . . ."

She crumpled into a heap, her sobs shuddering her body, huge breaths heaving in and out. Denser pulled her onto his lap, stroking her hair and whispering close to her ear, biting hard on his own sorrow lest it overcome him too.

"We'll help you," he said. "But you have to let us in. And you have to start to let go. Please let me in, Erienne. Please."

"How many of them were there?" Captain Yron wiped a hand across his face and looked over the scorched carnage in front of the temple. He had been very lucky, slipping round what was apparently a ForceCone and diving aside just as the doors exploded, killing thirty of his people in an instant. Even so, he'd had the hair scorched from his chin and half his head. It itched like hell.

"Nine, sir," said his just-promoted second in command, a drawn and scared youth called Ben-Foran. The boy had smears of black over his face and a long burn down the left side of his chin and neck.

"Dear Gods, is that all? Are you sure there are no more?"

"As sure as we can be, sir. But they can just melt into the forest."

Ben-Foran's eyes were everywhere. Yron couldn't blame him. In all they'd lost eighty-five men to wards, swords and poisoned arrows. Such ferocity he'd never known before. Yron was aware of the Al-Arynaar, of course, but they weren't supposed to be so fierce, unlike the elite TaiGethen. More a ceremonial guard. And if rumour and intelligence could be so wrong about the Al-Arynaar, what about their reportedly far more dangerous cousins?

"Well, let's make sure our perimeter defence is sound. As many as possible will sleep inside tonight," he said, jerking a thumb over his shoulder at the beautifully cool temple. "We'll be all right."

Ben-Foran looked past him. "Are they nearly finished in there?"

Yron looked round at his two remaining mages, searching for more wards and traps. They'd been in there hours, and the sun had been unrelenting since the predawn rains.

"Gods, I hope so, son," he said. He clapped the boy on the shoulder and turned him round. "Come on. Let's check the living and honour the dead, what's left of them."

An insect bit into his arm. He slapped at the creature, the third he had felt in the last few minutes. Gods knew how many had gone unnoticed. He caught the expression on Ben-Foran's face. Both men scratched at their arms instinctively. He knew what the boy was thinking. Cuts, blisters and insect stings meant nothing in Balaia but everything here. And only two mages to keep almost fifty men well. They would have to be very careful.

The pyre was still burning on the centre of the apron when Yron finally got his first look inside the temple that had cost them so dear. All but the two mages and Ben-Foran were outside, awaiting the signal that meant relief from the oppressive heat and humidity of the early afternoon.

Inside, it was almost cool, chilly in comparison. The stone was deep and carried little heat, and the flow of cold water into the pool, undoubtedly from some underground spring, gave the temple a refreshing atmosphere. It was, Yron conceded as he looked up at the splendidly detailed statue, a very pleasant place to be. At that moment almost perfect in fact.

"The light is beautiful," said Ben-Foran.

Yron turned. Ben was indicating the shafts of coloured light filtering through the glass blocks and windows at the top of the temple walls and set into the base of the dome roof. The effect had clearly been lessened by the destruction of the doors but he could see what the boy meant.

"Not just decorative, either," said Erys, a clever young mage archivist with very bright red hair he should have kept shorter. If he had been a soldier, Yron could have forced him to.

"Used in ceremony, you think?" suggested Yron.

"Much more than that. They open and close doors at the back of the temple."

Yron raised his eyebrows. "Really? I think you'd better show me that."

Erys led the captain around the statue into a short corridor. It was dark but for light spilling out from two open doorways.

"Both of these opened while we were in here, and a third closed," said Erys. "We thought it was a trap at first but Stenys is convinced it's the lights passing across particular areas of the statue. We'll monitor it."

Yron glanced into one of the rooms. It was a shrine of sorts. A carved figure sat in an alcove surrounded by incense sticks. A few parchments lay stacked on a low table. A single cushion was propped against the back wall.

"Anything of interest here?"

Erys shook his head. "I don't think so but we'll take everything anyway. There are some more likely papers next door but we'll have to wait for the real prize."

Yron stared at him blankly.

"There must be a dozen rooms at least," the mage explained. "And we don't know when they'll open."

Yron snorted. "Then let's take the walls down. I'm not waiting here a day longer than I have to. I'm being eaten alive. And some of them out there won't last. You've seen the fever."

"I know." Erys nodded. "And we'll do everything we can. But there's something you don't understand. Come and see."

He led Yron back through the temple to the doors. Ben-Foran had wandered back outside to organise something.

"Here," said Erys, indicating the stone lintel and the pillars that had once housed the doors. "Notice anything interesting?"

Yron gave the elaborate carvings and engravings on the stonework a cursory glance and rubbed a hand across the smooth insides where the door frame had sat flush. He shrugged.

"Well, it doesn't seem too damaged."

"Captain, it isn't damaged *at all*. I mean, there aren't even any scorch marks. Not here, not anywhere on the temple stone. I know that ward was focussed out but even so . . ."

"Meaning?"

"It's why we were so long earlier. We've probed the structure. Every stone in this temple is bound to every other by a force we can't fathom. It's magic of some sort, but ancient. Really ancient. The only thing not bound in is the statue they built this place round—presumably because it's marble."

"So you're saying it's strong, is that it?"

"Oh, it's much more than strong," said Erys. "If you scratch away the lichen and plant growth on the outside, it hardly even looks old. For one thing, I don't think any spell or tool we've got can do the job. And for another, if by some mischance we did damage the structure, the binding magic would snap any hole shut. Rather violently."

"Terrific," muttered Yron. "Welcome to your new home." He scratched at his arms, feeling the lumps of the insect bites. He faced the mage. "Right, I want you two to examine every parchment you find immediately each of these bloody doors opens. Finding a text on repelling insects would go down very well right now."

Erys chuckled. "We'll do what we can. Unfortunately, much of it's in an ancient elven dialect we can't read."

"Well, this gets better," said Yron dryly. "How will you know when you've found what Dystran wants?"

"We won't," he said. "Not necessarily anyway, though we expect to recognise enough to help us. But we're still taking pretty much everything that's not nailed down. Just in case."

Yron looked for a sign that Erys was joking. He plainly wasn't. The captain nodded.

"Right, I'll catch up with you later. Let me know about anything else you find." He switched his attention outside. "Ben! Get your arse over here!"

"Sir!" The new lieutenant jogged up.

"Right. Here's what I want. Log every cut, blister and infected bite. List every man with the fever. Give it all to Stenys to work through. Next, I need eight of the fittest to go back to the camp and bring back enough canvas to cover this entrance and set up a stores tent. They are also to bring shovels, wood axes and picks and I want as much food as they can load onto the pack animals, assuming the stupid things are still alive. They have a remarkably developed instinct for uncovering danger.

"Anyway. The camp guard and the mage are to stay there, look after the sick and the rest of the kit. If that dimwit girl can keep any of them alive, it would be a real bonus. I want the eight back here by midnight so they'd better get a move on. Meanwhile, you mark out pitching and shit-hole areas, organise a firewood party and set a ring of four fires around this entrance. I don't want anything unwelcome disturbing my sleep. Looks like we could be here for a while. All clear?"

Ben-Foran nodded. "Yes, sir."

"Good. I'll be inside exercising my rank privilege and watching you all get hot and tired. We'll all sleep in there tonight but anyone pissing in the pool gets staked out for the jaguars. Oh, and Ben, remind the firewood party to wear gloves and be careful where they're putting their hands. If it moves when you pick it up, it isn't a stick."

Ben-Foran grinned. "Yes, sir."

"Good. Now get to it. The light'll fade quickly." Yron turned and strode back into the glorious cool of the temple. "Dear Gods, what did I do to land this dog's arse of a command?"

CHAPTER 8

Erienne felt sick. The nausea spread through her whole body and made her head swim. It knotted her stomach and quivered in her limbs. The blood was pounding in her neck so hard she thought it would burst through her skin. She reached out a pale and shaking hand toward the door handle then let it drop, having to lean on the frame to steady herself. She wasn't sure whether this was fear or hate. Probably it was a mixture of the two. And she could let them see neither.

She gathered her strength, grasped the door handle and pushed open the door, stepping inside before her mind forced her body to run.

"Erienne, how delightful to see you at last."

And there they were, the two of them, sat in deep, fabric-upholstered chairs, their legs propped up on cushioned footstools. They looked frail and old and a sickness had disfigured their skin but their eyes burned bright. They should both be dead. Like her daughter. Yet here they were, greeting her like a grandchild, which to them she probably was.

"This is not a social call," said Erienne, hardening her voice. "I will not exchange pleasantries with those who orchestrated the murder of my daughter."

"We grieve for your loss—" began Myriell.

"Don't you dare!" Erienne's shout caused them both to flinch. She felt tears well up but refused to let her sorrow get the better of her. "Don't ever tell me you grieve. Dear Gods drowning, but it was you who let her die. And you didn't have to."

"We felt—"

"You didn't have to," repeated Erienne deliberately. "You panicked when the Dordovans attacked. I could have saved her. You should have trusted The Raven and you should have trusted me. But you didn't."

Two seasons she had been waiting to say these words. Two seasons where bottomless grief and gut-wrenching loathing had robbed her of the strength to face them as she wanted to. The nausea eased and the nerves steadied. She felt in control of herself.

"But you would have died doing so," said Myriell.

"To die for my daughter would have been the greatest honour of my life. I'm her mother. What the hell else would you expect of me?"

Erienne moved further into the room. The door to the kitchen opened but her scowl sent Nerane scurrying back.

"We expected you to fulfill your belief in the greater necessity of maintaining the One magic," said Cleress.

"My, my, how divorced you are from reality." Erienne's words dripped like venom as she advanced on the Al-Drechar's chairs to stand over them, looking down on their pitifully weak forms. "Did you ever have children of your own or have you always been as dried up and infertile as you are now?"

She rested her hands on the arms of Myriell's chair and leaned in close. "I would have done anything to save my child's life. Being prepared to die for her was easy. And your One magic didn't even figure."

There was silence as the two women stared each other out, Erienne finally straightening and stepping back as Myriell broke the gaze.

"So why have you come to us?" asked Cleress. "Just to vent your feelings or is there more?"

Erienne turned on her. "And do you not think I have the right? Do you really think in your senile minds that I might have come to see your actions as right? You sicken me."

"No, we don't think that," said Cleress. "And we don't expect your forgiveness either. And yes, we both bore children. But the One is bigger and more critical than any of us."

"Try telling that to Lyanna!" stormed Erienne, the tears threatening. She felt overwhelmed by their calm detachment. They were cold.

"And she lives on within you now but you deny it," said Myriell.

"Do you think me completely bereft of sense?" Erienne shook her head. "I felt what you forced from Lyanna into me and I understand why she had such difficulty controlling it. But it is not in any way some essence of my daughter. It is a malignant force, trying to overpower me. But I am too strong for it and so it lies dormant until I am ready, should that time ever come."

"But accept it you must," said Cleress, her voice suddenly gaining intensity. "It is the future for us all."

Erienne stared at her long and hard.

"If you deny it forever, it will shrivel and wither, but not before causing your death. Then you and your daughter will both have died in vain," said Myriell.

"On my terms if at all," said Erienne slowly. "If you so much as touch the outer reaches of my mind, I swear I will come back here and kill you both. I trust I make myself clear."

"Back?" Cleress's half smile stretched her face painfully.

"That is why I am here. The Raven are leaving here and I have been reminded that I am one of The Raven. Xetesk controls Herendeneth now. We have things to do, so my husband informs me. While I am gone, keep out of my mind unless by some miracle I invite you in. But more important, stay away from Lyanna's grave. Your foul presence would upset her rest. Nerane will tend her until I return."

Myriell and Cleress shared a glance.

"We will, of course, respect your wishes," said Cleress. "But remember we are dying. And even though you may hate us, you need us. Because the One will awake and only we can shepherd you through the ordeal you must face."

"If I choose to believe you."

"Believe me, girl!" snapped Myriell. "It is an enormous power. And if you awaken it without our help, your fate will be more awful than your daughter's."

Erienne was surprised at the vehemence of Myriell's outburst but still refused to be cowed.

"I know you want what lies dormant in my head. I know you think you can return the One to dominance through me. But for now it is lost to you. And you will suffer that loss as I have suffered mine. But at least you will have the one thing I do not. Hope."

"Be careful where you travel," warned Cleress.

"I will go where I choose and I will do as I please." Erienne turned and headed toward the kitchen door, suddenly hungry. She paused at the door as a final thought struck her.

"You do not own me, Al-Drechar. And you do not own what I host. You would do well to remember that."

Ilkar left Herendeneth with a mix of emotions that left him distinctly uncomfortable. He hardly knew where to start to sort it all out. He was happy to be leaving the island but deeply concerned by the overwhelming Xeteskian presence there. His desire to recruit, even temporarily, mages from Calaius to help rebuild Julatsa was tempered by his anxiety about returning to his Southern Continent homeland for the first time in over a century.

And perhaps worse than all of it, immediately at least, he was going to have to travel there by ship. Despite the pouch of the relaxing and settling drug, lemiir, that the Al-Drechar had given him, his memories of misery and sickness on the open ocean were all too fresh.

Scaling the netting covering the port side of the *Calaian Sun*, he dropped onto the deck and shook hands with the ship's master, Captain Jevin. The elven sailor smiled a little too knowingly.

"Hoping to develop sea legs a little quicker this time?" he asked.

"Just tell me it's not a long journey," replied Ilkar.

"Three days if the weather holds." Jevin's eyes sparkled. "Still, there's a healthy eight- to ten-foot swell out there and you know how capricious the weather can be."

"I'm so glad I asked."

Jevin laughed and gestured aft. "Same cabin, Ilkar. Make yourself comfortable."

Ilkar hefted his bag and moved off along the sleek vessel, nodding at any of the crew who had time to look up as he passed. All elven, the ship and her crew had played a pivotal role in stopping the Dordovans capturing Lyanna, risking their own lives for a wholly inadequate price to take The Raven across the storm-ravaged Southern Ocean. It was a debt that could never properly be repaid, not with mere coin though they were now pledged a good deal of that. But all Ilkar hoped for was a calm enough sea. Feeling the first twinges in his stomach at just the thought, he went below.

In quick time, The Raven were all aboard, netting and boats were stowed and the anchor was weighed. Ilkar joined Hirad at the rail to watch Herendeneth slip away aft, Jevin setting only topsail and foresail for the delicate journey out of the treacherous waters of the Ornouth Archipelago.

Above them, wheeling and calling in the sky, the Kaan dragons watched them go. Beside Ilkar, Hirad was smiling.

"Sha-Kaan having a few words, is he?" asked the elf.

Hirad nodded. "He's talking about you, actually."

"Oh, terrific."

Ilkar didn't get on with the dragons. Not that anyone really did. Except Hirad of course. Something about the thick skin they shared, or so went the joke. But then, Hirad and Sha-Kaan had a unique relationship, part of which allowed their minds to touch, facilitating telepathic communication.

"What's he saying, exactly?"

"Well, I mentioned that you were concerned about the Xeteskians on Herendeneth," explained Hirad. "He said he'd make sure they didn't step out of line, so to speak."

"Oh," said Ilkar. "I rather thought he might be coming along with us. Calaius would be very much to his liking, climate-wise."

"Come off it, Ilks. Wake up. He has to get home, so he's staying to work with the Al-Drechar and the Xeteskians. I'd have thought you'd be pleased— it gives us direct communication to Herendeneth. At least you'll know what's going on."

"I thought that was what Aeb was coming for?" Ilkar frowned.

Hirad turned to face him. "This has all really got to you, hasn't it?"

"What do you mean?"

"Well, it's just that it's unlike you to be so thick, that's what."

"Thanks for being so tactful."

"Sorry." Hirad smiled. "Look, Aeb is Denser's Given Protector, and anyway The Unknown likes him and needs him to fight on his left; that's why he's here. And, let's face it, his communication with the other Protectors is hardly going to be independent, is it? Any information they get will be from the Xeteskian mages."

"I suppose."

Ilkar turned and leaned his back against the rail. Hirad was right; he didn't feel clearheaded at all. And of course everything the barbarian said made perfect sense. He shook his head ruefully and looked about him. So, here they all were again, but it didn't feel quite right, not yet anyway. And the reason for that was clear enough and was surely why The Unknown was so keen that Erienne and Thraun were on the ship.

It was because they were travelling with people who would never be true members of The Raven. Ilkar could remember clearly when Thraun came to the group. Even though he had been a stranger, there was somehow no doubt he was one of them. To a certain extent, the same was true of Darrick, though he would have to learn to open up more. But Aeb, well, he wasn't Raven. He was a Protector first and that was wrong. The same went for Ren. She was with them because she loved him, was a Calaian elf, an archer of consummate skill and a useful fighter. But she didn't understand what being in The Raven meant. Her loyalty to the Guild of Drech, who looked after the Al-Drechar, was no training for the total belief she had to be able to show in The Raven to be one of them. The problem she had at the moment was that she thought the two were similar.

What made Ilkar anxious, despite his personal feelings for her, was that he knew she wouldn't have been invited to join Balaia's foremost mercenary team in normal circumstances. And that made Hirad and The Unknown particularly uncomfortable. Ilkar could see some difficult times ahead.

He sighed and turned back to the rail. The Unknown was to his left, still waving to Diera and Jonas who were watching from the beach. Another tearful parting. He patted the big warrior on the shoulder.

"Don't worry. We'll be back soon enough."

The Unknown looked at him and smiled rather sadly. "Now Ilkar," he said, "neither you nor I believe for one moment that is true, do we?"

Selik blamed the loss of Balaia's beauty on the curse of magic. In a lighter mood he might have added his own face to the losses, ruined as it had been by the bitch Erienne's IceWind six years before, but this was no time for levity.

He'd thought he'd seen everything, but riding at the head of his fifty-strong band of ever hungry but resourceful men into Erskan, he saw the hardest sight of all. On the outskirts of the once comfortable if not prosperous castle town, two boys were advancing on a girl, knives in their grubby hands. The girl was backing away, eyes wide and fearful, desperate for a way out but unwilling to give up what she had clutched to her chest. None of them was more than seven years old.

Selik ordered his men to stop before riding in alone, looking around for any local men or women who might have intervened. Apparently, though, this end of the cobbled main road into the heart of Erskan was deserted.

The two boys ignored him as he reined in and dismounted but the girl stared at him, not sure if he was saviour or robber. He stepped smoothly between them, shielding the girl, his cloak billowing, giving her assailants no sight of her. His hood he kept well forward. He had no intention of showing them his face.

"Must we steal from our sisters to survive?" he slurred through his partly paralysed mouth.

"She won't share," said one of the boys, his eyes sunken into a face gaunt with hunger.

"But does she have enough to share, I wonder?" asked Selik. "And would you have shared with her, eh?"

He turned his head to see the girl, dirty faced with short black hair and tiny ears, weighing up whether or not to run. He held out a hand. "Stand by me, child. They won't harm you."

Reluctantly, she did so, her hand small and fragile in his fingers. He smiled, happy she couldn't see what it did to his face.

"Now," he said gently. "Show me what you were so keen to have to yourself."

The other hand came away from her chest to display her prize. It was bread, a filthy crust, but there wasn't enough to satisfy one of these tattered children and what there was came covered in dirt and speckled with lurid mould. That they would fight over this . . .

"I tell you what," he said, trying to mask his disgust. "Why don't you give me that and I'll fetch food enough for you all?"

The girl gaped in amazement but the boys, who had been shifting about nervously, unwilling to desert any potential scrap to eat, frowned in concert.

"Why would you do that?" asked the other boy, a freckle-faced lad with filthy light brown hair and dried snot on his upper lip. He wasn't dressed in rags, it was just that his clothes had been worn too long. They were shabby, but not in tatters.

"Because you are hungry and we can spare food for the three of you. And because I am a good man, following a just cause."

"Who are you then?" asked the girl, simultaneously tightening her grip on his hand and proffering the repulsive crust.

Selik accepted it and began walking back toward his men, his horse following obediently behind him and the children. "Well, young lady, my name is Selik and I am in charge of a group trying to help people like you and your parents and all your friends. We're called the Black Wings. Have you heard of us?"

The girl shook her head. So did the two boys who walked the other side of him. Selik felt a grim satisfaction.

"Ah well, never mind. But I tell you what. In order for us to help you and all those you love get better and for there to be more food, when I give you something to eat will you tell me where some people are?"

The girl shrugged but nodded.

"Thank you. What's your name?"

"Elise," said the girl.

"A lovely name for a lovely girl."

"Why do you wear a hood?" one of the boys asked abruptly.

Selik stopped and glared at him, and saw the boy shrink back. His face might have been effectively hidden but the glint of his one good eye wouldn't be.

"Because when you fight evil, sometimes you get hurt. And now my face frightens little boys and girls and they think badly of me," he said, fighting to remain calm. "Now then, your food." He clicked his fingers at the nearest rider. "Devun, give some dried meat and some of that spring fruit you found to each of these three. They are hungry and their need is greater than ours."

Devun raised his eyebrows but unclasped a saddlebag and fetched out some wrapped packages. Giving each one a sniff as he produced it, he passed on three to Selik. The Black Wing commander unwrapped them and showed the contents to the children; two contained strips of dried meat, and one soft fruit, turning to overripe.

"Now, this food will last you a while if you're careful, and I don't want to hear that you have fought over it." He let his gaze linger on the two boys until both shifted and nodded. "Good. If we are to become strong again, we have to work together."

He crouched and passed over the food, which the trio grabbed hungrily, mumbling thanks as mouths watered and eyes widened in anticipation. The dividing up began immediately.

"And your part of the bargain," he said, dragging their attention back to him, "is to tell me two things. Is Lord Erskan still alive?"

"Yes, he is," said Elise. "But he doesn't come out of the castle anymore. My brother says he's sick."

"Or hiding from his people," said Selik under his breath. "And do you know if there are any mages still in the town?"

There was a pause.

"I think so," said the freckled boy, after sharing a glance with his friend. "But I don't know where they are."

"I'm sure you don't." Selik stood up. "I expect they are too ashamed to show their faces. Skulking about at night if they dare." He breathed deep. "Now, you three be on your way but remember this. All your hunger and all your pain was caused by magic and the people who use magic without a thought for those it affects. People like you and your families are the victims. If you find out where the mages are, you come and see me and I'll deal with them for you. Run along."

He watched them hurry away down the main street, their voices raised in squabbles about shares but their conflict over the crust forgotten, at least until their stomachs emptied again.

Selik turned to his men. "If there is a more eloquent demonstration of the evil we face, I have not seen it. Mount up; we're going to the castle. And we're going there proud and through the market place."

CHAPTER 9

Selik and his men rode slowly through the centre of Erskan, seeing in the human ruins of the once quiet and pleasant town a reflection of all the ills afflicting Balaia. Filth covered the streets, which were deserted but for a few scavengers out on the hunt for scraps they had little or no chance of finding. The Black Wings became instant targets for beggars, of which there were many. Some had been born to it and they now fared better than their once wealthier competitors, who looked sicker and thinner than those on whom they had so recently looked down.

The market tried to struggle on but Selik didn't see a single food stall. Silver and gold were barely in evidence either. What the traders wanted in return for their cut-price goods were bread, meat and grain. At its edges, inns were closed and businesses boarded up. Those not begging or attempting to ply a trade but just walking about did so with a kind of stupefied expression. Selik understood that too. The pace of what had befallen Balaia was staggering and all but impossible to grasp.

Down side streets, bodies rotted where they had been left, some obviously months before. And though the town stank of decay and disease, in some ways it was cleaner than before. Not a stray cat or dog ran, not a rat scuttled. All in the stomachs of the desperate by now.

Selik arrived at the castle and found exactly what he had expected: portcullis lowered, doors barred shut and guards on the gatehouse battlements, bows ready.

"We have nothing!" called a voice. "And what we have goes to our people. There's nothing here for travellers. Move on."

"I want nothing but the ear of your Lord for a few minutes. I am Selik and this is my Black Wing guard. We have food for ourselves and our horses graze the open pastures. Might I speak with him?" Selik's good eye roved the battlements. Erskan's pennants snapped defiantly in the wind, so at least he was at home.

"What is it you wish to discuss?" asked the same voice.

Selik saw him, on the left of the gatehouse, leaning slightly out. "Restoration of Balaia to its former glory. A subject close to all our hearts."

There was a short conversation. The man nodded.

"You may enter. Your men remain outside."

"Naturally," said Selik. "And thank you."

He heard the sound of the portcullis being raised and saw it rise above the gatehouse walls. The doors creaked ajar. Selik rode forward alone, seeing the killing ground beyond the doors lined with soldiers. Erskan was one nervous man.

Riding into the courtyard, Selik dismounted, his horse was led away to the stables and he was shown into the keep. A squire took him through a great entrance hall hung with deep-coloured tapestries, through a single door to the right and up a short flight of stairs. A further corridor revealed four or five doors and he was ushered through the first of them.

"Relax, sir," said the squire. "My Lord Erskan will be along presently."

Selik was in a small cold room. An empty grate dominated the far end and what light came in was through stained-glass windows in the wall to the right. A scattering of armchairs in front of the hearth was the only furniture bar two small low tables and the Erskan crest above the grate.

Deciding he'd rather be found standing, Selik walked to the windows and looked out. The town sprawled away beyond the courtyard, silent and grieving. He sighed and pulled his hood tight over his head. Behind him, the door creaked open.

"It wasn't so very long ago that I would have run you out of my town, Black Wing."

Selik turned to see Lord Erskan enter, attended by the same squire. The youth carried a tray with two glasses and a pewter flagon, placing them on one of the low tables. Erskan waved him out.

"Come and sit," said Erskan, moving slowly to the chairs. "I can offer you a glass of wine. That is something in which we are rich." A dry chuckle escaped his lips. "And do take that damn silly hood off. I am aware of the deformities it hides."

Selik swept the hood back, glad for the play of air across his head. He sat down opposite Erskan, who didn't flinch as he took in Selik's smeared left cheek, dead white eye and slack left jaw. He was a middle-aged man grown very old in just two seasons. Terribly thin and frail looking, his wisps of grey hair were oiled down on a scalp that topped a narrow, long-nosed face with a sharp chin and dull blue eyes. His hands, liver spotted and with nails bitten down to the quick, shook as he poured the wine and handed Selik a glass.

"So, Captain, or is it Commander, Selik. What great statement do you have to cheer the people of Erskan?" The Lord spoke as he put his glass to his lips.

"Captain, please." Selik smiled. "I understand your scepticism, my Lord. And I would concede that certain actions of the Black Wings have been, shall we say, overzealous?"

"A vast understatement," said Erskan.

"Be that as it may, we have all seen these past two seasons and more that our fears were entirely justified. More than that, the reality has far outweighed even my most fervent nightmares."

Erskan's nod was cautious. "But surely you are not attempting to justify murder or any of your lesser crimes."

"Murder is an emotive word." Selik bristled despite his determination to remain under control. "I'm only asking you to agree that magic must, as we have always said in the Black Wings, be monitored and regulated independently of the colleges."

Erskan rested back in his chair. A cloud came across the sun, dimming the tinted light in the sparse room.

"Well, I think that might be going a little far. Though a code of conduct might be a good compromise," said Erskan. "After all, one rogue child does not make every mage in every college irresponsible."

"But look at what she spawned, devastation and now war," said Selik. "And can any of us forget what has been caused in Arlen, or indeed in Julatsa, by the indiscriminate use of magic?"

"Well, I—"

"Have you been to Arlen, my Lord? Have you visited Korina or Gyernath, Denebre or Greythorne?" Selik's tone hardened. He could see he wasn't getting through.

"I must confess, no." At least Erskan had the grace to be embarrassed. "We have had problems of our own here."

"Arlen has all but been destroyed by the new conflict. But your buildings still stand and your farmers are planting new crops. For you, there is an end in sight."

Erskan's smile was thin. "And our families bury their dead daily, they report their sick in ever-increasing numbers but the healers are dead too and the mages have fled. By the time the harvest comes, I will have less than a third of my people alive. And I wonder if there will be anyone fit enough to tend the crops, let alone gather them in."

Selik took a long sip of his wine. It was a Denebre red, a wine that would soon command a very high price. Denebre and its vineyards had been swallowed by the earth. Erskan's eyes held depths of sorrow and desperation that should have melted the most frozen heart. But the Black Wings couldn't afford such sentimentality.

"Then now is the time to strike," Selik said. "To make the mages pay for the blight they've cast on our land. Where are they now, eh? In your hours of greatest need they are all at each other's throats.

"I need men, Lord Erskan. And I need them now. Do you think you'll somehow escape the war here? We have to make a stand. All the innocent people who have died because of the mages must be avenged."

Erskan frowned. "I sympathise with you in this, I really do. But all you have to do is look about you to know why I can't help you."

"Without popular support, where are we?" asked Selik, failing to conceal his disappointment. "Balaians have to stand up now. They weaken each other every day they fight. We can break their domination, but only if we do it now."

Lord Erskan drained his glass and refilled it. The clouds moved on and the light sharpened.

"You'll find men out there with the will, I have no doubt," he said, gesturing at the windows with his free hand. "Men who have learned to hate mages, magic and everything they stand for.

"But where will you find the strength, Captain? You want an army but those you see around you are struggling just to keep themselves and their families alive. I will ask no more of them and nor shall you."

"And your own guard?"

"I won't spare you even one. There are those within and without who would plunder what little we have. If I let that happen, I will have striven my whole life for nothing."

Selik finished his wine and stood up, feeling his frustration grow. It was a litany he had heard in half a dozen places but he had true support from many more.

"But unless we curb the colleges' power now, while we have the opportunity, you are lost anyway."

Erskan gave the slightest of shrugs but said nothing. Selik nodded and pulled his hood back over his head.

"We have all made sacrifices and we have all seen friends and loved ones die. But to make our futures worth living, magic must be tamed. And I will do it with you or without you. But be prepared for change, my Lord. And soon."

Erskan stood too, and began moving toward the door. "You will do what you will do. I cannot give you my blessing or my men but I can wish a brighter future for us all. If you are instrumental in bringing that to Balaia, then I will have nothing but respect for you. But be sure you are just, because Balaia's people have had enough of the unjust and power brokers treating them like pawns and playthings to be used and discarded on a whim."

"And that is why I will fight. The righteous are always just, my Lord, though those who do not see the path are often shocked at its turns." A thought struck him. "When did your mages leave?"

Erskan shook his head. "A day ago, perhaps two. Heading for Julatsa. They are long gone from you. I don't really remember."

"Thank you for your audience." Selik bowed his head.

"It wasn't just to hear you, Selik, it was to thank you."

"For what?" Selik couldn't disguise his surprise.

"What you did for the street children. Every little helps."

Selik smiled beneath his hood. "Well, well, the sign of a Lord in control. Eyes everywhere." He bowed his head again. "Good day, Lord Erskan, and if you have a change of heart, you will find me. I already have support from Corin, Rache, Pontois—such as it is—Orytte and too many villages to mention."

Erskan seemed unimpressed. "They are free to make their choices, as am I. Take care on your path, Selik. The emotion of the people might be with you now but it is fickle. And no matter how much magic is feared and despised now, most of us count mages among our friends."

"But while they conduct a war, you are nothing to them, believe me. You only have to see Arlen to understand that."

Selik turned and followed the squire back to the courtyard and his horse. He was irritated but not surprised at Erskan's reaction. But he couldn't let it bother him. He had to focus on what he could rely on right now. The speed of his horses on the open road.

After all, a day wasn't so much to make up. Not if you knew how.

Yron looked out over the fires into the impenetrable shadows of the rain forest and felt at ease for the first time since he had set foot on Calaius. His men had returned from the base camp reporting some improvement in the condition of the fever and snake bite cases and they'd all enjoyed a relaxed meal an hour or so after midnight.

Guards stood at the edge of the ring of fires in front of the temple, but with the stores tent built and everything edible off the ground and sealed, he didn't feel the need to post a permanent guard there. With wood enough to keep the fires going for two nights stacked in the stores tent and in the temple he even felt sanguine toward the rain, which fell periodically and with enough force to douse flames and send his men scurrying for cover.

He turned and wandered back inside the lantern-lit cool of the temple, allowing the canvas flap to fall back and hide the night. After failing to attach it to the stone, they'd hung it over a log balanced on the wide stone lintel.

There was a healthy buzz of conversation as his men unwound and began to believe they might make it back to Balaia alive. The hardest part was done now. All they had to do was wait for the various stone doors to open. Irritating but bearable.

Smiling, Yron walked up to the pool and trailed his hand through its cold pure surface. He'd stared at it a great deal during the day, imagining himself jumping into its cleansing embrace. He reckoned it was somewhere around eight to ten feet deep, and wide enough to accommodate a quarter of the men at a time. It was a gift and they'd earned the right to use it.

Standing up, he began to unbuckle his belt.

"Ben, the time has come," he announced.

From his right, a man cheered and a ripple of laughter ran around the circular room, echoing faintly.

"Divide up the group into four, first group to join me about as fast as you can strip!"

Another cheer, taken up by more of the men and accompanied by desultory handclaps, lightened the mood further. Yron pulled his shirt over his head, unbuttoned his trousers, dragged them and his loincloth off and, leaving them in a heap, jumped into the pool.

It was icy, invigorating and beautiful. He broke the surface and whooped, running his hands across his face and through his hair. He ducked under again, feeling the water edging grime from every inch of his body. Opening his eyes, he swam down a little, seeing the intricate mosaic of fish, plants and a single swimming figure at the bottom come alive in his shifting vision. He wondered briefly where the pool drained back into the earth but a slapping sound above him told of others joining his bath.

"Gods falling, but this is wonderful!" he exclaimed, joining the excited clamour.

And it was true, he'd never felt so good so quickly. As if the waters had cleansed not just his body but his spirit, his whole being. He felt lifted. Alive. He lay on his back and floated toward the statue and the water outflow under its outstretched hand. Drifting beneath it, he could see a main pipe made of stone and fired clay, which split into two, directing the flow to where it emerged from under thumb and forefinger.

There was a third branch too, a little further back, which led away toward the base of the statue. Strange that they should bother to limit the flow into the pool, he thought, but then he was sure they had their reasons. But lying where he was, he saw an easy enough way to get more of this beautiful water into the pool.

Yron swam to the side and dragged himself out, beginning to dry immediately in the relative cool of the temple. He fetched his loincloth and put it on but ignored the rest of his clothes. Looking down into the pool, he could see the waters already muddied by the filth he and his men had accumulated. Yet another reason to increase the flow.

"Ben, where are you?" he asked.

"Here, Captain." Ben-Foran appeared from the opposite side of the statue.

"Fetch me a pickaxe would you, I'm going to make the odd adjustment here."

Knowing enough not to question him, Ben trotted outside to the stores tent, reappearing a short while later, pickaxe in hand.

"Not thinking of dressing, sir?" he observed.

Yron looked at his pile of clothes and shook his head. "Once you've been in there, you'll know why."

"What is it you're going to do?" asked Ben-Foran, handing over the tool.

"Well, they've diverted half the water away back into the ground, as far as I can tell. And looking at the mess we're making in there, I think we could do with all of it." He walked round behind the pool and edged his way around the statue until he stood as close as he could get to the outstretched hand that fed in the water. "If we get rid of the hand, it'll take the pipes with it and give us what we want. What do you think?"

Ben-Foran frowned. "Honestly?"

"Of course." Yron frowned.

"I think it's a shame to damage the statue. It's a beautiful piece of sculpture."

"But needs must," said Yron. "And I don't think it'll be getting too many more visitors after we've left, do you?"

"Have you asked Erys? It might be trapped in some way and I've had enough wards to last a lifetime," said Ben-Foran.

"Fair point. Erys?" Yron looked about and quickly saw the mage in the pool, his red hair darkened by the water. "Any reason why I shouldn't lop the hand off this thing?"

Erys shook his head. "It's aesthetically harsh but there's no magical reason, no. Seems a pity to spoil it."

"Sod the pair of you," said Yron. "Right, clear away from here. Don't want any injuries from flying marble."

He took aim, raised the pickaxe and brought it down on the wrist of the statue. Shards of stone flew in all directions, spattering into the pool and across the floor. Some of the men moved further away. Yron could see a few cracks emanating from the point of impact. He struck again and the cracks widened. All eyes were on him, all conversation had ceased, the sound of the pick striking the marble slapping off the walls of the temple. A third blow and he was sure he felt it give. A fourth and the marble sheared, the hand, some four feet long, toppling into the pool.

It had the desired effect. With the pipes broken beneath, water poured with much greater intensity into the pool, the noise of the trickle gone, to be replaced by one akin to a jug being emptied into a bowl.

"Gentlemen," said Yron from his vantage point, "I give you the waters of life!"

He dropped the pickaxe and jumped back into the pool, the cheers muted as the water closed over his head.

Rebraal groped his way toward agonising consciousness. He was being dragged over the forest floor. It was full dark and the nocturnal denizens of the rain forest were all around him. He could sense their scuttling, their movement through the canopy and myriad wings of every size beating. Almost more alive than during daylight hours, the forest buzzed with activity.

He shook his head to clear the confusion encasing his brain. At the same time, his back connected with something sharp on the ground and he yelped. The dragging ceased immediately and he was laid gently flat. He heard footsteps and opened his eyes to see Mercuun leaning over him.

"Dear Yniss, you're really alive!" said the elf, a grin splitting his face.

"Just about," said Rebraal. Memories crashed through his mind and he struggled to sit up but Mercuun restrained him.

"Don't. I'm only moving you because we needed to get somewhere safer."

"But Aryndeneth? And what about the others? Meru, tell me."

Mercuun's grin vanished to be replaced by an expression close to despair.

"The strangers have the temple," he said. "All the others are dead and they have almost fifty guarding it now. They have fires and tents and they are resting inside."

Rebraal felt sick. Strangers defiling Aryndeneth by their touch and their very breath on its sacred walls. And to use the great temple as a dormitory. Not even the Al-Arynaar would presume such, choosing to sleep in netted hammocks under thatched shelters in a clearing behind the temple.

"We have to stop them," said Rebraal.

"We are but two," said Mercuun. "Alone, there is nothing we can do."

Rebraal pushed Mercuun's hand aside and forced himself into a sitting position. His left shoulder was aflame with pain and he gasped, moving his right hand there to investigate.

"I removed the crossbow bolt but it was deep," explained Mercuun. "They must have thought you dead, as did I when I found you. Shorth have mercy on the others. Those bastards just left you all in a pile on the forest floor. No ceremony, no respect, no honour."

"Then I was lucky. Tual has saved me for the task of retaking the temple."

As if quoting the name of Tual, God of the forest denizens, had sent a ripple through the canopy, a jaguar growled nearby and above them the shriek of a monkey was taken up by an entire troop.

"See?" Rebraal's smile was grim. "Tual hears me."

"And retake the temple we will, but I have to get you to the village or you will die," said Mercuun. "The bolt wound is already reddening under infection and you're cut all over. I've treated your skin with legumia but you need a mage to knit the muscle of your shoulder, and you've lost too much blood. You know the signs as well as I do."

"I don't want to go back there," said Rebraal.

"Please, Rebraal, this isn't the time to dredge up old animosities. You must be well."

Rebraal shook his head. "Just don't make me talk to them. They have no faith." He offered Mercuun his right hand. "Help me up, will you? I'm not too sick to walk."

But as soon as they started, he wasn't so sure. The pain in his shoulder built steadily as Mercuun's soothing poultice wore off, and his legs were cramped. He felt weak and light-headed and leant on his friend for support but refused to rest again until they'd put real distance between them and the strangers who had taken his temple, his life. Taking it back would be sweet. Every Al-Arynaar that had fallen would be avenged ten times over.

"Tell me how you fared, Meru," he said, when he found the energy to speak and the pain had dropped temporarily to a numbing thump.

"I have announced the alarm. The Al-Arynaar are alerted and the word is spreading. I have stressed the need for our people to be aware north and I have asked for information from anyone who saw these people land. There is confusion about how the strangers found the temple and remained undetected for their whole journey. We fear the worst for the watchers in the northern canopy and uplands. But the ClawBound are walking and the TaiGethen are closing. These strangers will never leave Calaius."

"How long before we are assembled to retake Aryndeneth?"

Mercuun sucked in his cheeks. "Remember, Rebraal, we weren't due to be relieved for another seventy days. The gathering has to take place and the prayers must be spoken or we will anger Yniss. There are gaps in the net; people are on hunting expeditions and it is the season of contemplation. So many of those closest by are at hermitage."

"How long?" Rebraal knew what Mercuun said was true, and knew the rituals must be observed. He felt a chill enter his body and a vision played across his mind of the desecration that could be visited on Aryndeneth in a few short days.

"Eighty will be ready to attack in twenty days' time."

"Twenty days!" Rebraal's shout put birds to flight, and in the undergrowth animals scampered from the supposed threat. "Gyal's tears, that is too long."

He stopped walking and leaned against the rough bole of a fig tree under attack from strangler vines that were slowly enmeshing it. Eventually, they would kill it. He would have understood ten days, maybe even accepted the delay as inevitable, but this . . .

"Please, Rebraal, the Al-Arynaar are moving as fast as they can. But we are not the reactive force of our fathers' days. Our mage numbers are small and we cannot afford to go in without their support."

"But in twenty days, all could have been lost. The cell of Yniss opens in fourteen. What if they are after his writings? Think of the cost. These aren't treasure seekers. There are too many of them. They want something they believe is inside the temple."

Rebraal began walking again, quickly, his eyes piercing the night as surely as any panther's. He denied the pain that thundered through him at every foot-fall, praying to Beeth, God of root and branch, to keep him from falling.

"We can't wait, Meru. We'll have to get people from the village. I know they aren't true believers but we have already been betrayed or how could the strangers have found us?"

He had expected Mercuun to be happy at his sudden insistence on enlisting help from their birthplace, the place where his family were treated almost as outcasts because they would not relinquish what were now popularly considered to be old ways. Although every elf on Calaius believed in the harmony, and in Yniss its highest deity, they did not believe in the sanctity of Aryndeneth enough to honour the village quota and send every fifth child to the calling of the Al-Arynaar.

They did not see the honour it bestowed on their families, nor did they appreciate the importance of keeping the calling strong. Rebraal shuddered at the thought that the strangers might actually damage the stones of the temple. If they were powerful enough, it was possible. Theft of the writings of any god was hideous enough, but the balance of Aryndeneth had to be maintained.

Mercuun, though, said nothing. Rebraal slowed and turned to see his friend twenty yards behind him, crouching on the ground.

"Meru?" Rebraal's head was thudding. He was hungry and thirsty and his blood loss sapped his strength.

Mercuun looked up, his face drawn and anguished. He tried to speak but coughed instead, a sick sound from deep in his chest. Rebraal hurried over to him.

"Meru, what is it? Snake? Yellowback frog?"

But it wasn't animal poison. Mercuun shook his head and raised a hand, asking for a moment. He caught his breath and coughed again, a great racking that shook his body. He raised his sweat-slick face to speak.

"I don't feel good," he managed, Rebraal refraining from telling him he was speaking the obvious. "Like a wave of something unclean washed through me. It clogged my lungs but they're clearing now. I thought I would fall; my balance went for a moment. I'll be all right. Don't worry about me."

"We should rest here. Neither of us is fit to go on. I'll bring you liana to lace for hammocks, then I'll fetch food and water. Give me your skins and jaqrui."

Mercuun made to protest but the relief on his face was all too evident. Instead he nodded. "But we must push on before dawn. I agree with you. I don't think we've very much time."

CHAPTER 10

The morning cacophony of monkeys, birds, insects, frogs and anything else that had a voice was in full cry when Ben-Foran decided to wash in the temple pool. Yron's rather clumsy work on the statue's hand might have eroded the majesty of the sculpture but it had had the desired effect. The much increased water flow into the pool had quickly cleared the grime from four dozen sweaty filthy bodies, and now, in the diffused light of dawn, it was crystal clear once again.

Yron was keen for his men not to get lazy and so, barring the sick and the mages, who were tending the ill and examining scrolls and parchments in a room that had opened up with the first touch of light, everyone was outside. Everyone, that is, except Ben, who was duty temple officer. While he swam, Yron and all the rest of the relatively fit were either on hunting parties, investigating the rear of the temple and the area surrounding it, collecting more firewood or preparing breakfast and making a stores inventory.

Despite the hardships of the rain forest, the loss of so many of those he'd travelled with and the feeling he couldn't shift that, despite his loyalty, this was a raid too far, Ben-Foran had to admit to himself that he was rather enjoying it. Partly it was because he had survived with barely a scratch and without catching the fever to which so many had succumbed. Mostly it was because he was with Captain Yron, a real leader and universally loved by the men in his charge. He commanded total respect because he treated all in his command as equals, whatever their rank; a very difficult balance to strike given his position of superiority. And he was a great teacher, constantly springing surprises and doing things by a book all of his own devising. His unorthodoxy didn't endear him to his masters and was, no doubt, why he had gained plenty of experience in places like the Calaian rain forests, but for his men, it was something they could always talk about. If they survived.

Ben-Foran was scared of swimming in rivers, indeed any open area of water where creatures might lurk, but this pool was relaxation itself. On a whim, he duck dived and swam down, drifting slowly over the statue's hand that lay at rest at the bottom of the pool, the living forest sounds muted as the water closed over his head.

He could see that part of the thumb had broken off where it had hit the bottom of the pool and was trapped underneath the rest. Bracing himself against the back wall, he half rolled, half pushed the hand aside to release the thumb, snatching it up and surging back to the surface with it held aloft like a trophy.

"Morning, Ben." The captain's voice rang out around the temple.

"Good morning, sir," replied Ben, turning in the water to see Yron silhouetted in the doorway, the canvas covering tied back.

"Glad to see you're putting your duty to good use. I can't imagine anything we'll need more in the days to come than an expert diver."

Ben-Foran blushed, splashed hurriedly to the side of the pool and hauled himself out to sit dripping at its edge, heart suddenly beating hard.

"Sorry, sir."

To his surprise and relief, Yron laughed. "Don't worry, boy," he said, slapping him hard on the shoulder, the wet crack echoing off the temple walls. "It's exactly what I would have done."

Ben got up and pulled on his loincloth, the thumb tight in his hand.

"Still, I see your exploration wasn't entirely wasted," said Yron, indicating his prize.

"No, sir. I saw it had broken off, you know, and—"

"—thought you'd have yourself a souvenir."

"Yes, sir."

Yron tutted and shook his head. He snapped his fingers then held out his hand. "Well, with one small amendment, it was a sound plan."

A little reluctantly, Ben handed over the thumb. Yron examined it closely. It was a finely detailed piece, a little over five inches long.

"Now this is a lesson it is my pleasure to teach you," said Yron, smiling broadly.

"What's that, Captain?" Ben felt the question was expected though he had no desire to ask it.

Yron leaned in a little closer. "It's something you'll no doubt be able to practise in the future when you have your own command. It's called pulling rank." He chuckled and slipped the piece into his pocket before spreading his arms wide. "There you are. Simple, isn't it? Now, get yourself dressed, there's something I want you to see."

Ben nodded, aware suddenly that he was already dry. He frowned and paused for a moment. It was definitely hotter in here than it had been yesterday afternoon. Odd. He shrugged and pulled on his trousers.

As leader of the task force, he knew it had to be him. Sytkan took the longest walk of his life up the gentle slopes of Herendeneth toward the needle. He walked alone as a show of peaceful intent but the only solace he could really take as he walked was that he could hope they thought he was here to help.

They watched him as he picked his way up around the graves of the ancients, their heads unmoving, eyes not blinking. Sytkan was acutely aware of his frailty, of the ease with which either of these incredible creatures could snuff out his life.

He'd had no real idea of their size, their sheer domination of the space around them, until he got closer. And there they lay, like two huge golden sculptures. They were each a hundred feet and more long from nose to tail, the mounds of their bodies higher than his house and their stupendous wings folded back along their glittering scaled flanks.

Sytkan was less than thirty feet from them, his steps tentative and nervous, his nose full of their sharp wood and oil odour, when they moved. Heads as tall as he was swept out on long graceful necks and arrowed down on his insignificance. It was all he could do to stay standing.

"Um . . ." he began, and all his planned words fell from his memory. His eyes fixed on the upper fangs of the larger dragon as it opened its mouth. Dear Gods burning, those teeth.

"I am Sha-Kaan, Great Kaan of my Brood. Nos-Kaan rests by me. And I understand from my Dragonene and friend, Hirad Coldheart, that you are Sytkan, mage of Xetesk. You and yours are here to find us a way home from this disagreeable dimension."

"I . . . yes," said Sytkan. "I . . . that is, at least partially. And that's why I—we—may need to ask you some questions. Is . . . um, will that be acceptable?"

The great dragon laughed. The breath blew Sytkan from his feet, the sound pounded around his skull and reverberated through ground and air.

"It is expected," said Sha-Kaan. "How else will you understand when you find Beshara?"

Sytkan got slowly to his feet and dusted himself down. "Beshara?" he ventured.

"Our home," said Sha-Kaan.

"Sorry, of course," said Sytkan, never having heard the word before. His gaze locked on to Sha-Kaan's, he saw deep into those bottomless eyes and the power they contained and his composure deserted him. "Well, I er, I came up here to introduce myself. I'm the leader of the Xeteskians and I assure you of our good intent as to wanting to work with you in the best way possible and is there a good or better or worse—if you see what I mean—time to talk to you?"

Sytkan gasped in a breath. Sha-Kaan regarded him for a long moment, the huge slitted black pupil narrowing very slightly. His eyes blinked slowly and he stretched his mouth. The mage fought the urge to turn and run.

"Well met," said Sha-Kaan without hint of warmth. "Ask us what you will, when you will, though I suggest when we are landed is your best time." Sha-Kaan laughed at his own lame joke. "Now go, unless there is anything more?"

"No. No, no," said Sytkan, relief flooding through him. "Thank you."

He turned but had taken only one pace before he found himself staring at Sha-Kaan again, the dragon's long neck curving away out of sight behind him.

"Tell me, Sytkan," rumbled Sha-Kaan. "There are but two Al-Drechar and two Kaan dragons on this island. Yet to research and gather information you have brought with you thirty mages and a hundred Protectors. Perhaps you would like to explain."

Sytkan felt cold all around his heart. "Well, there are many disciplines represented," he blustered. "Many strands to the research. The Protectors are merely—"

Sha-Kaan snorted derisively, dumping Sytkan on his backside again. "Do not presume to insult my intelligence." His head shot forward, his muzzle stopping inches from Sytkan's face. All the mage could see were scales, teeth and ire. "My flame ducts may be dry but these—" he snapped his jaws meaningfully "—are in perfect working order. I will be watching you. All of you. Do not give me cause to become disappointed."

Selik wanted to laugh out loud. Even though he'd ridden hard from Erskan and they'd stopped well after nightfall for only a few snatched hours of rest before setting off again at daylight, he hadn't expected to sight his quarries until the following day at least. Yet there they were, no more than a couple of miles ahead on the trail, the dust of their passage clouding into the warm late morning.

They were heading north on the principal trail that led to the ruined town of Denebre and then on into the mage lands. A fertile part of Balaia, the landscape here, like so much of the country, had been ruined. Trees lay snapped or uprooted, farms were abandoned and fields lay unplanted or with the remnants of rotted crops still in the soil. It was a gently rolling vista, with shallow slopes and vales crisscrossed with a lattice of streams and rivers. To the west, the Blackthorne Mountains made up the entire horizon, their gaunt majesty punctuated only by the eastern face of the Varhawk Crags, scene of one of the most famous victories of the last Wesmen wars.

But Selik wasn't concerned with the scene around him right now. He and his men had reined in at the top of a rise and were looking down onto a grassland plain. In the middle of it, a single covered wagon drove slowly on, the reason for the mages' slow progress obvious. Despite Erskan's assertion that he numbered mages among his friends, he hadn't been overly kind to these, however many there were. The carriage was being dragged by a single, fairly small horse.

"What's your guess at the numbers in there?" asked Selik of Devun.

The man blew out his cheeks. "Well, they're very slow but it's impossible to see what the horse's condition is from here. I reckon they're overloaded so, assuming there are two up front, there could be as many as four inside, plus baggage."

"That's assuming there were ever that many mages in Erskan."

Devun shrugged. "Best to assume more than less."

"All right." Selik nodded, then raised his voice to address all of them. "We're going to assume there are six but I doubt there's a warrior guard in there with them. You all know what to do. Let's not rush and they may not hear us until it's too late. It's time to make another statement. Let's go."

There was precious little cover and they would be seen as soon as anyone looked back; and with no magical defence, they were open to spell attack. But there were fifty Black Wings, all of whom knew the dangers of attacking mages, and their tactic was simple.

Pushing on at just under a canter, they narrowed the distance quickly, the carriage ahead bumping and rattling over the uneven ground. Selik rode front and centre of the formless group, feeling a thrill through his body as they closed. This would be a blow for Balaia. A blow for the righteous.

Perhaps half a mile behind the carriage they were spotted. The back of the square-framed canvas covering twitched aside, and though he couldn't hear it, Selik could imagine the shout of alarm and saw its result as the single horse was urged to a flat-out gallop.

The carriage began to pull away but Selik could see immediately that it wasn't sustainable. Resisting the urge to up the Black Wings' pace, he was content to follow, waiting for the carriage to slow when the horse spent itself and enjoying the desperation he knew they must be feeling. Even if they didn't know exactly who was following them, fifty men on horseback were never going to be good news at a time like this.

A quarter of a mile behind and with the horse slowing dramatically, the carriage slewed to a halt across the trail in a cloud of dust. Figures leapt from back and front to kneel motionless. Casting.

It was to be expected. Selik signalled spread and gallop, circling his arm above his head and splaying gloved fingers wide. Behind him, the Black Wings picked up the pace, driving into a rough double-rowed crescent. The quartet at the points, his finest horsemen, nocked arrows into bows, steering their mounts with stirrup and thigh.

The blood surged through Selik's body, sending pins and needles into the dead parts of his face and chest. He dragged in a huge breath and yelled a triumphant cry, the sound of two hundred hooves thrumming in his head.

In front of him the mages remained still, bar one who looked up, spreading his arms wide in an enveloping motion. At the points, his bowmen tracked in, loosed their arrows and wheeled away immediately, Selik seeing the shafts all bounce from the cast HardShield.

The sky flashed orange.

"Break!" yelled Selik, half a dozen FlameOrbs soaring out toward them.

The Black Wing lines broke and scattered, the globes of mana fire, each the size of a skull, arcing across the sky. The mages were good, individual Orbs following their targets faster than a horse could gallop and splashing down to cover two or three riders and mounts, the soundless impact rendered horribly real by the screams of men and horses.

Hunched low in his saddle, Selik looked back over his shoulder, eyes narrowing and anger building. He counted four men ablaze in their saddles, horses shrieking, plunging this way and that, stumbling and falling as they attempted to dislodge their riders. Another three were already on the ground, beating uselessly at the flames that consumed armour and flesh. And streaking across the plain, fire gorging on mane, back and tail, a horse trailed smoke as it galloped to inevitable and agonising death, rider already gone.

But if the mages expected their attackers to be dismayed by death so easily wrought, they were sadly mistaken. The Black Wings were on them. One more mage cast, her ForceCone punching out, stopping three horses in their tracks and smashing riders from saddles. Selik heard the snap of equine bones, shut the pain from his mind, drew his sword and plunged into the enemy.

Leaning down from his saddle, he whipped his sword through low, the blade carving into the mage's face, snapping the head back and cartwheeling her flopping corpse end over end. Not pausing, he rode down the HardShield mage and only then dragged at the reins to turn his horse round to a stop.

His men had done exactly the job required. A third mage was dead, body twisted unnaturally, a slick of blood already subsiding into the earth under his chest. The other two were being held while they were beaten into a state where they couldn't have cast if their lives depended on it. Shame, because for one of them, it did.

Selik trotted back to the wagon, which two of his men were already ransacking. He smiled and swept back his hood, dismounting when he reached his captives, the sound of their gasps and grunts of pain sweet in his ears. He spared a glance at the fires still smouldering a hundred yards away and the smile left his face.

"Enough," he ordered.

The rain of punches, sword pommels and kicks stopped, both men having to be supported to remain upright.

He nodded. "Good work," he said, seeing the blood running from noses and mouths, the puffed eyes and torn ears. But no amount of blood on their faces could mask the fear in their eyes.

"More mages running from their responsibilities," he said, standing close to them, letting the venom in his mind spit from his mouth. "Running from what they have created. Where were you going, eh? Away to join your armies for a new assault on the innocents of Balaia?"

He shrugged. "You're scum. Worthless, cowardly scum."

"We'd have stayed to help but your supporters wanted us gone," said one of the mages, voice thick through split and swelling lips.

Selik stepped up and grabbed him by the throat, pushing his head back. "The damage was already done, fool. What help could you give now?"

"So what is it that you want from us? To stay or to leave?" said the mage, desperation clear in his voice.

"I want you to face up to what your kind has done to my world," said Selik, not releasing his grip. "You know what I saw in Erskan? Three children who would have killed each other for a scrap of bread a rat would turn down. You have sapped the strength and the will from those who trusted you. You have broken their spirit. But I am going to give it back to them and you and your kind will never wield your unholy power so freely again."

"We could have helped, had we been allowed to stay," pleaded the mage. "We could have healed the people. Healed the ground."

Selik dropped his hand and stepped away. "You really don't understand what you've done to Balaia and its people do you? How blind you are to think that after magic has destroyed so much, people would allow you to cast a few more spells to put it right. You have lost their trust but still you think it is as easy as waving your hands."

He turned to the second mage, finding the man glaring defiantly back at him.

"Nothing to say?" he asked.

"To someone who would deny magic to an entire population because of a single rogue, no. It is you who are blind, Selik, you and the monkeys who follow you so slavishly."

"Some fight still left, at least," said Selik to the chuckles of his men within earshot. "Trouble is, I don't really think I want to hear your voice on the road. Because you won't listen. So you will stay as a warning and your friend here will accompany us."

He gestured to the men holding the mages. "Get him on that carthorse and away from here."

"I'm sorry," said the mage to his doomed colleague.

The man shook his head. "Don't be. These bastards can never defeat us."

"But you won't live to see whether that's true, will you?" said Selik.

"I am proud you think me so dangerous that you have to kill me."

"Kill you?" said Selik, a smile creeping over his face. "No, no, that would be too easy. All I can promise is that you will die unless you are very, very fortunate."

The Black Wings captain saw the mage's eyes flicker, his bravado punctured, and all he could do, while his colleague was loaded, hands bound, onto the carthorse and away with a guard of six, was watch while his fate unfolded in front of him.

Quickly, the cart was stood on its end and braced, its wheels facing in the direction of the mage lands to the northwest. The traces and lines from the harness were cut into four pieces and the mage strung upright between the four wheels with his clothes ripped from him to leave only a loincloth. Selik watched it all dispassionately, a slight twinge of disappointment at the bearing of the mage, who didn't struggle or protest. When he was secured, Selik unsheathed a dagger and walked slowly over to him, the mage's eyes never leaving his.

"There are people like you all over this land. Left as warnings to others of your kind that the Black Wings are growing. That we will pursue you relentlessly, that you will atone for what you have done and that we will not stop until the evil of magic is scrubbed from Balaia. You, at least, will not join the war."

The mage spat at him, the blood-veined saliva catching Selik on the cheek and running down the side of his face. He merely smiled.

"You'll regret that when your thirst becomes unbearable."

"Come closer and I'll do it again. I'm not afraid to die."

"Lucky for you," said Selik, his mouth bent into a grotesque sneer. "Our trouble is that there can be no warning without a message. And, since we've run right out of parchment, we need to use a somewhat different medium." He turned to his men. "Hold him still and shut his useless mouth."

Black Wings moved in and hands pressed on the mage's head, shoulders, knees and the top of his legs, rendering him immobile. Selik walked up slowly, staring deep into the mage's eyes, watching the fear begin to grow and the first cracks appear in his bearing.

Taking the tip of his dagger between his thumb and first two fingers, he began to carve letters on the mage's chest, letting the blade bite deep, feeling his human canvas heave and hearing choked cries through his closed mouth.

"Hold him, I'm trying to write," he said.

He bent back to his task, dragging the dagger in letter shapes, keeping the mage's chest and stomach skin taut with his other hand. Soon it was done. He backed up, wiped and sheathed the dagger and looked at his handiwork, which was a little lost in the streaming blood. With a flick of his hand, he waved his men away. The mage drew in shuddering breaths, his face dripping sweat and pale. He swallowed.

"You'll die at the hand of a mage, Selik," he managed. "And when you do, my death will seem painless by comparison."

Selik ignored his words. "I expect you're curious to know what I've written."

"I couldn't care less," said the mage, regaining some control over his wracked body. "You are worthless vermin, Selik. I'm surprised you can write at all."

"It says, 'Mages: fear the Black Wings.' Succinct, I think. To the point, if you will." He laughed. "Of course it isn't easy to read but I expect whoever finds you will fathom it eventually. And if you are very lucky, you'll be able to tell them yourself."

He swung away and strode back to his horse. "Mount up, Black Wings; we've a long way to go and a mage to educate."

"Burn in hell, Selik!" roared the mage, straining at his lashings.

Selik laughed again. "No, dear mage, I will not. Because the righteous are blessed, not cursed."

He kicked his heels into his horse's flanks and led the Black Wings away, the mage's shouts growing ever fainter in his ears. It had been a truly uplifting day.

CHAPTER 11

The *Calaian Sun* sailed slowly into Ysundeneth shortly after midday on the third day after leaving the Ornouth Archipelago. Even Jevin had declared himself surprised at the speed they'd made. A steady southerly wind had driven them through a light swell and the dolphins that had swum with them most of the journey added to the idyll.

Standing next to Ilkar as they cruised toward their berth at the heart of the docks, Denser could sense the relief in the Julatsan mage, shot through as it was with nerves. It mirrored Denser's own feelings, though his reasons were very different. The voyage had not been easy. Erienne had barely left her bunk the entire time, her heart rebroken by the ever-increasing distance from Lyanna's grave. And when she had walked the deck, the set of her body kept everyone away from her.

Denser could understand her reaction but was frustrated he wasn't being allowed to help. She had withdrawn into herself completely, ate little and said less. Ilkar had given voice to his concern the day before. Calaius and its climate were not like Balaia in any way. It drained and fatigued the fittest of bodies and sickness was so easy to contract, particularly for those not born there. Erienne, he said, would be seriously risking her health if she refused to keep up her strength for much longer. And if her capacity for casting was impaired, she could be risking the health of The Raven too.

As he had so often in the last three days, Denser had sighed and hoped she'd come back to herself once they landed. But, with the sun beating down hard from a clear blue sky, Denser found he could forget for a moment by simply looking straight in front of him at his first clear view of a new land. When they had first sighted Calaius and The Raven had run on deck to see, he'd felt vaguely disappointed. All he could make out were cliffs, the outline of the land where it met the sea and the very distant shapes of buildings.

Now, much closer to, it was stunning in its vibrancy and beauty. In front of them, Ysundeneth, the capital port city of Calaius, filled his eyes. Translating as "Ocean Home," or so Ilkar had said, Ysundeneth was a vast sprawling place whose dock area stretched for four miles along the winding coast; and whose buildings spread half as far back. It was almost the size of Korina but looked so utterly different. Where Korina's skyline was filled with low, sturdy brick and stone structures built against the gales that swept the city's estuary, Ysundeneth was a riot of spires and tall buildings, slim and sinuous but with an air of solidity. And every single one of them was made solely of wood.

Denser was astonished at the wooden buildings but Ilkar had only laughed and pointed beyond the city. Surrounding the port on all sides and covering the land for as far as he could see was a thick mat of green. Trees everywhere, punctuated by sharp rises, great sweeping cliffs and plunging soaking lowlands, but trees all the same.

Denser had stood and stared at it all for what seemed an age, only emerging from his reverie when Ilkar nudged him. He looked round to see the Julatsan arm in arm with Ren, both smiling at him.

"What do you think?" asked the elf.

Denser shrugged. "It's extraordinary. I can't believe how big this port is. I didn't think many of you lived in cities. More to the point, what do you think? Been a long time for you, hasn't it?"

Ilkar nodded, his smile fading. "It's odd, no doubt about that. But I still feel like I'm coming home. I mean, I hardly recognise this place, it's grown so much, but I was born here."

"Ysundeneth?"

"Well, no, not here exactly. About three days upriver by boat, but I spent a lot of time here when I was growing up and it was never this big."

"So how does it sustain itself?" The Unknown had come to the rail and was leaning out, his shaven head tanning deep brown.

"Trade with Balaia is important," said Ren. "But the real money's made trading around the coast. So much of the inland is impassable to boats of any real size that it's quicker to go around. But this is the biggest port by far. None of the others are even half this size."

"There have got to be well over a hundred thousand elves living here, haven't there?" said The Unknown.

"More," said Ren.

"I'm amazed there are that many on the entire continent," said Denser. "Given the very few we see, that is."

"Calaius is a very big continent, Denser, and you'd be surprised how many elves there are here," said Ilkar. "But as a race, we just like to keep ourselves to ourselves. No one's going to take you to their bosom when we land, I can tell you. And when I also tell you that the elves you'll meet in the ports are the most outgoing, well, I'll leave you to draw your own conclusions."

"The place must burn a lot." It was Hirad, standing just behind them. "All that wood."

Ilkar cupped a hand to his ear. "Hark," he said, a broad grin on his face. "The lilting sounds of a barbarian making a daft comment."

"Bugger off."

"Does the term 'rain forest' not give you any sort of clue?" asked Ilkar. "I mean it doesn't rain quite so much here on the coast but inland, well, you'll experience it soon enough."

Ren nudged Ilkar hard. "Tell him the truth. All of it."

Hirad's face hardened. Denser clapped his hands. "Gods, I love listening to you two."

"You could sell tickets to it," muttered The Unknown.

Ilkar puffed out his cheeks. "Fair enough, I was just taking a rise and am guilty as charged, although it does rain a lot."

"So what is the truth?" growled Hirad.

"That all the buildings are coated with flame-retardant resin. We just use nature's own defences out here. Smells a bit if you're not used to it but it's good against lightning and fire."

"Make a simple statement, I don't know . . ." Hirad let his voice trail off but Denser could see his heart wasn't in his anger. As it never was with Ilkar. It was one of the joys of travelling with The Raven. Those two could be pure theatre at times.

"So what's the plan?" asked Hirad.

"Simple, really," said Ilkar. "We're landing in about an hour, I think. We'll find a place to stay tonight and while you lot take a look at the sights, Ren and I'll hire a boat to take us upriver tomorrow."

"And you're quite sure your village is the place to start looking for these mages of yours?" The Unknown was frowning.

"It's as good a place as any. We used to send a lot of adepts to Julatsa at one time and there'll be people there who are sympathetic and, more important, who will know where to look for more. Just hanging up a sign here won't get us far. But of course I have personal reasons for wanting to go there, I'm sure you'll understand. You don't have to come if you don't want to."

"The Raven never work apart," said Hirad.

Ilkar smiled. "You won't regret it," he said. "It's beautiful."

"And flame resistant," said The Unknown.

The east gates of Xetesk opened and the massed ranks of refugees stood, their movement an expanding ripple across a human sea. Ten thousand and more with hope renewed that this time food and not soldiers would be disgorged.

From where Avesh stood on a patch of churned mud with everything he loved and everything he owned, he couldn't see the base of the gates. Couldn't see what or who came out, but he could rely on the mood of the crowd to give him the information he needed.

He pulled his wife and young son to him, their bony frames pressed against his, and stepped away from their pile of filthy blankets and scant possessions. How they hadn't died of cold, starvation or disease through the winter, having lost their farm to the storms, he would never know. But they had been spared and that was all he cared about.

The family all knew the drill. If it was food they would split up and run because if you were slow you got nothing. But if you were lucky, you got three shares. At first Avesh had been against that but he'd been forced to harden his heart as the death toll from illness and hunger rose daily. Rather them than his family.

And now, with spring coming to ease the chill and the first colours of new life pushing through the thawed earth, it looked like their persistence might actually pay off. Though they were all haggard and thin they were still alive. Today, Avesh was daring to believe they would live to rebuild their lives.

The noise built around them. Those with the strength made ready to run or swallow their disappointment. But something was different. Avesh caught it in the air just before he heard the shouts. A cry of surprise. Another of indignant outrage.

He watched for a few moments, feeling the unease whiplash through the throng. His first instinct had been to move forward but he held his ground, his heart querulous. He bit his lip and stood on tiptoe.

"Atyo, hop up on my shoulders. Let's look see." The scrawny lad scrambled up. "What can you see?"

"Soldiers," he said. "And riders. Lots."

"Coming along the path?"

They'd seen this a dozen times but the mood of the crowd suggested something new.

"No, all over. Everyone's moving."

And now Avesh could see it. The move forward had faltered, was already reversing. The noise of countless scared people was growing to a crescendo shot through with the harsh shouts of soldiers carrying on the breeze.

The boy climbed down and looked up into his father's eyes.

"What will we do?"

"Give me a moment, son," said Avesh.

The crowd was rippling again. No, not a ripple, a wave heading outward away from the gates.

"Gods falling," he breathed. He gripped Atyo and Ellin, turning them both to him. "They're trying to clear the camp, the bastards. If we get separated, we'll meet back at the crossing of the River Dord to the north. Can you both find that?"

"Why would we be separated?" asked Ellin.

He didn't have to answer her. The wave hit them instead. He grabbed them each by a hand.

"Come on, we've got to go."

The press was thickening but Ellin hesitated.

"Our things."

"Leave them. Come on."

Avesh could feel the surge through the ground now. A drumming like a thousand hoof beats. But this stampede was human. He swung them both around, stumbling against somebody who rushed past. He caught the briefest glimpse of an ashen face before it was lost in the throng.

They began to run. There was only one direction. To try and cross the path of the crowd would be suicide. Avesh held them firm, taking care to move at the same pace as his boy, but when the youngster tripped anyway, Avesh scooped him into one arm and ran on, his wife right beside him.

He could see nothing but flailing limbs, hair streaming and the backs of countless desperate people driven to run though they barely had the strength. It was a chase that would exhaust itself quickly, and already the weakest were falling, their legs powerless to keep them upright, their spirits unable to take them a single pace further. And those that fell were left. There was nothing anyone could do, not even family, as the packed horde fled on, dragging the crying survivors with it.

Avesh ignored the ache in his wasted left arm muscles where he clutched Atyo and dared a look down at his wife. Ellin's face was determined as she ploughed on, transmitting her fear through the painfully tight grip on his hand.

Through the screams, the shouts and the thrumming of feet across the ground, Avesh could hear horses and the rhythmic heavy thud of men running in unison, closing fast. The crowd gathered sudden extra impetus. Worse, it split. Avesh pulled left, Ellin went right. Their hands slipped agonisingly apart. Avesh tried to change direction and reached out his hand. Their fingers brushed but that was all and he caught only a glimpse of her gaunt face and despairing hand as the crowd swept her away from him.

Riders galloped through the gap, voices hoarse, shouting orders to move.

"Ellin!" Avesh yelled. "The Dord. Remember the Dord!"

"Mummy!" screamed Atyo, wriggling around, straining to see her.

Avesh saw her just once more, bobbing like a bottle in a stormy sea, helpless, unable even to struggle as she vanished from sight.

"Mummy!"

"It's all right, Atyo," said Avesh, head down and running again, breath heaving painfully into his lungs. "We'll find her. We'll see her soon."

Right in front of him, a man tripped and fell. Reacting fast, Avesh hurdled the sprawling figure. His left foot came down on slimy wet mud and slipped sideways. Hopelessly unbalanced, he pitched right, holding hard on to his son as he went down.

The sound of horses was very close again. He rolled over, people scrambling past him cursing, shouts chasing them, that rhythmic thump of feet mingling with hoof beats reverberating through the ground.

Avesh clambered to his feet, presenting his back to the streaming mob threatening to knock him back down again. His muddied and terrified son was screaming, out of control, clutching handfuls of his clothing.

"We'll be all right," said Avesh. "We'll—"

He was standing in a space that suddenly contained too much horseflesh to dodge. He turned left and right, his vision filled with black and brown flanks, greaved legs and riding boots. He felt a heavy impact as a stallion reared near him, its rider yelling at him to move, but he could do nothing more than fall flat on his back.

He lay still, hooves coming down close to his head and body on their way past, driving the wailing refugees further and further from Xetesk. The relative silence flooded him. He gasped a breath.

"We'll be safe now, boy, safe now," he said, stroking Atyo's head. His hand came away wet. Blood. He froze.

"Atyo?" The boy was limp in his arms. "Atyo?"

He scrabbled frantically into a sitting position and held the boy in his lap. Atyo's head lolled to one side, blood matting his face. And, just below the hairline, his skull was stove in, caught by a horse's hoof. He had never stood a chance.

"No." The word was barely audible. "No."

Avesh rose to his feet, holding his dead child to his chest. After all they'd been through, huddling in the intense cold, saving scraps of food from the ground and going days without. The boy had survived it all, only to be murdered by those he'd begged for succour.

The tears began rolling down his face, smearing the dirt as they came. Avesh fought back the nausea that swept through him, the blackening of his vision and the clouding of his mind.

His boy. Dead.

His vision cleared and he took in the litter of the camp, the scattering stragglers missed by the soldiers and the dozens, maybe hundreds, of prone forms lying where they'd fallen, clothes ruffling in the breeze. Some moved, most did not. And he saw the line of cavalry backed by the masked abominations that were the Protectors, their pace unremitting. Thump, thump, thump.

He looked down. He was standing on a tattered blanket. He laid Atyo on it and wrapped it around the boy's body. At least he wouldn't get cold. With a last look at that face so casually ruined, he kissed Atyo's forehead and closed the blanket. He stood.

The blank walls of Xetesk faced him. They could not be allowed to escape justice but he would not toss his life away in a futile attempt at vengeance. That would mock Atyo's death.

His body shaking. Avesh turned and walked away toward the north and the crossing of the River Dord, there to find his wife so they could bury their son together.

Then he'd be back. And he wouldn't be alone.

CHAPTER 12

B y the time they reached the canopy rope crossing of the huge sluggish brown force of the River Ix, Rebraal wasn't sure who was supposed to be rescuing who.

A night where they'd both slept long through sheer exhaustion had given way to two days where it seemed the rain was Gyal's tears, sweeping across the forest and drenching it almost incessantly. Sometimes it abated to a fine mist, but more often it fell in torrents with angry thunder cracking above the canopy.

Rebraal's shoulder was agony, his multiple cuts and scratches from being dragged to the pile of bodies by the strangers and away again by Meru itched in unison. They'd done what they could—legumia root paste for the deep crossbow wound, poultices of rubiac fruits for his scratches and long drinks of menispere to ward off the effects of fever—but he knew he was getting sick. He should be resting, not running home, wading rivers and climbing high into the canopy to use the hidden walkways and ropes to pass the great rivers and waterfalls.

His muscles were tortured, his back aflame with searing pain and his mind often muddied and confused. He'd mistaken bird and monkey calls more than once, had blundered into a swarm of ants and escaped a crocodile by a mere heartbeat.

But for all his many woes, his greater concern was Mercuun. His was a sickness that defied understanding or remedy and attacked him apparently at random, leaving him gasping for breath one moment and driven with manic energy the next, though the latter was becoming increasingly infrequent. Meru had assumed it was something in his stomach and they'd searched and found a good supply of simarou bark with which they made strong infusions, but it did no recognisable good.

Between his bouts of energy, he lost muscle strength and bulk, his balance was dangerously off true and, on the second morning, Rebraal had wakened to hear Mercuun coughing as if his organs were fighting their way into his throat. His friend could not disguise the blood that flew from his mouth in a spray every time he convulsed.

Later that afternoon, they'd rested long by the banks of the Ix, sheltered from Gyal's tears and prayed to Orra, the God of the earth's life blood, for an end to the illness that plagued Mercuun. Rebraal had looked at him where they sat close together under the great broad leaves of a young palm and seen death stalking across his face. He seemed to be collapsing from the inside out, and for all their herbal lore they could find no antidote.

"You're sure you haven't been bitten?" probed Rebraal, moving his back against the bole of the palm and feeling a new pain shoot through his legs and neck.

"I'm sure," said Mercuun, his voice a hoarse whisper, his throat raw from wracking coughs. Every time he breathed, he shuddered.

"Have you checked yourself? If not a viper, a brush with a yellow-back is all it would take."

"It's not poison," said Mercuun.

"Then what is it?" Rebraal was at a loss.

"I don't know." Mercuun shook his head and lifted his face to Rebraal. He was scared; his eyes betrayed him and tears of frustration and fear welled up before he could catch them. "Shorth is coming. I can feel it."

"You aren't going to die, Meru." Rebraal reached out a hand, which his friend grabbed and held tight. "We'll be in the village before nightfall. There is help for you there."

Mercuun dropped his head back to stare at the muddied ground. "There is nothing their healers know that we don't."

"But they will also employ magic should they have to," said Rebraal, giving Mercuun's hand a reassuring squeeze before climbing stiffly to his feet. "Come on. One more climb and it's all down from then on."

But as he looked up into the canopy and their hundred-foot climb, his confidence wavered. He had seen Meru stumble over the merest root. And he himself could only rely on one arm. The other was as good as useless, the strength of his grip diminished by the wound in his shoulder.

"It seems so high," said Mercuun, staring up and out over the river.

High above the muddy flow, where the canopy leant in on both sides, the practised eye could see a trio of tensed ropes among the leaves and branches. Used by elves and monkeys alike, the crossing spanned the one-hundred-yard width of the River Ix. Upriver, a waterfall more than five hundred feet high plunged into a huge sheltered pool, its outflow slackened by long lazy twists in the deep river. Way downstream, where the Ix narrowed, rocks hastened the water through a cramped ravine before the river spilled back out into its natural slow state. And everywhere along its length, death lurked beneath the surface.

"We can make it," assured Rebraal, leaving unspoken the fact that they would never swim the river. They were too weak and too much blood scent clung to them. They'd been lucky with panthers and jaguars. That luck would not hold out there in the water. "You go first. I'll watch for you. I won't let you fall."

Mercuun dragged himself to his feet, leaning against the palm to steady himself before following Rebraal down to the towering banyan around which the ropes were fastened on this side, lost beneath a tangle of vines and secured from rotting by resin, oils and the occasional spell. He breathed deep, clenched his fists, took a brief glance up and began to climb.

"There's something wrong here," said The Unknown. "Can't you feel it?"

Hirad shrugged. They were sitting in an eatery on the docks with Darrick and Thraun. Ilkar said it was a typical elven establishment, characterised by long tables and benches, high ceilings, plenty of windows and exotic-tasting soups and meats. It was busy but there was clear space between them and the rest of the predominantly elven clientele.

The Julatsan and Ren had agreed to meet them inside, while Erienne and Denser visited the city markets. Aeb, who had drawn the odd interested glance when they docked, was at the inn, speaking to his brothers, communing in the Soul Tank.

"Elves don't like us very much, you mean?" said Hirad.

"No, not that. And they've been perfectly civil so far, if a little reserved. No. There's an atmosphere, like a growing fear of something. I can't put my finger on it. You don't feel anything?"

"No." Hirad shovelled more soup-soaked bread into his mouth.

The Unknown shook his head. "I don't know why I bother. You've got a skull thicker than a dragon's. Darrick, what about you?"

"Hard to say," said the former Lysternan general, leaning forward. "There's an air of vague disquiet round the docks but that's just lack of trade, I'd say. Nothing really sinister in it."

Hirad looked at The Unknown, feeling a familiar sense of unease. Fifteen years he'd known the big man and he was hardly ever wrong. And since his, albeit brief, time as a Protector his instinct for trouble and danger had heightened still further. His expression told Hirad he was sure about this one.

The barbarian switched his attention to Thraun. The shapechanger had been feeding himself as though he'd not eaten for days but was now staring at The Unknown, mouth half open and next spoonful forgotten. The Unknown indicated him.

"Thraun knows what I'm talking about," he said. "Don't you, Thraun?"

There might have been the merest suggestion of a nod, but aside from that no reaction.

"So what is it?" asked Darrick.

"Just a hint at the moment," said The Unknown. "Like overripe fruit. Sickly sweet and on the way to rotting. Whatever it is, it's below the skin of the city now but won't be for long."

"I'm not with you," said Hirad.

A moment later, Ilkar walked in with Ren and confirmed everything.

"There are sick people all over the place," he said, sitting down and waving at a servant boy to come over. "It's weird. Everywhere we've been."

"Plague?" The Unknown raised his eyebrows.

"If it is, it's a new one on me. We've spoken to mages who can find no cause, just effects. And the traditional healers are struggling with the numbers. Only started a couple of days ago, apparently."

"You were right then, Unknown," said Hirad.

"Unfortunately." he said. "What's your view, Ilkar?"

The Julatsan shrugged. "Information's patchy but there's no obvious pattern or epicentre. Whatever, I think it's a good job we're leaving tomorrow."

"You've found a boat, then?" asked Darrick.

"And a guide. It's not easy to navigate. I'm glad I don't have to rely on my memory. Watercourses change, local landscape alters . . . you know."

"Not really, Ilks, no," said Hirad. "But then you've been around a lot longer than the rest of us, haven't you?"

"You could say." Ilkar smiled. It was always a slightly sad smile, Hirad thought. The subject brought home to Ilkar his relative immortality.

"How worried should we be?" asked The Unknown.

"People are scared," said Ren. "Not so much here—the dock doesn't seem affected yet—but fear spreads. They'll be looking for something to blame and it doesn't take much to figure out where the finger'll be pointed first."

"Better get yourselves elven ears quickly," said Ilkar.

"I'd rather take the abuse," said Hirad.

"No pun intended but can we return to the point?" The Unknown rapped his fork on the table. "Tell me who's getting this thing and what happens when they do."

"From what we've seen it's indiscriminate. Young, old, male, female, rich and poor," said Ren. "I don't think it's to do with living conditions. There are no outward signs—no sores or boils."

"No, nor any fever," added Ilkar. "From what we've been able to find out, it affects balance, brings on bouts of sickness and muscle weakness. One mage we found said she thought there was organ damage but it's too early to say."

"Strange," said Darrick. "And how many have died?"

"So far none, but it's early days," said Ren. "Perhaps it'll run its course and people will recover, but if there are deaths and no cure is forthcoming, it'll just accelerate the panic we've already seen."

"And you're hoping to get mages to leave here and travel to Balaia?" said The Unknown. "You'll be lucky if any ships are allowed to sail if this is a plague."

"The thought had crossed my mind. And no mage will leave here while there's work they feel they can do."

"I'd have thought it a great reason to leave," said Hirad. "They might be saving themselves, after all."

Ilkar shook his head. "You don't understand elven society, Hirad. It's honour based, not driven by profit and magic like Balaia."

"So you should stay too?" said the barbarian.

"That's a tricky one," said Ilkar. "If this is serious I'll have to think about it, but I don't belong here. My home is Julatsa. I feel no ties like elves who have lived here all their lives or only visited Balaia to train. It wouldn't be dishonourable to leave, but that won't make it easy."

"Don't even think about it," said The Unknown. "We have to find mages to help you raise the Heart of Julatsa or this disease, whatever it is, will seem a mere inconvenience by comparison."

Hirad could see they were attracting glances from further down their table and behind them.

"I think we should keep our voices down," he said quietly.

"We should do more than that," said The Unknown. "Let's get back to the inn and stay in our rooms until first light tomorrow. I don't like what I'm feeling. Anyone know when Denser and Erienne planned on getting back?"

Ilkar shook his head. "I shouldn't worry about them. They're mages and any elf will know it. They won't be harmed. Asked to help maybe but not harmed."

They stood up to go, Ilkar apologising to the serving boy who'd brought a plate of meat and cheese. He left coins for everything and led them outside.

"Will we catch it, do you think?" asked Hirad.

"No idea," said Ilkar. "It's not something we can really worry about right now, is it?"

He shrugged and walked on, trying to appear unconcerned, but Hirad could see that underneath anxiety was building. Not for himself, but for the ramifications of his mage-gathering mission. Hirad hoped dawn would bring some cheer but somehow he doubted it.

Mercuun's fall was as shocking as it was predictable. A terribly slow climb up the banyan to the rope bridge had preceded a clumsy, nerve-shredding drag across the River Ix, Mercuun's weakness and lack of balance a constant threat to them both.

Five times Rebraal had had to clutch the ropes of the yawing bridge as his friend slipped or stumbled, ignoring the fire that was his left shoulder to help Mercuun, or stand by him as he recovered his breath.

It was awful to watch. Mercuun had been the most sure footed of them all, moving with the stealth of a panther and the agility of a monkey. He could have been a TaiGethen. And now something they couldn't fathom had reduced him to a juddering height-shy oaf in less than three days.

Rebraal had breathed a premature sigh of relief when they'd reached the opposite bank and Mercuun, sweating and shaking, had wrapped his arms gratefully around a bough. Feeling dizzy with fever and the effort himself, Rebraal had begun to descend almost immediately, telling Mercuun to rest until he was sure enough to move, however long that took. It could have been days and he would have waited for his friend, but something about Mercuun told Rebraal that he didn't have days. Meru felt it too. That's why he moved too soon.

Rebraal had been twenty feet from the ground when a heavy branch had snapped above him. A dark shape had come hurtling toward him, leaves and wood flying everywhere. Soundless, Mercuun had fallen past him, arms and legs splayed to break his fall on every bough. It was an action, combined with the limpness with which he hit the ground, that undoubtedly saved his life.

And so Rebraal had found him broken but alive.

"Meru, talk to me."

"Hurts, Rebraal. It hurts."

"Of course it hurts. You've come down eighty feet."

Rebraal looked at him, not quite believing what he saw. Mercuun was moving and obviously aware but his left leg was turned behind him at an impossible angle and he lay stretched, his left arm beneath him and a trickle of blood running from his mouth.

"Lie still. I've got to get some casimir and get rid of the pain."

"Hurry."

Rebraal sprinted away, looking for the tell-tale bright broad green leaves and yellow-green ball-like fruit. He was heedless of his own condition, adrenaline banishing hurt and fever. He had to be quick. Not just because Mercuun was in agony but because the forest was full of predators and scavengers. And right now his friend was easy prey.

Mercuun had lapsed into merciful unconsciousness by the time he returned. Flies crawled on his face and a lizard sniffed at the blood from his mouth. In the trees above, birds were settling.

"Tual, spare him," whispered Rebraal to the God of the denizens, fishing in Mercuun's leather sack for his metal cup and small medicine skin.

He hurried to the river bank and scooped up some water, collected small twigs for kindling on the way back and built a tiny fire, using Mercuun's tinderbox to light the wet wood. He heated the water above the guttering flame, using a cloth to protect his hands from the hot metal.

When the water steamed and bubbled, he dropped some leaves into the mug, their rich fresh scent blooming in his nostrils.

"Almost ready, Meru," he said, though his friend couldn't hear him. He was moving though, and close to consciousness again, a low moan escaping his lips.

When the infusion was ready, Rebraal decanted the murky green liquid into the skin, added some seeds from the casimir fruit and kept back the leaf sludge. While the drink cooled, he tipped the sludge into a palm leaf, blew on it until he could just touch it and spread it on Mercuun's fractures, having cut his clothes where he had to. The remainder he smeared on his own shoulder.

Mercuun's eyes flickered open. "I'm dying, Rebraal."

"No, you're not. Now let me support your head while you drink this."

He knelt down and lifted Mercuun's head into his lap. The broken elf gulped down the infusion, knowing the powerful sedative would numb his pain.

"What are you going to do?" he asked when the skin was empty.

"Carry you home, Meru. You need healing."

"But your shoulder." Mercuun lifted an arm weakly.

"It'll be all right. Trust me."

"Yniss keep you, Rebraal."

"And you, Meru. How do you feel?"

"The pain is fading."

"Good, then let's get going."

Rebraal packed Mercuun's sack and slung it over his right shoulder before stooping to pick him up. He felt his own wound give and the blood start to flow but the leaf sludge masked him from all but a dull ache.

Mercuun hung in his arms like a dead weight, his head cradled against Rebraal's shoulder and chest.

"Not far now," said Rebraal. "Try to rest."

A chuckle trickled from Mercuun's mouth. "Don't lie. I may be sick but I haven't completely lost my senses. You're the one who should be resting."

Rebraal gritted his teeth and set off. It was almost ten miles to the village through dense rain forest, up steep hillsides, down muddy valleys and along a treacherous stream course. Offering a prayer to Yniss to give him the strength to survive, Rebraal left the River Ix behind him.

CHAPTER 13

D usk had fallen and the cacophony that greeted the night invaded the rain forest as it always had and always would. A persistent heavy rain was falling from low, deep grey cloud cover but the thunder and lightning had moved north, heading for the coast.

Not needing the sounds of the elements and nature to mask his movements, Auum walked forward, footsteps less than whispers on the forest floor, barely a leaf rippling as he passed. Five yards to either side, his Tai mirrored him. He had no need to look to know exactly where they stood. They were Duele and Evunn and, with Auum, formed one cell of the TaiGethen, the elite warrior hunters of the Al-Arynaar. There were fifty cells in all, spread through the rain forest. No single elf knew them all but every elf knew their purpose.

When called, they killed strangers.

And for Auum's Tai, their quarry was close. They had no orders but the word had reached them and they, like every cell, would comb their zone of the forest, exterminating any threat they found.

For Auum it was his first call, but he didn't think in terms of nerves, or reality versus training. This was what the TaiGethen were bred for.

The scents of the enemy camp had been in their nostrils for hours now as they had closed in. Like poison on the wind, wood smoke, waxed canvas, and cooked meat drifted where they had no right to. It was an affront to the Gods of the rain forest. To Cefu, God of the canopy; to Beeth, the lord of root and branch; and to Tual, who ruled the forest denizens.

The TaiGethen were willing slaves to the Gods and would do their bidding. The forest had to be cleansed and the balance restored.

The cell came together scant yards from the strangers' encampment to paint themselves and pray. The destruction of the forest to make the camp clearing offended and Auum could see the contempt in the eyes of his Tai. Not anger. Anger was a distraction and a waste.

Opening his pouches of black and deep green pastes, he traced broken stripes over Duele's deep brown face, his prayers sharpening their focus still further. And when the three were ready they rose to their feet, tan moccasins making no sound, green mottled jerkins and trousers blending with the tones of the undergrowth, faces now marked and hidden.

"Work for the Tai. Faith will keep us. Now string your bows and we will do the Gods' bidding."

There was a commotion outside the tent, but during his fever Sorys had heard so much that was strange he'd stopped trusting his senses. He'd been hallucinating giant spiders and plagues of snakes at the height of his four-day fever but at least now his mind was capable, or seemed to be, of rational thought. His tending mage, Claryse, said the fever had broken but that he was to rest another two days before joining Yron at the temple. She'd said very little but Sorys had the distinct impression they'd encountered serious trouble there.

So he lay in a platoon tent on a makeshift hammock, alone but for an oil lamp on the ground nearby. His night terrors were still too real and the pale yellow light was such a comfort.

He listened hard. There was something not right about what he could hear outside but he couldn't be sure if the fever had truly left him and he felt confused. So he just lay where he was, straining to pick up the sounds in among the raised voices.

The commotion died down. He thought he heard footsteps outside his tent but they were very quiet. And then, clear as the call of one of those damned howling monkeys, came a shrill wailing, passing left to right. It was the sound of loss, and it shuddered through his tired body. It scared him but he didn't cry out. Best to lie very still.

The wail came again and again. A man shouted but was cut off abruptly. Sorys could feel his heart beating very hard in his chest. Nausea rose. He reached for his water bottle just as the tent flap flew open. Claryse stood there, the lantern light illuminating a face drawn by some awful fear.

"Ghosts," she stammered, voice choked and broken. "Ghosts. We've got—"

The head of an arrow appeared through the front of her throat and her body jolted forward. She stumbled, blood pouring from the wound. She reached out, tried to speak and crumpled.

Sorys was too terrified even to scream.

He heard a whispering on the breeze and the tent flap moved again.

With the tent canvas shredded, all ropes frayed and cut, bodies laid out, fires extinguished and all metal buried, Auum led the Tai in prayer. They'd killed seventeen strangers and he felt at peace though the scything of the forest around him was a stain that only the gods could remove.

"Cefu, hear us. Beeth, hear us. Tual, hear us. We, your loyal servants who work according to your will, offer all that is around us to you and your denizens. May the flesh feed your creatures, may the cloth line burrows and nests and may the bones forever remind all who seek to destroy you that there is only eternal failure and damnation. Hear us and move us. Direct us to your will and so it shall be.

"To the greater glory of Yniss, who presides above all who walk this land. Hear us."

"And so it shall be," intoned Duele and Evunn.

Each of the Tai bowed his head in silent contemplation for a moment. Auum stood.

"Come," he said. "We have more work to do."

Yron and Ben-Foran were crouched by a small clutch of plants at the base of a balsa tree. Wide triangular green leaves sprawled out, seeming almost part of the tree but attached to a thick woody stem.

"Now," said Yron. "This is a young pareira vine. Notice the leaf shape. When it gets older, it'll flower and produce a red oblong fruit. Got that?"

Ben-Foran nodded.

"It's an important plant because a poultice of these leaves makes a good snake bite antidote and you can take a root infusion for the same purpose."

"Does it work?"

Yron gave him an old-fashioned look. "How do you suppose the forest elves survive day to day? So many of these plants have medicinal qualities. Learn. Because when you're without mage support, you might need to know. Now. One more thing. See that?"

He pointed at a flash of yellow under the leaves. It was a frog, barely bigger than his thumb.

"Yes, Captain."

Ben-Foran reached out reflexively but Yron slapped his hand away.

"Don't touch it. Don't let it touch you on exposed skin. This is the yellow frog. Remember my talk on the ship?"

"Yes, but—" began Ben.

"Small, isn't it?" said Yron. "But there's enough poison on its back to kill us all ten times over. You recall all of those who died from light puncture wounds? The elven arrows were all tipped with this poison." Yron grimaced. "Now, I know it's getting dark but I want as many of the men as possible to see this frog. It'll give them some sense of perspective."

"Yes, sir."

The two men stood.

"Captain Yron." It was Erys, running from the temple. He was clutching some papers and beaming all over his freckled face. Yron felt a warm glow, comforting despite the stifling heat.

"Good news, I take it?" He signalled Ben-Foran to stay with him.

"The best," said Erys as he stopped in front of them, handing over two leather-bound books and a scroll of parchment.

"Thanks," said Yron. "I'll acquire their accumulated wisdom the moment I've grasped ancient elvish. A decade of your close tutelage should do the trick."

Erys stared at him a moment before he got the joke. "Sorry, I just . . .

Well, never mind. The point is, I could understand enough of that to know it's what we're looking for. It's the key to the longevity argument."

Yron raised his eyebrows. "Really? And how many doors are there left to open?"

"Seven, I think. The Gods know when they'll open."

"Hmm." Yron clacked his tongue while he thought. "Never mind the frog, Ben; we'll find another tomorrow. Bring me the fittest sixteen men we have, barring yourself."

"Yes, Captain. Might I ask why?"

"You might, but it would be a waste of your breath."

Ben-Foran saluted and strode off, calling out names as he went.

"It's time we got some of this stuff away from here," he said to Erys.

"You think we're in some danger?"

"This is the centre of their faith, or so you told me. How long before it gets visited by more Al-Arynaar, do you think?" Yron hefted the papers. "These go tonight, and not via the camp. There's something not quite right about the atmosphere round here."

"I can't feel anything different."

"No indeed. But then you haven't been here before, have you? It's just a feeling. Trust me." He ushered Erys back toward the temple. "Show me everything you've got so far. We need an evacuation plan."

Thunder cracked across the darkening sky. The rains came again.

The next morning, Hirad was woken by The Unknown Warrior to a surprisingly cool dawn. A sea mist had rolled in and was suffocating the docks and large areas of the city, hemmed in as it was by hills. Over a meal of bread and herb tea, Ren assured them the mist wouldn't last.

Hirad didn't care if it stayed all day. He was anxious to get on and could feel the energy building within him. He knew where it came from and he looked around the table and drank in the sight. The Raven. Together and united in a single purpose. To watch them and hear the desultory conversation it was easy to imagine they were as they had always been but that was far from the truth.

Thraun still hadn't uttered a word and had the look of a man lost to the real world for much of the time. At the moment he was concentrating on food and was the most human he ever seemed. He followed The Unknown around like a faithful hound. Hirad was beginning to wonder if he'd prove a liability.

The dark patches under Erienne's eyes told of another night of precious little sleep. Hirad had heard her quiet crying through the thin walls of the inn and Denser's voice trying to comfort her. Neither had said much this morning but they had brought no good news back with them the previous evening. Though they'd not seen or heard of anyone dying, more and more were afflicted and to starkly varying degrees.

Some who had shown violent symptoms days before were now no more than tired, while others who had only just developed the disease were already too weak or unbalanced to walk, or else were struggling against sudden and severe internal bleeding. The Raven had done what they could, but without experience of the ways of elves had found themselves treated with coolness though not hostility.

Still, at least Darrick was with them now. Hirad remembered trying to get him to ride with The Raven during the final stages of their quest for Dawnthief. He'd refused then but Hirad had always known deep down that things would change. It was just a shame the circumstances of that change had been so bloody and tragic.

He looked forward to fighting with Darrick, if it came to that, back on Balaia. Aeb, of course, was a hugely powerful addition and The Unknown's left-hand defence now he couldn't use his double-handed sword. Ren worried him though. There had been neither the will nor the need to train her to fight in line and he worried about what that might do. He knew she enjoyed swordplay but perhaps they could persuade her to stick to her bow.

Time would undoubtedly tell. But on the trip to Balaia they'd have to get themselves back into fighting form. The Raven had survived for so many years because of their trust and unshakeable discipline as much as their skill. Hirad reminded himself to talk to The Unknown about it. He wasn't sure how much fighting the big man anticipated back on Balaia but one thing was certain. Right now, they didn't have their edge. They'd be fighting from memory, with two people who had only fought with them once, one who hadn't hefted a sword in The Raven ever and one complete enigma.

Hirad drained his tea and stood up from the table in the inn where they'd gathered for breakfast. All that was for later.

"Come on then, Raven. Let's get moving before the sun clears this mist."

There was a concerted move stalled only by Thraun, who was determined to finish every last crumb of bread.

"What's he planning to do, hibernate?" said Ilkar. "Don't bring too much. We're in one boat. It's got oars, a sail and forward decking for stowing gear. I'll introduce you to the guide when we're on our way. Until then, keep quiet. He's already nervous about taking strangers upriver."

"Strangers?"

"Yes, Hirad. If you're not elven on Calaius, you're a stranger. Remember that. Especially inland."

They walked down to the river jetties in almost total silence, the thick mist giving the streets an eerie feel. Ysundeneth was very quiet. It shouldn't have been, not even this early, but word of the illness would have spread fast and people weren't anxious to open their doors and face the uncertainty of the day ahead.

The sun was barely beginning to penetrate the chill of the mist. Hirad shivered, wishing for his heavy leather or furs, but on Ilkar's advice he, like all of them, had bought new clothes in the markets yesterday. Light leather armour and boots, lightweight cloaks and shirts. Everything dark brown, black or green, the colours of the forest.

"It must be a drab place," Hirad had said.

Ilkar had laughed. "You have never seen anything like it."

Hirad determined to remember that. He'd better be impressed.

Ilkar took them through twisting paved streets with houses and buildings close in on either side. Above the mist, seabirds called and answered. The jetties were a couple of miles inland from the docks and above the estuary. They were built for shallow-draught riverboats, and as they approached Hirad could see dozens of the boats tied up or hauled onto the muddy shore of the River Ix, which was named after the elven God of mana, or so Ilkar said.

He could smell the water. It was not altogether unpleasant, and although brown and its flow soporific in its sluggishness, it had none of the fetid stagnancy he associated with city rivers back on Balaia. The elves, it seemed, didn't use theirs as dumps or sewers.

The wooden jetty echoed under the tramp of their feet, the odd timber creaking as they passed, water lapping against the piles driven into the river bed. Ilkar strode confidently over the damp and slippery surface, stopping in front of a quartet of identical craft each some thirty feet long with a single mast in the middle, sail furled horizontally against it. An elf was stretched out across a seat at the stern of one of the vessels, smoke curling from a pipe in his mouth. It reminded Hirad that he hadn't seen Denser smoking his pipe in ages. Perhaps Erienne had cured him of the habit.

Ilkar hailed the elf and he sat up and waved them all on board, keeping his eyes down, not wishing contact with the Balaians invading his boat. He was old for an elf, his hair long and greying, his face full of sharp lines and heavy wrinkles. He had huge hands and powerful shoulders and possessed little of the natural grace of so many of his kind. He and Ilkar held a brief conversation in a dialect Hirad couldn't understand before he untied the stern rope and pushed them into the flow with an oar, where there was a breeze getting up, clearing the mist.

"Get the sail up, would you someone?" asked Ilkar, taking up station at the tiller with their guide, Ren, close to him. "Kayloor thinks there'll be enough wind to take us up against the current but if we could have oars ready, it might help if things get slack."

"No problem," said The Unknown, bending down and untying the oar beneath the bulwark. "You relax."

"Someone's got to relay what he's saying," said Ilkar, a smile on his face.

"Right." The Unknown sat down, Aeb taking up the position beside him. Thraun looked on in some confusion but The Unknown just waved him to a seat and he seemed to understand. Denser and Erienne sat in the prow looking out, still saying nothing. It left Hirad and Darrick to raise the sail, which filled enough to push them gently out into the current.

"Now it starts," said Ilkar. "Keep your eyes on the banks and don't trail your hands in the water."

"Fish got sharp teeth, have they?" said Hirad.

"Oh it's not the fish that should be worrying you, Hirad. There's far worse than mere fish in here," said Ilkar.

"You're so reassuring."

"Just realistic," said Ilkar. "This isn't like anything any of you have ever experienced. Don't treat it like Balaia or even Herendeneth or you'll come unstuck."

"'Coming unstuck' meaning?"

"Dead, usually," said Ren.

"Great place," said Hirad. "How surprising you left."

"But it is great, Hirad," said Ilkar. "Just dangerous for strangers."

Hirad shared a glance with Darrick, who raised his eyebrows.

"All right, General?" asked the barbarian.

"Never better," replied Darrick.

A booming bellow echoed across the river from the opposite bank. Through the clearing mist, a flock of birds scattered into the sky, their calls piercing and shrill. Hirad jumped. The boat rocked. In the stern Ren and Ilkar were laughing.

"Gods, but I'm going to enjoy this," said the mage.

The sail snapped and filled as the breeze stiffened in the centre of the channel. Choosing to keep his thoughts to himself, Hirad looked away into the depths of the rain forest.

CHAPTER 14

Selik, forty Black Wings and their mage prisoner galloped into Understone after a hard three-day ride through yet more devastated countryside, abandoned farms and desolate villages. Their horses were exhausted, riders saddlesore and Selik himself was experiencing severe pain in his face and across the dead parts of his chest. It was something he'd never understood. The nerves had been frozen by the bitch's spell so why could it hurt so much? Phantom pain, he'd been told. He preferred to believe it signalled some regeneration of his damaged body but in six years his condition hadn't improved.

Understone had never recovered from its central role in the last Wesmen wars. A small garrison town, it had been run-down when the war began and the battles it saw had left it burned and battered. It was now barely a shell. And to think what it had been when first built: the great defence against Wesmen invasion through Understone Pass.

The Black Wings rode down its rebuilt but again abandoned main street, past boarded-up houses down to the small stockaded garrison itself, reining in by the open front gates. Less than four hundred yards away, the black mouth that was the pass yawned large. Under the control of the Wesmen once again, the pass was the only passable land route east to west across the Blackthorne Mountains.

Selik turned his attention to the guard who hurried out to meet them. He was a raw recruit wearing old shabby leather and chain armour and carrying a rusting pike. His helmet wobbled on his head and his white, pinched and hungry face held frightened eyes.

"State your business," he said, his voice wavering.

Selik dismounted and walked over to the guard, his arms spread to indicate peaceful intent.

"Please don't be nervous. We mean our defenders no harm," he drawled through the ache in his face and mouth. "We merely seek a place to billet for the night before riding on south tomorrow morning."

The guard's eyes narrowed a little. "Why south?"

"We're on a humanitarian mission," said Selik. "Perhaps I should speak to your commanding officer."

"I will see if he's available," said the guard, the tremor diminishing in his voice. "May I take your name?"

"Of course. I am Captain Selik and these are the Black Wings."

The guard took a step backward. "I'll go and get the Commander."

Selik shook his head and turned to his men.

"Dismount. Go and find yourselves places to sleep. I'll organise feed for the horses and make sure the garrison have nothing to fear from us, if you know what I mean. We'll talk later. Be ready for my orders."

He watched them disperse, one of his lieutenants taking his horse for him. His gaze fell on the Julatsan mage, his puffed face and bound hands, as he was pulled from his mount. The elf leant against his horse while the strength returned to his legs. Selik was forming a grudging respect for him. Despite threats, frequent beatings, smashed fingers and toes, the mage hadn't even told them his name.

Selik would normally have broken a mage by now, frightened him or her into doing his bidding. But this elf had enormous mental strength. It couldn't go on, of course. Selik had a message he wanted delivered. He didn't want to wait until he returned from Blackthorne to dispatch it and, right now, one thing he was certain of was that this mage would not obey him. Turning to watch the garrison commander walk toward him, the scared guard at his shoulder, he pondered what he might do.

"Captain Selik," said the Commander gruffly, not offering a hand. He was a lean man, more from hunger than fitness, Selik suspected, with very short grey hair and a well-trimmed beard of the same colour. His armour was obviously looked after if a little old and he carried himself with pride. "I am Anders, commander of this garrison. My private tells me you're looking to travel south."

"Tomorrow morning, Commander Anders. I was hoping you'd allow my men to rest until then in the town."

Anders raised his eyebrows. "Help yourself. I can offer you nothing in the way of food or bedding though we have a well in the compound here that you're welcome to use."

Selik smiled. "Many thanks. I appreciate the gesture."

Anders' face was stone. "It was not offered in fellowship. I care more for your horses than I do for you or your band of murderers."

Used to the polarised reactions he inspired, Selik kept himself deliberately calm.

"We are all entitled to our beliefs, Commander. Much of Balaia's population would not agree with you, I fear."

"I have heard the reports, Selik. You are attempting to deny Balaia the very people it needs to drag itself out of this mess."

"A mess created by magic," snapped Selik.

"I won't debate this with you," said Anders, holding up a hand. "You are wrong and unwelcome, and were it not for your horses, you would not be staying here."

"Exactly what I would expect from a college lackey."

Anders laughed. "Don't try to rile me, Selik. I am proud of my college. And I am proud of the force I command here, small though it is. There may be conflict between the colleges at the moment but not here. We are, and ever will be, mindful of the Wesmen threat and we also police the trails north and south of here."

"Conflict? What are they telling you, Anders? Let me guess. The Xeteskian and Dordovan contingents had to be recalled but they have failed to explain why, am I right? I'd hate you to have to test their commitment right now."

Anders stepped forward and ushered Selik away from the gates to the compound.

"Let me advise you of a couple of things, Selik. First, the four colleges all hold to the pledge to supply a considerable force should there be any attempted incursion. I and my fifty charges are here to maintain defences, wards and to keep up trails, food and water supplies.

"Second, I have mages inside that compound who I rate as friends. They will be very unhappy you are here even for a night but very happy that you are travelling south in the morning. I have no idea why you're going and I don't care as long as you leave at first light," he said, coming to a halt. "But if Blackthorne is your intended destination, I have no doubt he will be even less accommodating. He, like me, believes in both mages and magic."

"I'll bear your warning in mind," said Selik.

"I sincerely hope not," said Anders. "Now, I don't expect to see you at my gates ever again. Only two of your men will collect water at a time, and they will ask permission at the gates before entering. And should any of my men or mages be abused verbally or physically by any of your men, I will seek you out and kill you myself. How do those rules sound to you?"

"Whatever makes you happy, Commander. Good day. We will not speak again."

Selik walked on, not sparing Anders another glance. He picked up his pace as he strode down into the town, noting the temporary picketing of horses and the boards levered off wrecked buildings to fuel fires. He snapped his fingers at a nearby Black Wing whose name escaped him. No more than a thug, the man, with thick neck and bald head covered in tattoos, ambled across, a stalk of grass hanging from his mouth.

"Where is Devun?"

The man shrugged and pointed. "In the old inn, I think."

"See that Edman and Callom join us there immediately. And then start ferrying water, two men at a time, from the compound. And keep your mouth shut. They may be college scum but we need them until we get back, understand?"

The man looked at him with sullen eyes but nodded. "Yes, Captain."

"Then get on with it."

Selik marched to the inn, identifiable only because of the brace on which the sign had once hung. Inside, he found Devun and Edman talking with another two. They were among a litter of splintered timbers but had found a serviceable table and bench.

"You two, get out of here. See to your horses and wait for orders," said Selik, jabbing a thumb over his shoulder. "And if you see Callom, get him in here quickly."

He watched them until they disappeared through the door out to the street.

"Right. Where's the mage?"

"Callom's got him. We're still working on him," said Devun. "Gods, but he's a tough bastard."

"Keep going. I want him cracked by the morning or his corpse in the ground."

"Yes, Captain," said Edman, a Black Wing veteran; tall, well built with dark brown hair and a bushy beard flecked with grey.

"Right, I've learned two things. First, the garrison here is small but has reasonable mage strength. However, it is isolated. Second, Blackthorne is definitely harbouring mages.

"Things need to move fast now. It's eight days' ride to Blackthorne and I'll be leaving before dawn tomorrow. Give it half a day to talk to the Baron and scout the area and another eight days back and you have your timescale."

"Is it worth visiting Blackthorne, sir? After all, he won't join us," said Edman.

"I have to know the threat he poses to us, and I have to canvass opinion of our crusade in the outlying villages. Yes, it's worth it. And I have to try to convert him before declaring him an enemy. Think if I could persuade him against his beliefs."

"And the rest of the plan still holds?" asked Edman.

"Yes. You and Callom each pick five good men. Mobilise support. Bring supply. Bring it here. I want the first true Balaians here by the time the garrison is cleared. I can give you a maximum of twenty days. Think you can do that?"

"Yes, sir." Edman nodded. "And what about the garrison?"

"Leave it to me. Don't worry. By the time you get back, we'll be in charge of Understone. Now pick your men, brief Callom when you see him, since he's obviously otherwise engaged now, and get some rest. You're leaving before me."

Edman nodded and trotted out of the inn. Selik turned to Devun and breathed out long.

"Any alcohol in here?"

"No, sir." Devun smiled. "We've looked."

"Cellars?"

"Empty."

"Dammit." Selik sat down heavily on the bench, which creaked alarmingly.

"Are you worried, Captain?"

Selik looked up into Devun's eyes and shook his head. "Not really. But this is our best chance to bring down the colleges and I can't afford it to go wrong. We've got to crack that mage, make sure he takes our message. Their divisions need deepening."

"I'll see what I can do, Captain." Devun cracked his knuckles for effect.

"You're a good man, Devun," said Selik. "I'm glad you're with me. The sacrifices are many on the path to righteousness. Get to it."

Devun beamed, saluted and left.

Selik smiled at his retreating back.

Heryst, Lord Elder Mage of Lystern, slapped his riding gloves down on the table in the great hall of the college's vast tower complex and poured himself a large goblet of wine. He stared around at the tapestries of his forerunners while he calmed himself and waited for the council.

Galloping through the quiet streets of Lystern in the early hours of the morning on the last day of his ride from Dordover, Heryst had felt the anger redouble in him. This city was dragging itself back from the brink of famine. Its people had worked hard and believed in the rationing that had kept them alive. They had taken in refugees by the thousand, gone without to do so, and still there had been little disorder.

The streets were clean, the markets still bought and sold, trade was just beginning to show some recovery and he had seen real optimism in the faces of those he had passed.

And now it was being threatened. Pointlessly threatened.

Draining his goblet, he poured more, enjoying the taste of the wine so early in the day, feeling it warming his mind and easing his frayed temper. He walked to one of the great arched windows and looked down over his college.

The great hall sat at the top of the wide low tower that was the centre of Lysternan magic. Only forty feet high, with a plain tiled conical roof, it had a diameter three times its height and an intricate beam system bound by magic that kept the roof from collapsing. Beneath the great hall, ceremonial chambers, lecture theatres and laboratories were dug deep into the earth surrounding the Heart of the college.

Like the spokes of a wheel, seven stone corridors spread from the tower to an outer circle of offices and classrooms, and between the corridors were seven stunning gardens, places of contemplation reserved for the senior mages of the college. Orchards, shrubberies, rock gardens, pools and fantastic arrays of flowers; the mood of the mage and the season dictated where one might be found walking or sitting.

Linked to the outer circle, arcs of buildings spread hundreds of yards in all directions: the library, refectories, cold room, mana bowl, long rooms and chambers of those resident. Only Heryst himself had his rooms and offices in the tower. All built to a focused design, Lysternan magic found power in the geometry of its buildings, their precise architecture and the angles of walls and roofs. Heryst didn't claim to know a great deal about the origins of the knowledge, he only knew he was not going to let it be torn apart.

He sat in his luxuriously upholstered and very high-backed chair, all deep greens and blood reds, and looked around the circular table, with its diamond-patterned marquetry and its hollows where the elbows of ages had worn its scratched but polished surface. What decisions had been taken here over the centuries, what great projects had been discussed. History hung in the air; you could all but smell it. But no subject could have been more important than the one about to be aired now.

Doors opened all along the semicircular corridor that bordered the great hall on one side and in came the council. Thirty men and women, expectant but a little anxious at being called from their beds so early. Each took his or her allotted place at the table. Not a one spoke aloud though Heryst could feel the odd surge of Communion as some tried to get a hint of what was to come from friends they thought in higher places than themselves.

"My friends, I apologise for the intrusion on your rest this morning and for my appearance," said Heryst, when all were seated. He had no doubt the fact he was still dusty and sweaty from the road had raised a few eyebrows. "But there are things I need to know and you need to hear."

There was a murmur around the table. Heryst looked to his immediate left, straight into the eyes of his mentor, Kayvel. He touched the arm of the white-haired strong old man, smiled and nodded.

"It has come," he said quietly.

Kayvel sighed, his grey eyes sparkling in the sun and lantern light. "And in my lifetime."

"And I thank the Gods you are here to advise me."

"Speak," Kayvel said.

Heryst turned to the council table and spoke.

"My friends, you will know I am just returned from Dordover. I had thought to seek assurances from Vuldaroq that the conflict at Arlen was at an end before riding to Xetesk to seek the same from Dystran.

"Instead, I find that we are facing our gravest crisis for hundreds of years. We have suffered animosities and skirmishes in my lifetime but all these disputes were settled by negotiation. What we are facing now, my friends, is war. War between powerful colleges at a time when the very existence of magic is being questioned on Balaia. At a time when surely we should be pulling together to repair the damage magic has done to our land, two colleges seek to rip us all to shreds. All over a dead girl and the information two dying elves can give.

"Should we have been surprised? Possibly not. After all, we have seen Xetesk and Dordover battle over Lyanna; we have seen Dordover betray Erienne, one of their own, to the witch hunters; and we have seen our own General Darrick so sickened by our liaison with Dordover that he deserted his command. And the results of what Xetesk's Protector army did to Arlen are there today for all to see."

"But is it war?" A voice sounded from the far side of the table. "Could this not be another flexing of muscles?"

"I rode here and probably killed my horse in the process because it *is* war. Both colleges want it and we will be swept up in it, whether we like it or not. I fear for us and I fear for Julatsa because I do not believe this fight will end when either Xetesk or Dordover is beaten. The balance of magic will be irrevocably altered and the victor will inevitably desire dominion.

"Vuldaroq informs me that Xetesk has cleared its refugee camps by riding the people out like animals. They have scattered, many toward the Dord to the north. Some will inevitably come here.

"Kayvel, I need you to contact our deputation in Xetesk. Make sure they are unharmed and free. Are there any questions?"

He looked around the table. No one spoke.

"Good. I am going to rest and change. You are going to stay here and begin planning. And remember, if war comes to our borders and our negotiations come to nothing, we may have to defend not just ourselves but Julatsa too."

The doors at the end of the chamber opened with a crash.

"My Lord Heryst, council. I apologise but I must speak."

Heryst stilled the irritated murmur with a hand and acknowledged the head of his mana spectrum monitoring team.

"Go ahead, Dunera."

"My Lord." She nodded. "We've got a problem in the spectrum over Arlen."

"What is it?"

"I don't know," she said. "But whatever it is, people are going to die. Lots of them."

"And the signature?" asked Kayvel.

"The mana is in flux, density increasing. It's huge, or it will be. And it's offensive in nature, no doubt of it."

"Who's casting it?"

"Xetesk."

"Do we have anyone in the vicinity?" Heryst kneaded his forehead.

"Yes. We have representatives with the Dordovans," said Dunera, head dropping to her chest. "They have refused to leave and I have already commended their souls."

Commander Senese ran along the back of the Dordovan lines, urging his men to greater efforts. Three days they'd repulsed comfortably the Xeteskians' attempts to push them out of the northern streets. But now this.

Dawn had seen fierce fighting on three fronts, with Protectors in every attack. His men were holding but only just, keeping key intersections secure as well as the southern edge of the Park of the Martyrs. But in the mana spectrum, something much, much worse.

They'd been following its development for hours; a cooperative spell that must be taking the combined stamina of over fifty mages. And planning defence and reaction was taking most of his magical resource, leaving this as a battle almost entirely without spell attack. Somehow, though, he had to break the enemy onslaught.

"Don't falter!" he called. "Push on. You can break them."

The power of the Protectors was awesome. Huge men, masked and silent, their dual sword and axe attacks directed by the soul mind so quickly and accurately. But Dordover had to stand up to them. To be exact, the scared men in front of him had to.

One of those men took an axe in his chest. He was cast into those behind, threatening for a moment to cause a breach in the line, but Senese filled it, sword deflecting a low strike.

"Keep going!"

Their commander's presence fighting alongside galvanised those near him. The din of order and weapon increased, and the Xeteskians' grinding advance was halted. Senese wheeled his blade and drove it at a Protector's heart. Without looking, the masked man whipped his axe across to block, following up with a sweep of his sword. Senese ducked, yelling a warning. The blade whistled just over him, slicing through stray hairs on his head and burying itself in the skull of the man next to him at the end of its arc.

Blood and brain sprayed into the air. The victim tumbled sideways to the ground. The Protectors stepped up their pace. Senese moved to block and thrust again and felt a presence at his right shoulder.

"Sir!" It was one of his field captains, a brave young man named Hinar. "Drop back. You're needed at command!"

Senese flat-bladed a Protector across the mask, sending him staggering. Hinar saw his opportunity and thrust forward, his point piercing the enemy's armour and penetrating his stomach.

"Go, we can hold!" Hinar regathered himself to turn away an axe, the heavy blow making him gasp.

Senese forced a regular Xeteskian soldier back and ducked out of the combat, another man immediately moving to take his place. He ran back toward the ruined bakery in which he'd set up his command post. The lead mage met him halfway.

"We've got to pull back," said Indesi, his face terrified, his hands grabbing at Senese's jerkin. "We can't defend against this spell."

"Find a way," barked Senese. "We are not running."

"It's too big, it'll destroy us."

"Then combine your shields and talk up your mages." Senese stopped and spun Indesi round to look at the fighting. "See those men? Up against it but they believe. Start believing yourself."

"But—"

"And where will we run to, eh? Those bastards will chase us all the way to Dordover. We can't let them run the supply route from here to Xetesk. I will not yield."

"Then break through right now or they will win anyway." Indesi's voice was toneless, dead almost. "You don't understand."

"I understand we cannot afford to lose this town. That's what I understand."

A piercing scream from inside the command post went straight through Senese.

"What the—"

But Indesi wasn't listening. He turned and ran to the door, shouted into its lantern-lit interior.

"Weave the defence grid. No gaps, dual skin." He looked back over his shoulder at Senese before disappearing inside. "It's coming. I warned you."

Senese shuddered and began to run back toward the line. Perhaps there was still a chance. There were still men running across the small courtyard to the line he was defending. The enemy mages had to be right behind the Protectors. Surely the spell would be targeted by line of sight.

He opened his mouth to shout but swallowed it. A blue glow, brighter than the sun, washed over the buildings ahead, casting stark shadows down alleys, behind trees and across the courtyard. The fighting changed in tone. Voices lost their authority, blades fell with less power.

"No!" he shouted. "Fight. Now you've got to fight!"

He began to run forward again but his men were wavering. The Protectors would slaughter them. But they weren't moving, satisfied to stand by and watch. And the reason became all too clear.

Above the level of tree and building rose a globe of fire, tinged deep Xeteskian blue and ringed by sparks and sheets of what looked like lightning but Senese knew was unstable mana.

"Oh dear Gods," said Senese, staring up as the globe rose smoothly, its radiance glaring harsh, its size, bigger than a ship, awesome and stupefying. His men were starting to break. "Stay under the shielding. It's your only chance!"

But while the Xeteskians stood and watched, the Dordovans scattered beneath the globe and the stillness that accompanied it.

"Stand firm!" screamed Senese, but they weren't listening to him.

Weapons fell from nerveless hands, brave men stumbled and sprawled, legs pumping as they tried to flee, not heeding the most obvious fact. There was nowhere to run. Hinar came to his side.

"Where are the mages?" he shouted into the pounding of feet and cries of fear.

"Trying to shield us. Pray Gods they can make it stick."

Hinar nodded as the two men backed away, watching the globe gathering speed and, impossibly, size as it rushed over the heads of the Xeteskians.

"Come on, Indesi," breathed Senese. "Come on."

The globe struck the Dordovan outer shield. Mana flared and spat, the globe flattened over the curved surface, bulged down over them. Senese felt a sudden intense heat as the shield gave way.

He put his hands above him and crouched reflexively but the globe didn't travel far, striking the second skin, but hard. The temperature was like the inside of an oven, the blazing heat of the Southern Continent desert and increasing. From the command post, Senese could hear screaming and voices urging effort.

"They aren't going to do it," said Senese, breaking at last. "Run."

The two men turned, but at the same moment the second shield collapsed, the great globe crashing down into the courtyard. Senese was blown from his feet by the rush of displaced air and connected hard with the wall of a building. It jarred his back and he crumpled into a half seated position, winded and groggy. He focussed his eyes as the globe struck the ground.

Fire washed across the cobblestones, surging up the sides of buildings and blasting through windows and weakened timbers. Across the courtyard, a damaged tenement shattered under the blast, the rending of wood and squealing of nails torn from stays lost in the roar of flame. Everywhere, men, helpless under the spell, were rolled over or plucked from the ground, clothing and flesh charred in a heartbeat.

The heat in the courtyard intensified still further. Sword metal glowed red, stones blackened, timber disintegrated, glass dissolved. Roof tiles flew high into the sky as the globe breached another building, tearing it apart. A great pall of smoke billowed in the superheated wind, which took the screams of the dying and whipped them away like chaff in a breeze. A burning corpse struck the wall by Senese and broke apart, gaping skull pleading.

Indesi had been right; this was no ordinary FlameOrb construct. There was too much heat, too much energy. It consumed everything in its path, scoured the ground clean as would the fires of hell.

And as the heat lashed the moisture from his body Senese's last view was of the Xeteskians, standing and waiting, their fire breaking over their mana shields which glowed blue and dissipated its power.

"What have you done?" he rasped.

The flame wall rolled over him like an angry sea.

CHAPTER 15

It was night. Yron was standing alone in the centre of the stone apron outside the ring of guard fires. Behind him, his men either stood nervous guard or tried to rest as best they could in the increasing humidity and heat that had penetrated the temple in the last few days. Presumably, the atmosphere had been spoiled by the removal of the doors but Yron thought there was probably more to it than that. It was like the ambience in the rain forest; he couldn't put his finger on it but he knew all was not well.

He had come beyond the guard fires to listen and to think. Out in the forest the sounds of the night echoed around him; the growl of big cats, the calls of monkeys and birds under threat, the buzzing of an insect swarm under the canopy, awoken from rest. A spider scuttled across the apron right by his feet. The size of his hand, he watched it go, pursuing some prey he couldn't see, perhaps one of the myriad frogs croaking all around him, or the cicadas rasping as they tried to attract mates.

Yron felt uncertain and that was a condition with which he was unfamiliar. The runner he'd sent to the base camp earlier today hadn't returned and that worried him. He knew he should have sent two men but Pavol was very fit and wanted to see whether he could run all the way. Yron was a man to encourage endeavour and had loaded him with water skins and sent him at dawn.

Now he needed him back with news. There was danger coming and he was anxious about the sick in the camp. He needed to start moving back to the coast where his ships lay at anchor, and he was not about to leave anyone behind.

Erys finding the vital writings earlier that evening was good news in the extreme and Yron's first squad was ready to go before first light the next day. He had outlined for them a different route based on his incomplete charts of the forest. It would take them up to six days to reach the ships, assuming they stayed healthy. They were a quartet in which Ben-Foran had faith and that was enough for him, yet he still felt nervous for them. The rain forest was a danger to all of them but more so now. Their invasion could not go unnoticed for long and inevitably the elves would seek revenge.

The elven guard at the temple had surprised him with their ferocity but there was much worse out there and it was those elves he feared and those elves that he was sure were coming. He knew his men didn't understand why he was splitting his force. They had been taught there was strength in numbers, but in the depths of the rain forest it didn't always hold true. Small squads of men, quiet and careful men, would have more chance of survival out there.

Yron blew out his cheeks and swatted at a fly that buzzed around his head. How long before the enemy got here? Should he call up the reserve from the ships to cover his retreat? How long could he give Erys and Stenys to research? Should he cut his losses now? After all they had the main prize, if Erys was right, and all but those papers were leaving for the ships tomorrow. Erys would take the most valuable material himself.

Looking up into the heavens, Yron could see it was clouding over again. Thunder rumbled distantly. Another downpour was on its way. He turned to go back to the watch fires but a crashing in the forest stopped him. He spun round, cocking an ear. Whatever it was was blundering wildly. Probably a wounded animal. Whatever it was was coming straight toward them. He backed up and drew his axe, listening to the snap of branches and the calls of distress that set off the howler monkeys and the wild shrieks of birds in their nests.

He reached the ring of fires.

"Crossbowmen ready. If it's injured, we need to take it down. It'll attack anything that gets in its way and that includes us."

A heartbeat later and those cries of distress resolved themselves into something that set his heart racing.

"Stand down!" he ordered.

He was already hurrying toward the path when the figure stumbled out of the forest, ran a few unsteady steps across the paving, slipped and sprawled on its damp surface.

"Erys!" Yron shouted, running to the fallen figure. "Get out here now. Bring me some light. Move!"

He slithered to a halt by the man, who was heaving in great ragged breaths, coughing and shivering the length of his body. He knelt and put a hand on the man's shoulder.

"Calm down, Pavol. You're safe now," he said.

Pavol tried to push himself up on his hands, his head shaking violently.

"No," he managed through a clotted throat. "No."

"Shhh," said Yron. "You're scared and hurt. Take your time. Come on, let me help you over."

Using his knees as a pivot, Yron turned the young man over so his head lay in the officer's lap. One of his men brought over a lantern and the two of them gasped.

Pavol's face was shredded. The left side had been clawed away, taking his eye with it. Bite marks covered his neck, the punctures oozing blood, and there was a flap of skin hanging from a deep gash in his forehead that had poured blood over his face. His clothes were ripped and torn in a dozen places, his right hand was mangled and broken and across his stomach more claws had gouged their paths.

"Erys!" yelled Yron. "Where is that bloody mage?"

"Here." Erys ran up with Ben-Foran.

"Get to work. See what you can do, then we'll get him inside," said Yron. "Ben, remember those leaves I showed you earlier? Not the snakebite ones, the others. Take one man and a lantern and collect as many as you can. Get them in a pot and boil them. Make a drink but don't throw away the paste you have left behind. All right?"

"Yes, Captain." Calling a man to him, Ben-Foran hurried away.

"Erys?" asked Yron.

The mage shook his head. "It's bad, Captain. He's lost a great deal of blood and he'll be infected from all these gashes and cuts. There's nothing I can do about the eye but we should wrap him up. He's in shock. I'll put him to sleep."

"N-n-no," stammered Pavol. "Let me sp-speak."

"Later," said Yron, smoothing back his blood-matted hair. "You have to rest now."

Pavol reached round and gripped Yron's arm fiercely, his single eye boring into his captain's face.

"They killed all of them," he said, each word dragging from his mouth. "The camp. All dead."

Yron tensed and put a hand out to stop Erys casting.

"Wait," he said. "Pavol, carefully now, tell me what you saw."

"Something," said Pavol, and he coughed blood which sprayed on to Yron's face, "moved so quickly. I should have helped. But I just watched."

"What were they? What did they do?" urged Yron. "Animals?"

"No. Elves. Just one or two. I just watched them all die." The young man's eye filled with tears and he blinked furiously. An ooze of gore slipped from his ruined orb. "Then I crept away and ran like a coward."

Yron's heart was thumping in his chest. What he feared most was about to come to pass.

"You're not a coward," he said. "You did exactly the right thing. There was nothing you could have done for our people. But you might just have saved all our lives." He looked down at Pavol's torn body. "What did this? Jaguar?"

"Panther," he rasped. "Big. Black. Stalked me for hours."

"A panther? But there are no . . ." Yron's voiced trailed away.

"Attacked me only once. And those eyes. It looked at me. Almost . . . human."

"And it left you for dead?" Erys's curiosity got the better of him.

"Yes," said Yron, his eyes scanning the dark cloak of the rain forest all around them.

"Why?"

"Because, Erys, that panther was not hunting for meat." Yron rubbed his mouth and chin. At least it couldn't get any worse now.

"Please," said Pavol. "It hurts."

"I know, son. We'll save you."

But Pavol was suddenly dead. Yron laid his head gently on the ground and turned to Erys, his mind racing with possibilities, a shiver of fear running down his back.

"How's your stamina, you and Stenys?"

"Pretty good. Your herbs do a better job than I'd thought."

"Right. Get yourselves linked and commune with the ships. I want the reserve out now; I want them to establish defensive positions in front of the estuary entrance. Tell them we're coming in teams. Get to it."

"That panther—" began Erys.

"Later. Go." Yron turned away. "Ben-Foran!"

His lieutenant ran over. "Sir."

"I want to see all the squads with cargo ready to go now. Any that aren't ready, get them so. That includes the two with Erys and Stenys. They're leaving now and there'll be a change to their routes. We've just run out of time here."

"And the rest of us?"

Yron shrugged. "We get to buy them as much time as we can before we die."

Rebraal stumbled again and crashed heavily into the trunk of a tree, only managing to turn his body at the last moment to avoid Mercuun taking the damage. His shoulder sang out its agony and a cry forced itself out of his mouth. He rested a few moments, panting hard, his pulse pounding in his head, his body soaked in sweat and his limbs shaking with exhaustion.

He had no idea how far he had travelled or for how long. All he knew was that it wasn't far enough and that now, with night full around him, he was fading fast. His eyesight wandered in and out of focus and every step was a trial. He felt constantly nauseous and faint and he was waiting for his body to give out and for Tual to offer him up to the rain forest. Him and Mercuun.

He pushed himself away from the tree and plodded deliberately on, seeking vegetation he could force through without a blade as he had done all day. It added to the distance but there was no way he could do otherwise.

Once he put Mercuun down, he didn't think he'd have the strength to lift him again.

He ducked under a stand of broad leaves, his vision swimming again, the colours he could usually pick out so cleanly in the dark all washed out and running together. Again he was forced to stop while his head cleared, each time taking longer than the last, and it was then that he heard what he had most feared. The quiet padding of feet. The almost imperceptible movement of vegetation at odds with the ambient breeze. The careful placement and sinuous movement that spoke of the consummate hunter. Tual had spoken her wishes.

Rebraal was being stalked.

Shivering, his body wracked with the fever pumped around his bloodstream by his exertions, he forced himself on. Mercuun, unconscious for much of the time and incoherent the rest, was a draining weight in his arms. Rebraal knew he hadn't the strength to fight the jaguar, if such it was, and his only hope was to carry on, hoping and praying the animal was diverted from its hunt.

He upped his pace, his body screaming at him to stop, his mind fogging and new blood seeping from the wound in his shoulder. He tripped across a root, dropped to his haunches under a low branch and drove himself upright, gasping. He broke into a trot, imagining the jaguar's footsteps increasing, the shoulders moving under the sleek fur, the eyes piercing the night and the nostrils twitching as they caught the scent of blood.

Behind him, he heard the crack of a twig and the rustle of leaves. He ran, praying for respite or a hiding place. Mercuun bounced in his arms and moaned in his unconsciousness, the pain of his broken limbs finding him even there. Liana and vine slapped Rebraal's face as he went; he twisted this way and that, jumped more roots, slid down a slight slope and forced himself up its other side. He dared not look behind him.

The sounds of the rain forest filled his ears, their volume increasing tenfold, twentyfold, as he ran. The croaking of frogs, the rasping of lizards, the scurrying of ants and spiders. He could hear it all so loud, mingled with his ragged breath as he fought for air. He heaved them over the lip of another incline, not stopping, rushing onward, splashing through a stream, his skull echoing painfully to the awful noise that built and built.

He felt his legs half give but drove himself for another pace. And another. He ignored the shuddering of his arms and the lancing stabs through his back every time his foot went down. He had to escape the jaguar, he had to get to the village and warn them. The temple. By Yniss, the temple had to be retaken. He couldn't fail or the harmony would be lost.

He raised his head to look for his route, his vision clouded again and a branch caught him squarely across the forehead.

Rebraal felt himself go as if in slow time. Even as his head rocked back from the impact, his legs carried on forward a pace. Impossibly unbalanced, his grip on Mercuun was lost and his broken friend tumbled out of his hands and away. He circled his arms desperately but still he fell back, landing in a tumble on the soft muddy forest floor, his head a mass of sparks, his senses all but gone.

He heard the sound of those feet running toward him, could feel their vibration through his tortured body.

"I am sorry, Meru," he managed as he waited for the end. "I have failed you."

The hot breath of the cat fired into his face. He looked up into the eyes of Tual's creature to see the wonder of creation even as it tore his life from him but it was no jaguar. It was a panther, black as night with the light of sentience in its eyes. Its head darted in and licked at his cheeks and forehead, an impossibly comforting feeling as the rough tongue dragged at his skin.

He frowned, the last vestiges of his strength gone, too weak even to raise an arm, but as he faded to nowhere he heard a voice.

"How fast you ran, brave Al-Arynaar. But now you can stop. We have found you. We will take you home."

Ilkar had told them it would be different but he hadn't managed to get across the magnitude of that difference. The rain forest was vast. Unbelievably vast. It covered everything that they could see and, the Julatsan assured them, a thousand times more that they couldn't.

Sailing gently up the River Ix, they were hemmed in by walls of green on either side. The tallest trees towered over two hundred feet into the sky; their shorter cousins hung their branches into the water, sucking up the life that gave their colours such verdancy. But just as the forest seemed about to overwhelm them, the bank would cut suddenly away on one side, and the roaring they had been hearing for an hour would reveal itself as a waterfall, many hundreds of feet high, falling sheer down moss-covered rock into a deep plunge pool that fed straight into the Ix. And elsewhere they would glimpse huge gentle slopes, running away from shallow banks and up the sides of hills, that gave way in turn to spectacular mountains, thrusting through the all-conquering forest and up into the heavens.

And everyone but Aeb stared, stunned by the majesty of the land. The Protector betrayed no emotion and Hirad wanted to rip off his ebony mask and implore him to look, to laugh in delight at the beauty and to drink in his freedom. But to remove the mask would be to subject Aeb to torment at the hands of the demons who controlled his soul and the path between it and his body. Such was the curse of every Xeteskian Protector.

So Hirad tried not to think about it, and felt happy instead that some of what they saw brought light even to Erienne's eyes.

Everywhere was gorged with life. From the vibrantly coloured birds that flew overhead to the jaguars they'd seen lapping at the water's edge; to the snakes that curled around so many boughs of so many trees, and the lizards, rodents and huge hairy pig-like mammals that watched them with nervous eyes and snuffling snouts as they journeyed by. Below them yet more lurked and Hirad was glad of Ilkar's warning.

The lazy flop of fish at the river's surface was occasionally counterpointed by the thrash of the great armoured reptiles that swam the Ix and basked on its muddy banks. Some of them had to be more than thirty feet long and the only animal not scared of them was even bigger. These giants, only their frog eyes visible, watched The Raven pass from their submerged positions. One slip, Hirad thought, and any man would be prey, though Ilkar swore to him that these lumbering aquatic animals ate only plant life.

Still, the river had yielded food for the night's stop. Before midday, the travellers had caught enough fish for a feast; they thrashed in a water-filled sack at their irascible guide's feet.

As the day wore on, tempers began to turn. Where the morning had seen the mist burn off and the rains come to cool them, the afternoon took on a heavy stifling quality that dampened spirits and leached strength. And when the clouds had stormed over them, and the lightning flashed under the dark grey mantle with thunder the prelude to yet another savage downpour, it had failed to clear the air and the heat was like a wall.

When at last, with light fading quickly, they'd steered for the bank and made camp forty yards from the river, the smiles were a fading memory.

Hirad sat on a log in the tiny clearing they had made under the patronising instruction of Kayloor who, Ilkar translated every now and again, was apparently appalled at the damage they were doing to the forest. Hammocks were strung in a loose circle around a shallow fire pit and wood burned there, lit despite its damp by Ilkar's FlamePalm.

Kayloor had produced a spit and stand from the boat's storage locker and was making himself useful cooking the fish. On another part of the fire, water boiled in a sizeable pot. Ilkar sat next to Hirad and the two of them looked around the campsite in silence for a time, watching. Aeb cleaned and sharpened his axe and sword. The Unknown was doing likewise with blade and daggers. Denser and Erienne sat on the other side of the fire, she constantly kneading her neck and trying to cover everywhere at once with her eyes and he scratching at an itch below his skullcap. The other three were out in the forest, collecting more wood and, so Ilkar said, some useful herbs, if they could find them.

"How are you doing?" he asked Hirad.

"Bloody awful," said Hirad. "I feel knackered but I haven't done anything. I'm already dreading another day in that damn boat, and if that guide of yours makes another clever comment he's going to find himself a snack for one of those great reptile things in the river. Oh, and my hands hurt from rowing."

"They're called crocodiles. And quiet," hissed Ilkar. "We can't afford to upset him."

They both looked at Kayloor but he didn't seem to have heard them.

"Look," continued Ilkar. "I know it's difficult to understand, but it's not personal what he's saying. It's how elves think. They tolerate Balaians in the trading towns and ports, but inland it's different. They don't think you understand the lore of the forest and of course they're absolutely right. Now, let me see your hands."

"They'll be fine," said Hirad, not convinced by Ilkar's defence of Kayloor. As far as he was concerned, the elf was just plain insulting.

"No, they won't, Hirad. You haven't listened to me, have you? This isn't Balaia. Are you blistered?"

"Well, what do you think, Ilkar?" Hirad raised his voice, feeling suddenly irritated. "While you were sitting chatting with king smart-arse there, some of us were putting our backs out trying to move us upriver more quickly. And looking around here, I fail to see why we bothered. I mean, is this the best you can do?"

"Frankly, yes," said Ilkar. "Now let me see."

"Gods, all right," said Hirad, holding out his hands. "You're worse than my mother."

"I'm surprised you can remember," said Ilkar shortly.

"Oh, and I'm sure you saw yours only just the other day. Or was it a hundred years ago? I'm easily confused."

Ilkar didn't answer but grabbed Hirad's hands roughly, stretching his damaged skin.

"Ouch," he said.

"Sorry," replied Ilkar brightly. "Right. It's not too bad but you've broken the skin in a couple of places. Assuming Ren brings back some rubiac, I'll make you a poultice that you should apply to each hand for an hour, all right?"

"Why don't you just do me a WarmHeal or something if you're that bothered? Can't imagine a few wet leaves is going to do much good."

"They'll kill the infection and help the skin to heal over. Don't argue. Don't put your hands in the dirt if you can help it, and try not to row tomorrow."

"Tell our great captain that," said Hirad, pointing a finger at Kayloor. The elf said nothing, merely turned the fish skewered on the spit. Whatever Hirad thought of him personally, whatever the sort of fish he was cooking, it smelled fantastic. Hirad had forgotten how hungry he was. "I just don't see why you're so concerned. They're just a few blisters."

Ilkar breathed out loudly. "I don't know why I bloody bother. Look—and I want you all to listen to this, not just cloth-ears, here. Worry about every cut, sore or blister you get. Worry about every rash, every stomach pain and every headache. For the last time, this is not Balaia. Infections are so easy to get, particularly if you weren't born here. Never drink water before you've boiled it or before a mage has cleansed it. But you must eat and drink well. I can see how tired you all are and you've been sitting in a boat all day. What if we end up having to walk? You have to give your bodies time to get used to the heat, the humidity, everything. Please tell me you understand."

Ilkar's impassioned speech was met with a few muttered affirmatives.

"Two other points, if I may," he said. "First, Aeb, you need to bathe your face every night. Ren or I will make you a balm, though it would be easier if you'd let someone help you."

"That is not possible," said Aeb. "I am the only Protector here. I will attend to myself alone."

"Understood. The other thing, Erienne and Denser, is please look after your mana stamina reserves. No matter how hard we try, someone will most likely get sick and we will all get bitten to pieces. There are snakes that can kill in a couple of hours and anything that bites will infect you."

"So glad you brought us here," said Denser. "I mean, is there anything we can do that won't result in death or serious illness?"

"Just take extra care. You'll soon get used to it," said Ilkar. "And I should remind you that no one was forced to come here."

"Oh, really?" Denser raised his eyebrows. "If you cast your mind back you'll find there was considerable pressure."

"That's because we're The Raven. We work together and Ilkar needed our help," said Hirad. "I didn't hear you object."

"But there was never any choice, Hirad, was there?"

Hirad snapped the twig he was holding and threw the ends into the fire.

"This again? Gods drowning, Denser but I don't remember you giving us any choice when you needed us to help find Erienne and Lyanna."

"And look what good it did us," whispered Erienne.

Hirad felt a pit open in his heart. "Oh, Erienne, I didn't mean it that way—"

"I'm sorry we were such a burden on your time," she said, voice rising. "Perhaps if you'd stayed at home with your damn dragons all this wouldn't have happened. And perhaps if we weren't The Raven I could be where I belong. At my daughter's graveside."

"It was no burden, Erienne," said Hirad. "You know that."

"Let's just leave it, shall we?" said The Unknown. "We're here because we're The Raven and Ilkar asked us. It's how we've always done things and how we always will. Choice does not necessarily enter into it."

"Well, don't tell me that, tell him." Hirad pointed at Denser.

"Grow up, Hirad, for Gods' sake."

"I'm not the one complaining about choice or the lack of it, Xetesk man," said Hirad. "In case you hadn't noticed, none of us is exactly comfortable here but you don't hear us making smart remarks. Just deal with it."

"What the hell have we come here for anyway?" asked Denser. "Ysundeneth was full of mages."

"Yes, Denser, busy ones," said Ilkar. "And I know none of them. I thought I'd explained that I had to go to my home village to start. Find contacts, establish a line. You have to understand how it works over here. Nailing up a sign offering money to lapsed elven mages won't work."

Denser slapped at an insect that had settled on his hand. "One more bite," he muttered.

"Want me to show you all mine?" Hirad stood up.

"Hirad, enough."

"No, Unknown, you know what he's doing. It's bloody typical," said Hirad, feeling his muscles tense. "When he needs us to find his daughter it's fine. When the position's reversed he'll go on letting us know it's all done under sufferance. Why can't you just do something for someone else for a change, eh?"

"*For a change?*" Denser gaped.

"Denser, please," said Erienne, laying a hand on his arm. He ignored her.

"Who was it cast Dawnthief to save us from the Wytch Lords, eh? Who was it defied the Lord of the Mount to get The Unknown back from his Protector calling? Who was it lay with you and Ilkar to keep you both alive when you—you, Hirad Coldheart—were dying?"

"That's what being in The Raven is all about," said Hirad calmly. "Those are great things you did, Denser, and I'll love you forever for doing them. But this is now. And I don't want to hear you bleating about how difficult it is for you."

"Don't patronise me, Hirad."

"Did you have anything better to do with your time?" snapped Hirad. "Aside from sunbathing and gardening?"

"Stop it! Stop it!" yelled Erienne, surging to her feet, hands about her head. "How dare you bring my child's grave into your infantile row! I came here to try and forget, don't you understand? Not for The Raven. For me. When will you let me start?"

She turned and ran from the camp, Denser making to follow her. Before she'd got five yards she ran into the hulking form of Thraun, who dropped his huge bundle of wood and caught her round the waist in one arm.

"Let me go, Thraun."

The shapechanger just shook his head. He traced a hand down the side of her face and looked very deeply into her eyes.

"Not forget, Erienne," he said, his voice rusty, gruff and croaking. "Grieve. Live. Not forget."

CHAPTER 16

The fish had been excellent but The Raven had paid little attention to its succulence, so stunned were they all by Thraun's words, his first in more than five years. Where they had come from and what barrier had fallen in his mind to let him form speech they'd probably never know but he had spoken and that was enough.

In truth he'd done much more. Not just understanding Erienne's feelings but defusing the whole stupid argument. Now, Denser and Hirad were chatting away like it had never happened and Ilkar looked at them across the fire and shook his head.

"I know what you're thinking," said The Unknown next to him.

Ilkar had noticed him studying the ants that swarmed over the fish bones at his feet, breaking down anything useful and carrying it off. It was the way of the rain forest. Everything was used.

"I don't understand those two and I probably never will," said Ilkar. "What is it with them? Put them round a campfire and they're at each other's throats about something trivial."

"It wasn't trivial, though, was it?" said The Unknown. "Hirad's right."

"But he can't communicate it, can he?"

"And Denser should know that by now and stop rising to the bait. You should have a word."

"And do you think he's got the right attitude?" asked Ilkar.

"Who, Denser?"

"Who else?"

The Unknown shrugged. "Hard to say. He was only trying to protect Erienne, I think. He's just looking for an outlet. He'll be fine when we get back to Balaia and he can feel more useful."

They fell silent, watching Thraun and Darrick. Since his first utterance, Thraun had said very little and much of his confusion seemed to have returned. But they were all working on him now in turn and Darrick was once again trying to get him to accept a sword. It was looking a lot simpler this time.

"What brought it on, do you think?" asked Ilkar.

"Erienne," said The Unknown. "Or, more precisely, what she said. His words came from very deep, didn't they?"

"I'm amazed he can remember what happened to Will."

"Like I say, it came from very deep. Maybe we shouldn't be surprised at what he retains from before he was a wolf those five years."

"Maybe not." Ilkar stretched out his legs. "Any more tea on the go?"

"Just some muck you're boiling down," said Hirad from across the fire. "Is it really all necessary?"

Ilkar smiled. "You'll be glad of that muck tomorrow."

But he had to admit he and Ren were monopolising the fire. Three pots hung from Kayloor's spit. Hirad was already clutching cloth balls steeped in rubiac fruit and there was more boiling away for Darrick, who had suffered similar blistering. Next to it, Aeb's legumia was infusing and the last pot held a dozen mashed gentian plants that Ren was boiling to a paste to dry out and use as an insect repellent. It wasn't a perfect solution but it was the best they had.

"Can I ask you something?"

"Yes, Hirad, you can," said Ilkar. "And I say that with a due sense of foreboding."

"You keep going on about us not understanding how elves live over here, and according to Captain Miserable snoring in his hammock over there we even cut the brush down wrong. Are we upsetting something by just being here, is that it?"

Ilkar couldn't hide his surprise. "How unusually perceptive of you. Let's make some more tea and I'll fill you in on some useful detail. It might stop you getting yourselves hurt."

"I've got a better idea," said Hirad, reaching into his sack. He threw a sealed pouch over to Ilkar. "I've been saving it."

Ilkar unclasped the pouch and sniffed. He smiled. "Coffee."

"That comes under critical equipment, does it?" Darrick's head had snapped up at the word.

"Indeed not, General, but any that think I shouldn't have it can relieve themselves of the trouble of drinking any."

Ilkar laughed into the silence. "Is there room for one more pot on there, I wonder?"

They made room, and soon, with the smell of the grounds pervading every nostril and steaming mugs in every hand, Ilkar spoke.

"At the core of elven life on Calaius is their belief in the balance of life. The closest translation is 'harmony.' They believe that all elements—air, earth, fire, water and mana—exist in this state of perpetual harmony and that it is a delicate balance that must be protected. I can't emphasise enough how deeply these beliefs are ingrained in the elves who live here and the energy with which they uphold them. To this end, every elf believes him- or herself to be a guardian of the harmony to a greater or lesser degree and that is why you should be mindful of loose comments or careless actions."

"And what happens if this harmony is disturbed?" asked Denser.

"Well, that depends what you believe. There are writings that predict floods being sent to cleanse the land, or cloud shrivelling the canopy before allowing the sun through to grow new life. There are also writings about the demise of the elven race but, when all's said and done, you have to take all these things with a pinch of salt. They're just warnings to look after the land, if you want my opinion."

Beside him, Ren was nodding. "Most elves use the teachings to educate the young to respect the forest. It provides their food, clothing, shelter . . . everything. Abusing it is not an option."

Ilkar resumed his explanation. "Take Kayloor, for instance. He felt your clearance of even this small patch of forest clumsy at best and an affront to the harmony at worst. That's why he doesn't like you; because you don't understand and never can. It's nothing personal; no stranger can. So we had to accept certain conditions before he'd carry us."

"And pay him over the odds, no doubt," said Hirad.

"No, Hirad, you're missing the point. We've paid him a fair price for his time and the use of his boat. He doesn't want any more. People like Kayloor live to serve the rain forest families, not the port paymasters. Like I say, you don't understand and, coming from Balaia, you never will."

"And what were these conditions exactly, Ilkar?" The Unknown said quietly, meeting the Julatsan's eye. "We may not be risking our lives here but that doesn't mean you can keep us in the dark about anything that might be material."

"I know and I'm sorry," said Ilkar, acknowledging his transgression by raising his hands. "But it was either acceptance then and there or a very long and uncomfortable walk. If you refuse one guide, you refuse them all."

"Even so, your negotiation was last night. The Raven don't do things that way."

Ilkar nodded. "Point taken, but the conditions aren't in any way onerous. Common sense if anything. We've undertaken to respect the lore of the forest, not to cause wanton damage, to kill only for food or to avoid death, to make reparations as we go and to leave the lands of any family or village should they require it."

There was little reaction bar the shrugging of shoulders.

"So we shouldn't swat any flies, then?" asked Hirad, doing exactly that.

"Absolutely not, Hirad," said Ilkar. "And you'll burn in hell for that."

"Really?"

"No, not really," said Ilkar. "What do you think? There are a million flies for each one you squash. The ratio is altogether smaller for snakes, rabbits and jaguars. Just use your judgement."

"Hirad doesn't have any judgement," said Denser.

"Let me do the jokes, Denser," advised Hirad.

"You've said that before."

"And until you're funny, I'll keep on."

"Another mature debate begins," said The Unknown, silencing them both. "Presumably, this balance and harmony structure has its roots in religion."

Ilkar nodded and leaned forward to refill his mug. Ren took over.

"There are Gods at every conceivable level but there's little temple worship outside the larger towns and cities."

"Mind you, the grandest and oldest of them all is out here," said Ilkar.

"Mainly, houses have shrines to their favoured Gods and most elves believe the forest to be temple enough for worship. At the top of the tree, if you'll pardon the term, is Yniss, God of the harmony, who pulls all the elements together. Beneath Yniss there are Gods and lords of the canopy, its roots, the animals, the wind, rain, death, fire . . . you name it. The ones you'll mostly hear about are Tual, who controls the animals, including elves, by the way, Cefu, God of the canopy above, Gyal, who sends the rain, and Shorth, the death God."

"There are hundreds of minor deities," said Ilkar. "It's all rather well structured for an ancient religion, if a little complex. The point, I suppose, is don't underestimate the power of these beliefs and the lengths some elves will go to to protect what they have in the name of that religion."

Hirad shifted and drained his mug. "Funny thing, Ilks. In all the years I've known you, I've never once heard you use any of these Gods' names."

"That would have been hypocritical," said Ilkar. "After all, if I really believed, I'd have come back to do my part, wouldn't I?"

"Was that the idea, then?" asked Hirad.

"Something like that," said Ilkar, feeling suddenly uncomfortable. "Look, can we leave this for now?"

"Ilkar's got some embarrassing secret, I take it," said Denser.

Hirad nodded. "Must be."

"Can we? Please?" Ilkar's raised voice caused Kayloor to shift in his slumber, but he didn't wake and it served as a timely reminder.

"Another long day tomorrow," said The Unknown.

"Yes," said Ilkar. "Look, can I suggest that you put the nets over your hammocks. It'll feel a little odd but you'll thank me in the morning."

With a little grumbling, The Raven and Ren took to their beds, leaving Aeb to take the first watch and bathe his face. After him, they'd watch in pairs.

Lying in his hammock, shifting to try and find a modicum of comfort, Ilkar felt the anxious silence around him as an alien night closed in around the group. He could sense his friends straining to hear danger now that the camaraderie of the campfire was broken. But all they'd be hearing was the rasping, croaking, buzzing, rustling and cawing clamour that came from every direction.

"Doesn't this ever stop?" asked Hirad.

"Never," said Ilkar.

"Wonderful. Could have told us to bring ear bungs or something. I don't want to have to sleep with my fingers rammed in my ears."

"Believe me, Hirad. Not hearing things is altogether worse than hearing them." Ilkar smiled to himself. "Sleep tight."

"Fat chance."

In the grey light of dawn, Selik could see the smirk on Devun's face. He'd been wearing it ever since they'd ridden out of Understone, like a child who'd escaped punishment for some misdemeanour.

"So," he said, finally addressing Devun. "You've been itching to tell me ever since we rode out of that slum. What was it you did to that mage that so changed his mind?"

Devun laughed. It was an uncomfortable sound, without humour or soul. Selik sighed inwardly. Like most of the Black Wings Devun was useful muscle but eminently dispensable. Of Callom and Edman, he hoped for better things.

"The threats weren't working," said Devun. "He didn't believe us, I don't think he ever would have. So I told him the truth."

"Which was?" asked Selik, not sure he wanted to hear the answer.

"That Xetesk was so intent on control of Balaian magic that they would march on Julatsa when and if they beat Dordover."

Selik looked at him with a little more respect, wondering if he'd misjudged the man. "Well, it's a view rather than the definite truth," he said, smiling a little. "It's not exactly the message I had in mind for him to take to Julatsa, but still."

"Oh, I don't think he'll be taking it there."

"Why not?" The doubt was back.

"Because I advised him that he needed to tell the people best able to do something about it. So he's going to Dordover."

"Are you sure?" Selik had to admit to himself that this was a far better solution than he'd planned.

"The look on his face," said Devun. "He believed me. I said they wouldn't believe us, but they'd believe a mage. I left it up to him how he said he learned the information."

Selik scratched his neck with an index finger. "I am genuinely impressed. Let us hope he doesn't get cold feet at the gates of Vuldaroq's college, eh?"

"Always a risk." Devun shrugged.

"Indeed."

Selik spurred the Black Wings on, his spirits lifted in a way he had not anticipated. The Blackthorne Mountains glowered down at them from his right as they rode, heading through the Varhawk Crags and then Blackthorne Town. He knew it would be a difficult meeting, but the warming early dawn sun on his face effectively masked the problems of the future.

CHAPTER 17

It was almost dawn. A violent cloudburst, accompanied by spectacular lightning and resounding thunder, had doused the watch fires and woken everyone from nervous sleep.

Yron called for the guards to be relieved and fresher faces trotted out to the two camouflaged elven platforms still standing and to four other concealed positions a few feet up in the trees. Anything to give them even a hint of warning.

The captain hadn't slept at all, standing at the door of the temple all night, feeling his anxiety grow as the inevitable attack drew closer. Four quartets of men had left camp hours before, skirting well away from their established path before heading north for the boats they'd left a couple of days downriver or on the longer walk direct to the ships moored in the Shorth Estuary.

With them they carried critical information from the temple. It was a gamble but, not knowing exactly who and what they faced, Yron felt he had no choice. He had entrusted the most valuable information to the group containing Erys.

His quick briefing of those left behind had been both poignant and uplifting. He hadn't sought to fool them, to lie or to soften the blow. They were there to hold on as long as they could and die for the greater glory. The elves they would face, he had told them, would be few but extraordinarily lethal, and he had cautioned them against being mesmerised by the speed or grace of what they saw.

And their fight would be entirely without magic. Stenys had also been sent with a group of runners, his magical skills better used in ensuring survival of the booty than staving off the inevitable at the temple.

Yron took Ben-Foran on a last tour of the hurried defences they'd set. Thorn traps dug perhaps a little shallow, twisted woodpiles positioned in the hope of driving their attackers down certain overlooked ways and a couple of snap nooses. Little more than glorified animal traps, these last were strung using tensioned saplings on the approach to the apron. Yron was surprised that they had not been attacked during the night. It was a blessing of sorts. Bought them and their runners precious time. Always assuming they hadn't already been hunted down. If he was honest, he expected only one of the groups to succeed and Erys's was the most likely.

"You should have left, Ben," said Yron, more proud than he would ever admit that the young lieutenant had refused to leave his commanding officer.

"I'm a soldier," said Ben-Foran. "I'm not stealthy, I'm clumsy if anything, but I fight well. My skills are better used here."

"So you keep saying."

"So stop reminding me, Captain." He sipped from the mug of tea he carried.

"You could have chosen life."

"I chose soldiering," said Ben-Foran. "That sometimes includes death. It's an occupational hazard."

Yron bent to check the snap mechanism on one of the nooses, wondering if Ben-Foran was as calm as he appeared. Gods knew, Yron wasn't, but then he had a greater knowledge of their enemy and still couldn't quite believe they hadn't arrived yet.

The noose was excellent. He didn't expect it to trap anyone but it would certainly give the elves pause for thought. He drained his own mug.

"Very good," he said. "Who set this?"

"I did."

Yron smiled. "Bloody waste of time teaching you though, wasn't it? Who're you going to pass it on to, some subdeity in the afterlife? Gods, but I should have been a career drinker. It's so much simpler when you're pissed."

"Teaching is never a waste," said Ben-Foran. "You never know when it's going to be your time to die."

"Not a waste, eh? Then come and see this and learn. Unless you've something better to do."

"Nothing pressing, Captain," said Ben.

Yron led him away from the apron to the small natural clearing where they'd taken the elven bodies after the assault on the temple. He heard Ben take in a sharp breath.

Not four days ago, they'd left nine bodies there. None had questioned Yron on why. What was left were a few scattered bones and remnants of clothing. Everything else was gone.

"The forest takes everything back," said Yron, his voice quiet and reverent. "They deserved that respect from us."

"I don't understand," said Ben.

"It's an elven belief. One of many. All life returns to the forest in death. Everything is used. We owed them the respect of not burning them."

"Oh, I see."

"No graveyards in the rain forest, Ben. Burying corpses is a waste."

Yron heard a sound at the far edge of his hearing. Ever so slight but not made by an animal, he was sure of it. He put a finger to his lips and gestured Ben-Foran into the shelter of a broad-leaved plant growing in the lee of a palm. The youngster knew better than to question him.

Stunned he wasn't dead, Yron watched the lithe shapes pass by scant yards from him. He couldn't help but be impressed by their economy of movement; it rendered them all but invisible, mere shadows across the forest floor.

With his heart loud in his chest, Yron turned his head to Ben-Foran, gesturing him to be still. The young soldier looked at him questioningly and nodded his head after the elves, a hand on his sword hilt.

Yron responded with a shake of his head and a frown. He scanned the ground at his feet and took the pace between them very slowly.

"We've got to warn the others. Help them," whispered Ben-Foran.

"We wouldn't get twenty paces," said Yron, his head almost touching Ben's, his voice very, very quiet. "It's hard, I know, but the Gods have spared us for a reason or we'd already be dead. When the attack starts, we'll move. Go after Erys." He paused and looked Ben in the eye. "This isn't going to be nice."

Auum moved smoothly across the forest floor, Duele and Evunn his shadows. They'd rested to eat and pray not far from the strangers' camp in a place free of their stench. Ignoring the crudely hacked path the forest was already beginning to reclaim, they kept to the natural trails, aiming to see the temple at dawn when Cefu was at her most magnificent and their strength was at its height.

They could sense the strangers at the temple long before they could smell them. The forest was askew, Tual's denizens confused by the destruction so carelessly wrought. The balance was disturbed but there was more. The TaiGethen could feel it deep within them. It was as if Yniss had turned away, His attention deflected. The imbalance caused by the strangers in the forest was just one small part. What Auum and his breed could feel went deeper, to the base of everything on which the elven races built their existence. He could feel it in the air and taste it on the rain. It ran through him on the mana trails and was heard in the rustling of the wind through the canopy. It was everywhere.

Auum experienced an unusual frisson of anxiety. The harmony was at odds with itself. He knew it was serious but it was a matter for prayer and contemplation later. The Tai had their task for the present, as did the others he knew would be approaching from the south. Others were surely near too. And Al-Arynaar. Drawn by the unease that must have swept through all of them, though some would feel it more keenly than others.

In the last few hundred yards, Auum's senses heightened, bringing him an awareness of his immediate environment no stranger could possibly conceive.

Again they stopped for prayer and to mark their faces. Again they strung their compact high-tension bows. Again they headed toward their target, their total focus broken only by the two strangers outside the attack perimeter.

The Tai ignored them for now. Once their task was complete and the temple returned to the Al-Arynaar, they would be tracked to their destination. Just to be sure all the invaders died.

Auum stepped easily over a snap noose of fair quality. Interesting that they should attempt such crude traps. It suggested desperation, as did the thorn pits they skirted immediately after. A hiss brought him to a standstill. He looked left. Duele indicated trees ahead where men were concealed, two of them on the approach to the temple. Auum pointed to himself and then to the trees before indicating Duele and making a sweeping motion, pointing to his eye and up again into the branches.

Duele nodded and darted away. To the right, Evunn was a statue, barely visible even to Auum. He directed Evunn further right, both elves nocking arrows. The forest stilled. It was time.

The two bows sang together, arrows whipping away, striking their targets with deadly accuracy. One man was taken through the throat, the other's heart was pierced. Auum was already running, another arrow in the string, ignoring the bodies as they fell near him. To the left, a jaqrui crescent whispered away, the thud of its strike reaching Auum's tuned ears. Duele was at the platforms.

Twenty yards ahead, another stranger was staring out from a hide in the trees right by the stone path to the temple. He knew something was coming but could see nothing. As he opened his mouth to call a warning, Auum and Evunn both loosed arrows, the impacts in the enemy's head and neck punching him out of the tree to crash into the foliage below, dead before he felt the fangs of the viper he disturbed.

A third arrow was in Auum's bow before he broke cover at the side of the apron, sprinting round its left-hand side while Evunn took the right. He heard a shout from within the temple, an echoing scared voice. It was as they wanted, the expected reaction to his plan. Four crossbow bolts flashed out from the temple doorway.

Auum held up four fingers. Across the apron, Evunn mirrored his gesture, having seen the same number of bolts. In front of them, canvas fell across the opening, hiding the strangers inside the sacred trap they'd made for themselves and desecrated by their very touch. He heard voices from within; he couldn't understand the language, but knew it jarred in his ears.

He and Evunn moved back into the edge of the forest either side of the apron. Duele appeared by him.

"Five are dead," he said. "There are no more outside."

Auum nodded. "Climb."

Duele ran to the temple, keeping out of sight of the breaks in the canvas.

He found footholds where there should have been none and climbed swiftly up the side of the building, moving onto the domed roof, arms and legs splayed for purchase, easing up smoothly. His route took him left and then right, allowing him to look down through six of the small tinted windows. At each one, he shaded his eyes with a hand. When he seemed satisfied, he came down to the stone lintel and sat just above the log that held the canvas covering in place.

Auum nodded he was ready. Duele lifted up two fingers, made a trigger gesture and indicated immediately left and right of the doorway. Next, four fingers twice and a spread of his arms describing a rough crescent. Finally, four fingers again and a flat-palmed sawing gesture left to right signifying a line. Auum nodded again and looked across to Evunn. He pointed at the doorway and swept his hand to the right. To Duele, he repeated back his own sawing gesture.

Loading his bow, Auum ran at the doorway, Evunn likewise, their footsteps nothing over the slick stone and vines of the apron. They were six paces from the temple when Duele heaved the log from its mounting on the lintel. Auum fired into the gloom, his bow discarded, light short sword and jaqrui in hands before he'd gone another three.

Together, they dived over the log, turning low forward rolls, crossbow bolts slashing empty air above their bodies. Duele swung down over the lintel behind them. Auum came to a crouch, his eyes adjusting quickly to the light in the temple. Shouts echoed off the walls and ceiling, men moved, swords before them, crossbowmen struggled to reload. His arrow had missed its target but no matter.

He darted left, surprising those immediately in front of him, who took a reflexive pace forward directly into the path of Duele as he rushed on. Auum's jaqrui moaned away, its double edge whipping into the face of a crossbowman, who shrieked as he stumbled backward, blood pouring from the bridge of his nose, one eye gone. Hand fishing in his pouch for another, Auum came up to his first opponent, seeing the fear in the stranger's eyes. His blade licked out, slicing across the man's shoulder and upper body before he could organise a defence. Auum kicked out straight, the blow taking the man in his midriff and catapulting him back against the temple wall.

Left, another jaqrui, this one clashing against the blade of a stranger, sparks seething as the edges connected. Auum rolled again, coming up and stabbing straight into the groin of another. A third roll right to avoid a blade that swept into the stone floor and he was standing again. A stranger came at him, hefting a longsword. The clumsy half-paced blow was turned easily. Auum punched him in the face, his blade flickered out and sliced the man's throat, a kick sending him to the ground.

His movements fast and sure, Auum ran at the surviving crossbowman, who had loaded his weapon and was bringing it to bear. Auum leapt, his legs shooting out straight, catching his target in the chest. He felt ribs crack beneath the force of the blow and the man grunted his pain. Auum landed and rolled again, spinning around as he stopped to plunge his sword through the man's heart and finish his cries for help.

He stood, able to take in the whole scene from his position by the wall of the temple. Ten were down. Duele and Evunn fought side by side, swords a blur, the clashing of metal echoing sharply in the enclosed space. Blood slicked the floor. Two men were coming at him, one with an injured shoulder. Both were wary. It would be their undoing.

Stepping back, Auum snapped out another jaqrui, this one whipping into the injured man's sword arm just above the wrist. He dropped his blade, turned and ran for the door. The other came on. Auum rushed him, dropping at the last moment to sweep his legs from under him. The man crashed to the ground, sword swiping uselessly at thin air. On top of him in an instant, Auum's punch crushed his windpipe.

The Tai leader tore from the temple after the fleeing stranger, eating up the ground between them. Jaqrui in hand, he cocked his arm but did not throw. Ahead of him, the man screamed, slithered to a stop at the edge of the apron and started to scrabble backward. From the shadows padded a panther, its eyes locked on him. And behind the beautiful animal came an elf, dressed in jet black, face painted in halves of black and white. Elf and panther were one. A pairing of the ClawBound, their minds interlinked, their consciousnesses irrevocably combined.

Auum nodded at them and turned back to the temple. The stranger had nowhere to run.

Inside, all the enemy were dead. Evunn had sustained a slight cut to his shoulder and Duele one on his thigh. It was nothing. The forest would provide healing and Yniss would keep them safe for what they had done.

Auum strode up to his Tai. "We will scour this temple of their blood and present their bones to Tual. We will rest. But first we will pray."

The Tai turned to kneel before the statue of Yniss and stopped. As if dragged against his will, Auum walked forward, stepping over the body of a stranger. He crouched by the pool and cried out. A fury rose within him that he had no desire to contain. His heart sounded doom in his chest, his face burned and his muscles tensed. His body shook. But he could not drag his eyes from the stump of the statue's arm. He saw it as if through a haze, his mind unable to fully comprehend the enormity of what was before his eyes.

Duele dived into the pool and swam down, surfacing when he had finished his search of the bottom and heaving himself back out of the water. His face was streaked where his paint had run, his eyes were narrowed and he seemed to struggle to get his words out.

"The hand is there."

"Then the statue can be remade," said Auum. But his relief was short-lived.

"Part of the thumb is missing. It is not in the pool."

Auum sat back on his haunches, staring at the ruined stream that fell uselessly into the pool from the smashed pipe under Yniss's wrist. The flow was wrong.

"Then we will find it," he said. "Search the temple. Search the bodies, search everywhere."

Outside, a low growl was followed by a scream, cut off abruptly.

"The ClawBound will help," said Auum.

"And if we can't find it?" asked Duele.

"Then we will take one of the strangers alive. And he will be but the first to pay for what they have done here."

Auum pushed himself to his feet. The Al-Arynaar would soon arrive. And more TaiGethen cells. Much could be done to cleanse the temple and raise the hand from its resting place but the statue would not be complete until the thumb was returned. And until then, Yniss would forsake them.

Auum felt a chill dread creep over his body. He knew the writings. He knew the consequences. A tear ran down his cheek.

CHAPTER 18

Captain Yron had been frozen in terror, suddenly sure he'd never truly experienced the emotion before. Originally, he'd planned to make their escape once the temple was attacked, but the attack had been so swift and sure he'd kept Ben-Foran hidden by the scattered bones of the elves. At the same time, he'd heard a big cat advancing along the path.

He could just about see it in the shadows. The panther was fifty yards from him and directly behind it stood an elf whose face was painted half white. It was the only part of him Yron could see. They had moved toward the apron; there had been a commotion, a scream and the panther had pounced. Yron had closed his eyes, hearing his man's cries cut off, and had prayed that he and Ben would be spared such a fate.

Now, with all four elves and the panther in the temple, or at least very near it, he signalled to Ben and they moved. Rising to their feet, the squawking of birds masking at least some of their noise, he took the most careful pace of his life, his foot coming down soundlessly. He indicated that Ben should step directly into his prints and moved off, all the time waiting for the whisper or wail of one of their throwing crescents or the thud of a bowstring.

With agonising slowness, he reached the path his trailblazers had hacked through the forest and started down it, still staring at the ground immediately in front of him, hardly daring to breathe. He could feel the sweat pouring down his back and face, he saw it drip onto the ground beneath his chin. Over and over, he told himself to keep calm, to resist the desire to run. They had to get out of earshot before they did and he had no real idea how far that might be.

Pausing and looking back over his shoulder, he saw Ben-Foran's drawn and pale face. It too was slick with sweat and the young soldier reflexively clasped and unclasped his hand around the pommel of his sword. Yron raised his eyebrows, Ben replying with a nod. They walked on.

Just a little further, he told himself, just a little further.

The path was alive; countless ants scurried to and fro. He was careful to step over them as well as he could. Tiny though they were individually, they packed painful bites and he didn't need them up his legs and in his boots. It was impossible to find silent footing now. The debris of the crude path lay on the ground and cracked beneath his feet, the reports like thunder in his ears.

He stopped again and looked up. The light was going fast. He couldn't see the sky but knew cloud must be boiling up from the south. He let Ben-Foran catch up and whispered, "When you feel the first raindrop, run. Run as fast as you can for as long as you can. Don't stop until you think you're going to die."

"Where are we going?"

"Toward the camp, then east to the river, any river. We've got to throw them off the scent or we'll be dead before nightfall."

Thunder rolled in the distance. The humidity climbed. Yron was soaked beneath his clothes. Rain would be refreshing. It came suddenly and very heavy, thudding into the canopy and driving through. A drop landed on the ground in front, immediately joined by a thousand others. He ran.

With Ben behind him, he ran faster than he ever had, fear driving his limbs. Though he tried to listen for noise, he could hear nothing but the sounds of his feet slapping on the ground, the rain drumming overhead and his breathing loud and fast. It was exhilarating, uplifting. Ahead the path was already being overgrown, and he brushed aside lianas, creepers, and spiders' webs. All around him, he knew the smaller animals would be seeking shelter while the larger ignored the deluge, accepting it with stoicism.

Sloths, monkeys, monitor lizards, tapir. All would sit it out wherever they were while he and Ben sprinted past, heedless of root and low branch, of striking snake and angry spider. Because what was behind them, Yron knew not how far, was infinitely more dangerous. Distance alone wouldn't save them; distance and a river in flood just might.

Calling on everything he had left, Yron dragged another breath into his protesting lungs and ran on.

Rebraal wasn't sure if he was awake or asleep. He knew he was lying down but had no idea if he was floating or not. He fought his mind, tried to drive it to think, but all he got were snatches of scenes of which he wasn't even sure he'd been a part. Of ClawBound carrying him. Of Mercuun crying out. Of the rain pouring across his face and of people crowding, looking down on him and frowning.

He was inside, he thought. It was dark. But maybe that was because he couldn't see. He felt hot. Very hot. He could smell the scents of menispere, casimir and of pokeweed mixing in the still air. And he'd felt the touch of a spell, too, though he might have dreamed that also. It was so hard to tell.

A shaft of light stabbed through the darkness and he realised at least he wasn't blind. A face swam into view in front of his and leant over. It was fuzzy and he didn't recognise it but he could see the smile that didn't mask the concern. She spoke words but he couldn't hear them, only a murmur as if he was underwater. He tried to move his head but his neck was locked and pain scorched down his back and across his shoulders.

She pressed her arms on his chest and shook her head. She was quite old, he thought. He wanted to speak. He knew his mouth was open and moving but whatever tumbled out was not understood. Maybe they were both speaking underwater. The random thought amused him.

Cool on his forehead. Wet. He opened eyes he hadn't realised he'd closed and saw her dabbing him with a cloth. It felt good but the burning soon came back. He wanted to touch her but his arms were leaden. He wanted her to know he was thankful but he was locked inside himself.

A second figure joined them. Another woman. Younger. She laid her hands on his shoulder. She was talking too, and as she did the ache that hammered there diminished to nothing and a gentle warmth suffused his body. He thought he saw them withdraw but then wasn't sure if they'd been there at all.

He closed his eyes and the nightmares came.

The TaiGethen used water from the pool itself to cleanse the temple. Auum was possessed of an anger he could not quench as he scrubbed at the floor with palm leaves soaked in lime. The juice stung his fingers but he ignored the irritation. Every hint of stranger blood had to go. Every boot mark, every careless scratch had to be expunged.

Duele, Evunn and the ClawBound were outside, dealing with the bodies, offering them up to Tual. Auum couldn't bring himself to join them, unsure whether those that had perpetrated this crime against the elven races should be consumed by the forest denizens. So he stayed to clean and he wouldn't be satisfied until the floor ran with the blood from his own raw hands.

It was late in the afternoon when Auum had scoured the temple enough and the stone shone clean. He and his Tai had raised the marble hand and it sat next to the stump to which it had been attached. They had collected every chip of marble from pool and floor. All that remained missing was dust and the thumb fragment. And Duele had reported many writings gone from the temple's chambers of contemplation, compounding the desecration.

Examining the tent the strangers had pitched to the left of the apron before tearing it and its contents to shreds, the Tai had found food and equipment for more than the twenty-one they had killed and the two they would soon hunt. It seemed clear that others had run too, and almost certainly north. It was critical that all these strangers were found, killed and searched. This was too big for one TaiGethen cell and one ClawBound pair. Auum brought his Tai together, and after their prayers had been offered and their fast of the day broken, he told them of his decision.

"We will track the two we saw," he said. "They will lead us to others. The

ClawBound pair can start now if they will. We will wait for our brother TaiGethen and the Al-Arynaar. Many are close, I can feel it."

He stopped to chew a mouthful of food.

"Yniss has set us the stiffest of tests and we must not fail. Every elf depends upon us. All that was taken from here must be returned. Let no one and nothing stand in our way. But do not indulge in retribution or revenge while our task is upon us. Those may come later. Rest now, for when we begin again we must not pause until the harmony is restored. Are you both full well?"

They knew what he asked them, whether the spiritual unease they felt had affected them physically or mentally. Both nodded their heads.

"Do not be silent if you should change. I will talk to the ClawBound."

Auum flowed to his feet and walked across the apron to where the elf and panther sat at the edge of the forest. The heavily muscled sleek black feline had her paw on the bones of a large rodent and was chewing the flesh. Beside her, the elf crunched on raw vegetables.

"You saw the two?" asked Auum.

The ClawBound turned their heads to him as one, their eyes on him, the panther's yellow and hooded, the elf's a deep dark green. The elf nodded.

"You understand what we seek? All must die. All that was taken must be returned. Will you track the two for us?"

Another nod.

"Tual watch over you. We will not be far behind you."

Auum returned to his Tai. Behind him, the ClawBound slipped silently back into the forest.

Chapter 19

Two more days. Two more days of heat, rain, sweat, flies, snakes, lizards, spiders, rats and bickering men. Erienne hardly slept a wink that first night and the next was no better. She spent the days staring into the waters of the River Ix as the guide took them away from the main flow and up countless turns, branches and tributaries. By the end of the second day, she was so unsure of their overall direction, she had to keep checking their position by the sun.

This was surely some form of elaborate torture designed for a purpose she couldn't guess. The land was hell above ground, the skies disgorged rain that stung her head through the hood of her cloak, and everywhere there were animals large and small obsessed solely with killing her should she make one false move. Even the brightly coloured frogs, Ren had told her cheerfully, could unintentionally end her life.

And so, when they did land, for a break or for that dreaded second night, Erienne was scared every time she put her foot down, stretched out an arm to steady herself or sat on a log to eat around the fire. Even had she wanted to, she couldn't have sustained a conversation. Her concentration was broken by every rustle and crack in the undergrowth and every call of every animal. It made her temporarily useless as a mage, and already Denser and Ilkar had become a little irritable that the cleansing and gentle healing spells they had to cast were not being shared equally.

She tried telling herself that the threat couldn't be everywhere, that she was simply overreacting to an alien situation. She stared long at Ren and Ilkar, who seemed so completely at ease. And at Kayloor, respectful of the forest but comfortable. At Hirad and The Unknown, who accepted their situation with trademark phlegmatism, and at Thraun, who absolutely loved it and whose hunting instincts were sharper than ever, back beneath trees where he felt he belonged.

But she could turn to Denser and Darrick because she knew, without having to ask, that the strangeness affected them too. Her only other option was to retreat into her mind alone, which was even more distressing filled as it was with Lyanna. Being apart from her daughter's grave had broken the direct association but nothing would ever dim the memories. Her desperation was as keen as ever, and those scant moments when her memories brought her joy were scarce jewels in the desert. But she couldn't cry. Not here. This place didn't understand her pain, and her tears and rage would be wasted.

To distract herself as they sailed, she tried to imagine what lay beneath them. Ilkar and Ren had been fulsome in their descriptions and she had bought it all, fuel for her fears. The shoals of flesh-eating fish that scented blood from ten miles' distance. The thirty-foot crocodiles with jaws strong enough to pierce plate mail. The invisible creatures that burrowed into flesh and laid their young to grow fat on host blood.

She imagined war beneath the impenetrable surface. The flashing of scales in the dance of life. And seeing one of the armoured beasts surge from the river to take a tapir as it drank fed her fantasies until she expected a fanged head to spear through the floor of the boat and take them all to the terrible drowning death that dominated her nightmares.

But instead they landed for good in the late afternoon of the third day at a shallow beach fringed with palms and waving grasses, home to three dozen and more fishing boats and open canoes.

"Home," said Ilkar, leaping onto the land and staring up the beach.

"About bloody time," said Hirad, following him to stand with hands on hips.

Erienne felt a rush of relief. She needed to lie under a roof, in something more substantial than a hammock. The light was beginning to fade, she was tired, hungry and could no longer ignore the growing pulse in her head as a passing ache. It had been coming on for days. At least now she could hope for a little privacy and security to sort it out.

"It's beautiful," said Ren, slipping an arm around Ilkar's waist.

A flight of red-backed parrots passed over them, heading for the cloud-shrouded green heights and the falls they could just make out in the distance.

"Naturally," said Ilkar.

"He's going to tell us it's a five-mile swamp hike through snake-infested forest to his front door," grumbled Denser, though he was smiling. He looked down at Erienne, his expression sobering. "Are you all right, love?"

"Damn fool question," said Erienne, feeling the comfort of his closeness and empathy.

"You know what I mean."

"Later," she said.

"The village is literally just over the rise here," said Ilkar, pointing up the bank through which a path had been well trodden, its shingle all but covered in mud.

Erienne followed his arm and could see the odd plume of smoke rising into the heavy sky. It was getting very hot again. She felt the sweat prickling on her and had a sudden longing for winter and the cold. Even the rain here was hot enough to bathe in.

The Unknown and Aeb had hauled all of their kit from the boat under the scowling gaze of Kayloor.

"Let's get going," said Hirad. "I can feel rain." He shouldered his sack and glared at their elven guide. "It's been a real pleasure."

"Respect the forest. Cefu watches you," said Kayloor in halting Balaian.

"It speaks," said Hirad.

"Yes, and so do you," said Ilkar. "Too much. He's just giving you sound advice."

"Who's Cefu again?"

"God of the canopy, Hirad," said Erienne.

Ilkar smiled. "At least someone listens to me. And remember what I told you before. People will stare at you. They won't want you to be here. Don't react; let Ren and me guide you. And Hirad, no staring back."

"Me?" Hirad's expression was pained innocence.

"Yes, you," said Ilkar. "Prolonged eye contact is a challenge. Don't make it until they accept you. Really. Come on."

He led the way up the bank, The Raven and Ren close behind him as the rain swept across the river and soaked them yet again. It wasn't even worth hurrying. They'd learned that much. And at least it discouraged the flies.

Taanepol, Ilkar's home village, which roughly translated meant "town on the river," was a cluster of approaching two hundred wood and leaf-thatch buildings in an elf-made clearing somehow in total sympathy with the forest around it. Trees overlooked it on three sides, with the fourth largely open as the ground fell away toward the river.

It was not an obviously organised settlement to the Balaian eye because there was no discernible centre or dominating structure. Groups of buildings were gathered loosely around cleared areas in which fire pits sat, tables and benches were arranged, and cooking and hunting paraphernalia lay scattered. Every house had a wide covered porch, roofs angled to take the rain into shallow channels that ran away downhill and back to the Ix.

As they approached, the rain smearing their faces, Erienne thought she could see what looked like a moat along the edge of the village, bridged by lashed-together logs. Ilkar was speaking for all their benefits.

"There'll be about five hundred in all here, though at any one time half are fishing, hunting or farming. Or on Balaia mage training, if they feel the calling. I know it looks a bit jumbled, but like every other village, it was originally settled by one family and has grown as others were accepted and joined."

"Why did it happen that way?" asked The Unknown. "Protection presumably."

"That's right. The elves of Calaius have a tribal history no less torn by war than the Wesmen's. Even so, this is one of the biggest settlements you'll find this deep in the forest."

"So how come you're allowed to hack down the forest but when we break a twig Captain Miserable has a fit?"

"Because, Hirad, it's our land. We were born to it and we husband it. This isn't wanton destruction. We benefit the forest; strangers destroy it," said Ilkar. "Like I say, just respect elven beliefs and you'll have no trouble."

It was a moat. Dug square, and she could see as she neared that it was the best part of six feet deep and around eight feet wide. Log bridges crossed it in five places.

"Expecting attack, are you?" she asked.

"Not exactly," said Ilkar, turning and smiling through the downpour, his black hair smeared on his head. He stopped on the bridge. "It keeps our animals in and some of the undesirables out."

Erienne caught her breath. The moat was lined with an inch or so of water and seemed to be teeming with life. Lizards, rodents, snakes—she could see them all in there—scuttling or slithering here and there or testing the sides of the moat. There had to be dozens of the things in the stretches she could see to either side.

"It's hardly going to stop a spider, is it?" said The Unknown.

Ilkar shrugged. "Probably not, but we fill it periodically with a mild alkali. Creatures don't like it. Then, in the morning, we clear it out and get them back into the forest where they belong."

"Is it that bad?" asked Darrick.

"Unless things have changed radically, it varies," said Ilkar. "It's just a safer environment, particularly for the young ones. They need to be taught to treat animals correctly to avoid trouble. Some of these things don't give you a second chance."

Erienne walked briskly across the bridge, feeling altogether safer. It all made perfect sense to her. But, like crossing from light into shadow, the hostility hit her immediately too.

All activity had stopped in the village. Children came running out until voices stopped them. Adults moved deliberately and with common purpose. There were no weapons evident. None was needed to convey the message. Most of the villagers were dressed simply in dark-coloured tops and trousers. All were dark skinned with pronounced cheekbones and deep frowns.

"Always this welcoming, are they?" asked Hirad.

"Now's the time to be quiet," said Ilkar sharply. "Remember, most of these elves have never seen a nonelf. I suggest you stop and let me see what's going on."

The Raven did so, each of them assessing the threat. Erienne saw The Unknown move to the centre of the group, Aeb to one side, Hirad the other. She found herself behind them with Denser. Darrick had seen the line forming and came to Hirad's right shoulder. Thraun too moved instinctively into the line, his hand resting easily on the pommel of the sword he now carried, mimicking Darrick's stance. Only Ren stood apart, caught between Ilkar and The Raven, unsure what to do. None of them fingered weapons but they were ready.

Despite herself and the clouding of her mind, Erienne was impressed. Well over two seasons since they had last fought together and the instinct was as strong as ever. And for the first time for so long, she felt a release in the comfort of their close company. Perhaps Denser was right. Perhaps this would be the beginning of her recovery.

Knowing she'd be unable to understand what Ilkar said to his people, she moved so that she could see the villagers clearly and tried to gauge their body language. She looked at Ilkar, seeing him ramrod straight, and felt total confidence in him.

It was not shared by Ilkar. The Julatsan mage, who had last seen his home before any of The Raven's parents had been born, had rehearsed this moment in his mind over and over since they'd boarded ship at Herendeneth. In his dreams, he'd seen smiling faces and open arms as he strode across the bridge to his family group of homes, the lost son returned. But in his waking thoughts, he'd known suspicion would hide the smiles and that those arms would not be opened to him or those he brought with him.

But he'd expected nothing like this. There was no confusion on their faces, some of which he recognised although others were too young for him to know. There was no surprise either. What he could see were anger and fear. He scanned those in front of him, seeing neighbours and members of his wide family group, some of whom had aged, some not. Of his immediate family, his parents and less surprisingly his brother, there was no sign.

Ilkar glanced behind him and saw The Raven's formation. It was unnecessary, of course, but it gave him security and faith. And more than anything else it reinforced who his family really were. They stood behind him, not before him. Ren looked at him a little helplessly. He smiled at her, gestured her to stay just where she was. To Hirad he nodded and mouthed his thanks before turning back to his family group.

He made a wide angle with his arms in front of his face, fingers linked at the first digit to mimic the canopy. It was an ancient greeting, and was returned by most of the thirty or so in front of him, more in reflex than friendship.

"Hello, Kild'aar," said Ilkar, settling on a middle-aged elven woman, distantly related to him on his father's side. She was standing near the centre of the group, arms folded firmly under her breasts, her jet-black hair covered by a soaking cloth and her light clothing sticking to her thin body. She looked very tired, her slanted oval eyes red around her pupils, the crow's feet deep and pronounced. "I've come back seeking help. May I and my friends enjoy the hospitality of Taanepol?"

Ilkar was glad of the traditional opening speech required of any visiting an elven rain forest village, which included reasons for the visit and a request for lodging should it be desired. Kild'aar stepped forward, her face severe.

"As a child of this village, you are welcome, as is the child of Drech with you," she said, cocking her head at Ren behind him. "But these strangers must go. Now."

Ilkar started at Kild'aar's vehemence.

"What I ask affects us all," said Ilkar. "Calaians and Balaians alike. Julatsa stands on the verge of extinction. The Heart is buried and not enough mages remain on Balaia to raise it to beat life through the college again. What consequences for the elves of Calaius if it should fail? Please, let us all get out of the rain and talk."

"Julatsan magic has nothing to do with those who stand near you," said Kild'aar.

"Until you hear me, you will not know how wrong you are," said Ilkar. "Kild'aar, have things changed so much in my absence that you cannot even begin to extend the hand of friendship?"

"Perhaps they have," said Kild'aar. "A great crime has been committed here. Strangers are to blame. And now illness is sweeping the village. You saw the fishing boats tied up; it's because there are too few fit to crew them. Who's to say the strangers didn't bring the sickness with them? Who's to say those you stand with don't support the desecrators?"

Ilkar held up a hand. "Wait, wait. You're losing me." He looked at Kild'aar and then past her into the scared and angry faces of those behind her. "We saw evidence of illness in Ysundeneth when we landed there three days ago, but what's been desecrated?"

"Ysundeneth has sickness?" Kild'aar ignored his question and looked around at her village folk. "Strangers visit there." She shrugged.

"But not here," said Ilkar. "And it may not be the same sickness. Why don't you let our mages see? We helped elves in Ysundeneth."

Kild'aar sighed. "In truth, we're stretched," she said. "We can't find a reason or a cure and it strikes at random. Tomorrow the victim could be me, any of us. Our people have started to die."

"Then let us try and help you," implored Ilkar. "These people behind me, they're much more than just friends. I love them like family. They are good people and I swear on every creature in the forest that they have nothing to do with any desecration." He paused. "Kild'aar, what has been desecrated?"

The elven woman looked older and more exhausted as she looked at him then, biting her lip. "Aryndeneth," she whispered.

"What?" Ilkar's mouth was suddenly dry, the drumming rain on his head forgotten. "How?"

"We don't know," said Kild'aar. "But we know Al-Arynaar have been killed." She stopped. "One moment."

Ilkar nodded and watched as she turned and spoke in low tones to a group of young and old elves. He saw nods and shakes of heads, he saw fingers being pointed and he heard sharp tones. In the end though, it was clear Kild'aar had got her way.

"Take your friends, if such they are, to your father's house. They can take drinks from the firepot if they are so inclined. I'll wait for you. There's something you have to see."

"And what of my parents?" asked Ilkar, knowing it was the question she had been waiting for and he had been avoiding.

"What do you think, Ilkar? You've been away too long." She shook her head. "We needed people like you here and you didn't even send word that you were alive."

She turned and walked away, taking the crowd with her, a murmur growing as they dispersed into smaller groups. Ilkar turned back to The Raven, catching Ren's eye as he did.

"Did you hear all that?" he asked her.

She nodded and put a hand on his arm. "Are you all right?"

"We didn't get on," he said. "Or else I might have come back when I was supposed to."

"That wasn't what I asked."

"I know," he said, but in truth he wasn't sure how he felt. He hadn't worked out whether he expected his parents to be alive or not; and finding out they weren't had left him immediately saddened but hardly gripped with grief.

"Hey!"

Ilkar looked over at Hirad. The barbarian was standing with his arms outstretched and palms up, his long dark hair dripping with the rain that still fell with no sign of letting up.

"Sorry, Hirad."

"When you've quite finished nattering in elvish, I wondered if there was any danger of you letting us in on the big secret. Are they going to run us through or let us dry out a little?"

"Well, I had to haggle," said Ilkar, wandering back up to Hirad and patting his soaking wet cheek. "They were concerned that you were too ugly to be allowed into such a beautiful setting. There are children here after all."

Denser laughed aloud, hugging Erienne to him. She too could not suppress a smile. The comment had been worth it just for that. Hirad swung round to the Xeteskian.

"You haven't heard what they said about you and that miserable mould you call a beard," he said to Denser.

"At least it doesn't frighten children."

"Only because they don't understand," said Hirad. "Scares the shit out of me that you think it's attractive."

"Let's get in out of the rain, shall we?" said The Unknown. "I don't know about you but I'm getting a little tired of this particular shower."

Ilkar nodded. Once again, a couple of sentences from the big man and they all fell into line.

"Follow me. And don't make a mess. This is my house you're about to see."

He took Ren's hand and led the way into the village, uncertain of what they were about to face and with the sceptical eyes of the people upon them. There was so much more to be done than he'd hoped. He sighed. It had seemed so simple. Just show up, get trained mages and gather a friendly support network. He should have known. When The Raven were involved, somehow things were never simple.

CHAPTER 20

"Why won't you let Denser and Erienne help you?" Ilkar was fast losing his patience.

He'd seen The Raven to his house—it had been almost exactly the same as when he'd last seen it—and had sought out Kild'aar very soon after, suddenly anxious to be anywhere else than in his past. But his enquiries into how many villagers were actually sick were met with vague estimates and his offers of help with a blank refusal. The house they were headed for was no more than fifty yards across the village but this was the third time he'd asked.

"Because you must understand first," said Kild'aar.

"I understand already," he replied. "People in my village are dying and you won't let two brilliant mages try and save them because of your intractable distrust of every nonelf. I don't remember it being this way when I left."

"Ilkar, you have been away a very long time. And you've been with strangers for all that time. You are the one who has changed, not us. Even your skin is light. And now we're seeing good reasons why we've been ever suspicious."

"But you need help."

"It can wait," snapped Kild'aar. "Gyal's tears, Ilkar, you come wandering back into our village a hundred years after you left it and you expect us to accept you with open arms? And your Balaian friends? Maybe over there people are quick to trust. Here, as you well know, trusting the wrong people has led to so much harm."

Ilkar had to concede the point though he would never admit it to her. They had never seen eye to eye. Truth was, Ilkar hadn't seen eye to eye with anyone. Except his brother. And even that bond was gone now. Buried under a hundred years of separation.

"What happened to my parents?" he asked.

Kild'aar stopped briefly. "They died of old age, not knowing whether their son was alive or dead. Whether he had made a success of his talent or whether he had perished in the Mana Bowl or in some petty conflict of the Balaians. Perhaps the question should be, what happened to you?"

"It's a long story," said Ilkar.

"And one we don't have time for at the moment," said Kild'aar, setting off again across the soaking village. The rain was beginning to ease at last, blue cracks in the heavy grey sky.

"What is it you want me to see?" Ilkar struggled to keep up with the sudden pace, slipping on the muddy ground, unused to the texture under-foot, his reactions dulled by his absence. Kild'aar, of course, looked as if she were walking on flat dry rock.

She led him to a house on the southern periphery of the village. On the porch sat an elf dressed in jet black with a face painted in black and white halves. At his feet a panther lay, licking its paws.

"What the hell is going on?" demanded Ilkar. "What are they doing here?"

"Waiting for answers," replied Kild'aar.

"Fine," said Ilkar. "So what's inside?"

"You'll see."

"Gods, but you're frustrating, Kild'aar."

"Any particular God? Or just that amorphous deity Balaians always invoke?"

"Now I'm remembering why I didn't come back sooner."

Kild'aar pushed open the door. "I'd hate to disappoint your memories, Ilkar. Room to the left."

She waited while he went in. The room was lit by heavily scented can-dles set on the floor and on low tables. Otherwise it was bare but for a high-legged bed in its centre on which lay a shrouded figure. Ilkar turned, frowning, but was ushered on. He walked to the head of the bed, the sweet scents filling his head, and pulled back the shroud.

On the bed lay an elf of about his age, though it was hard to tell in truth. His face was wrinkled as if the moisture had been leached from it, a trail of blood ran from his nose and another from the corner of his mouth. There was no relaxation in death, as if the pain that had gripped him as he lost his fight for life had endured beyond. Ilkar knew him.

"There was nothing we could do," said Kild'aar as Ilkar replaced the shroud. "He was all but dead when he was brought in. Nothing we did, mag-ical or herbal, did anything at all bar relieving his pain a little. Everyone here knows the agony in which he died and they know our helplessness. All that lie sick know their fate unless we can find a way to save them. That's why we're so scared. Who's next?"

"Then let Erienne help," urged Ilkar. "She is the best healer mage I've ever met. She's saved my life before now. Let her examine him, find out what she can. Please, Kild'aar, trust me on this."

Kild'aar shrugged. "We'll see. Come." She led Ilkar to the room next door. It was similarly bare though the shutters had been opened to let in nat-ural light. On a table under the window sat a bowl of water draped with cloths. A single bed was pushed against a wall and on it an elf lay on his stomach, head to one side. A sheet covered him to his waist and his back was largely swathed in bandages, heaviest on his left shoulder.

"Oh dear Gods," said Ilkar, rushing to the bedside and kneeling down to stroke the hair away from his face. It felt hot. "Not him too."

"No," said Kild'aar. "His fever was caused by an infected wound and it's broken now. He'll live. For now at least."

Relief flooded Ilkar and he exhaled heavily, his breath playing over the prone elf's face.

"Rebraal," he whispered. "Can you hear me?"

The elf's eyes flickered open, narrowed against the light and steadied. He frowned.

"Are you real?" he asked, voice no more than a croak.

"Yes, I am. What happened to you?"

"You're not real. I'm still fevered. You're a shade." He seemed to be talking to himself, his words barely distinct.

"No. The fever's broken. Kild'aar says you're recovering. It really is me, kneeling in front of you." Ilkar smiled.

Rebraal's face darkened. "Shade or real, let me tell you this. You're too late. A century too late. Where were you when the strangers came and took Aryndeneth? Where were you when I was shot? We needed you. You promised to return. It was your destiny as it is mine. Get out of here. I don't know you."

"Rebraal, I understand your anger. But my destiny changed. There was other work I had to do. But it doesn't stop me being your brother."

"You betrayed me. You betrayed the Al-Arynaar. You are not my brother." He turned his head away. "Go back to your other destiny."

Ilkar put a hand on Rebraal's back.

"Please, Rebraal. I can help you. I've brought people with me. We'll take the temple back."

"I want nothing that you can give. We don't need your help. Go."

Ilkar felt Kild'aar's touch on his shoulder. He looked up, his brief joy at seeing his brother extinguished. There was a lump in his throat and he shook his head to clear his mind, a cascade of emotions surging through him. His parents were dead, as he had expected, and he felt little grief at their passing. But Rebraal. Rebraal was only a little older than him and Ilkar's love for his hero had never dimmed though his brother had often been far from his thoughts. And now he had been dismissed. Disconnected. He stood and strode from the house.

"What did you expect?" asked Kild'aar after him. "He thought you'd abandoned him. You were supposed to join the Al-Arynaar. It's why you went to train in Julatsa."

Ilkar rounded on her. "No, it isn't!" he shouted, then checked his voice. "It's what you all assumed. You, him, my parents. You never let me speak my mind, you never considered what I actually wanted. I never, ever wanted to follow Rebraal and my father into the Al-Arynaar. I admired them for their sacrifice but I didn't want to do the same."

Kild'aar frowned. "So why did you go to train?"

Ilkar almost laughed. "Because I wanted to be a mage. Because I felt the calling so strongly I could never deny it. You have no idea the release I felt when I left here and the elation I felt every day I was training. I knew what you would all feel when I didn't return but I couldn't come back to explain because you'd never have let me leave."

"Didn't you believe in what the Al-Arynaar represented?"

"Of course I did," said Ilkar. He pushed a hand through his hair, searching for the words that would help her understand. "But I was never driven enough to spend my life defending something I thought would never be attacked. I know how hollow that sounds now but I wanted more."

Kild'aar shook her head. "How can there be anything more than the honour of defending your faith?"

"It wasn't what I wanted. Why can't you understand that? Why can't Rebraal?"

Ilkar felt like telling her his life story, or at least the last decade of it. But she wouldn't want to hear about how his and The Raven's search for Dawnthief halted the Wytch Lords, or how their sealing of the Noonshade rip stopped Balaia being overwhelmed by dragons. Both actions had done more to protect the elven faith than guarding Aryndeneth. The trouble was, they were too isolated here. To Kild'aar, and to so many rain forest villagers, events on Balaia were of no importance.

All they knew or cared about the Northern Continent was Julatsa and the training it could give elves who felt the mage calling. And even then, most village elders would shrug at the demise of the college, blaming the elves who had stayed there for their stupidity in doing so. It was a paradox, but one the elven elders would face comfortably.

"Your head was turned from true sight on Balaia," she said. "And Rebraal will blame you in part for the loss of the temple."

"Then persuade him to let me help put it right," said Ilkar. He pointed at his father's house. "You don't know it, but in that house you've got the most talented warriors and mages on Balaia. They are The Raven and they can make a difference."

"We have heard the name," said Kild'aar, unimpressed. "Our mages who did return as they promised brought word of you. We don't need the help of mercenaries. We need believers. Rebraal is right, you should go."

Ilkar felt his cheeks colouring, very aware that his paler skin tone from decades on Balaia now set him apart from his own roots. It was useless talking to Kild'aar. And while to a certain extent he could understand their sense of betrayal, he couldn't fathom their obduracy in the face of a genuine offer of help.

"Let me tell you exactly how it's going to be," said Ilkar, his frustration getting the better of him at last. "We're here to take mages back to Julatsa, because if we don't there will be no college for you to send your precious defenders to train at. Then where will your Al-Arynaar be, eh? And we will find mages with or without your help. Secondly, we *are* going to help the sick in this village and we *are* going to help return the temple to the hands of the Al-Arynaar. We are The Raven and this is what we do. Now you can try and stop us, but consider who is betraying the elven race and faith then.

"Now, if you'll excuse me, I have some organisation to attend to."

He turned and strode back to his father's house, his desire to prove Kild'aar wrong, to prove that those he loved were not mere strangers to be despised, burning hot within him.

Heryst rubbed his hands over his face and leaned back in his chair in the great hall in the tower of Lystern. He seemed to have spent most of his time here in the last few days, meeting senior mages, desperately seeking a solution.

He felt the weight of responsibility bearing him down. In the many clear and frightening moments he experienced when he was alone, he saw himself as the only man truly capable of halting the appalling spiral of the war. But the chances for peace were slipping through his fingers and there was seemingly nothing he could do. His delegation in Xetesk was making no progress and all he heard from Dordover were demands to ally to save Balaia. And they were demands he was finding it increasingly hard to refuse.

"You're tired, Heryst," said Kayvel, who sat next to him, an unfailing support. "You should rest."

"It's not even dark yet," he replied. "How can I be tired?"

"It might be something to do with the fact that, to my certain knowledge, you haven't slept for three days, my Lord," chided Kayvel gently. "Take an hour. It won't hurt."

"I'm afraid there isn't time," said Heryst.

He could feel war advancing like a virus. The hideous events in Arlen were still so fresh. The spell Xetesk had used was a statement, if any such was still needed, of their intention to crush Dordover. And would they stop? Vuldaroq was sure they would not. Heryst was scared he was right.

The violent clearance of the refugees from the gates of the dark college was another clear message and now there were reports of the fighting moving into college lands. Dordovan and Xeteskian supply hamlets and farmland were being fired, college militias were strung out defending vulnerable lands and the opportunities for conflict were growing by the day. And behind it all was that nagging feeling that Selik and the Black Wings would be the only real beneficiaries if the four colleges were dragged into all-out conflict.

It was time for big decisions.

"I'm going back to Dordover," he said.

"My Lord?"

"I want you to contact Rusau in Xetesk, make sure he keeps up the pressure to meet the Lord of the Mount. But mind him to leave the moment he feels he is under threat."

"And what will you be saying to Vuldaroq?"

"That we have to look to protect what is left of the balance of the colleges. That we must dispatch forces to the defence of Julatsa and that we must consider a blockade of Xeteskian lands. It may be the only way to force them into negotiation. We all understand what they are trying to do and we cannot let them have free run of everything they need through Arlen. And that includes the return of the mages from Herendeneth. We are not strong enough to take them on alone."

"You will ally?"

"I will take practical steps to ensure Lystern is not destroyed."

"Ever the politician."

"I have entered alliance with Dordover before. I will not make the mistake of such a formal arrangement again."

Yron didn't know how long they been running when they at last collapsed off the path, legs like jelly and lungs heaving in tortured chests; he thought they had at least bought themselves an hour or two. But he knew they couldn't stop. Heading off at a gentler pace once they'd got their breath back, he led Ben-Foran east, away from the camp and toward a tributary of the River Shorth that would lead them eventually to the main force of the river and then to the estuary itself.

As they moved, he urged Ben to be as quiet as he was able, to disturb as little as he could and to keep his eyes peeled for anything that might indicate they were being followed. He knew all were futile gestures but it kept Ben from thinking about what had happened at the temple.

He wondered if Ben thought they had left the threat behind them, whether the boy considered the possibility of others in their path. This consumed Yron now, as they tramped through dense forest, ducking branches, vines and great dangling leaves and picking a path as best they could, trying to follow the sun through the thick canopy above when the cloud cleared.

Yron looked at his hands, thankful he'd ordered Ben to don his gloves too. The leather was caught and torn by thorns and bark and the Gods knew what else. His leggings had fared no better and he was pretty sure some snags had penetrated the material to scratch his skin. His light leather coat had kept the worst from his upper body and arms but his face was cut in half a dozen places he could feel and no doubt marked in many others he couldn't. It raised a problem. Two problems, actually.

At their next rest stop, perched on a hollow log that Yron first checked for anything poisonous, he tackled them.

"Ben, look at me," he said. "Now, describe every cut you see."

"Eh?"

"I'm going to do the same for you. We don't need infection and we don't need blood traces."

"Eh?"

"Are you practising some primate mating call, Ben?" asked Yron. "And it's 'Eh, Captain.'"

"I'm sorry, sir, but don't we just have to rest and go? You've nothing but a couple of thorn scratches. Nothing to waste time over."

Yron cleared his throat and stood up, stepping over to a rubiac plant he'd just spied and plucking the fruits from it. "Ben, take this as more teaching. Teaching which won't be a waste of time because we're both going to survive this. Always, always plan to survive. And in an environment like this planning is everything. Now tell me, what are we going to do when we get to the river?"

"Jump in, you said," replied Ben-Foran dubiously. He shivered. "Something like that. To shake our scent from those panthers."

"Correct. And it's a dangerous enough move at the best of times. But these aren't the best of times. I counted eight scratches on your face that have drawn blood. Eight scratches that unless we treat before we jump in the river will attract not only every water-borne disease you can think of and twenty you can't, but the even more unwelcome attention of piranhas. And believe you me, these are not the sort of little fishes you want to go swimming with if you're cut."

"Oh, I see."

"I'm glad," said Yron. "So we take half an hour here. Count our cuts, pick the fruit, make the poultices and apply. All right? Good."

"Sir?"

"Yes, Ben."

"Are we going to survive this?"

"Do you consider yourself lucky, Ben?"

The younger man shrugged. "Recently, yes."

"Me too. So I think we can. As long as our luck holds. And if you believe that, you'll do something else for me right now."

"What's that, sir?"

"Keep your hands exactly where they are," said Yron. "Don't put the left one down because there's what I believe to be a taipan sliding right by your thigh."

CHAPTER 21

A uum waited all day while they gathered. The TaiGethen, the Claw-Bound and the first of the Al-Arynaar relief. As each arrived, he ushered them into the temple to show them the desecration of the statue. And the news had continued to get worse. More of the daily and weekly contemplation chambers had opened to reveal their contents plundered. Auum's mood, already dark, plunged into new depths. Every stranger would be made to pay for the crime.

He did not begin his chase immediately. The ClawBound pair had already departed to follow the two he had spared temporarily. But now the need to find the others was just as important. So he waited all the day, praying with his Tai or alone. Or sitting in quiet contemplation both inside and outside the temple, focussing his energies, honing his mind to peaks of concentration to allow him to connect with Tual's denizens.

Finally the Al-Arynaar came, those who had first heard the calling from their brothers. Their numbers would grow but their task was here for the time being and would only take them northward should the TaiGethen fail to catch all the strangers.

When the light had begun to fade and the late afternoon rains had cleared for a moment, Auum called all those present to order. Ten TaiGethen cells, eight ClawBound pairs and fifteen Al-Arynaar. The forest was quiet around them, even the wind seemed to have ceased. Everything beneath the gaze of Yniss was listening.

"We have trained all of our lives for the protection of our forest and the defence of our faith. Yet, as we can all see, our network was pierced by a large force intent on desecration of the temple and destruction of the forest. That we were all guilty of complacency is not contended. That our sleeper cell defence needs to be changed is not in doubt. But these are subjects for another day when, with the blessing of Yniss, we can gather and discuss the protection of the lives of all elves in peace.

"For now, our response must be swift and without error. We are chasing between fifteen and twenty strangers of apparently varying skills. We have discovered four routes from the temple and the fifth pair we are tracking directly.

"The ClawBound are abroad in the forest to the north. More TaiGethen cells will be alerted. We can close this net on them. We must close it."

Auum paused. Every eye was on him. Every thought was focussing. The gods would soon be busy receiving prayer. Now for the tasks.

"Two TaiGethen cells will take each group of strangers. The ClawBound I ask to find the tracks that we cannot. To be our messengers in the days ahead. To bring down those that elude us. You will, of course, decide on the course that best serves us all. The Al-Arynaar, be ready to move on signal. Until then stay here, repair what you can, rebuild the defence and pray that we are successful.

"My brothers, this is the biggest ever threat to the elven races. These strangers have taken sacred writings; you all know the tally. They have stolen the thumb of Yniss and broken the harmony in so doing. We must recover every page, every fragment. We know where they will head. First to the rivers and then to the northern coasts.

"They must not reach their ships. Now join me in prayer."

Auum prayed aloud for them all and all prayed for Auum. They prayed to Yniss to repair the harmony, to Tual for the denizens to help them in their search, and for Shorth to exact revenge through all eternity on the perpetrators of the desecration.

And when all their prayers were complete, they melted into the forest, leaving no trail and making no sound. In their wake, the forest began to sing again. Justice would be done.

Yron and Ben-Foran didn't make the river until late in the afternoon. They were both tired and hungry, having been unable to spare the time to search for food. Ben-Foran hadn't fancied the taipan that Yron had skewered with a dagger through the top of its head, and in truth the gruff captain hadn't felt hungry at the time either. They'd moved quickly enough but the route to the tributary of the River Shorth had been tortuous and beset with swamps and one very steep climb and drop.

They had heard the fast running water an hour before they reached it and had stood on the bank for a time, just gazing at the beauty unrolled in front of them. They'd slithered down a water runoff and were standing ankle deep in the flow. Across from them, some fifty yards away, a sheer cliff rose what had to be five hundred feet straight up.

Creviced and cracked, it was home to a mass of clinging vegetation. Birds by the thousand flew its length, gliding and spinning on the eddies in the air it created, and at a dozen places along its length that they could see before it swept away into a fine mist, water cascaded over its edge. The falls tumbled down glittering into the river, plumes of spray leaping at their bases, plunge pools gouged out of the rock by the erosion of ages.

Before them, the river ran quickly through the narrow strait. Further up, it had been faster, thundering through a defile and bouncing off the rock before settling down into the gentle but pacey flow. Yron couldn't see too far into the mist north and to his left but he was left hoping that the silt-laden water calmed further around the next bend. Either that or they were in for a bumpy ride.

"Good news or bad news?" he asked Ben-Foran.

"Bad," said Ben.

"It's going to hurt."

"And the good?"

"You won't have to paddle, and until it settles down no crocodiles."

"Piranhas?"

"I'll let you know." Yron grimaced. "Now, we need to find something to hang on to. Shouldn't be too difficult."

He waded upstream, through the relatively still waters at the edge of the river, looking for a pocket pool. After thirty yards or so, he found one, filled with silt scum and, as he expected, plenty of driftwood. Heaving out his axe, he hacked free the largest log and floated it back down to Ben-Foran, trapping it between his leg and the bank and guiding it with a hand.

Despite his confidence that there would be no crocodiles in such a fast-flowing stream, he kept an eye out ahead and behind, looking for telltale ripples and those bug eyes creeping above the surface. He shivered and blew out his cheeks at the thought of being stalked by something so merciless and efficient but forgot his fears when he saw Ben. The boy was white as a sheet, hugging his body and staring out into the river as if hypnotised.

"Ben?" The boy turned and tried to smile. It was a feeble effort. "Are you all right?"

"Is it really necessary?" he asked. "Can't we lose our scent just wading down the side?"

Yron laughed. "Depends if you think you can outrun a panther or an arrow."

"Surely they're well behind."

"You have no idea, do you?" said Yron. "In some quiet moment out there in the middle, I'll explain who these people are and why we should be as far from them as is humanly possible."

Ben cast a frightened glance over his shoulder back up into the deep green mass of the rain forest.

"What are you worried about, Ben? Can't you swim or something?" Yron's encouraging smile died on his lips as Ben raised his eyebrows and pursed his lips. "Oh, no. Out of all the people I could have escaped with, I've chosen the sinker."

But to his own and Ben's surprise, he didn't lay into his second in command for his lack of training, he just laughed, the sound booming off the rock opposite and then lost in the roar of water.

"It isn't funny," said Ben. "I just don't like open water. Not to swim in."

Yron crooked a finger and reluctantly Ben waded out the yard or so to him and the log.

"I'll let you into a secret," said Yron. "You won't need to swim."

"No?" Ben's face brightened.

"No. When the croc grabs you, you don't get the chance."

"It's not funny, Captain," repeated Ben. He was breathing hard and chewing his top lip. Yron saw him shiver.

"Sorry, Ben, bad joke," said Yron. "But I was right about you not having to swim. All you've got to do is hang on for your very life. Reckon you can do that?"

"Do I get a choice?" Ben managed a weak smile.

Yron shook his head.

"Then I'll try," he said.

"Good lad," said Yron. "You'll be fine. Now let's get out into the stream. Snap the lock over your scabbard. Don't want you losing your sword."

With that, he pushed the log away and plunged after it, Ben scrambling after him. The boy grabbed on tight, changing his grip again and again. Yron felt the tug of the current as they edged out into the flow. Gods knew if they'd survive but one thing was sure. If they didn't put some distance between them and those chasing, they'd be dead in a day. Yron just prayed they didn't escape one lot just to fall into the hands of those spread through the rest of the forest.

"Oh well, only one way to find out."

"Sir?"

"Nothing, lad. Just hang on, and keep your legs up as much as you can. This is going to be interesting."

The main force of the current took them, the log gathered speed and they were dragged along in its wake, out of control and into the hands of the Gods. Yron wasn't a religious man by nature; to him religion was a matter of convenience and a support for the weak. But there are some times when you are so small and helpless that you need something to hang your life on, however briefly.

So while he watched the cliffs rush by, the water crash down from high above, and the bank they'd left begin to rise sheer as the river narrowed again and angled down, he began to pray.

He hoped the Gods, whoever they were, were listening.

It was not the sort of news Blackthorne wanted. He was walking through the marketplace with Baron Gresse, talking to the fresh produce stallholders, who were seeing their profits shrink and their livelihoods threatened. He'd worked out a compensation scheme based on the prices he'd previously paid all suppliers for foodstuffs and was trying to ensure that those who sold what was grown or bred were not left high and dry. It was difficult to be fair and some felt aggrieved.

Still, it had been good having Gresse here to discuss the problems facing the country. He was into his late sixties now but had the vitality of a man two decades his junior. And with that mischievous twinkle in his eye and his disdain for the trappings of wealth, Gresse was a popular figure. He had stepped in to help his people much as Blackthorne had done.

Walking back to their horses and just about to ride out to an outlying hamlet on a cloudy and cool early afternoon, the two barons were hailed by a young squire racing through the marketplace on foot. He was barely in his teens, tall and thin as a rake and instantly recognisable. He skittered to a clumsy halt in front of them and bowed.

"My Lords, sorry to call you in such a manner."

Blackthorne nodded. "I take it this is an important message, young Berrin."

"Yes, my Lord. Luke sent me personally, said you would want to know right away."

"Well don't keep him guessing, young man," said Gresse, a half smile on his face. "Or me for that matter. At my age patience is in short supply."

"Sorry, my Lord," said Berrin, blushing bright red below his cropped brown hair. "It's just that some of the mounted militia have intercepted a group of twenty riders heading for the town. They demand an audience with you, Baron Blackthorne."

"Demand, eh? Who are they and where are they?" asked Blackthorne.

"Black Wings, my Lord, two miles north on the main trail. Selik is with them."

Blackthorne cursed under his breath and swung into his saddle, his mood darkening. "I will attend immediately. Tell Luke where I have gone."

"Yes, my Lord." Berrin ran off toward the castle.

"Coming, Gresse?" asked Blackthorne.

"I think I need to hear what you have to say to Selik. I wonder why he's chosen to come here. Surely he knows where you stand."

"The man's arrogance knows no boundary," replied Blackthorne, feeling some anxiety. Gresse was right. Selik wouldn't come unless he felt he had real weight on his side. Truth or lie, Blackthorne was worried what he might hear. He signalled to his guard of six to accompany them and put his heels to his horse's flanks.

Blackthorne rode quickly, Gresse at his side, his well-armoured guards in a loose circle around him as they passed along the north trail out of the town. To the east, the skyline was dominated by the Balan Mountains but in front of them the land was flat, covered in bracken and coarse grass. It was a cool if dry day but there were clouds massing on the mountain peaks. Rain was not far away.

They could see both militia and Black Wings from over a mile away as they rounded a bend in the trail through a small area of devastated woodland. Blackthorne could see eight of his own men, who would have a mage with them, mounted and watching over the Black Wing riders who had all dismounted, leaving their horses to graze at will.

The Baron, feeling irritation at the waste of his valuable time but happy that his increased security had intercepted the Black Wings, reined in by the militia sergeant and dismounted.

"Stand off but be ready," he said.

"Yes, my Lord."

Blackthorne and Gresse walked the short distance to the Black Wing captain, obvious by his wrecked face, and his men. Selik did not smile as he saw them.

"Baron Blackthorne, a pleasure I'm sure. And made all the better by the presence of the famous Baron Gresse. You have saved me a further journey." He extended a gauntleted hand which both barons ignored.

"You have nothing to say that I want to hear, so make it quick and be on your way," said Blackthorne. "I am a busy man."

"I thought it only fair to visit you, Blackthorne, and offer you the hand of alliance."

Blackthorne folded his arms and frowned. "Against what?"

"Well, magic of course. The scourge that has brought this great country to its knees, that threatens to destroy our land and that must be stopped from regaining its dominance over the people."

"A country that you would clearly like to see flat on its back with its eyes staring sightless at the sky," said Blackthorne.

"No, one that I would see return to rude health without the ever-present fear of magical devastation."

Blackthorne exchanged a quick glance with Gresse, who raised his eyebrows and shook his head.

"You want me, us, to ally with you to throw down the colleges, is that it?"

"It is a crusade of the righteous," said Selik. "You are respected men. Your presence could stop unnecessary bloodshed."

"Respect that alliance with you would destroy in a moment," said Gresse. "The Gods only know what bullshit your supporters swallow, but don't treat us as fools. Your ultimate goal is the murder of every mage in Balaia. There is no unnecessary bloodshed for you, and while I have breath I will oppose you."

Selik's eye narrowed and his expression clouded. "The people are sick of magic. They want rid of it, they want it exterminated or controlled. And those who support it are the enemies of Balaia."

"And these people are the same ones who wallow in filth right now while their families die of hunger and disease and the only thriving creatures are rats," said Blackthorne.

"And all brought upon them by magic."

"And magic will save them," snapped Blackthorne. "My town is free of vermin. It is free of disease. The people are fed. They can see an end. But only with the help of magic. Who will save these people should you succeed in your sick aim?"

"Healing is a natural process and cats can catch rats," said Selik smoothly. "Breed more cats."

Blackthorne walked forward. He was a head taller than Selik. He looked down at the Black Wing captain and saw a brief fear in his eyes that undermined his air of confidence.

"You will not hasten an end to the college war by intervening. I want to see magic returned to balance, not exterminated. We must end this war by negotiation and strength of will. And while I am angry that there is war and disgusted at the actions taken by Xetesk and Dordover, I will not condone opportunists like you attempting to weaken the colleges to the point of collapse. Balaia must have magic."

"The colleges have no will other than to tear each other apart and damn the consequences for this country," said Selik, the fire back in his eyes.

"And I and the barons that are with me will pressure for peace at every stage. You well know Heryst is a force for that peace and my allegiance is with him. Meanwhile, my borders are strong and my mages are loyal to me and wish the conflict ended as fervently as I do."

"The righteous will prevail," said Selik.

"Yes, they will," said Blackthorne. "And you are not among them. This country has magic running through its veins. It is part of all of us. It makes us strong. You will never end magic, Selik, but I sincerely hope you die trying and before you consign more innocent men and women to their deaths. Now, leave my lands immediately. Any further incursion and you will be taken. Do I make myself clear?"

Selik laughed, a rattling unpleasant sound. "I have made my point, I have offered you alliance and now I know your allegiance. The people will not forget where you stand, Blackthorne. Nor you, Gresse. And when the army of justice rides south, remember my words."

"Leave." Blackthorne turned away to his sergeant. "See he leaves our lands and pass the word. They are not to be tolerated here again."

"Yes, my Lord."

Blackthorne and Gresse walked to their horses.

"So why didn't you arrest him then and there?" asked the older baron.

"My dear Gresse, there are times when you must gamble and this is one of those times. Something must be done to draw the colleges together, for them to unite as they did when the Wytch Lords threatened. And I can think of nothing better than a Black Wing attack, can you?"

"And the innocents that die in the process?"

Blackthorne sighed. "Regrettable. Regrettable but inevitable. Come, Gresse, we have places to be and I want to wash the taste of that meeting away with a good drop of ale."

CHAPTER 22

Ilkar's quick summary of his conversations with Kild'aar and Rebraal had given Erienne new focus. Leaving Hirad to berate the Julatsan for never revealing he had a brother, she, Denser and Ren hurried over to the house Ilkar had indicated, wary of the panther and its extraordinary keeper who sat silent outside. They were stopped at the door by Kild'aar. The elven woman spoke briefly. Ren turned to them.

"She says you're not welcome. She says you will not defile the body of the Al-Arynaar."

"Tell her I agree, I will not defile his body," said Erienne. "But if she wants us to help save her village, she'd better let us through now."

It was late and Erienne was tired. The ache in her head was growing and it pulsed like a reminder, nudging her to do something, fulfill an obligation she didn't feel. Ren was talking to Kild'aar. It was a curt exchange. At one point the older elf pointed meaningfully at the panther who so far, like its keeper, had paid them no heed whatever. Eventually, she stepped from the doorway, her contempt clear in the set of her body and expression.

"She says the panther will claw out your eyes if you do wrong to the body."

Denser looked at Ren with the expression Erienne recognised whenever The Raven were threatened. Utter disdain.

"It wouldn't get within five yards," he said, and stalked inside.

They went left as directed into a candle-lit and chokingly scented room containing a single bed on which lay the shrouded figure of Mercuun. Kild'aar followed them in and stood to watch, arms folded in silent disapproval.

Erienne knelt by the bedside and Denser pulled the shroud gently from the body, folding it back to expose his head and bare chest. In the flickering light, Erienne could make out a young, angular face. No bruising was evident on the dark skin.

She placed her hands on his chest, hearing a hiss of indrawn breath from Kild'aar. The skin was cold, hard and waxy. She ignored the unpleasant sensation and tuned herself to the mana spectrum, directing a sheet of mana across the body slowly from head to toe, her fingers picking up everything it touched and penetrated.

Almost immediately she felt a surge of nausea, like gulping rancid air. She fought to keep her concentration, focussing hard on her task, driving her mind to analyse what the mana stream fed back to her. The construct she was using borrowed heavily from the BodyCast spell, but Mercuun couldn't have been saved even by this most powerful healer casting. It could knit bone, repair muscle and organ, stop bleeding and soothe bruising. But it couldn't reverse rot and decay.

She withdrew from Mercuun's body, nodding at Denser to replace the shroud. For a moment she remained on her knees, rubbing her hands slowly down the top of her thighs. She breathed deeply to clear her head of the fetid sensations she'd experienced and returned her mind to its normal state.

"All right, love?" asked Denser, squatting down beside her and stroking her cheek.

"Yes," she said, and looked across at Ren. "I need to know some things. Ask her how long he's been dead."

Ren nodded and asked the question.

"Two days," she relayed. "They are waiting for Rebraal before they commit his body to the forest."

Erienne shuddered. "So recent?" She spared Denser an anxious glance. "Ask her if his bone breaks were tended to."

"They were," came the delayed reply. "They could be treated and they responded. Still he died."

"That's because they weren't the problem," said Erienne grimly. "What else do they know?"

"Nothing," translated Ren. "He never regained consciousness."

"And what about the others who are sick?" Erienne got to her feet, helped by Denser.

There was a longer delay, Ren listening to what she was hearing with a frown deepening on her beautiful features. She asked a couple of questions then took a deep breath and turned to Erienne.

"It sounds horrible," she said. "Loss of balance, bleeding from ears, nose and anus, grinding pain in the gut and chest, loss of vision and hearing, muscle weakness and the clawing of hands and feet. I think there's probably more but that covers the most common symptoms. The worst thing is, nothing seems to reverse or even ease the symptoms, and death has occurred in as little as four days. No one has survived yet."

"I'm not surprised," said Erienne. "How many are suffering at the moment?"

"A hundred and thirty-three."

"Oh no," said Erienne, putting a hand over her mouth, the size of the problem sending her reeling inside. "No wonder she's been so hostile."

Erienne walked up to Kild'aar and gripped her folded arms with both hands. She saw a pleading in the elf's eyes behind the stern mask, a barely repressed fear born of a lack of any answer.

"I'm sorry, Kild'aar," said Erienne. "But I need you to show me one of those still alive."

Kild'aar nodded but didn't understand her words, only her expression and the emotion in her voice. Ren translated Erienne's words and was asked another question.

"She wants to know what you found."

Erienne bit her lip. "He was rotten inside," she said as calmly as she could, recalling the feelings of decay and disease that had pervaded her so strongly. "All his organs just so much mush inside his body, some of them barely recognisable. His brain was the same. His bones were brittle, no calcium, like he was an elf hundreds of years older than he was. I've never seen anything like it. Outwardly, he was fine. On the inside, like he'd been dead for weeks. But I need to see a live patient. Someone I can talk to. Quickly."

Ren was momentarily dumbfounded by Erienne's description. She pulled herself together but shivered as she related the awful symptoms to Kild'aar, who gasped as Mercuun's fate was relayed to her. She looked across at Erienne, all the anger replaced with shock and sadness. She spoke a few words.

"Kild'aar asks if there is anything you can do."

Erienne shrugged uselessly. "I don't know. I hope so but I don't know. I've never encountered anything like this."

Kild'aar didn't need her words translated. Beckoning them, she made to leave the room, only to stop at the sound of the door opposite opening. Leaning on the frame for support, a half-naked elf shambled out of the room and across the narrow hallway. His right hand was clamped over his left shoulder and his brow was furrowed and covered in a light sweat. His eyes burned as he took in Erienne and Denser, sparing Ren a brief glance before focussing on Kild'aar and launching into a stream of invective.

Erienne moved reflexively back until she felt Denser behind her, watching Kild'aar stretch to touch the wounded elf and having her hand slapped away. She responded to his words, her voice calming, but this only inspired him to shout, nodding into the room, his neck straining with his anger. Erienne felt her heart beating fast, the vehemence of the verbal onslaught shocking. She reached out and found Denser's hand.

The elf wasn't letting up. Whatever Kild'aar said, it wasn't mollifying him. Ren was following the argument. Again and again she looked about to jump in but something she heard stayed her. The noise in the room was intensifying, Kild'aar shouting now. In the end, Ren did finish it. Erienne saw the young elf clench both her fists, step firmly between the two combatants and yell directly into the wounded elf's face. The shock of the intercession stopped him and he glared at Ren with interest. Seizing her chance, Ren spoke, her tone firm but calm. She pointed behind her at Mercuun, at Erienne, and out past the elf to the front door. The only word Erienne picked up was "Ilkar," but whatever Ren said had instant effect.

The elf nodded, spoke two words and Ren moved aside. He walked slowly into the room, Kild'aar next to him, an arm about his back. He pulled the shroud aside and gazed down at Mercuun, Erienne seeing his shoulders hunch and fall. He whispered words of prayer, knelt very awkwardly and placed his left hand on Mercuun's forehead, bowing. He was silent for a time, lost in contemplation or memory.

Denser nudged Erienne and whispered.

"Looks like a tanned version of Ilkar, doesn't he?"

"There's some resemblance," agreed Erienne.

"So there should be," said Ren quietly from beside them. "That's Rebraal, Ilkar's brother."

At the sound of his name, Rebraal pushed himself slowly and painfully back to his feet and turned to Erienne and Denser. The anger was gone from his face and Erienne was surprised to see fear in his eyes. He spoke and Ren translated.

"He says he has to go back to the temple. It must be returned to the hands of the Al-Arynaar. He's leaving at dawn tomorrow."

"Tell him we'll be with him," said Denser.

The mage tensed as Rebraal snorted in derision at Ren's translation. Erienne put a hand on his arm to calm him.

"Going to do it on his own, is he?" asked Denser.

Rebraal snapped out some words. Ren held up her hands, replied and got a terse one-word answer.

"He's going to kill strangers. Why would he want more there?"

"My question still stands," said Denser.

"His brother Al-Arynaar will join him in a few days. He hopes it will be soon enough," said Ren.

"And if it isn't? He's left the best chance he's got here mopping sick brows. Put this to him. We're coming. We can help, and whatever it is that's got him so scared will be solved that much more quickly."

Another short elven conversation.

"He says the forest will kill you."

"I know I speak for us all when I say this. We want to help. We have to get mages back to Balaia quickly so anything we can do to speed that, to get the elves to trust us, we will do. And does he really have a choice? Right now, we're all he's got and, Gods burning, one of us is his brother."

Erienne could feel the passion in Denser. It was a belief she knew well.

She only hoped Rebraal saw it too. She watched Ren talk to him, saw him respond while looking over her shoulder at Denser. He shrugged, his expression hardened but he nodded.

"So we're all right by him now, are we?" Denser was terse.

"No," said Ren. "You're here, that's all. The Raven. He knows that he needs all the help he can get. Ilkar is the key. Without him, you would not be allowed to travel with him."

Erienne felt a crawling sensation across her chest. "Just what is it that's so wrong he thinks us worth risking?"

"Rebraal knows what's causing this. He's studied the texts at the temple. He's dedicated his life to preserving the harmony."

"And?" pushed Denser.

"Rebraal says the harmony has been broken. That the strangers who took the temple have done it, but he doesn't know how. That's why we have to go there. Because you can't cure this sickness with magic or herbs, and unless harmony is restored the elves will die."

Erienne frowned. "Which elves?"

"All of us."

Aeb was unsettled. Protectors were used to being alone, travelling with their Given Xeteskian mage. But in times of conflict the Soul Tank, deep in the catacombs of Xetesk, was always troubled. The souls of those Protectors who could not be physically together communicated their thoughts and their fears for one another. Aeb had been hearing much and the anxiety was rising.

Aeb's position was unique. Officially he was the Given of Denser, the Dawnthief mage. A high honour in itself. But in reality he was more the defender of Sol, The Unknown Warrior, the only man to have been a Protector and returned from the calling, his soul repatriated to his body.

If Protectors could genuinely feel pride, then Aeb would have been proud. But it didn't change the fact that he could hear the agitation of the souls of his brothers in his head. They weren't scared. They were bred to fight and defend. But when they were split they were inevitably weakened, and so anxiety filtered across the Soul Tank.

Aeb had been sitting silent in his room, having bathed his face and let the air play across his maskless features in the dark, calming those he could and listening to the thoughts of others. But now, with the voices still whispering in his head—he could never shut them out and would never want to—he strapped the mask back over his face, ignoring the discomfort, and went to find Sol.

The Unknown Warrior was standing alone but turned when the Protector approached.

"Aeb," said The Unknown, nodding to him.

Aeb could see immediately that he could sense something. It had been a mystery long cherished in the Soul Tank. How Sol, with his soul in his body and not in contact with his Protector brothers any more, could still sense them all and pick up on feelings, though not fully grasp them. It gave them hope that should they ever be released from thrall they would still be joined in some indelible way. It was what they prayed for.

"I apologise for disturbing you."

The Unknown shook his head. "You are still close to me," he said. "And something's worried you. You should be at rest."

"Yes."

"Then speak freely. Denser has granted you that freedom gladly."

"It is still difficult," he said. "All these years . . ."

"You've heard something in the Soul Tank," guessed The Unknown.

"Yes," said Aeb. "It is not information I can volunteer, Sol. You know the strictures of the calling."

"But you cannot knowingly lie to a direct question from your Given," said Denser, joining them. "Sorry to overhear."

Aeb swung to face the mage.

"So ask," said The Unknown.

"Aeb, take The Unknown's questions as coming from me. Answer us both," said Denser.

"Yes."

Denser looked across at The Unknown to speak.

"The Protectors are engaged in combat?"

"Yes."

"Where?"

"Arlen."

"And Xetesk are in control of the town?"

"Yes."

"How far have the Dordovan forces been pushed back?"

"They have been eliminated."

"What?" The Unknown gaped and looked across at Denser.

"Were they given the option of surrender?" asked the mage.

"No."

"And the Protectors were ordered to kill them all?"

"All that survived the magical attack. Cavalry were dispatched to deal with outlying forces."

The Unknown and Denser exchanged another glance. Aeb was comforted by it, seeing in their expressions a reflection of his own unease. He would relay this to his brothers later.

"Describe the spell and its effect," ordered Denser.

Aeb paused, consulting with the Soul Tank.

"A cooperative FlameOrb. Mages called it a FireGlobe. Large area effect. It destroyed the northwestern quarter of Arlen. At its splash point, the heat is still too great to bear, even after a day."

The Unknown cursed. "They're clearing a path," he said. "And riding roughshod over the rules of engagement. It'll escalate the conflict."

"Clearing a path for who?" asked Denser.

"The mage researchers and my brothers on Herendeneth," said Aeb immediately. "They will return to Balaia soon."

"So," said Denser, staring at The Unknown. "Which of us gets to tell Hirad that Xetesk has no intention of helping his dragons?"

The Unknown raised his eyebrows and walked back into the house.

CHAPTER 23

Ben-Foran was asleep. It was born of exhaustion, both mental and physical, and the knowledge that Yron wanted more of the same from him the next day. For the Captain himself though, sleep was the farthest thing from his mind. He wasn't sure how long they'd clung to the log. Two hours, maybe more. All he knew was that when the tributary eventually emptied out into the River Shorth, he'd never been so glad to feel the ground beneath his feet.

They'd been swept through gorge after gorge, across rapids, their bodies grazing rock and sandbar, through swirling currents and over one mercifully low waterfall. Yron's only consolation during the whole bruising ride—apart from the knowledge that they were putting good distance between themselves and the elven hunters—was that no serious predator could be after them.

And the whole time Ben hadn't said a word, just clung on to the log, keeping his head above water and his legs stretched out behind him as well as he could. His teeth had chattered from chill and fear but he hadn't complained. And even though the journey must have drained every ounce of energy from his body, as it had from Yron, when the waters suddenly slackened and they joined the two-hundred-yard width of the Shorth, it was Ben who had kicked for the bank harder.

They had barely stopped even then until, with the evening beginning to close in and the light fading fast, they sought a place to rest. Yron hadn't liked the look of the forest where they'd landed. It was very dense and heavy, the ground rising sharply away, and neither he nor Ben wanted to climb. So they'd walked along in the shallows, mindful of crocodiles but seeing none except those basking on the mud of the opposite bank.

With night almost upon them and an evening deluge keeping them drenched, they'd come to a section of bank where rock rose sheer from the water to a height of some two hundred feet. Opposite, the forest tumbled away up a long, gentle and beautiful slope, revealing the full glory of the rain forest canopy. Thousands of birds flocked above it, filling the air with their cries, while closer to the bank the trees rustled with a troop of monkeys, on their way to a new feeding ground.

Ben had seen a ledge up in the rock face and they'd pushed themselves to one more climb. It was about thirty feet but worth it. There would have been enough space for six men on its flat surface, and once they'd swept its crevices for snake, spider and scorpion, they settled down to rest, safe from most that the forest could throw at them.

The unyielding rock had clearly been to Ben's liking and he was almost instantly asleep, but Yron had no desire to lie down and instead rested his back against the rock face and looked out over the river and into the vastness beyond. Above him the clouds rolled over incessantly, keeping in the heat of the day— for which he was grateful despite the rain they brought. They couldn't have risked a fire. To those following, it would be an unmissable beacon.

Through occasional gaps in the cloud, moon and starlight filtered down, illuminating the forest with a grey light. As his eyes adjusted to the gloom, Yron could make out the herbivores that came to drink at the water's edge, hidden by the night. He could see the nocturnal birds soaring and swooping overhead. It was a truly stupendous land. Primeval in so many respects but so *close*. Everything worked together. The elves were right to call it harmony. It was like perfectly arranged music and dancing. The greatest show nature could provide. He wouldn't upset it for anything and, as he had done many times since they'd landed, he regretted the necessity of their actions.

But, he assured himself, the forest would recover from the small damage they had caused and the papers would one day be returned. He had no great fondness for elves but didn't wish them ill either. He had experienced their coldness too many times to think of those who lived here as anything more than half civilised. Strange that their Balaian-dwelling cousins were so friendly. Perhaps it was a function of shaking off the manacles of the rain forest. Or perhaps Balaia really was a better place to live.

Right now he certainly believed it was. He would have given almost anything for a soft bed somewhere he wasn't liable to wake up covered in bites and burrowing insects. Still, they'd be at the ship in a few days. If they could outwit the TaiGethen.

He shifted and moved to the rim of the ledge, hanging his legs over the side and banging them gently against the rock while he thought.

"Where are you?" he whispered. "How do you think? How do you hunt?"

So little was known about the TaiGethen bar their fanaticism. Indeed he was fortunate to have even seen one. They shunned towns and cities and bothered no one unless they felt threatened. He had hoped to avoid them but now he had to think around them. Do what they wouldn't expect.

They'd assume he'd travel downriver but he might have fooled them by taking to the stream. But they would catch him. They'd be watching the rivers at key points. They'd probably already guessed where the ships were. What he really needed to do was find Stenys or Erys but that would be well-nigh impossible. Either of them could commune with the reserve and ensure they didn't come too far, keeping themselves to a defensive line up across the river estuary in which the ships lay at anchor. It was the action he had ordered but they might get twitchy enough to send out search parties. Trouble was, it was as good as sending the unfortunates to their executions.

Knowing there was nothing he could do, he thought back to the plans he'd given the groups for their escapes. Almost immediately he had an idea. Ben wasn't going to like it, but then Ben wasn't in charge.

Relaxing now he had something definite in mind, Yron swung his legs back on to the ledge, scrambled in a little way and lay down with his hands behind his head to doze, a smile on his face.

"You are not in a fit state to be out of bed, much less travel to Aryndeneth," said Ilkar.

He and Rebraal were sitting alone around a fire in the centre of the village, drinking a healing herb tea. It was late and very dark and the fire had drawn insects from everywhere. What Rebraal had learned made him talk to his brother but it hadn't changed his opinion.

"And you are not fit to be in my sight at all. You will not tell me what I can and can't do. This is something that must be done, and it is betrayers like you who make it necessary."

"How did you work that out?" Ilkar hadn't thought to be blamed for the shortcomings of the Al-Arynaar.

"Because those such as you did not believe. You thought you knew better, that what the Al-Arynaar and the TaiGethen believe in had no foundation. And because you refused to join us, you weakened us. And here is the result of that weakness."

"How many of them attacked you?" asked Ilkar.

"A hundred and thirty or so." Rebraal was matter of fact.

Ilkar was stunned. "How many?" He had imagined a lightning strike by some very skilled raiders, not an armed invasion.

"And nine of us killed almost a hundred."

"Nine?" Ilkar swallowed.

"Yes, Ilkar, nine. Including two mages. Because there are not enough of us. Barely enough to keep the net working. You've forgotten so much. Where did I go wrong?"

Ilkar heard regret and disappointment in Rebraal's voice. And the net hadn't worked. Neither the Al-Arynaar nor the TaiGethen nor the Claw-Bound had detected a large raiding group.

"You didn't go wrong," said Ilkar quietly. "It was me. I didn't believe, not deeply enough."

"Do you not pray to Yniss, Ilkar?"

Ilkar dropped his gaze and stared into the fire.

"Then truly I have failed," said Rebraal. "I couldn't even teach you what binds us to the land and our Gods."

"I know the teachings," said Ilkar. "I just didn't feel the power as you or Father did. I didn't have it within me to be Al-Arynaar."

"But you had it within you to be a mage," said Rebraal. "Why didn't you come back?"

"Because I didn't belong. I wanted to be a great mage, not one just adequate to guard Aryndeneth or scout the forest all my life."

"You follow different Gods," said Rebraal. "I hope it was worth it."

"Yes it was."

"And now? Now that elves are dying because of what strangers from Balaia have done?"

Ilkar had reached the limit of what he was prepared to accept. This was where he began to lose it. Funny. Denser and Erienne seemed more willing to listen to Rebraal than he was on this.

"How can that be? How can we be so vulnerable that a hundred thieves can bring us to the brink of disaster? There has to be another explanation. There has to be a cure."

"Idiot!" stormed Rebraal, pushing himself up from the bench, pain spearing across his face as it must have through his shoulder. "It has always been this way. Why do you think the Al-Arynaar exist? The TaiGethen? Why? To protect the elves from exactly this possibility. I have read the texts as you have not, Ilkar. I bothered to learn the one weakness in the glory of the harmony, of Yniss, Tual, Orra and every God in which I place my faith and trust."

"And what is it?"

Rebraal's face fell and comprehension dawned on his features. He sat down very close to Ilkar.

"You really don't feel it, do you? And that's why you never came back as I did."

"Feel what?" Ilkar could sense the disappointment in his brother.

"I see it now. And you're probably not alone, are you? Every elf who stays on Balaia must feel like you do." Rebraal sighed, understanding bringing him a little peace.

"Like what?" Ilkar wanted to shake him but calmed himself, letting Rebraal order his thoughts in order to explain. He'd seen this in his older brother before. He had always been so thoughtful, so deep in his belief. It was one of the things Ilkar admired about him most.

In front of them the fire hissed and crackled as a light rain began to fall. Ilkar looked up into the heavens. The cloud wasn't heavy; it would soon pass.

"There is a text you will have heard of. That handed down by Yniss to Tual and from Tual to the elves when they were spawned from the rain forest and built Aryndeneth."

"The Aryn Hiil." Ilkar nodded.

It was the text the priests and then the Al-Arynaar guarded most jealously. The Words of the Earth, if you believed it, written by Yniss himself. Only those of a certain attainment were allowed sight of it. Rebraal would be one of them.

"Yes. The Aryn Hiil describes elves and their place in the world. It tells that elves should be the guardians of the forest. That we should be the denizens blessed by Tual and charged with keeping the land and its creatures safe. That with this honour was given long life—so the ways of the forest could be learned and passed to the next generations—but that we would not be numerous, only wise and careful. And that we would be further honoured by being one with the forest and the air and the magic. That we would feel all these energies within us and this would give us the strength to fulfill our task for Tual.

"But with it came a warning. That should we stop believing and let vine and rat gain dominion over our sacred sites; let sloth govern our minds and ignorance guide our hands, then this gift would be taken from us. And we would shrivel and die, our long life taken and our families lying dead beside us where they had lived. It would be the Sorrow of Elves, and only by turning back to Yniss could we be complete again.

"It is happening, Ilkar, and we must put it right."

Ilkar pondered. Parable it may be but it made awful sense. This was no contagious plague. It struck at random. At the young and old, the sick and healthy. It had no rhyme or reason. It just happened.

And even if he couldn't quite bring himself to believe that this was some kind of divine retribution, it was enough that Rebraal and Kild'aar did. It meant elves everywhere would not rest until the balance was restored, until the harmony had returned. It meant that not one elf mage would leave these shores to help Julatsa.

"And what is it that I don't feel?" he asked.

Rebraal smiled. "The forest and the sky and the air. It doesn't suffuse you. Only the magic does. That is why you didn't come back. I had no choice. I was pulled by the strings of my life." The smile faded from Rebraal's face. "But do not think it makes you immune from the Elfsorrow. You are still one of us. Next heartbeat the Sorrow could take you, or me, or Ren'erei."

Ilkar hadn't considered the possibility of his own death and it was an uncomfortable thought. He took a sip of his drink. "And you think that whatever these strangers have done is enough to spoil the harmony and bring this warning to pass?"

"It is the only explanation. We may be low in numbers but there is no turning from Yniss. The elves of the towns and cities and villages all pray as they have always done, and respect as they always have. The coincidence is too great."

"The Raven will help you, Rebraal, I swear it. We will kill them as we would any enemy."

"Hmm. The Raven. We are not so distant that we haven't heard of you, some of us. We always ask for news of you when one of us returns from training in Julatsa. Your name is famous, isn't it?" He stood up. "A big reputation. Let's just hope it isn't all so much muscle and tits."

Ilkar laughed and dragged a dry chuckle from Rebraal.

"I can assure you it is not," said Ilkar. "And, with a turn of phrase like that, perhaps you spent too long in Balaia too."

"A day was too long. But I had to learn, though I could not be a mage."

"It might pay you to brush up your Balaian, if you can remember any." Ilkar stood too. "I was always sorry I didn't come back, you know."

"No, you weren't. You didn't believe. It will be a mark on my spirit forever."

"I was, but not for that. For you. I knew I'd let you down."

"I had a hundred years when I didn't think I had a brother. I'm still not sure I have."

"Take your time," said Ilkar. "And get Erienne to see to your shoulder. If you want to leave at first light you need a WarmHeal cast by an expert."

"You don't perform this spell, great mage?"

Ilkar ignored the jibe. "Not like Erienne. Come with me; she's in the house."

The brothers walked from the fire, one driven by a fervour that would never be extinguished, the other by a growing sense of guilt that he might just have been wrong and let down not just his family and his calling, but the entire elven race.

Hirad lay back on his bed and closed his eyes, relaxing his body and opening his mind the way Sha-Kaan had taught him. He had missed contact with the Great Kaan and, as his Dragonene, should have made this effort before. It was possible that the hugely powerful mind of the dragon had probed his and discovered it not sufficiently at rest for him to risk communication. He wouldn't be surprised. The last three days had hardly been his most restful. Nevertheless, he felt a nervousness. The Great Kaan wasn't going to like what he had to say.

"Sha-Kaan, can you hear me?" he asked, letting his thoughts flow as though adrift on the sea.

Almost at once, he felt the surge as Sha-Kaan's mind touched his, filling him with a slightly piqued warmth.

"My memories of you were dimming, Hirad Coldheart," said Sha-Kaan, his mood definitely light.

"And mine of your poor jokes," said Hirad. "It is good to feel my mind touch yours again."

"And I yours," said Sha-Kaan. "You are troubled. You have a question for me?"

"We need to know the progress the Al-Drechar and you have made with the Xeteskian researchers," said Hirad.

"Ah," said Sha-Kaan. Hirad's mind filled with intensified warmth and an emotion that was easily defined. Hope. Hirad's heart beat faster. "The Ancients know so much. And the Xeteskians have sound theory on which to rely. I can almost smell the forests of Teras and see the mountains of Beshara."

Hirad bit his lip. "Have they told you how long?"

"Half a season, they say, before they can be confident of the position of the dimensions again. But they are discovering much else in the meantime."

"Oh really?"

"My hearing is a little more acute than the Xeteskians realise," said Sha-Kaan, and Hirad felt more humour. "After all, I am but a reptile, is that not right?"

"Their mistake," said Hirad.

"Yes," agreed Sha-Kaan. "Most humans are fools. But they believe they have isolated a power they can use in interdimensional space and they are excited at reestablishing a linkage to your closest relative dimension, though I am at a loss as to why. The Arakhe, the demons." He paused and Hirad felt the edge come off his mood. "You are keeping something from me. Do not."

"They are preparing to leave," said Hirad. "They want to use everything they've found to win the war on Balaia. We don't think they intend to help you."

The silence in his mind was total, and for a time Hirad thought the dragon had left him. But a brooding fury grew in the space so recently filled with hope. He felt it like a weight, pressing down on his brain. It hurt.

"You are sure of this?"

"The Protectors are sure," said Hirad, his breath a gasp.

"Then we will ensure they do not leave."

"Be careful," said Hirad. "They are a powerful group."

"Better to die fighting for a way home than slowly on an alien hillside," said Sha-Kaan. "No one uses Kaan dragons."

And he was gone. Hirad breathed easier, the pressure gone but leaving an ache in his head. The dragons were awesome fighters, but without their fire were weakened. He prayed that Sha-Kaan heeded him. If he didn't, Xeteskian spells could finish what the Dordovans had started two seasons before.

Denser slipped between the rough woven but clean sheets and blew out the single candle that illuminated the small room. He lay on his back and Erienne moved across to him, putting her head on his chest. He stroked her hair and she breathed deeply.

"It doesn't get any easier, does it?" he said.

"No," said Erienne. "Though at least I can distract myself here. The dark though. That brings it all back."

"I know, love. I'm no different."

His heart was as heavy as the day they had left Herendeneth, and he knew Erienne's must be too. And now here they were charged with something they didn't expect. The elves were dying and Ilkar was at risk. And if he sickened, the only humane thing to do would be to kill him. More death of those they loved. They couldn't let that happen. Bugger the rest of them but Ilkar deserved every day of his long life.

"Funny though, isn't it?" he said.

"What?" He felt her head move as if she were trying to look up at him.

"We came here to help Ilkar look for mages and now we're off to fight at a temple to save the whole elven race. It's horrible, I know, but I feel better for doing it."

"The Raven needs a purpose," said Erienne. "Shepherd to a flock of reluctant Julatsan elves wasn't enough, was it?"

"No." Denser chuckled. "How was Rebraal?"

"I don't think he enjoys the touch of a human," said Erienne.

"Good."

Erienne slapped his shoulder. "But he was fine. He'll sleep till just before dawn. I only hope it's enough. His determination is incredible. I think he'd have left tonight if Kild'aar and Ilkar hadn't stopped him. And by all accounts two days ago he should have been dead."

"Like brother, like brother," said Denser. He paused. "And how are you?"

Erienne didn't answer immediately, just lay silent, listening to his heart beating and the sound of the rain hammering on the leaf thatch above.

"I miss her," she said, her voice trembling but controlled. "Every quiet moment her memory floods me."

"I'm sorry," he said. "It wasn't quite what I meant though. How's your head, the One?"

"It hurts more every day," admitted Erienne. "Sometimes a pulsing pain, sometimes a dull ache. But it never lets me forget it's there."

"And have you thought of opening yourself to it? And seeking the advice of the Al-Drechar?"

Denser expected an angry response and was pleasantly surprised.

"Every day," she said. "When the pain is bad and Lyanna fills my mind. Then I wonder if I shouldn't get started."

"Then why don't you?"

"Because they are causing the pain," said Erienne, tensing suddenly. She pushed herself up on her arms and looked at him. He could just see her face in the dark, surrounded by her mass of long curls. Gods, but she was beautiful. "I know it's them. Somehow, they're putting pressure on me and I will not dance to their tune."

"If it is them, you'd think they'd have realised that by now," said Denser. "Didn't take me long, did it?"

He saw the flash of a smile. "But they're old and fearful of dying before they can ensure the One survives. I'm just not ready and I wish they'd respect that. I could handle the learning; I just can't handle them inside my head. Not yet."

"I understand. Just don't do it on your own," said Denser, his hand rubbing her upper arm. "I'm here. We're all here."

She lay back down, her fingers running up and down his chest and stomach. His gut muscles tensed.

"That tickles," he said.

"I know." She carried on. "It's good to have something approaching a proper bed again, isn't it? I bloody hate hammocks."

Denser laughed. "Can't say I got used to them either."

"This feels great though." She raised herself up on her arms again. "Want to put it to some proper use?"

He didn't answer, just dragged her face to his, kissed her deeply on the lips and let the mana cocoon them and their passion sweep them away.

CHAPTER 24

The Raven, led by Rebraal and flanked by the mysterious painted elf and his companion panther, set off toward Aryndeneth as first light began to pierce the morning's heavy cloud cover. Just before dawn, they'd witnessed a deluge harder than any they'd seen before, accompanied by a spectacular lightning storm and splitting reports of thunder.

There was something indefinably powerful about the pair that Ilkar had named ClawBound. They were linked in mind, he'd said, and utterly dependent on each other. The panther had sized up and dismissed The Raven immediately. All bar Thraun. Shapechanger and panther had stared deep into each other's eyes, Thraun crouching to stroke the animal's head, the panther responding by licking his hand and face. An understanding passed between them, that was certain. And when Thraun had stood, Hirad saw the painted elf nod at him. Very slight, but there nonetheless. Thraun showed no emotion bar the slightest of smiles.

Crossing the log bridge, they could see the trench had claimed the lives of many small rodents while the lizards and snakes kept their heads above water while they searched for a way out.

Rebraal led them south, occasionally pausing to look over his shoulder, shake his head and offer prayers to whichever God he thought was listening before slipping away again through the dense forest, leaving almost no mark. The same couldn't be said of The Raven. Rebraal had given Hirad and The Unknown a short, angled chopping blade each and told them in halting and very rusty Balaian that they should only use it when they ran out of room.

Through the morning, the heat grew and Hirad finally understood what Ilkar had meant by the sapping conditions in the forest. Sailing and rowing upriver, they'd been outside the oppressive heat-trapping weight of the canopy and a light breeze had kept conditions tolerable. Now though, only a few hours into their walk, he could see the wisdom of the light leather Ilkar had insisted they buy for armour.

Sweat beaded and ran on his face, it dripped down his back and soaked the backs of his legs. He felt as if he'd dipped his head in a hot stream, and the more he wiped it away the more it came. They were plagued by clouds of flies the magnitude of which they certainly hadn't seen when camping on the way to the village. For a brief moment, Hirad wondered if he shouldn't wear the fine net that covered his hammock at night. Imagining himself dressed in it brought the only smile to his face the whole morning.

Holding aside a draping plant, Hirad looked behind him. Denser and

Erienne walked together, faces set and anxious, eyes darting everywhere, following every noise. But they'd drawn closer again and for that Hirad was grateful, even if the sounds of their lovemaking had kept him awake last night.

Darrick looked miserable, waving incessantly at flies or scratching at his legs and arms, while Aeb betrayed nothing and Thraun, bringing up the rear, was smiling, loving every moment of it. He still hadn't said much but Hirad could see in his eyes that he was coming back to them. And the way he'd formed up in The Raven's line outside the village had set Hirad's heart singing. There was still pain there, though. The pain of the loss of his pack and of his friend Will Begman's death, for which he blamed himself so unfairly.

"Come on, Hirad, keep up," called Ilkar from up ahead.

Hirad turned to see Rebraal, Ren and Ilkar watching him. He held the plant aside until Denser reached it and then strode on, scowling.

"God, I hate patronising elves," he muttered at The Unknown's broad back.

"Just don't let it get to you too much," said The Unknown over his shoulder.

"Too late. Just because they're bloody born to it. I don't have to be here, you know."

"Of course not, Hirad," said The Unknown. "After all, I've never heard you mention how The Raven never works apart."

"Some rules you live to regret, don't you?" he said.

"No, you don't," replied The Unknown. He upped his pace a little, Hirad responding. "What a place."

Rebraal kept up a hard pace all day. The going was difficult and in the afternoon they tired quickly. A brief stop for food after the third rain of the day hadn't brought much respite. Interrupted by having to move smartly away to avoid a foraging mass of inch-long ants, the meal of cold dried meat and bread was as tasteless as it was hard to eat.

Hirad had heard the sounds of water for some time before Rebraal brought them to a stop on the banks of a wide sluggish river. He could see the dirty brown water through the bankside vegetation and could just about make out the opposite bank some hundred yards away. Light was fading fast and he didn't know about anyone else but he was exhausted. Soaked by sweat and rain and with blisters irritating in his boots, he was ready to string up his hammock, confident that nothing would keep him awake once he got his head down.

"Which way?" he asked.

They'd gathered under the branches of a huge tree which soared up into the canopy and leaned out over the river.

Ilkar pointed across the river. "That way."

"How, by boat?"

Ilkar smiled. "No, a bridge."

"Really?" Hirad peered through the leaves and branches again. "Where is it?"

"Hirad, this isn't Korina. You're not going to find a stone arch across the river. You're not even going to find lashed logs. You're looking in the wrong place."

Ilkar tilted his head skyward. "We do things by rope here. That way, people that shouldn't know crossing points don't find them."

Hirad followed his gaze. He could see nothing. "How far up?"

Ilkar asked Rebraal. "About a hundred feet. It's an easy enough climb. Rebraal will show you."

"Wait a moment . . ."

But Rebraal was already climbing. Favouring his right arm, he stormed up the trunk, his agility leaving Hirad open mouthed.

"Hirad, light's fading. We need to get across tonight. The opposite bank is far better for camping."

"Why?"

"Less crocodiles, more space," said Ren. "And Rebraal doesn't want to stop here. This is where Mercuun fell."

Hirad sighed and spread his hands. "Let's do it. Anyone else not looking forward to it?"

"Didn't you ever climb trees as a child?" asked Denser.

"They weren't miles in the sky and full of snakes," said Hirad. "What are you two smiling about?"

Erienne and Denser had the look of people reprieved from execution.

"Tell you what," said Denser. "I'll try and catch you if you fall."

Hirad frowned. "You'll what?"

And then they were casting. So was Ilkar. In moments, all had Shadow Wings at their backs.

"Bastards."

Erienne laughed, her fear of the forest forgotten for a moment. "One clear patch of bank is all we need. You should learn a bit of magic, Hirad."

"I should choose new friends." Hirad shook his head. "You'd better have a good fire going by the time I get across. Make yourselves at least a little useful."

"What, and miss the chance to see you wobbling on the rope bridge?" said Ilkar.

Hirad ignored him, turning instead to The Unknown. "Who's first?"

"Don't be an idiot," said The Unknown. "Denser, Ilkar. Carry us. Let's show your brother we aren't so helpless."

Hirad smiled. "Great idea."

"It was always the plan," said Ilkar. "And so was winding you up."

Hirad laughed as he was lifted from the ground, arms locked around Ilkar's waist.

"What is it?" asked Ilkar

"Thraun," said Hirad. "Just look at him." The shapechanger was scurrying up the tree, his agility a match for Rebraal's. "Your brother's got a lot to learn about us."

Yron was woken by distant thunder and opened his eyes on a day kept dim by heavy cloud. He could see a swathe of blue over to the north but didn't hold out any hope of avoiding a soaking before the break arrived. Not that it would make much difference, given his plan for the morning.

As if to prove him right the heavens opened, drowning out the dawn chorus he had come to expect and now didn't disturb him at all. He shook Ben-Foran, the youngster coming to wakefulness with a start and groaning as he stretched his limbs and back, stiff after an uncomfortable night on the rock. He eyed Yron with a scowl but managed to force a smile onto his face as he stood up.

"What's for breakfast?" he asked.

Yron patted him on the shoulder. "You know the rules of my army. Exercise before nourishment."

"Why am I not surprised, Captain?" said Ben. He got to his feet and stretched again, arms high and back arched. "Which way are we walking, then?"

"Same direction as yesterday. But there's nothing better than a healthy swim first thing, I always say. What say we race to the other side?"

Ben looked at him in total disbelief. "You are joking, I hope, sir?"

Yron shook his head. "Got to put something more impressive between us and them than distance, if we're going to survive this."

"Captain, if I may make a couple of points that may have slipped your mind," said Ben, face pale in the falling rain. "First, I'm scared in open water, and second, when we hit this calm stretch, you said we had to get out quickly to avoid crocodile attack. And now you're suggesting we jump back in? Are you really sure?"

"If we don't, they'll track us down and kill us before we get to the ships, unless we are incredibly lucky."

"And if we do, we're breakfast for crocodiles."

"Not necessarily," said Yron. "It's all a question of timing and appearance."

Ben shifted and frowned. "You're really scared of these elves aren't you?"

"More scared than I am of a crocodile or a piranha shoal," said Yron.

"How can they be so good?"

"When we get across to the other side, I'll tell you," said Yron. "It's time you knew what we're up against."

"What about the others, then?" asked Ben, jerking a thumb back into the forest.

Yron smiled. This boy would go far if he survived. About to risk his life in the water, he still had enough wit to be worried about the other men.

"They had a good head start," said Yron. "They have a chance."

"Really, Captain?"

"Don't stop believing," said Yron, though inside he had very little hope left, none for the groups travelling without mages. "Come on, let's find ourselves a float and a place to cross."

Yron led the way back down the short climb, dropping the last couple of feet to stand ankle deep in the water. He cast an eye over the river, looking for telltale ripples or the eyes of a crocodile just above the surface. Ben was descending slowly, favouring his left leg. He looked clumsy.

"You all right, Ben?"

"Yes, sir."

"What's wrong with the leg?"

"Just a little stiff I think. I must have lain on it bent or something."

"Right," said Yron. He looked closely, watching as Ben jumped into the water by him, landing on his left leg only. "Are you sure?"

"It's fine, really."

"Right," said Yron again. "Stay here, watch the opposite bank. Count the crocodiles on the mud and tell me if any take to the water before I get back with the flotsam. Think you can do that?"

"Yes, sir."

Yron hurried back upstream to the pocket of still water they'd finished their river journey in. The log was still there and Yron greeted it like an old friend. He edged it from its lodging place and shepherded it downstream much as the day before, smiling as Ben came into sight. The young lieutenant was staring across the river sixty yards to the mud slope where four or five of the big reptiles lay.

Yron knew they couldn't see them from that distance but they'd sense vague movement and see clearly from about halfway across.

"Anything happen?" he asked.

"Nothing at all. They haven't moved a muscle."

"Glad to hear it. Right, follow me. And tread lightly; anything in the river will be able to sense movement, so take slow easy paces, all right?"

Ben nodded and Yron set off, keeping the log slightly ahead of him and brushing the rock face. His nerves began to tingle. Here there was no quick escape. Here they were vulnerable. But he really had no choice. Crocodiles were predictable to a point. TaiGethen were infinitely more dangerous.

There was no movement from the opposite bank. He didn't necessarily expect any. Of course they wouldn't all be resting, but it was early yet and reptiles that size would be sluggish until they warmed up. It was imperative they get across at the earliest opportunity.

About two hundred yards further downstream, the river took a bend to the left and narrowed to forty or fifty yards. The bank just before the bend was grass covered and sloped sharply upward but would be easy to scramble up in a hurry if necessary. The distance was as good as they were liable to get but the negative was that the river flowed that bit quicker here. It would take a lot of effort and noise to ensure they landed before drifting past the bank and into the next cliff-sided stretch.

"You ready for this?" asked Yron.

"I'll never be ready for it," said Ben. "So I'm just going to do it."

"Good lad. We're headed there." Yron pointed downstream. "Anywhere along that stretch and we can get out quick. Now here's what we're going to do. Like yesterday, we're going to push gently out into the stream and swim up a little way against the current. Once we're across the middle of the river, I want you to stay quite still. Be part of the log. If you're inert, you won't attract attention. We'll drift down a way before pushing for the bank. When we do, don't thrash, for God's sake. Do you understand?"

Ben-Foran nodded. "Sir."

Gently, Yron pushed the log out and entered the water after it, hearing Ben do the same despite his care. With long slow sweeps of his legs, Yron moved them out from the bank, heading toward the crocodiles. It was uncomfortable but necessary. Fortunately the current was slow and they reached the middle of the river quickly. There they turned and began to drift downstream.

"Now's the time, Ben," he said, voice quiet. "Try not to move at all. Search the surface. Tell me what you see. Breathe slow."

The rain had stopped and the cloud was breaking up quickly, for which Yron was not grateful. Heavy rain upset natural senses, cloud kept cold blood that way. Conditions were changing fast but out here peace was total. The water was cool beneath the immediate surface, and the sounds of the myriad rain forest creatures muted somehow. He forced himself to relax, to listen and to watch.

Beside him Ben was admirably silent, his eyes forward. Yron turned his head. Nothing he could see. The mudbank remained still. It was exactly as he had prayed.

Ben jerked back, his leg twitching. "Dammit!"

"What was it?" Yron, tense all over again, looked immediately behind them.

"Nothing, I . . . ow!" Ben slapped the water with a hand. "Something bit me."

Yron went cold all over. They were twenty-five yards from the bank. It could prove a very long way. Something bumped into his boot. He felt another impact on his leather. He knew this behaviour. This was the vanguard of an invasion. The army would not be far behind and they were unstoppable. Piranha.

"Swim, Ben!" he shouted, thrashing his legs to action, driving them across the river. "Pump those legs and don't you fucking stop! Swim!"

He knew it gave out distress signals but they had no option. The fish had scented blood from somewhere and he and Ben were the targets. As he swept his legs through the water, bringing the log around to steer them straight for the bank, he saw the mudbank was empty. The crocodiles were already in the water, heading downstream. Their thrashing had been like a call to feeding time and none wanted to miss out. They had a start of a hundred and fifty yards or so. It was going to be very close.

Ben was under concerted attack. His heaving legs made purchase difficult but piranha were quick and their jaws awesomely strong. He cried out again and again as they bit clean through cloth and into his flesh, every bite pumping more blood into the water, attracting more of the voracious killers.

From their left, the crocodiles closed in, strong tails powering them through the water faster than any man could hope to swim. The bank was nearing, moment by moment. Yron felt a sharp bite on his ankle through the leather of his boot. He thrashed his legs harder.

Ben moaned.

"Keep going, son, almost there," urged Yron. "You can do it. Don't you give up on me, lad."

"No . . . intention," gasped Ben, but he was weakening quickly.

"So much more to teach you, Ben. Don't let go now, don't let go."

Yron's legs struck the bottom. Reacting instantly, he plunged his feet to the bed of the river and stood upright, dragging Ben with him. He forced his way through the stomach-deep water, feeling the press of the fish around him, their incessant probing, feeling the brush of teeth and the tearing of cloth.

With Ben practically under one arm and barely able to stand, he scrambled up the mud at the edge of the river and pushed Ben ahead of him, the boy stumbling through the shallows and falling forward onto the grass. His right leg was a bloody mess, his trousers shredded; one of his boots hung by its laces and his jerkin was ripped and torn around the waist.

"Don't stop, Ben." He heaved in a breath. "Not safe."

Ben tried to get to his feet, made it to a crawling position and dragged himself up the slope of the bank. Behind Yron the water boiled. A crocodile erupted from the river, hammering at them with extraordinary speed. Yron slipped on the bank, fell onto his backside and pushed himself backward, his back against Ben's floundering body.

The crocodile came on, head still, running at its intended prey. Behind it, others fought each other in the shallows but it ignored them. Its jaws snapped once, missing Yron's foot by a hair. The captain lashed out with his boot, catching it across the snout. It hesitated then came on. He kicked again, another good contact. The crocodile stopped and hissed.

"Ben, go!" he yelled. "Go!"

Below him, the huge reptile shook its head from side to side, gave Yron one last malevolent look and retreated into the water. He looked down on it from the top of the bank, stood and dragged Ben further into the forest and under cover. He laid the boy down and stared at his wounds.

"Damn you, boy," he said, though his tone carried no anger. "You were cut, weren't you?"

Ben nodded feebly then slumped back to lie prostrate. He was a mess. Ignoring the scratches and bites on his own body, Yron assessed his charge. Blood poured from Ben's ravaged right leg, and oozed from more other places than he could count. Flesh had been ripped from bones, which showed through where the piranhas had got to work. Back home the leg would have been amputated; here it had to be patched up.

One thing was clear. If Yron didn't bathe and dress the wounds with the right herbs, the boy was going to die.

Auum led his Tai along the banks of the River Shorth, his frustration growing. These men he'd ignored near the temple had proved to be difficult prey, and within his frustration there was a sense of grudging respect. A respect, though, that didn't lessen the outrage at the crime for which the strangers would pay.

They had followed the easy trail north and then east to the banks of the river. Footsteps had dragged down to the shore and there the trail had gone cold. It was clear they had gone downriver but how far was currently not known. Duele had found a disturbed pile of driftwood just upstream and it was then that Auum had to confess his surprise. The tributary was quick, with rocks not far under the surface. Even with driftwood to cling to, the chances of injury were very high, and where the flow eased, the predators massed.

They moved on at speed, never more than five yards apart in a line that gave them a view across the river and deep into the forest eastward.

"Thoughts," he asked of them.

"The ClawBound has sensed nothing of them north to Shorth's Teeth rapids," said Duele. "I suggest they are back on land upstream of the rapids, possibly on the opposite bank."

"They moved quickly to the river yesterday," said Evunn. "They have direction and they are unharmed. They may have reversed, leaving a false trail."

It had to be considered, but Auum dismissed it. "Not that good," he said. "But quick, yes. I suspect one of them knows of us."

"So he would take great risk to escape," said Duele.

"Speed is nothing without guile. We will always be faster," countered Evunn.

"To a stranger, distance is safety. They chase the goal of escape," said Auum. "We should alert the ClawBound west of the river. These strangers must not escape."

A roar lifted above the buzz of the forest. It was echoed at greater distance. The Tai stopped, waited. It was communication. A series of calls circled out, some elven, some animal. Growls, whistles, wails, grunts and barks. Auum understood none of it. Despite the closeness of their alliance, the ClawBound never revealed any of their secrets. The TaiGethen would know what was relevant soon enough.

The discordant messaging went on, silencing the forest denizens. This was noise at odds, noise that meant trouble and the determination to find a cure. None of Tual's creatures would interfere. Most would be scared by what they heard; an instinctive memory cowed them where they stood, caused them to land on the nearest perch or hold themselves still in the water or high in the canopy.

The moment it died away, the forest buzzed once more and a ClawBound pair emerged from the shadows to Auum's left. The panther trotted in and stood in Auum's path, its eyes glistening, asking him to stop.

"Tai," said Auum and they came to him.

The ClawBound elf, very tall, his face impassive beneath his paint, bowed his head and spoke, the voice unused to speech.

"We have one group. Two trails are new. The fourth is west. The fifth group has crossed the Shorth. They are hurt. We will follow."

He turned to go. Auum's question stopped him.

"Where are they running to?"

"Verendii Tual," said the ClawBound. "Many strangers wait. We watch."

He turned and walked away into the forest, the panther sniffing the Tai's scent on the air before growling low and trotting after him.

"Verendii Tual," said Auum. "We haven't much time. The ClawBound will not lose them as I did. We'll wait for them at the estuary."

His Tai knew better than to question him and they followed him away from the tributary, which would soon carve away west to join the Shorth, the combined river flowing on to its mouth at Verendii Tual, the staggering high-cliffed inlet that bit deep into the forest.

All the groups were tracked and one would be down by dawn tomorrow. The net was closing.

CHAPTER 25

Just before dawn, Erys had woken experiencing a dread fear. Barely a day and a half out from the temple and the calming influence of Captain Yron and, while the group weren't lost, their minds were full of the terrors of the forest and their thinking wasn't straight. He'd tried to bring them back to themselves time and again in their ill-disciplined march toward the coast. He'd reminded them that Yron had trusted them to escape and had bought them time by sacrificing his own life.

And it had worked, brought them all back to what they had sworn to do. For an hour, maybe. Time was so difficult to judge. And then the bickering had started again. The backbiting and the fights about who was to lead. Erys had kept out of it. Let the egos of the other three battle it out. He gave up trying to reason with them and consoled himself by reflecting that it was he who carried the vital cargo. When it came to it, only he had to survive. Everyone else was expendable. He hoped they all went to hell.

It had been the previous dawn that they realised they were being followed. Tracked. There was nothing they could point to. No evidence. But it was there all the same, the indefinable feeling that they were being watched. Perhaps it was a change in the quality of a shadow; perhaps a branch cracked at a quiet moment in the din that was the forest day, or maybe the call of a bird didn't ring true. Whatever it was, it had destroyed any semblance of order and the day had been little more than a blind rush north.

Heedless of where they had run, they had suffered cut, bruise and sprain. Only Erys, who had seen their charge for what it was, had kept a reasonable pace, kept up with them easily and so avoided injury. The Gods only knew how they had escaped broken bones or snakebite. And worse than it all had been the unearthly chorus of growls, barks, grunts and calls that had echoed from all around them, dimming the rest of the forest din for what seemed like an age. None of them had spoken of it, too scared at what it represented to give voice.

The night had been unbearably tense, but despite the determination of everyone to stay awake because they didn't trust each other, Erys had slumped into an exhausted sleep. But now he was awake and his heart was thundering in his chest. He tried to quiet his breathing, lay completely silent in his hammock and listened. He turned his head slowly from side to side and in the thin light he could see one of the soldiers lying asleep. From where he was, Erys couldn't see the other two. He couldn't hear anything out of the ordinary.

But something had woken him. He was sure it hadn't been a dream. Erys shuffled out of his hammock, slipping on the wet ground under his feet. A quick look round and he shuddered. There was no one on duty. An eerie quality lay over the camp. Walking quickly toward the nearest of his colleagues, Erys genuinely didn't know if any of them was still alive, such was his feeling of impending dread.

He shook the soldier's shoulder and was rewarded with a grunt. He shook it again.

"Wake up," he hissed. "Can't you feel it?"

"What?" muttered the soldier, a surly young individual called Awin.

"Just get ready. We've got to go now," said Erys.

He hurried across the camp and woke the other pair, whose hammocks were strung close together. Once he'd got them moving, he ran back to his own bed and began to unstring it, his eyes flicking into the forest as the watery light grew in strength. He stuffed the hammock into his pack, checked the wrapped parchments were secure and slung the bag over his shoulder.

Straightening, he met Awin's eyes.

"What's got into you?" asked the soldier. "There's nothing anywhere near. I—"

He stopped and looked past Erys's shoulder. The mage swung round and saw it too. A shadow flitting across his vision, fast and low. Erys backed off.

"Get behind me," said Awin, drawing his sword from his scabbard. "Trouble, you two, look lively. To your left. Get a shield up, Erys."

The other two scrambled to shrug on leather armour and grab swords but Erys didn't even begin to form the shape for a HardShield. He could see more figures moving. Upright this time. Like darker patches of shade and moving impossibly fast in the dense, overhanging, choking growth. He kept on backing away, his ears roaring with the clamour of his fear, praying that none of the shades were behind him. He'd have turned to look but he didn't really want to know.

Awin was crouched low, snapping out what he could see as he scanned the dark depths. The others were circling round slowly, swords and daggers drawn, armour untied and flapping. Erys saw the shadows move. He heard a growl. Something black, sleek, low and full of muscle flowed from the forest. It slammed into one of the soldiers whose name escaped him in the muddle of his mind. The scream was inhuman.

Awin and the other soldier ran in opposite directions, the latter stopping suddenly as the forest moved in front of him. Steel glinted and his head snapped back, blood misting into the dawn. Awin saw him go down and ran back.

"The shield, Erys, now!"

Erys desperately tried to clamp onto some concentration. He knew what he had to do. The shape was simple but its edges kept getting away from him and he had to lose himself before he could save himself. The shape formed. He dragged it together, blotting out Awin's panicked shouts and the sounds of the sleek shadow ripping the life from a man he'd heard laughing the night before. He cast as Awin turned a despairing face to him. CloakedWalk.

He stepped back and knew by Awin's expression that he'd disappeared.

"Bastard!" yelled the soldier. "Coward!"

He was almost crying; he knew his death was imminent. Erys edged further away. Awin turned at more sounds, a whimper escaping his lips. The black cat was gone, returned to the shadows. And from the forest they came.

Three of them, moving smoothly into the campsite. Tall, lean and with faces painted black, green and brown. Two carried short slim blades, the third had a hand in a pouch at his belt. Erys tried to contain his breathing and the urge to run. He heard movement and the black cat, the size of a war dog, stopped beside him. It sniffed the air, knowing something was amiss but seeing nothing with its keen eyes. It moved on, a low growl in its throat. And after it came another elf. White and black halved face, the stark contrast in the dark was terrifying, like the half-face was floating, ghostly. He too looked square at the delicately retreating Erys but didn't stop.

Poor Awin was surrounded. He straightened now and dropped his sword. He held up his hands.

"Please," he begged. "I surrender."

But they said nothing, just carried on advancing. Two came to his sides and grabbed an arm each. The third stepped up, pushed Awin's chin up with one hand and drove his blade through the man's neck with the other. The cat roared, the black and white elf exulted.

It was all Erys could do to stop himself crying out. He put his hands behind him, feeling his way. They found the trunk of a tree. Erys carried on, edging himself around it. His foot came down on a twig which snapped with a report like thunder in his ears. Elves and animal looked toward him. Awin's body dropped to the ground and he died ignored.

Erys fought the urge to stop moving, to become even more silent. He saw them speaking to each other. They couldn't see him. One of them came toward him, his eyes piercing green, catching the first shafts of sunlight. Erys kept on taking his gentle steps. He wanted to turn and run but was fearful of letting them out of his sight.

The elf came on but he was shaking his head. He said something then turned and rejoined the others. Another brief conversation and the cat and the spectral elf ran off to the north. The three others bent immediately to their task, and as Erys watched and the forest slowly obscured his view, packs were torn apart and bodies were searched. Erys's last memory was of the elves systematically shredding every item of kit and clothing.

Wanting nothing more than to find a place to hide, Erys clung onto the CloakedWalk, turned and walked forward at last, hoping to find the river to follow all the way to the coast.

Yron had done everything he could. Dragging Ben-Foran into the obscurity of the forest, he'd laid him down on a clear patch of ground and used his soaking leather jerkin as a pillow of sorts. He'd lit a fire using rubbed bamboo and fashioned a rough tripod from damp wood. They both still carried the mugs they'd run from the temple with; Yron had forbidden Ben to discard his, knowing they might prove vital. He'd filled both from the river and balanced them on the tripod.

Taking off his shirt, he'd cut it into strips and put them in the water to boil. Finally, hoping no predators were attracted to Ben's bloodied body, he made a quick hunt for legumia bark, rubiac fruit and vismia stems. He found none of the latter. He could have done with its antiseptic qualities and reminded himself to keep looking, assuming Ben survived.

The youngster was conscious when he returned and incredibly was struggling to sit up.

"Lie back, boy," said Yron. "Best you don't look."

"It's bloody agony," said Ben.

"I know. I got the odd nip myself." It was an understatement. Though the piranha had concentrated their attack on Ben's legs, the Captain had been the victim of more snaps than he could count. Most were little more than exploratory attacks but enough were full-blooded bites to cause him serious pain. He mustn't forget to treat himself. Ben would not be served by his own death.

Yron dropped the bark into the mugs and waited as it bubbled and spat.

"You'll be fine, Ben," he said. "You've broken nothing. It hurts like hell but I can numb the pain later. For now I have to clean it. That'll sting but you'll know it's doing the job, right?"

The commentary was as much for Yron as it was for his frightened lieutenant. Yron stared up at the sky, seeing the smoke trailing up into the canopy. The cloud had disappeared and strong light was shining down, bringing with it humidity and heat. He was aware they'd have to try and move soon. The smoke, while keeping away the flies, was a beacon for any watching TaiGethen and their silent ClawBound brethren.

When he'd waited as long as he could, Yron took the mugs from the tripod and placed them by Ben. He cut the remnants of Ben's trouser legs

away, took a deep breath at what he saw and gave the stricken man a reassuring smile.

"It's not so bad," he said.

"Liar," replied Ben. "Sir."

Yron hooked a piece of cloth from a mug with a stick, let it cool a little
in the air, then dropped it into his hands where he balled it up.

"Try not to cry out," he said gently. "I have to do this."

He began to clean the right leg, beginning at the foot. At the first touch
of the infused cloth, Ben tensed and bit down on a scream. Yron pressed on;
he really had no choice.

He had no real idea how long he worked. Meticulous and tireless for hour
after hour, he cleaned each wound separately, biting his lip as he looked at the
torn flesh, the flaps of skin and the deep bite wounds. The right leg was torn
to bits. Bone and muscle were exposed and he covered what he could with the
makeshift bandages. Perhaps magic could save it but they were far from such
help and Ben's survival chances were already low.

The left leg was better but his buttocks had both taken bites as had hips
and lower stomach. Yron cleaned and bandaged, refilled the mugs again and
again, kept the fire going and, finally, made rubiac poultices for himself to try
and combat any infection.

Finally, he dressed Ben in the remains of his trousers, helped him back
into his leather armour, having used his shirt for bandages too, and sat him
up. Ben-Foran was shivering in the heat as the shock of the attack began to
set in. It was after midday.

"We can't stay here, Ben," Yron said, keeping his face close to the boy's,
forcing him to focus. "We don't have to go far but we do have to go. Now I
want you to prepare yourself, all right? Think strength, and know I'll be supporting you. We can still make it."

"If you say so, sir," said Ben. His face was pale and sheened in sweat.

Yron smiled as best he could. If the infection didn't get him, the blood
loss or the shock just might. He turned from Ben to the fire, noting how the
blood was already soaking through the boy's bandages, and put out the blaze,
trying to minimise the smoke as he did so. Ordinarily he'd have hidden the
site, the embers and the remnants of the tripod to put off any pursuit, but
with the TaiGethen it was pointless. Even without the fire these elves would
have enough signs to track them easily.

Yron put his leather jerkin back on and stooped over Ben. "Come on,
son. One arm around my shoulder, let's get out of here."

Gasping in pain, Ben hauled himself up Yron's body. He leant heavily
against the captain, not daring to put his right foot on the ground.

"You should leave me, sir," he said. "You could make it on your own."

"To what purpose?" said Yron as they moved slowly off, Ben in a half hop, half drag, wincing at every movement. "My duty is to my men. You represent my men."

"But—"

"Decision's made, Ben. Let me assure you, if I was carrying anything important I'd have left you. But I'm not. So shut up and save your energy for shambling."

Through his pain Ben-Foran chuckled. "Thank you, sir."

"No problem."

CHAPTER 26

The east gates of Xetesk opened on a mild cloud-strewn morning. Three hundred cavalry and mages trotted from the portal, followed by fifteen hundred foot soldiers and dozens of wagons.

At the front of the column, riding with the Xeteskian commander, Chandyr, was Rusau, senior mage and member of the Lysternan delegation. He looked with dismay on the litter of bodies and rags that covered what had once been the refugee camp, now brutally cleared. Carrion birds took to the sky as the horses passed, clouds of flies buzzed angrily over the flesh left to rot and the air was tainted with decay.

"Look at what you have wrought, Commander Chandyr," he said as they rode past. "They were human beings and you have driven them away like animals. You killed so many."

Chandyr looked across at him, no hint of remorse evident. He was a career soldier in his early forties and had seen a great deal of action in the last decade. His face was pockmarked and he sported livid scars on his chin and forehead. Clad in mail-covered leather, he was a ferocious sight and his views were simple.

"First they were victims, now they are parasites. We have to look to our own problems, not take on other people's. Dordover is a powerful adversary."

"But you could have chosen to help these people cut wood for new homes, plough fields for new plantings. Your blacksmiths' wagons could have been the forges that made new hope."

"Building is preferable to dying in battle," said Chandyr, "but we have to defend ourselves before we can disperse ourselves across Balaia helping the people. Have you travelled the country in the last season?"

"No," confessed Rusau. "My duties kept me in Lystern."

"You should talk to the mages who come in. It is true that the Black Wings are feeding the flames of hatred for us but the country is not quite as destroyed as they would have us all believe. There are blacksmiths out there. There are woodmen too. There are builders and farmers. The regeneration of the country must come from within. We as a college army are duty bound to protect our borders."

"But this is a fight that can be solved around a table. By reason and discussion. War only feeds the fires of hate. And, after all, the issues are trivial, aren't they?"

"The issues do not concern me. The protection of Xetesk does."

Rusau took a breath. In front of them, the gentle sweep of the Xeteskian mage lands stretched northeast to Lystern and north to Dordover. It was undeniably beautiful. Shades of green dappled the landscape; trees, shrubs, brackens and grasses. And everywhere were splashes of colour as the first spring flowers pushed through the soil, a symbol of the enduring strength of nature.

"I can stop this," said Rusau, and inside he firmly believed that he could.

"Really?" asked Chandyr. "Like the Dordovan delegation, perhaps? What have they managed so far apart from outrageous demands that do nothing but lighten the mood in the officers' mess?"

"It is the nature of negotiation to begin at an unattainable level and settle for compromise."

"Compromise!" Chandyr spat the word. "We are defending ourselves from unwarranted aggression."

"And Xetesk is blameless in your view?"

Chandyr's face darkened. "You ride at my side because I like you, Rusau. And because my Lord of the Mount, Dystran, wants independent reporting of what we find. But we are not the aggressors. We did not invite this conflict, it was thrust upon us. It is not our forces herding refugees into neighbouring lands. It is not us using innocents as pawns. But we will not stand by and watch it happen. Dordover will not be allowed to encroach on our lands. We will fight to preserve what is ours."

"I meant no offence, Commander," said Rusau. "But when we find the Dordovans I urge you to stand off and let me speak, whether they are on Xeteskian land or not. Words are one thing, significant loss of life is another. When they see you and hear me, they will think again."

"You are naive to believe that," said Chandyr. "But I pray you are right. Remember, though, that soldiers go where they are ordered and fight as directed. It is accepted that not all those who enter battle will leave it alive. I don't think you will find anyone in the Dordovan force able to make the decision to stand down."

"Perhaps not, but would you choose not to fight if I could negotiate a truce to allow the rulers to speak again?"

"I will assess the situation when we encounter the Dordovans," said Chandyr. "But we are at war, Rusau, and I will not take any decision that risks our borders."

"But I must be allowed to cross the battle lines," said Rusau.

"Enough," snapped Chandyr. "I go to defend my lands. And I will take such action as I see fit in discussion with the senior mage. If you get in the way of such action it will be on your own head. I trust you understand. Now I must think. Please fall back to the centre of the column."

He looked at Rusau, and for the first time the Lysternan mage felt a pang of doubt.

"Now, Rusau. I don't want to have you removed."

Rusau did as he was ordered, and for the rest of the day's march and the day following he kept his distance from the Xeteskian commander. Late in the afternoon of the second day, with light cloud covering what had been a warm spring day, he was summoned forward.

He found Chandyr in conversation with the senior mage, Synour, a man fast rising through the echelons of Xeteskian power. They were riding toward the crest of a low hill and Rusau knew that beyond it a shallow valley swept away to the River Dord, which flowed through Dordover and eventually let out into the River Tri just to the north of Triverne Lake. The Dord marked the northern border of the Xeteskian and Lysternan mage lands.

"Commander," he said, as he rode to Chandyr's free side.

Chandyr acknowledged his presence but finished his conversation before turning in his saddle.

"My scouts have reported," he said, voice matter of fact, "a force of perhaps eighteen hundred Dordovans setting up camp just north of the river. There are an estimated five hundred refugees there too. They are corralled by the Dordovans but are south of the river. On Xeteskian land. You will see that they have been very careful to allow no one to occupy Lysternan land. I think their message is quite clear."

"And what are your intentions?" asked Rusau.

"The refugees must be freed immediately to return to rebuild their homes. The Dordovans must not stand in their way. I am sending a message to that effect to their commander, whoever he may be. You are welcome to ride under the parley flag but you will not interfere with the delivery of the message. We are not negotiating this point. Those refugees will not be used against us."

"I will see what I can do," said Rusau.

"Try not to endanger your own life," said Chandyr. "I am not responsible for you and neither are the Dordovans. My messenger will return with their answer as soon as he is able. If that answer is negative, we will advance immediately, while there is daylight enough."

"Commander, you have to give me a chance," implored Rusau

"No, Rusau, I do not," he said. "I sympathise with you but my orders are quite clear. Dordover has invaded us. I will repel that invasion. The time for talking is when they are north of the Dord. I suggest you work quickly or get yourself to a place of safety."

Rusau nodded. "I had hoped for more understanding from you. Where is your messenger?"

"He is being briefed by the sergeant at arms now. You'll find them to your right." Chandyr indicated a pair of riders slightly apart from the rest of the column. "And Rusau, I understand very well. We didn't ask for war but we will wage it. Perhaps you can talk sense into the Dordovans, but if you ask me, the time for talking is done."

Rusau joined the messenger as he cantered up the the rise and over the crest into the valley. Below them a wide grassy plain fell away down a shallow slope to the banks of the River Dord a mile and a half away. A mass of humanity waited on the south side. "Corralled" was the right word. They were in a tight group, Dordovan cavalry and foot soldiers guarding them. To the north of the river, tents were pitched, fires burned and pennants flew. The sound of hammering and the whinnies of horses filtered up to them as they rode in silence toward the Dordovan army.

As they passed the refugees, a Dordovan cavalryman detached himself from the guard and fell in beside them.

"You're wasting your time, Xeteskian," he said to the messenger. "You should have saved your horse's legs and your breath. While you still have it to waste, that is."

"What is the name of your commanding officer? I have a message for him."

The cavalryman laughed. "Very disciplined, I'm sure. Turn around. Mark my words, boy."

"His name," said the messenger.

"Master Mage Tendjorn," said the cavalryman. "He'll eat you for breakfast."

He peeled away and rode back to his companions. They shared an over-loud laugh.

"Commendable," said Rusau to his companion.

The messenger didn't reply. He kept his pace even, riding through the shallow waters of the Dord which, though thirty yards wide at this stretch, barely reached his boots. Unchallenged, they rode to the centre of the camp, where they dismounted. The command tent was obvious, its sides pinned back. A table inside was bare but for a scattering of goblets and a few bottles. Five men stood inside and waited for them to enter.

"You took your time," said one. Rusau supposed him to be Tendjorn. He was an ugly man with a wide nose, small ears and thinning unkempt dark hair. "And you? Sent a Lysternan lackey to beg, have they? We've enough of your sort plaguing us already."

"I am Rusau of Lystern," he confirmed. "I seek peace, as I believe ulti-mately we all do."

"Well there's your first mistaken assumption," said Tendjorn. "Xetesk's protection of the Nightchild was the first act of aggression in this war and now we are delivering the consequences of their invasion to their door for them to deal with."

"These people are not consequences of this dispute," said Rusau. "You cannot use them as such."

"Can't I? Xetesk prevented us from dealing with the Nightchild at the earliest opportunity. They were complicit in her prolonged survival, hence the prolonged elemental attacks on Balaia. Therefore these refugees are their problem."

"Your memories are coloured," began Rusau, but Tendjorn cut him off with a snap of his fingers.

"Your message, Xeteskian," he said.

The messenger pulled a leather envelope from his breast and handed it over.

"I would take your reply at your earliest convenience, my Lord," he said.

Tendjorn untied the envelope and took out the single sheet of paper it contained. It was a brief message, and the mage smiled and shook his head as he read it.

"Gracious me, how predictable," he muttered, and handed it to the quartet of soldiers and mages grouped behind him. He slapped the empty envelope into the chest of the messenger. "Tell your commander that we will not withdraw until he agrees to take charge of the people whom his college has made homeless. Tell him that any move to force them across the river will be met with an appropriate response."

"Yes, my Lord." The messenger bowed, his face expressionless.

Rusau grabbed his shoulder. "Wait a moment. You can't deliver that. This is madness. Tendjorn, I beg you to reconsider."

"You must remove your hand, sir," said the messenger. "You may not impede a messenger under the parley flag."

"I know but . . ." He removed his hand and immediately the messenger turned and walked from the tent. "Think what your message means. Men will die."

"Quiet your bleating, Rusau, and face reality," said Tendjorn. "This conflict is about far more than just Herendeneth. It concerns balance. Something Xetesk is determined to upset."

"All it takes is for you to withdraw your forces and let the refugees move to their homes to rebuild their lives. It will give us a basis for negotiation. Please, Tendjorn. Someone has to make a gesture for peace to have a chance."

Tendjorn walked the pace to Rusau and looked square into his face, holding his gaze.

"There is but one way to stop this and that is for Lystern to stop dithering and join us. Isn't it obvious to you? Xetesk always wanted war; we have merely upset their timing. Without you, they may well beat us. With you, they may well not.

"Heryst is cautious. But what price that when Xetesk marches up to his gates, eh? You have done your best, Lysternan, you and your negotiators. Has Xetesk listened to you? Join us now. We don't want to destroy Xetesk, we need them in balance. They want to dominate, don't you understand?"

"I understand that war will leave all of magic seriously weakened and will draw in the population who surely have suffered enough. More innocents will die in this conflict and hatred will grow. Do not assume nonmages are too weak to fight. Look at what the Wesmen did to Julatsa."

"Yes, Rusau," growled Tendjorn. "And look what that has done to the balance of magic. Even now we are protecting Julatsa from the inevitable Xeteskian invasion. Where are Lystern, their supposed friends, eh? Xetesk cannot be allowed to win."

"Heryst is on his way to discuss that very matter with Vuldaroq, have you not been informed? Wait for them to reach accord. Must you fight today?" Rusau was exasperated in the face of such closed-minded determination to let blood.

"Gods, man, are you blind?" shouted Tendjorn. He strode away a pace and threw up his arms. "You've been in Xetesk; surely you've seen?"

"Seen what?"

"I don't believe it," said Tendjorn. "They are arming and armouring every man of fighting age in the city. Every man. They are drilling women and children in battlefield supply. Their forges work day and night. They mean to win this war and they will not hear peace. And whether you believe it or not, the information they will get from Herendeneth will merely make them stronger. Now out of my way; I have a battle to organise."

Rusau ran from the tent and jumped back on his horse. He fought his way through the army coming to order. Shouts were ringing through the camp, horses were being saddled and mounted, weapons given a final taste of the whetstone. Mages planned offence and defence. He was ignored as he surged across the river. To his right the refugees were being moved away from the likely battlefield. He could hear their fear now. Ahead of him the messenger was galloping hard up the slope. As he went, he waved his parley flag and then angled it vertically down.

"Damn it," said Rusau.

A line of Xeteskians breasted the hill to stand silhouetted on the horizon.

Avesh stood with his arms around Ellin while she wept. It had been so since he reached her at the Dord and they had buried their son together. She had refused any sustenance, drinking only water from the river. He could understand. Her son lay dead and she couldn't even escape to grieve because the Dordovans had blocked their progress. Not just across the Dord but anywhere. They had provided food and spoken gentle words but there was no doubting the hundreds here were prisoners to be used against Xetesk. How, he didn't know and was scared to guess.

All he wanted to do was take her away. Somewhere where he knew she would be safe so that he could do what he had to do. Strike back. But right now he was helpless. Caught between two colleges, neither of whom cared whether he lived or died.

He had watched the two riders gallop over the rise to the south and cross to the Dordovan camp. He had watched them ride back separately, the one with the flag in advance of the other. And then he had watched the line of soldiers and horsemen appear, ready to charge. He shivered and cursed under his breath, not even having the strength to be scared like so many of those around him. He now had so little to lose.

He hugged Ellin tighter, kissing her on the top of her head.

"Be strong, my love," he said. "And listen to me. We are going to have to run once more."

CHAPTER 27

Chandyr had been organising his men from the moment Rusau and the messenger had disappeared over the crest. He'd split his cavalry into two wings, leaving his foot soldiers to take the central ground. Mages were dispersed along the line, providing offensive and defensive cover. Chandyr's aim was simple. His men would not put one foot in the waters of the Dord, that was not their brief. But they would push every enemy across those waters.

He called his forces to order. Flags waved their readiness from the left flank cavalry. He would lead the right.

"Archers ready?" he called.

"Aye!" came the shout.

"Soldiers ready?"

"Aye!"

"Engage only armed men, shoot at armed men only. I want as little refugee blood on my hands as possible. No one is to walk on Dordovan land. We are not mounting an invasion. Not yet. Lieutenants, sound the march."

Orders were barked along the line, which stretched for about a third of a mile. Chandyr trotted back to his cavalry. It would be a classic pincer if he could close it but he expected the Dordovans to be aware of the tactic. If not, he had movement orders waiting and his command team had been fully briefed, orders ready to be passed down to all levels of the army. Chandyr had studied Ry Darrick for a time and had learned a few truths about effective battle. He wondered if he could put any of them into practice.

The army advanced at a walk up the incline, the cavalry keeping pace. It was steady and ordered, as it had to be. And interrupted by a scout tearing back over the hill on foot. He sped down toward Chandyr.

"Messenger approaching, sir," he said, breathless. "Flag down, sir, flag down."

"Get your breath and fall in."

"Yes, sir." He saluted and ran off round the side of the cavalry.

Chandyr looked to his left. "Flagman, signal the full advance."

"Sir!"

A thin red flag was held aloft and swept around in a long circle twice. The order was taken up along the line.

"To a trot!" ordered Chandyr.

The line quickened its pace, trotting up the slope, cresting the hill and carrying on down at an unbroken pace. Chandyr could see the refugees being herded left but not fast enough. He could see the Dordovans forming up on the north bank, cavalry in loose formation behind their foot soldiers, scattered horsemen that had to be mages among the rank and file. And in the middle of the empty plain, one rider. Rusau.

"Dear Gods, you fool," muttered Chandyr. "You bloody fool."

There was nothing that could be done for him now. Chandyr's warning had been clear enough, though he felt a stab of regret.

To the left, the refugee group had seen the approaching army. There was trouble in the mass and the Dordovans were having difficulty containing it. People had got away from the guards. Some carried on running to the left, others unbelievably were coming up the plain toward them but most were making for the river.

"Keep it tight!" roared Chandyr. "Keep it tight!"

As they descended the slope, the Dordovans were fording the river, their line re-forming on the near bank and moving slowly, keeping to the flat ground, unwilling to give the Xeteskians any slope advantage. The forces closed, Rusau still between them.

"Get out of the way," whispered Chandyr, then shouted, "Get out of the way, Rusau!"

His voice echoed out. Rusau pulled his horse round and drove headlong toward Chandyr. He was shouting but the Xeteskian couldn't hear him until he closed to a few yards and slowed hard.

"Stop this madness!" he yelled.

"Out of my way, Rusau. Get behind the lines. There's nothing you can do now. Go back to Lystern."

"Damn you, Chandyr. Make it stop."

"Last chance, Rusau. Please go." He looked to his lieutenants and signalled with a clenched fist. They were a hundred yards from the Dordovans. Spells were prepared. "Flagman! Stand ready!"

"Sir!"

"Chandyr."

"Leave."

Rusau wheeled his horse again and sped back toward the Dordovans.

"Archers!" called Chandyr. At the back of the lines his archers stopped and knelt. The Dordovans were doing likewise. "Deploy shields." Each order was relayed by his command chain. Hard- and SpellShields came on instantly, deployment confirmed across the line. "Fire at will!"

Arrows flew away, volley after volley, soaring overhead to clatter against the Dordovan shields and answered by the enemy. Across the divide, Rusau was being pushed away by Dordovan soldiers. Chandyr had no time to look at him any more. Dordovan cavalry had broken left and right and were galloping along the back of their line, which bristled with pikemen.

"Waiting," yelled Chandyr. "Waiting."

He watched the cavalry closely. They were spread quite thin and out-numbered by the Xeteskian horsemen, their tactic as yet unclear. Thirty yards. It was enough.

"Engage!" he shouted.

The flagman flung his flag forward, the foot soldiers roared and charged, his cavalry sprang to the gallop. Archers dropped their bows and joined the fray, spells filled the air. And in the midst of it all, Rusau, seeing his folly, began a desperate gallop to the right. He was never going to make it.

A few Xeteskian FlameOrbs soared out into the late afternoon sky, targeting mages and archers and splashing down in their midst, fizzing and hissing over shields or detonating on the ground where there were none. HotRain fell from the sky in a brief torrent over the Dordovan foot soldiers. The enemy mages were ready; their shields held, as did the Xeteskians' under the entirely predictable response.

But Chandyr had held something back. As they had been drilled, the Xeteskian foot forces, still just ahead of the cavalry, suddenly slowed for four paces. Unexpectedly, the Dordovan line was exposed to Xeteskian spell attack and more FlameOrbs fell in a concentrated burst on their left. At least one SpellShield cracked under the sudden and focussed barrage. Magical fire tore into armour and cloth. It melted faces and ate through furs and flesh, the unquenchable flames leaving their victims helpless as they died.

"Push the right. Watch the cavalry flank!"

Chandyr rode headlong into the Dordovan cavalry, horsemen to his left driving at the disoriented and weakened line, to his right fanning out to guard against a flank attack.

Rusau was caught in the chaos, wheeling his horse left and right as swords rose and fell all around him. Chandyr leaned left and swept his sword over his horse's head to clash with an enemy's. He let go the reins and dragged at the man's shoulder with his left hand as he snatched his weapon back. Pulled off balance, the Dordovan didn't see Chandyr's blade whip back and across to take him on the top of his helmeted head. Stunned, he fell from his horse, as good as dead under the churning hooves.

The Xeteskian commander glanced along his line. They had forced the Dordovans well back on the right flank and a breach wouldn't be long coming. More spells flashed across the space above his head, keeping the opposition casting mages busy with shields. A detonation told of at least one more failing under pressure.

"Rusau!" he yelled, but his voice was lost in the roar of battle, the ring of swords, the screams of dying men, the calls of fifty lieutenants and the stamp of myriad hooves.

A sword swung toward him. Reflexively, he blocked right. It was a good stroke. The Dordovan was knocked back in his saddle and took a second thrust through his gut.

"Push on, push on!" he urged, seeing the Dordovan line falter.

Chandyr dragged his horse left, swinging down to connect with the shoulder of a pikeman whose weapon was trapped underfoot. In the mêlée all order had disappeared; men fought for their lives moment to moment. But Chandyr chose to fight for someone else's. Rusau. Unbelievably, the Lysternan was still upright in his saddle, blood spattering his cloak and robes.

"Pull back, damn you!" Chandyr knew the mage couldn't hear him; he was caught right in the middle of the fiercest fighting. His horse was cut and terrified, rearing and bucking, Rusau demonstrating remarkable skill to stay in the saddle.

Chandyr hacked his way toward the helpless mage, his own mount, bred and trained for the fray, kicking out as it moved, head butting low, driving enemies aside and giving its rider clear vision and sword arc. The Xeteskian kept his legs back, kept his sword forward and never gave an enemy a flank target.

"Rusau! To me!"

Chandyr swept his sword into the face of a foot soldier. To his relief, the mage heard him.

"Bring him round. To me!"

But Rusau's mount wasn't responding. The mage hauled at the reins, searching for space. There was none.

"Help him!" Chandyr leant over the shoulder of his horse and smashed his sword down. Another foot gained. Around him, his men pushed. Hard. "Go! Go!"

This was the time to trust. It was the only way. Orders to men beyond five yards were pointless. Local leaders picking up on the course of battle were vital. Men of better vision in the thick of metal and blood, of panic and death. Darrick had taught him that and he had trained his own. In this battle, it was making all the difference. All along the line, Xetesk held formation and Dordover fell back.

He heeled his horse again, it kicked a man aside and plunged forward.

"Rusau!" He was almost within touching distance. "Behind me, jump on."

From nowhere, pikes thrust from both sides, freed by the movement of bodies. As it had been trained to do, Chandyr's horse stepped smartly back and reared to use its forelegs as a shield. Rusau's panicked creature reared too, but pitched its rider off. The mage fell calling out, grasping desperately, straight onto the point of a Xeteskian pike.

"No!" cried Chandyr, but it was done.

The blade speared straight through the Lysternan's back and out of his chest, breaking his rib cage as it came. Blood rushed from Rusau's mouth and he died, the pikeman dropping the staff and snatching out his short sword, too scared for his own life to realise what he had done.

Chandyr wheeled and galloped from the battle to check progress. The day would be won. The Dordovans would be forced back across the river. But Chandyr didn't care much about that. Enough Dordovans had seen Rusau die. A neutral on a Xeteskian pike. He would tell the truth. The Dordovans would not. He could only guess at the consequences.

It was night and the battle was done. The Dordovans had been crushed and driven back across the river but not before herding many of the refugees to their deaths, caught helpless between the opposing forces.

Three miles west, the surviving refugees had regrouped, huddling together for comfort around fires. Another blow had been struck against their fragile spirits and here they were again with no food, shelter or hope.

The flight from the fighting had been terrifying. Once the Dordovan guard had deserted them to shore up their fractured line, Avesh had got Ellin away from the panic and those who ran to the Dord, or those who decided to throw themselves on the mercy of the Xeteskians. Many had followed him, and as the day wore on yet more joined the group.

They sat in almost complete silence. A misty rain was falling from a clouded night sky and in his arms Ellin was unmoving. He rocked her gently, cursing those who had reduced her from bright light to traumatised shell. He had to strike back but had no idea how to contact those he wanted, but then three of them rode into the camp just as he was fighting back sleep.

Alarm rippled through the exhausted refugees but the riders sought to quell it quickly, assuring them they were not from any college. Avesh sat up, fatigue fading, and as a hush fell, one of the riders spoke.

"I and my men had sight of the events of today and I want to pass on my sympathy at your plight and my fury at those who treat you no better than animals. But the reason I am here is to offer you hope and a way to make a difference and to end the persecution of ordinary Balaians.

"My name is Edman, and I am an emissary of the Black Wings."

He waited while renewed nervousness coursed through the cold, wet and hungry refugees.

"Please," he said, raising his hands. "I know our reputation but I want to assure you we mean you no harm. We seek to restore what has been lost but we need people to make it happen. I can offer you food and shelter. It is a long walk from here but we will help you every step of the way. We will keep you from contact with our common enemy and we will help your sick and your wounded.

"Any of you who want to return to rebuild the lives the colleges took from you go with our blessing. But any who come with us will make sure that those lives can be lived in security in the years that follow.

"Who is with me?"

There were questions, there was suspicion, there was fear. But Avesh was not alone in feeling a surge of purpose. By him, Ellin reached up a hand to stroke his face.

"You must go," she said. "Avenge our son for me. And when you are done, find me at the broken timbers of our farm and we will start again."

Avesh gazed down at her, tears standing in his eyes, and knew he had never loved her more than he did right now.

"I won't let you down."

"Just come back to me."

"You know I will," he said and, kissing her gently on the lips, he heaved himself from the ground and went to hear what Edman wanted of him.

Heryst rode into Dordover with the night full and cool. He and his delegation were tired from the trail but Vuldaroq wasn't in the mood to give them much time for food and rest. Still feeling dusty, Heryst met the fat red-faced Dordovan Arch Mage in a small warm reception chamber hung with dour portraits and with a roaring fire in a large grate.

The shake of hands was perfunctory but the wine Vuldaroq gave him was very welcome. The two men sat in large leather chairs either side of the blaze.

"So, come to your senses finally, my Lord Heryst?"

"I have always been in full possession of my senses, Vuldaroq. I had hoped that Xetesk and yourselves might rediscover yours."

"Exactly what was it you were hoping for?"

"A way to peace through diplomacy, what else?"

Vuldaroq smiled indulgently. "You know I respect your skill as a politician and mage but in this you are being as naive as a child. Surely you cannot close your eyes to what is happening now. Peace is only possible when both sides desire it."

"I have never been naive, Vuldaroq," said Heryst. "I simply choose to seek a less bloody path."

"You think we wanted war against them?"

"I think Dordover was angry enough at its defeat on Herendeneth to view conflict as preferable to negotiation. You as much as they have brought us to this juncture."

Vuldaroq was indignant. "Preposterous, Heryst. We sought justice for Balaia and the sharing of the treasures discovered on that island."

Heryst blinked slowly, having to make a deliberate effort to keep a scornful smile from his lips.

"Who exactly do you think you are talking to here? We formed an alliance, if you recall, with the express intention of stopping the Nightchild realising potential beyond her control. Her death was always a possibility we had to consider. But you had darker motives. Nothing would have survived there had The Raven not intervened, would it? Wasn't that why you involved the witch hunters?"

"They were the only people capable of finding those we sought."

"Damn you they were not!" Heryst spilled his wine on his hand. "And you gave Erienne to them. One of your own."

"A betrayer," said Vuldaroq smoothly. "A little like your own General Darrick, wouldn't you say?"

"Darrick's actions were regrettable, I admit, but he was not prepared to stand shoulder to shoulder with those who would see us all dead, as apparently you would. He will account for his actions, have no fear. He, at least, is a man of honour."

Vuldaroq sipped his wine. "And I am not? I and my college, alone, stand between Xetesk and their dominion of Balaia. Remember why we allied. We cannot let the power rest with one college alone; it would return us to the wilderness."

"I agree utterly. It is the method to use that has been where our differences lie," said Heryst, knowing tit for tat accusations would get them nowhere fast.

"And do you also agree that the war, whoever you believe is to blame, now threatens you as well as us?"

"And Julatsa, yes," said Heryst. "That is why I am here. I am appalled by the actions of Xetesk around Arlen and at their own gates. At least you have respected the rules of engagement and the rights of refugees."

Vuldaroq inclined his head. "From you that is compliment indeed."

"I want to make it abundantly clear, however, that I am not proposing a formal alliance," said Heryst. "But we have a joint obligation to shore up the defences of Julatsa. I also believe we must put in place a blockade of Xeteskian lands to prevent movement of troops and materials."

"There also we arc in accord," said Vuldaroq. "But how is this not an alliance?"

"Because Lystern is not at war with Xetesk and that is the way I want to keep it. My soldiers will not be under any command of yours. I am suggesting a sharing of responsibilities in order to pressure Xetesk to the negotiating table. I will be telling Dystran the same."

"Of course, I respect your wishes," said Vuldaroq, and Heryst could see the gleam of satisfaction in his eyes.

"Do not betray this. I will be seeking assurances you will not use this goodwill to advance the conflict."

Vuldaroq held up his hands. "Heryst, please."

"Good. I suggest we break and let our respective teams discuss my proposals. We can reconvene later to iron out points of difference."

An urgent knocking on the door was followed by two of Heryst's mages running in.

"Excuse the interruption, my Lords," said one, a young mage named Darrow. "I have grave news."

He looked over to Vuldaroq. Heryst waved him on.

"He will hear it anyway, best firsthand from you."

"Kayvel has contacted us," said Darrow. "As you know, Rusau travelled with a Xeteskian force riding to engage the Dordovans at the Dord crossing. It seems he was caught in the middle of the conflict. I'm sorry, my Lord, but he was killed."

Heryst closed his eyes. He had feared this. He took a deep breath before speaking.

"How did it happen?"

"The story we have heard from Dordovans in the field was that he was killed by a Xeteskian pikeman."

Heryst dashed his glass into the fireplace. Liquid hissed and spat. He fought to regain control but his mind churned and his pulse ran high.

"He was a diplomat. A neutral," he said, hardly able to get the words out.

"Yes, my Lord."

"He was also my friend." Heryst put his head in his hands for a moment. "Are you sure the reports are true?"

"That he's dead?" asked Darrow.

"No," snapped Heryst. "That he died the way it is told."

"As sure as we can be. He was caught in the battle. In the centre of the line. He was in the way and Xetesk removed him." Darrow shrugged.

"But could it have been an accident? Battle is confused," said Heryst. "You understand I have to be sure. Could it have been a Dordovan pike?"

Darrow shook his head. "No, my Lord. The picture is reasonably clear. A Xeteskian pike was driven through his body from the back. The battle continued. Xetesk pushed Dordover back across the river and their forces are now guarding the whole stretch and apparently sending more patrols out to secure their entire border with Dordover."

Heryst looked across at Vuldaroq, whose expression of sorrow appeared genuine enough, but the Lysternan knew that somewhere in that mind of his he was smiling at the news.

"And what have we heard from Xetesk?" he asked.

"Denials, as you would expect," said Darrow. "Kayvel has spoken to the rest of our delegation there and they aren't under any duress or arrest but the story they are relaying just doesn't have quite the ring of truth about it."

"And what is it?" Heryst straightened.

"That the Xeteskian commander was trying to get Rusau out of the battle and didn't make it before his horse threw him and he landed on a pike."

"Pure fantasy," muttered Vuldaroq. "I am sorry to hear of the loss of your friend, Heryst, but it casts new light on what we have just been discussing, does it not?"

Heryst held up a hand to silence the Dordovan Arch Mage. "Don't you dare try to put pressure on me, Vuldaroq. At the moment I am not interested in what you think. Perhaps you would grant me the favour of leaving me for a moment."

Vuldaroq nodded and rose. Heryst watched him go.

"This changes nothing as far as Dordover is concerned," he said to Darrow. "You will continue negotiation as if this desperate event hadn't happened. Do you understand?"

"Yes, my Lord, but—"

"But nothing, Darrow," said Heryst, keeping his voice quiet. "I do not trust Dordover any more than I trust Xetesk and I suggest you take my lead. I want to leave to return to Lystern tomorrow, so the pressure is on you. There, we will find the truth of this. All I will say is that it must hasten our deployment of forces.

"Damn you, Darrick, where are you when I need you most?"

CHAPTER 28

"Ow! Dammit!" shouted Darrick, jerking his leg at the sudden flare of pain. "That hurt."

"I'm really sorry, Darrick, but they won't be persuaded out with softly spoken words," said Ilkar. "Now keep still, you broke my concentration."

"Feels like you broke my leg."

"Well, I can leave them in there if you'd prefer," said Ilkar, meeting the Lysternan's gaze in the firelight.

Darrick shook his head. "What on earth possessed me to join you lot?"

"The glory and excitement," said The Unknown.

"That'll be it."

The Raven had stopped for the night before walking to the temple the following morning. They'd endured two days in the dense rain forest which had tested the nerve and patience of them all. Stultifying heat had been punctuated by torrential rain; and the close attentions of seemingly every bug that hopped, crawled, flew or burrowed had been utterly relentless. They'd been tracked by a pack of small wild dogs, had to move their fire pit when an army of ants had chosen their site for a route to somewhere, and had interrupted an enormous constrictor devouring a young adult monkey.

It was hard to gauge which had been the most unsettling event so Darrick didn't bother, concentrating instead on Ilkar and his ministrations. He knew what the mage was doing though he could see nothing: targeted needles of mana lancing into his legs to kill the burrowing insects and the eggs they laid. Every tiny wound was cauterised instantly and, with dozens from his ankles to his thighs, Darrick felt like he'd been showered with hot embers.

He felt a little aggrieved too. In the nightly checks that Ilkar insisted the mages carried out, whereas the others had largely escaped the tunnellers, having bites and blisters instead, he seemed to have been singled out. Unsurprisingly, Hirad found his discomfort a source of some amusement.

Rebraal, he'd noticed, had looked on with an expression of knowing mixed with distinct satisfaction. He'd concocted an insect repellent herb drink for them all but it only seemed to help the elves. And Thraun, for some reason. All the other humans needed magical intervention and the three mages were beginning to tire from the drain on their stamina.

"You are sure it's necessary?" said Darrick.

"Darrick, you have no idea what this country can do to you. How sick you will be if these insects' eggs hatch. They'll feed on you until they're big enough to burrow out. Rebraal has immunity. Wonder why they eat you? It's because you haven't."

"What about the others, are they immune too?"

"No, but you're just a tastier target. At least you haven't got boils behind your knees like Hirad. Just keep using the herbs we give you and remember you won't have to be here for too much longer."

Darrick knew Ilkar was right. He'd watched Denser and Erienne looking after cuts, blisters and bites under Ilkar's instruction and had his share of the herbs Rebraal made them eat, drink and spread on themselves. Rebraal took no healing save for Erienne's care of his shoulder. He belonged here. The Raven did not.

Not for the first time, Darrick yearned for the camaraderie of his officers, the obedience and respect of his men and the order of his life as a Lysternan soldier. Trouble was, the pull of The Raven was irresistible. Their energy, their delight in the challenges that faced them. And their belief in what kept them alive. The knowledge that they would prevail no matter what. You couldn't bottle it, you had to breathe it. And Darrick had breathed deep.

"Whatever you say, Ilkar."

Ilkar nodded. "And I say quiet to let me work."

And in these acts as much as in battle, Darrick understood The Raven. This was no macho brotherhood of arms. This was a group of people who routinely sacrificed themselves for their own. Because it made them stronger. Simple, really.

That night Darrick slept easier.

Erienne's head throbbed. It was an increasing and incessant thump that no spell could diminish. Any energy she had, she spent on keeping The Raven fit. But it was hard. She felt drained and found it ever more difficult to concentrate. Her mind refused to focus clearly.

At the same time the ache didn't feel like an illness. She knew what it meant and that soon she would be unable to deny it any longer. The knowledge crawled within her and she hated it. Loved it. Every pulse brought her fresh memories of Lyanna. They had taken on an unusual clarity in the days since they'd left the village. And they were good, as if her mind was filtering the dark visions. Erienne had her suspicions that the Al-Drechar were feeding both the ache and her memories though, in truth, she hadn't felt them in her mind.

"Are you feeling all right?"

It was The Unknown, with whom she was sharing the early watch. She'd been asleep but the ache in her head had forced her from her hammock. She found the fire comforting, and next to her The Unknown's frame represented total security.

"I'll live," she said.

"I've been watching you wince," he said. "Have you told Denser you're in this much pain?"

Erienne shook his head. "I've burdened him enough."

The Unknown chuckled. "I don't think you could ever overburden Denser."

"You weren't there. You didn't see the worst."

"And you think he doesn't understand why, or blames you, or something?"

"Lyanna was his daughter too," whispered Erienne. And there it was still. The dread feeling of loss that dragged at her soul. It would never go. But at least it didn't threaten to swamp her now.

"Erienne, you've been through something entirely and tragically unique. Don't add guilt to everything else you're forced to endure."

"I can't help it." Erienne shrugged.

"But you know he's forgiven your every action. Never blamed you in the first place. We all feel the same."

"I know." Erienne gazed at The Unknown in the firelight and recollected her surprise at the sensitivity that existed beneath those hard features. But those eyes that gazed back brimming with compassion and understanding could be so cold.

He was the most brutally effective warrior she'd ever seen. Had been. The smashed hip that had forced him to hang up his trademark two-handed sword must have reduced his effectiveness. On the other hand, looking at the power in his arms and shoulders, she thought he'd compensated. It was easy to see why his enemies feared him and equally easy to know why she and everyone else he cared for loved and trusted him without question.

"I hated the lot of you for forcing me out here. Away from Lyanna."

Another chuckle. "Right though, weren't we?"

"I don't know," said Erienne. "I can't shift the longing for her. I don't want to."

She stopped and looked around the quiet campsite—at Denser, Hirad and Ilkar sleeping in hammocks above the teeming life that dredged the forest floor—and she understood again what being with these men meant.

"But you're all with me now, aren't you? All of you."

"We never left," said The Unknown.

"I can see when I'm with you," she said, trying to explain herself.

"That's why you had to leave that place. We were there too but you wouldn't see us."

"She was my life," said Erienne.

"And she would have been your death too," he said.

The words stung but she knew he was right. But they were words she wouldn't have taken from Denser.

"I will never forget her."

"No one is expecting you to, Erienne," he said, and turned and covered her hands with his. "None of us ever will. But you had to get away from Herendeneth. You had to stop fuelling your grief."

"And that's why I'm here?" Erienne was taken aback, not quite understanding what he was saying.

"No," said The Unknown. "Not really. You're here because you're Raven and Ilkar needs you. The Raven needs you. But no one is denying the fortunate circumstance."

Erienne laughed. "Fortunate? Is that what you call it? Think I'd have entertained this if I'd known I'd be sleeping above snakes?"

"Think you'd have made that comment ten days ago?"

"No," said Erienne. "Gods, what is it about you?"

The Unknown squeezed her hands. "Simple. We love you. We wouldn't see you come to harm and you were coming to harm on Herendeneth. We understand your pain and we understand you are greater than it. And we all know what you carry inside you."

Erienne looked into the fire, unable to speak.

"At the risk of sounding like Hirad, this is what The Raven is about," said The Unknown. "No one has what we have. You can't explain it but it's why I'll leave my wife and child to do what I must with The Raven, and it's why Diera understands. I hate to sound superior but we are unique. And you're hurting at the moment so you should use us. We expect it. We want it."

Erienne flung her arms around The Unknown's neck and sobbed into his shoulder. She felt his arms crush her to him even as within her she felt release. She held on for a while, unwilling to leave the security of his embrace.

"Thank you," she said.

"You don't have to keep it burning inside you." The Unknown moved her back so he could look into her eyes. "Let us take some of the weight."

She nodded, but in her gratitude was the lonely realisation that they couldn't take any of the burden of the One.

"Now I think you should sleep, if that headache will let you. Your stamina reserves are low, aren't they?"

"It'll be a problem before long," she admitted.

She kissed his cheek and stood up, brushing herself down. Above them, the rain was beginning to fall again. She barely noticed.

"Erienne?"

"Yes?"

"You'll have to let them in, you know. The One isn't going to remain dormant. Only the Al-Drechar can help you with it. Talk to Denser again, all right?"

It was like he saw straight into her mind, finding in there the thing that worried her the most. She gave a tired smile. "I'll think about it."

"That's all I ask."

"Good night, Unknown."

"Sleep well."

The rain fell for hours until just before dawn but by the time The Raven had eaten a light meal of wild mushrooms and hard bread, they were as dry as the humid conditions would ever allow. Hirad walked at the head of the line on the third morning with The Unknown, just behind Rebraal and Ilkar. The brothers had clearly had another disagreement. The set of both their bodies spoke volumes and Rebraal repeatedly failed to hold branches aside for Ilkar as they moved through an area of forest far more dense than anything they'd encountered so far.

In the trees above them, monkeys called and hooted and birds sang, the songs of a myriad throats mixing to a magical crescendo.

"No one's going to hear us coming, at least," said Hirad.

"That's why elves don't rely on their ears here," said Ilkar, who was just ahead at the time. "If there are elves nearby, chances are they know about us already."

"And what does Rebraal think?" asked The Unknown.

"He's suddenly decided that we shouldn't have come and that he and the Al-Arynaar are able to handle everything perfectly well on their own."

"That's not what I asked."

Ilkar shrugged but he didn't look round. They'd all learned that looking at who you were talking to was the easiest way of sustaining a graze or falling over a root.

"So?" prompted Hirad

"So, he says the forest has a bad taste to it, that the harmony is damaged and he can't feel what he should. He's not sure what we'll find at the temple and he doesn't know if more Al-Arynaar are close," said Ilkar.

"And doesn't he think some of his people might not have retaken the temple already?" asked Hirad.

"Apparently the forest wouldn't feel this way if they had," said Ilkar.

"He's scared, isn't he?" said The Unknown.

Ilkar said nothing but Hirad saw his head nod.

"Then give him some room," said the big warrior. "This is his land far more than it is yours. We need him on our side as far as possible."

Ilkar tensed across the shoulders. "Thanks for your input, Unknown, but I think I understand my own brother."

"You are not behaving as if you do."

The Julatsan didn't respond and The Raven walked on in silence. The large insect bites on the back of Hirad's knees itched and chafed and the constant sweat down his arms wasn't helping the healing of the blisters he still had from his first day rowing. Not enough to worry him if it came to a fight but uncomfortable nonetheless.

After something like two hours of walking, Rebraal brought them to a sudden halt and beckoned them to group around him.

"Close," he said, pointing forward. "Quiet now."

"Talkative soul, isn't he?" said Hirad.

"Just a little rusty," responded Ilkar. "He hasn't had to speak Balaian for three times longer than you've been alive."

Rebraal scowled and put a finger to his lips. "Quiet," he hissed. "You must um . . . I lead." He looked to Ilkar and spoke quickly in elvish.

"He wants you to follow his lead. He says he'll direct us where we need to go."

"Tell him if there's a combat situation, we'll assess and do things how we think they should be done," said Hirad. "You know the way it is."

Ilkar smiled. "Anything to antagonise."

Rebraal hadn't caught the conversation and shook his head when Ilkar translated. Another sharp exchange ensued, ending when Rebraal threw his arms up, stabbed a finger at Ilkar, spoke what sounded like a threat and turned his back on them.

"So he's in full agreement then?" said Hirad.

"I've just tried to explain that we'll listen to him, but when it comes to it we'll decide on any attack or defence tactics. All I would ask is that you don't do anything precipitate. He will be able to perceive threat far better than us and the last thing we need is to start fighting friends. All right?"

Hirad nodded and turned to The Raven. "Fair enough. But let's assume we need a line before we set off. That means mages to the rear of the group now. Everyone knows their places. Ren, keep your bow handy and stay behind the sword line. We can protect you there."

Swords drawn, The Raven moved off behind the sullen Rebraal and it was immediately evident that the elf had a new purpose about him. They thought he'd been moving quickly before but now he glided through the forest ahead, his feet sure, his passage obviously quiet even given the din of life surrounding them.

Hirad tried as best he could to mimic his movements, keeping low, head flicking from ground to directly ahead continuously. He felt a thrill course through him as they advanced. He had no idea exactly what lay twenty yards ahead, let alone at the temple, but his excitement at the thought of action drove him on. He felt himself detach from the world outside The Raven and his senses took on the clarity a warrior needed to survive the fight.

He could smell the sharpness of the plant life around him, the sweetness of fruit. He could hear their footsteps and their breathing and he could see a path where none had been before, obscured as it had been by his untrained eyes. But he never took his gaze from Rebraal for more than a few heartbeats. The Al-Arynaar was the barometer for what lay immediately ahead. He took them across a crudely hacked path and back into the forest, turned to his right, entered a small clearing and stopped dead. Behind him, Hirad held up a hand and The Raven were still.

Rebraal turned briefly, took them all in, one of his eyebrows perhaps edging up very slightly. Hirad looked down at his feet. He was standing on a human bone.

"I can hear nothing," Rebraal whispered. "Follow. Slow."

He set off again, Hirad and The Unknown in his footprints, Aeb, Darrick and Thraun close by and just in front of Ren and the mages. The slightest murmuring was heard as mana shapes were formed. Slowly, slowly, the vegetation began to thin and the building that loomed out of the forest was enough to take the breath away.

A great green-gold dome rose, partly covered in liana, lichens and mosses. It was a huge structure that should have been completely at odds with its surroundings yet somehow fitted them perfectly. Harmony, supposed Hirad.

That there was much wrong, though, was evident in Rebraal's reaction to the place he apparently knew so well. He waved them hurriedly to a stop, crouched low to look either side of some obstruction, ducking his head this way and that, and finally stood and strode away.

"Rebraal!" called Ilkar, and broke position.

"Get back in line, Ilkar," ordered The Unknown.

Ilkar complied immediately but Ren, right behind him, did not listen.

"Ren!" barked The Unknown, but she had gone on after Ilkar's brother.

"Raven, form up," said Hirad. "Let's get after that idiot."

All pretence at silence was gone. Ahead of them, Rebraal was calling to someone, his elvish urgent and strained. The Raven came on, slicing away vegetation, revealing more and more of the temple as they advanced, Ren in front, calling Rebraal's name, her bow slack in her hands.

"HardShield up," said Erienne.

"SpellShield up," said Ilkar.

Secure, Hirad began a trot, The Unknown to his left and just ahead of him, Darrick to his right. Aeb and Thraun ran the other side of the big man. They burst into the stone apron clearing in front of the temple a few paces behind Ren, who had stuttered to a stop.

"Get behind me now!" roared Hirad.

The elf started and began to back off, head switching to either side. Rebraal was in the centre of the apron, walking slowly toward the temple doorway which was closed by rough wooden planking. From both sides of the apron and from behind the temple, elves were emerging.

Hirad stopped The Raven.

"Check left," he said.

"Twenty targets," said Aeb instantly. "More probably in shadow."

"Check right," said the barbarian.

"Similar," said Darrick. "Bows and swords."

"Be calm," said Ilkar, voice quiet with concentration on his spell. "They're Al-Arynaar."

"I'm taking no chances," said Hirad. "Keep focussed, Raven. Move slowly. Keep them in front of us if you can." Ren took her place in the line under Hirad's glare. "Never again or you walk."

"But—"

"Later." Hirad cut across her protest and returned his attention to the situation in front of them.

The Al-Arynaar—there were over thirty of them on the apron now—were clearly confused by what they saw. Their anger at the strangers in their midst was obvious enough but it was tempered by the sight of Rebraal. Hirad shuddered at the thought of what would have happened had he not been there. He'd had no inkling the elves were there until they appeared from the shadows. All that bothered him now was that they might decide Rebraal was an escaped captive. Shields or not, he didn't fancy taking on this lot.

"Rebraal?" he called.

The elf held up a hand. "Quiet." But he looked round and the suggestion of a smile crossed his face. His next words were in elvish and Hirad heard Ilkar's name mentioned.

"Shield down," said Ilkar, and moved out from the line, stopping in front of Hirad. "Keep your guard up but don't be aggressive. There's no magic here but I'd keep the HardShield up if I were you. Some of them look a little twitchy."

"Be careful," said Hirad. "You're vulnerable."

"I'll be standing next to my brother," said Ilkar, but he didn't appear convinced himself.

"Yes, and not us."

Ilkar nodded and walked onto the apron, Al-Arynaar eyes following him all the way. All Hirad could do was watch. Rebraal spoke quickly to an Al-Arynaar who had come forward to embrace him. He indicated Ilkar, gestured at The Raven and at the temple. Hirad saw him nodding, then start violently before running to the temple door, Ilkar right behind him.

The Raven took an automatic pace forward. The elves moved across the apron, blocking their route to the temple. Hirad held up a hand to calm them. He could see the hate dripping from some of their faces, the desire to kill clear in every gaze, the grip on every weapon and the intent in every stance. Perhaps fifty stood before them now. Too many.

From within the temple Hirad heard an anguished cry. Shouting echoed out into the forest. The rough doors were pulled aside and Rebraal came storming out, Ilkar pacing beside him, voice raised, talking into his ear. But Rebraal wasn't hearing whatever it was Ilkar was saying.

"Trouble," said Ren.

"What's he saying?" asked Hirad, not turning.

"Something's been damaged in there. The statue. Rebraal's blaming every stranger. That includes you."

The tension spiralled. The Al-Arynaar bunched and moved forward as Rebraal and Ilkar passed them. Arrows were nocked, belt pouches unclasped and swords raised.

"Ready, Raven," said Hirad. "Don't strike first. Block away. Denser, you got something that doesn't involve fire?"

"Plenty," said the Xeteskian. "I'm ready."

Rebraal's face betrayed the blindness in his mind. He was pushing Ilkar away but the Julatsan kept on coming back, casting very anxious glances at The Raven. A handful of paces in front of them, with the Al-Arynaar bearing down, Ilkar got between Rebraal and his targets, shoved his brother back and snapped out a stream of elvish that stopped him a moment.

Hirad knew enough to realise it was a challenge.

"Raven," he began.

"Stay there," said Ilkar. "Trust me."

"Unknown?" asked Hirad.

"Be ready."

The Unknown's blade tapped on the stone in front of him, sending a chilling toll across the open space while his mind cleared for battle.

Ilkar grabbed the flaps of his own leather jerkin and pulled them apart, daring Rebraal to kill him. Hirad watched Rebraal's eyes narrow, heard his words grate out and saw his gesture ordering Ilkar aside. Ilkar shook his head. Laid down the same challenge again. One word Hirad heard this time as clear as a bell at dawn. Raven.

The brothers stared at each other. Rebraal's eyes didn't flinch and didn't blink. The forest around them faded in Hirad's consciousness. All he could hear was the sound of The Unknown's sword tapping on stone, all he could see were the two elves in a standoff that would decide The Raven's fate. He felt a drip of sweat run down his back and gripped his sword tighter, aware of his slick palm.

In front of him Ilkar was perfectly still, his nerve not faltering. He spoke again, quietly now into the relative silence. His words carried utter determination. Rebraal said nothing in response but there was a flicker across his face. He glanced briefly at The Raven, back to Ilkar and nodded once, curtly, before spinning on his heel and taking the Al-Arynaar into the temple.

Ilkar turned to The Raven, his face pale but a smile spreading across his face.

"Thank you," he said. "We're safe for now."

"Shield down," said Erienne.

The Raven surrounded Ilkar. He was shaking now and he put his face in his hands.

"Oh Gods, it's bad," he said.

"What is?" asked Hirad.

"Give me a moment," said Ilkar.

"What have they gone to do?" asked Hirad, flicking his head at the departed Al-Arynaar.

"Pray," said Ilkar. "And if you had any sense, you'd be doing the same."

CHAPTER 29

The bandages boiled once again in the mugs above a small fire consisting mainly of embers. Smoke spiralled into the bright dawn sky, cloud clearing after the latest burst of rain. Yron had made Ben-Foran as comfortable as he could in a cut-in above the sloping banks of the River Shorth late the night before, after walking into the evening only because Ben had dredged energy from somewhere and didn't want to stop.

Yron had boiled the blood-soaked bandages that night and replaced them, and now he was repeating the procedure he still refused to believe was futile. But Ben was dying. The fact would have been obvious to a blind man. His night had been full of delusions. He'd cried out and Yron had forgone any rest to be at his side, to soothe his fears. Infection was setting in quickly despite Yron's best efforts and his knowledge of rain forest herbs.

He'd been without food too. They both had, existing only by chewing on the scraped bark and leaves of guarana, which provided basic energy. It had to be enough. They didn't have the time or the energy to hunt, or forage for anything other than medicinal plants.

And Yron himself was beginning to succumb. His bites from the piranha weren't healing and the insects had done their work too. He thought he might make it back to the ship but only if he was unencumbered. Trouble was, there was no way he was leaving Ben.

While the bandages bubbled, he fed Ben guarana and made him drink menispere to fight the fever. He laid boiled leaves of the same plant on his horrible leg wounds, apologising for the thousandth time as the pain ravaged his lieutenant. But as usual Ben didn't cry out or complain. Indeed he even managed a smile.

Throughout the previous day, as they'd walked with agonising slowness along the banks of the river, Yron's admiration for the young man had grown. His spirit was amazing. Unquenchable. He remained as alert as he could. He still talked, still wanted to learn. Even for a determined soldier like Yron, it was truly inspirational. Ben would be a great leader of men. Would have been.

"You respect them, don't you?" asked Ben suddenly, his words coming through short breaths.

"The elves?"

"The ones chasing us."

"Oh yes," said Yron. "Their skill is extraordinary."

"They will catch us, won't they?"

"Yes," said Yron. "Unless our luck holds, that is. Hard to think we've been lucky so far, but we have. They are utterly ruthless and we have committed a crime that carries the death penalty in their eyes. If they do catch up with us, there'll be no mercy shown."

"So why do you think they haven't caught us yet?" asked Ben.

"Because they aren't absolutely certain where we're going. When they know, they'll move." Yron stirred the bandages and began hooking them out. "And that's the game for us and for anyone else still alive out there if they did but know it. Keep the TaiGethen guessing, keep alive. Simple."

But it wasn't. Soon, if not already, the TaiGethen would know their exact destination and the ClawBound would confirm it.

"You ready to go?" he asked.

Ben laughed, coughing at the same time. "Never better, sir. Get the bandages on and let's run."

"Whatever you say, son."

Auum completed the prayers and stood, his Tai around him. They turned to the small fire and unwrapped the fish that had been cooking in its embers. Swallowing the succulent flesh, Auum's mood darkened. There were mages out there with the running strangers and though ClawBound and a full Tai had attacked a camp of four, they had not found the mage and the writings were still with him. A scouring of the camp had revealed nothing.

Elsewhere, a mage shielded another band of desecrators from the eyes of the panthers and the TaiGethen. But the two groups with no magical support were caught and dead, their prizes given up and even now being returned to Aryndeneth. But the mages worried him. Because mages could fly faster than a panther could run and a TaiGethen cell track. And on his own, with no companions to protect, a mage might well choose that option. It all depended on his energy in the stamina-sapping conditions of the rain forest.

"Is there a ClawBound near?" he asked.

"Yes," said Duele.

"Bring them."

Auum sorted more fish from the fire while Duele was gone and took one of the fresh catch from the pole resting against the tree at his back. He laid it on the ground for the panther, which darted in to snatch it, retreating to the shadows to eat. Auum turned and handed the tall ClawBound elf the baked fish.

"We risk losing our writings and our artefact," he said. "You are certain of the direction of travel the strangers are taking?"

The ClawBound elf nodded.

"All the TaiGethen must reach the estuary by the quickest means. The Al-Arynaar must join us. And we will let the desecrators come to us. Tell your people. Spread the message. This must happen now." He paused. "And the man who is travelling the east bank of the Shorth. He is too clever. Kill him."

The ClawBound nodded once more and looked at his panther. The big cat tore another bite from the fish trapped beneath its paws and walked over to him, muscle and bone fluid beneath its glossy black coat. Cat and elf stared at one another in silence, the communication that passed between them in a language and form closed to all but the bound pairs themselves.

And once they were done, they disappeared back into the forest. Auum turned to the Tai.

"Yniss speed us to the mouth of the Shorth before our enemies," he said.

Out in the forest, the throaty growl of a panther rose in volume and pitch, spanning the miles of land between it and its fellows spread throughout the northern sectors. The growls grew to a roar, climbed to a high-pitched whine and then descended back to the original deep guttural sound before repeating over and over. Within the complex of sounds, Auum knew the message was being carried to his people.

He led the Tai in prayer again before they began their run to the estuary.

Erys flew high above the canopy, following the course of the River Shorth. He had never known such fear in his life as when the elves had attacked their camp. He had been amazed that he had been able to cast but had later reflected that the fear hadn't really settled on him until some hours later. Then, hiding in the branches of a banyan tree, he had shivered and shuddered and tried to still his heart and the moans that escaped his mouth.

He knew he was no coward but it was right to fear something against which you had no defence and no hope. The snakes and lizards that came by him as he sat held no fear whatever. Indeed he had hoped in the dim recesses of his terrified mind that one of the snakes would bite him and he could die in a relatively painless way. But he was no threat to them and so they left him alone.

Eventually, the fear released its grip and he dozed fitfully through the night, tied to the branch on which he had sat all the day. The morning had brought fresh rain and fresh fear but he had been driven by the memory of Captain Yron, exhorting him not to fail. So he had climbed as high as he dared, into the tall exposed branches of the banyan that were the home of eagles. And here he had gathered every scrap of concentration his tired mind could muster and cast ShadowWings to bear him up into the safety of the sky.

He was secure up here but somehow he couldn't shake off his nagging anxiety over what lurked below. The ship was two days' flight away, more like three given his state of stamina. He was having to fly slowly and keep his mind fixed firmly on the mana shape that kept the wings at his back. ShadowWings was such an easy spell to master. Even after half a night's sleep he should have been able to partition his mind enough to think ahead, but it was all he could do to keep from plummeting into the river.

Midmorning, he was looking for a place to land and rest for a while, to refocus his mind. He was constantly staggered by the scale of what lay below him. Right now, the sun was shining fiercely down on the river-veined mat of almost unbroken green that was the forest canopy. It rolled up hillsides and into deep mist-filled valleys from which the light bounced in dazzling rainbow colours. Great faces of rock sheared up, punctuating the green, and he knew that behind him spectacular mountains bordered the forest, silent sentinels gazing down on all they protected.

Blinded by the vastness, he flew lower, travelling directly along the river course and about seventy feet above the water, keeping clear of the overhanging branches that sought to snag him and send him tumbling.

A growl emanated from the forest. From his left and behind at first. And quiet, from a single animal, he thought, and far away. But the intensity gained, the pitch climbed and dropped. It was alien and it sent Erys's pulse racing. Moments later it was taken up by other throats, the calls ricocheting across the rain forest. Birds scattered into the sky, a tumult of wings scrabbling at the air, their squawking momentarily drowning the roars.

But they came again, one very near. Erys rose sharply, the sound uncomfortably close. Looking down as he passed the bank of the river, Erys could see the source. He shivered again at the memory. The panther and elf, standing close, the animal lost in the chorus, the elf listening, intent. Fascinated, Erys circled, watching the pair set off at speed into the undergrowth. He lost them quickly but followed the direction of their travel, moving a little higher into the sky.

He badly needed rest but their movements had worried him. Like they were homing in on something. He flew forward, scanning for a likely quarry, and what he saw almost took the wings from him. In a tiny open space and hurrying to their feet were Yron and Ben-Foran, though something was very badly wrong. Ben-Foran leaned heavily on Yron, who seemed to be trying to push him toward cover.

Erys circled, losing height fast. Yron had half dragged Ben away from the open space. His axe was in his hand and he was searching the forest but it was plain he couldn't see anything. The panther would be on them in moments.

"Oh, hell."

Erys flared his wings back and landed hard in the clearing, scattering the embers of the dying fire.

"You're looking the wrong way," he said, already forming the simplest shape next to ShadowWings.

"Erys, I—" began Yron.

"Keep back," said Erys, took his courage and concentration in both hands and waited.

Not for long.

Eighty pounds of sleek black muscle exploded from the forest. It took a bound to see its target and leapt straight for Erys's throat. The mage almost lost it. Almost. Yellow fangs, long and sharp, mouth gaping and eyes boring into him, the panther powered forward.

Erys braced himself and cast at the instant of impact, his hands clamped around the huge jaws. Fire erupted in the panther's mouth, scorched along its nostrils and into its eyes. The panther howled in agony and rolled off Erys as it landed, running blindly toward the river, dying as it went, limbs beginning to buckle, all grace gone as it blundered into trees and bushes.

An inhuman wail emanated from the forest. It scoured the depths of anguish and dredged pain like Erys had never heard. It was a sound that clawed at his ears and lashed at his mind.

Below, at the river, the panther thrashed and roared, trying to extinguish the magical flame. From the forest stumbled its master. The elf clawed at his face, seeing nothing, his mouth bellowing agony, his legs boneless. He stumbled and fell, arms a blur as they sought to dull the phantom fire.

"Dear Gods."

Erys scrambled to his feet, a crushing pain in his chest. He looked down on the convulsing screaming body, searching for a way to help. Yron stepped from behind him and smashed his axe into the elf's chest. The screaming stopped, as did the thrashing at the water's edge. Erys took a pace back, gaping at Yron and the dead elf at his feet.

"Believe me," said Yron. "You didn't want to face him when his mind cleared. Now tell me you've got enough stamina to help Ben. He's dying."

"I'll see what I can do," said Erys, walking to the slope to look down at the body of the panther, already food for piranha. He felt shaken and clutched himself around the chest, taking in a pained breath. "Trouble is, I think that cat broke most of my ribs."

Ilkar stood in the temple again with Rebraal. The desire to kill had dissipated but the anger remained. They were shoulder to shoulder not far inside the doors, which had been hastily rebuilt and rehung on the original hinges by the Al-Arynaar, six of whom were now lying inside, the Elfsorrow killing them. Rebraal could not take his eyes from the statue. Ilkar could not take his eyes from Rebraal.

"I understand your anger," he said.

"No, you don't." Rebraal stopped but Ilkar knew there was more to come. "I never dreamed this. We fought so hard, Ilkar; you should have seen the magic and arrows fly. But they were so many. Meru saved me even though he was dying. Even then I thought we had time to regroup and kill the rest. Why did they have to do this? Why this?" He gestured at the disfigured statue. "Yniss save me but I have failed the elves."

"Rebraal, you took on one hundred and thirty with nine. At the end they had a hundred dead," said Ilkar.

"So I failed. And here is the result."

Ilkar opened his mouth to argue but could see instantly it was pointless. It wasn't Rebraal who had failed, it was the Al-Arynaar as an organisation. They and even the TaiGethen were guilty of complacency. It was tragic that so many elves would pay for the mistake without ever knowing why.

"So let's put it right," said Ilkar. "Now."

"Who did this?" Rebraal shook his head. "Who did it?"

"I don't know," said Ilkar.

And he wanted to. Badly. Because if he didn't find out, all Balaia was liable to pay.

"They are your people," spat Rebraal.

Ilkar regarded him blankly. "No, Rebraal, they are not. The Raven are my people and we will help you catch whoever did this."

"You. Your clumsy Raven. Leave it to the TaiGethen."

"What?"

"They will cleanse the forest and then we will all exact revenge."

"Dear Gods, no, they won't cleanse the forest. Rebraal, this was no bounty raid. You were attacked by a highly organised small army and they will have serious backup. Can't you see that? The TaiGethen are brilliant hunters but they're up against something big here and they need to think differently. As do you."

"'Gods.' And which God is it today? Another of the nameless?"

"Who cares, Rebraal? But we need to remake the statue and reclaim the writings. Gods do not enter into it."

"So you believe."

Ilkar grabbed Rebraal's shoulders and turned him. "Listen to me, big brother, because this is how it is. There's a plague engulfing the elven race. Eventually, maybe tomorrow, you and me will both die. Either you can ignore The

Raven and trust to your old ways, or you can live in the present and believe the best mercenaries in Balaia can help you. And we will make a difference. We will."

"Why should I believe you?"

"Because I'm your brother and I only want to help you. Just come and talk to us."

Ilkar could see the desperation in Rebraal's eyes conflicting with his native pride and mistrust.

"It can't possibly hurt just to listen," urged Ilkar.

"Quickly then."

Ilkar smiled. "Come on."

Outside, The Raven were gathered in the shadow of the temple. The sky was an unbroken blue above and a breeze was keeping humidity at bay for a few glorious moments. The idyll, however, was broken by raised voices. Hirad and Ren.

"I thought he might be in danger," protested Ren.

"And you thought the best way to help him was to put yourself, and so us, in the same position, is that right?" said Hirad.

"He needed cover," said Ren.

"We were providing cover," snapped Hirad. "We were shielded, we had a line of swords, we had offensive magic ready to go and, we thought, a bow."

"You weren't fast enough. He needed quicker help."

"Gods burning, I don't have to listen to this." Hirad's face darkened. "Let—"

"There's only one thing you have to understand, Ren. If you fight with The Raven, you do it our way. Our way works. You do not break the line over because that causes people to die. Am I getting through?"

Ilkar watched Ren react. Saw her stubborn folded-armed stance and the sullen expression on her face.

"I did what I thought was right," said Ren.

"And it could have killed us all," returned Hirad. "What if the apron had been trapped? Or there were fifty enemies in the trees? What then, eh?"

"I just—"

"Ren." Hirad lowered his voice a little though the passion remained. "No one is doubting your skill or your desire. But the reason The Raven are still alive and still the best is because we trust each other and we can rely on each other. Utterly. If I don't trust you and I can't rely on you to be where you should be, it means I won't die for you. And then I can't fight with you. That's The Raven's way."

Ren was silent. There really wasn't much to say after that. The eyes of them all were upon her. Her gaze flicked toward Ilkar.

"Doesn't matter who shares your bed, either," said Hirad. "He agrees with me, I can assure you of that. Erienne and Denser understand. In battle, there are no favourites, there's just dead and alive. And we do things our way because it's the right way. Either deal with it or go away. That's the choice."

"Are you going to stand there and let him talk to me like this?" Ren demanded of Ilkar.

"I never stop people when they're right," said Ilkar. He shrugged. "It's something you had to hear."

Ren's expression told him the debate was far from over but she backed away from Hirad nonetheless.

"What was all that about?" asked Rebraal, who had been looking on with a carefully neutral expression. "I didn't catch too much of it."

Ilkar smiled. "Call it administrative guidance. Come on, we've got things to discuss."

With Ilkar translating where necessary, The Raven got to work.

"What's the story up to now?" asked Hirad.

"Apologies if I'm repeating any of this for any of you," said Ilkar. "The temple was attacked by a force of around one hundred and thirty strangers. Probably a hundred were killed but enough survived to take the temple. The TaiGethen cleared the temple three days ago but at least five groups got away carrying writings and, more crucially, the thumb from the statue of Yniss. The TaiGethen and the ClawBound are hunting the escapees."

"Is that it?" asked Hirad.

"So far."

"It's not enough," said The Unknown instantly. "How many people are in each group? How many mages are there with them and where are they headed?"

"Very little is certain, but it looks odds-on that they're heading for the Shorth Estuary to take ship."

"Then that's where we have to get to, and very quickly by the sound of it," said The Unknown. "I mean, if regaining all these things is so important, then we can't risk one of those bastards getting away. Not one. And chasing them through the forest, that's exactly what you're risking."

"The TaiGethen have the skill. They will catch them," said Rebraal.

"You can't take that chance," said The Unknown. "Believe me. Look, your TaiGethen can chase if that's what they want. But we have to get to the estuary. If a hundred and thirty came here to attack, you could be looking at a similar number held in reserve. We have to put ourselves between them and the runners. Close off their escape. That way, we can catch them. All of them. After all, they've nowhere else to go. The TaiGethen risk driving them into the hands of their helpers, don't you see?"

Rebraal did see. It was clear in the relaxation of his expression. "What should we do?"

"Get there and get there fast," said The Unknown. "But be mindful the enemy reserve could be in the forest, not just confined to their ships. You need the TaiGethen and any other forces in the forest to try and slow up the runners. Catch and kill them if they can but not spook them into a dash because they might just make it. Now I'm praying you've got boats nearby because we need to be on them as soon as we can, with as many of your people as you can spare from here."

Rebraal bit his lip. He could see the sense but his mistrust ran deep.

"You've got to make your people understand," said Ilkar, dropping back into elvish. "We want to help. Not just to save the elves but because Balaia needs mages freed so we can rebuild Julatsa for the future. You must trust us. You must."

Roars of big cats, growing in volume, echoed through the forest, punctuated by growls, whines and almost dog-like barks. The Raven surged to their feet, spinning to find the source of the noise as two throats took up the calls from very close by. Across the apron and around the temple all work ceased. The Al-Arynaar, calm, stood listening and waiting as the sounds reverberated all around them, as did Thraun, that smile as if he understood on his lips. The calls cycled over and over before dying away, leaving a few moments of silence before the rain forest creatures rediscovered their collective voice.

Almost immediately a ClawBound pair emerged from the forest at their left. The panther trotted straight into the temple while its elven partner scanned the faces before him, passing briefly over The Raven, nodding at Thraun, before settling on Rebraal. He walked over to the Al-Arynaar leader and the two elves walked alone, talking quietly. As they did, the panther, muzzle soaked in water, walked from the temple and came to stand by The Raven—not threatening, just looking, gauging.

Ilkar couldn't help but be taken by the beauty of the animal and the power it represented. Like every elf, he had been taught total respect for both the ClawBound and TaiGethen elves but panthers held an almost mystical position in elven lore. Even so, he found himself moving slowly backward into the protective crescent The Raven warriors had automatically taken up.

"She won't attack," he said, as much for himself as for any who could hear him.

"She's beautiful," said Erienne.

Thraun knelt by the panther, his hands rubbing her flanks, her head nuzzling into the shapechanger's chest, rocking him on his heels.

"Big teeth," remarked Hirad. "Thraun's got a knack, I'll give him that. Still, never mind that, I wonder what they're talking about?"

Attention moved to Rebraal and the ClawBound elf. The two had stopped. Rebraal was nodding. He bowed his head to the elf and walked quickly back over to The Raven, his hand trailing over the panther's back. She looked at him and licked his hand before rejoining her partner. Rebraal was smiling. Ilkar translated.

"It would appear the TaiGethen share our conclusion, so it's time to move. But remember, we're here under sufferance. We aren't welcome and our actions have to be careful and considered. Any perceived threat will put us with the strangers, whoever they are."

"And you've got to wonder who, haven't you?" said Denser.

"We'll find out soon enough," said Hirad.

CHAPTER 30

Auum led Duele and Evunn along a shallow stream bed into which a run of low waterfalls fed when the rains were at their height. The stream led through a series of gullies, and the crags and rock faces either side were slick with algae and moss. A heavy smell of damp hung in the air and birds circled ceaselessly, looking for stranded fish in the pools, which cut off quickly when the rains ceased.

The stream, which flowed eventually into the Shorth, made travel easy, and the Tai moved quickly, keeping up a run for hours on end, bows slung across backs, boots slapping down on the wet rock. Auum felt an exhilaration through him as he ran. He could feel his hair flowing out behind him, his heart beating hard and fast, his legs pumping, his arms the perfect balance. Even though the harmony all around him was torn and bleeding, he could sense the energy of the forest and the sounds of Tual's denizens filled him with hope and belief.

Trotting round a gentle left-hand bend, leaping a deep pool and splashing down into the ankle-deep water on a fine silt bed, Auum saw two from another Tai cell ahead. He recognised them instantly. Marack, the leader, stood over the seated form of Nokhe. Both her hands were on Nokhe's shoulders and she was speaking to him, or was she praying?

Auum spread his arms and his Tai slowed to a stop by their colleagues. As they did, Marack looked up, her face a picture of anguish. Auum's exhilaration drained from him and shifted his gaze to Nokhe. The chest of the TaiGethen's shirt was covered in a fine mist of blood.

"Yniss save us," he gasped, dropping to his knees in front of the stricken elf. "Nokhe."

"It is the Sorrow," said Marack, her voice quiet, robbed of its usual confidence.

"When did it start?" asked Auum.

"At dawn today," said Nokhe, his breathing rasping painfully through ravaged lungs. "It is a pain like no other, Auum. I'm dying and there is nothing you or Yniss can do."

"I will do all that I can," said Auum, fighting the urge to scream his frustration at Yniss and his hatred of the strangers. "I will pray for you and all those afflicted. This is a test of our faith and I will not fail it."

Nokhe's smile was bloody. "Just find the desecrators. And their masters. Before the TaiGethen are gone and our people left defenceless."

"Walk with me in the forest," said Auum.

"I can sense all I need from here," said Nokhe, his breath hissing suddenly, his face lined and his colour drained and weak. "I cannot stand for now. My stomach is shivered and the pain is too much. I am so glad it is you I see with my last clear sight. You and Marack."

Auum looked up at Marack. "And Hohan. Collecting herbs for the pain?"

Marack shook her head and her face fell still further. "He is not coming back," she whispered. "The Sorrow took him yesterday. He is giving himself to the forest while he still has the strength."

Auum rocked back on his heels, stunned. Only now did he take in that TaiGethen would also die. No one was safe, not even Yniss's most faithful servants.

"And you, my brother?" asked Auum.

"I do not wish to die alone as Hohan," said Nokhe. "When the pain passes, I will walk the forest a final time with Marack. Soon, I hope." His acceptance of his fate could not mask his fear.

"And I will also be at your side."

"No, Auum. Only Marack may see me die. You must remember me in life."

Auum nodded and leaned forward. He cupped the back of Nokhe's head in his hands and kissed his forehead, cheeks and finally, tenderly, his lips. "May Tual choose you as her champion in paradise."

He stood and turned to Marack. "Strength," he said. "When you have walked alone and the contemplation is done, join us. I fear many Tai will be shorn of numbers."

Auum signalled his Tai. Duele and Evunn paid their respects to Nokhe, exhorting Shorth to speed his passage to the heart of Yniss. But before they began to run again, Auum drew them close.

"If you should be taken by the Sorrow, I will not hesitate to escort you into the embrace of the forest. And you will do the same for me. Now come, we have work to do."

Yron and Erys supported Ben-Foran between them now but it scarcely made travel any quicker or easier. Moving away from the bank of the Shorth for the time being to avoid being seen from the other side, they had found no respite deeper in the forest. The lianas hung everywhere. Huge spiders' webs drifted in any clear space and the trees were so close packed they had to back up and change direction constantly.

With every pace Yron feared the sound of a jaqrui, its ghostly wailing as it scythed toward his back or his head. Erys's arrival had surely exhausted their luck and came close to the miracle for which he'd been hoping, but the death of the ClawBound pair, when it was discovered, would intensify the hunt. And they were still two days from the estuary and—he hoped— the welcoming embrace of the reserve force and the ship back to Balaia.

He still hadn't let himself believe they would make it because he was sure it would dull his focus. And with the TaiGethen after them, that was something he could not afford. Yet slung between him and Erys was a man whose cries would surely attract the hunters. Ben-Foran's legs were festering. The bandages were mostly torn off now, exposing his terrible wounds to the elements and a new host of remorseless insects and burrowing worms.

How the boy was still alive was beyond him. Erys had intimated the same and had expended what little there was left of his mana stamina trying to numb the pain and fight the infection. But there was so much damage and he was already exhausted. Yron was grateful he had the strength to support some of Ben's weight.

They'd walked without stopping for more than an occasional short breather until well into the afternoon. Ben had drifted in and out of consciousness but had kept up his questions and talk whenever he was alert. But thirst had overcome them and Yron had boiled water and herbs together for them all, scraping guarana into the mixture to disguise its unpalatable texture and taste.

Following the inevitable rainfall, they'd continued, and now the sun was waning in the sky as the clouds gathered for another soaking. Like them all, Yron suspected, he had come to almost welcome it.

"Do they do anything else, the TaiGethen?" asked Ben suddenly.

Yron hadn't realised the boy had regained consciousness and he laughed.

"Mind still going, is it, son?" he said.

"About the only thing that is, sir."

"Anything else than what?" Erys joined the conversation.

There'd been a lengthy and deepening silence between them all and the sound of their own voices lifted their spirits from the pit into which they had fallen.

"Well, I don't know. Looking after the temple and the forest, I suppose," said Ben.

"No, they don't. And actually they don't look after the temple directly. That's the elves we fought, the Al-Arynaar. They are the keepers. They rotate their duties and live in villages much of the time. The TaiGethen never leave the forest. Not ever."

"So what do they do?" asked Ben.

"Well, besides the obvious it's actually rather hard to explain. They have a complex set of beliefs built around the harmony of the forest, the earth, the sky and magic. The TaiGethen are effectively the most zealous priests of the religion and they spend their lives dedicated to maintaining that harmony. Whatever it takes. Hunting people like us they believe have wronged them, monitoring animal populations, keeping tabs on elven settlements and logging. That sort of thing."

"Like a city guard," said Erys. "But in the forest, if you see what I mean."

"Hardly," said Yron. "That's like saying—I don't know—that Protectors are like city militia, only better trained. The TaiGethen have tracking and hunting skills like you wouldn't believe. Or maybe you would, Erys. They are silent, they're impossibly quick and you never see them until they're about to kill you. They don't want pay or glory. Bloody hell, they make Protectors look clumsy and slow, that's how good they are."

There was a contemplative silence. They walked on, skirting a particularly thick web in which a huge spider was wrapping up its latest catch, and ducking under the moving branches of a balsa tree. Above them, a young python watched, too small to consider them likely prey. The air was getting heavier as rain neared.

"And you think we can make the ship?" asked Ben yet again.

"If our luck holds," replied Yron, same as always. "I know what you're saying, but they really are that good. There just aren't very many of them in relation to the size of the forest."

"Will they chase us across the sea, do you think?" asked Erys. "Gods, I want this to be over when we get on board."

Yron shook his head. "Not them. We've only taken a few papers, when all's said and done. It's a crime, but when we're out of the forest the harmony can be restored. No, we'll get delegations from the Al-Arynaar and probably the race elders." Yron chuckled. "Don't worry, Erys; you won't have to spend every day looking over your shoulder."

Another silence but it had a clearer quality to it. Yron might have scared them with his description of the TaiGethen, but the thought of the safety of the ships was a spur to the mind and body, and for a few hundred yards the forest didn't seem so dense. And then the rain came, and the world closed in again.

With over a dozen Al-Arynaar staying at Aryndeneth, there was plenty of room in the boats at the moorings two hours east of the temple on the River Shorth. Word was that more Al-Arynaar were coming from all directions. They would be sent immediately downstream to the estuary, or toward Ysundeneth along the Ix in case any of the strangers broke that way. Hirad thought the latter unlikely, given they'd have very little knowledge of anything other than their original route, but it kept the net tight.

Four of the shallow elven craft began the race to the Shorth Estuary, which cut into the north coast of Calaius perhaps three days' sail east of Ysundeneth. The Shorth was one of the three principal rivers draining the rain forest, but unlike the Ix and the Orra none of its feeder streams connected with its sisters. Three boats carried a dozen elves each and one The Raven and Rebraal, who was none too pleased to be forced to travel with the humans despite their grudging truce.

Hirad found it all a little comical if irritating. The Raven were shunned almost completely—tolerated only because Ilkar was Rebraal's brother—and assumed to be inferior. It was also clear that Ilkar and Ren were somehow lessened by their association with the humans. That The Raven might actually be able to help the elves hadn't occurred to them at all as far as he could see.

"Don't let it get to you," said The Unknown, seeing Hirad scowl across at the nearest boat full of Al-Arynaar.

"We're ready to fight a battle for them," said Hirad. "We won't get paid although we might get hurt and they're treating us like shit. Sorry, but it *is* getting to me."

"They can't discard centuries of prejudice just like that," said Ilkar from further forward, beneath the billowing sail. There was no need to row just yet, the breeze angling across the Shorth driving them at a good speed on the back of the prevailing current. "Particularly with what's just happened to them."

"But we aren't anything to do with the temple raiders," said Hirad. "Do they assume all elves are the same? Is it so difficult for them to understand people can be different from one another? Gods, Ilkar, but if you weren't an elf I wouldn't be putting up with this."

"So do it for Ilkar alone," said The Unknown.

"I am," said Hirad. "And Ren. And any elf I know that's still alive back on Balaia. I would just like some recognition from this ungrateful bunch that we're on their side and trying to help. Not too much to ask."

"They aren't like us," said Denser. "You just have to accept that."

"That doesn't make it all right, Denser." Hirad looked along the bench to where the Xeteskian sat with Erienne in his arms. "I'm not like them. Don't see me being a tosser do you?"

"Not yet, anyway," said Ilkar.

Hirad shrugged and rubbed at his unshaven chin, then at his legs. "Glad we're out of the forest for a bit," he said. "What about you, Darrick?"

The Lysternan general looked around with pursed lips. "I was loving it," he said. "Nothing I enjoy more than being eaten from the inside."

Hirad laughed, knowing the Al-Arynaar would look round. "It's that pasty pampered cavalryman flesh of yours. I told you years ago you should have joined us."

"And then I'd have had to put up with boils and bites. How are yours, by the way?"

"Very well, thanks," said Hirad.

"There's a serious point to be made here," said The Unknown in that voice none could ignore. "We've got a couple of days of relative calm now. We should use it. Mages should get as much sleep as possible, and the rest of us should look after ourselves as well as we can. Only ask for a spell if you're getting sick. Agreed?"

Hirad looked over at Aeb, who occupied the back of the boat with them. The Protector had attracted no special interest from the Al-Arynaar. And that in itself was telling about how self-centred the temple defenders were. Someone of Aeb's size and appearance got attention everywhere.

"How's the face, Aeb?"

The mask turned toward him, the eyes fixing him neutrally. "I am not inconvenienced."

"Good. So does that mean you're clear of sores and bites or that they're under control?"

"I am not inconvenienced."

"Leave it, Hirad," said The Unknown. "It is Aeb's business and he will seek assistance should he need it. That's all you need to know."

"Whatever you say." Hirad was already bored despite the fact they'd only been on the boat a short time. "Hey, Thraun, you all right?"

The shapechanger had been silent since climbing the tree for the crossing of the River Ix. Hirad had watched him from time to time and there was no doubting his love of the rain forest. Thraun listened intently to the sounds and took pleasure in the creatures they encountered. He'd been the only one not surprised by the ClawBound communication and Hirad suspected he understood it.

What went on in that mind of his none of them could fathom. Darrick, who had taken on his blade training, had elicited almost nothing from him, and The Unknown, whom Thraun often shadowed closer than a Protector, couldn't persuade him to talk. Despite his silence, however, his fighting instincts were clearly there and Hirad had total confidence in his ability to do the right thing. Something he didn't yet have in Ren.

Thraun looked over and shrugged. His body was almost free of bites.

Either the drink Rebraal made them worked particularly well for him or his skin retained its lupine toughness. Seeing he wasn't going to get anything more, Hirad turned his attention to Ilkar, a smile returning to his face.

"Hey, Ilks, your girlfriend all right, is she?"

He saw Ren stiffen where she sat in the prow, looking determinedly forward. Ilkar, though, needed no goading.

"Drop it, Hirad," he warned, his ears pricking and reddening in irritation.

"Just wanted to be sure everything was all right between you two, you know. I'd hate there to be bad feeling."

"Everything will be fine as long as you keep your nose out of it," said Ilkar. "Just leave it alone."

"You're sure there's nothing I can do to help?"

"Besides throwing yourself over the side?"

"Sorry I spoke," said Hirad.

"As are we all," said Erienne. "Hirad, you can be such a child. You're giving me a headache."

"Erienne?" asked The Unknown.

"It's all right, thank you."

The Unknown grabbed the scruff of Hirad's jerkin and pulled him back, putting his mouth close to the barbarian's ear.

"We love your banter, Hirad," he said, "but sometimes silence is preferable to your incessant babble. Now is one of those times."

Hirad shook himself loose, sat back up and looked round, seeing the warning in The Unknown's face. "Roll on the estuary," he muttered.

It was two days before Hirad's wish was granted.

Chapter 31

The Shorth Estuary was a confused conjugation of half a dozen channels feeding off the main river flow. The low-lying land had created a wide shallow swamp on the margin of which brackish water filtered into the silt-filled estuary, which was bordered by stunning waterfall-strewn cliffs. Far out beyond the estuary mouth, where the water ran deep, calm and sheltered, would lie the enemy ships.

The Raven had left their boats hidden well upstream and had been brought along the west bank of the Shorth to the edge of the dense rain forest where it merged into the largely open but mangrove-bordered swamp. Past it, the outflow to the estuary was just about visible.

"This isn't going to be easy," said Hirad.

Darrick concurred. He'd been imagining a wide shallow sand plain washed by tidal waters on which a battle could be organised and won by superior tactics. What he was faced with was his worst nightmare of close-quarters combat on uncertain and possibly deadly terrain. The only saving grace was that he had no horses with him. They would have been a pure encumbrance.

"What do you think, Darrick?" asked The Unknown.

Even though he shouldn't have felt flattered by the question he was, but he'd not exactly been looking forward to answering it. With the Al-Arynaar spread out to cover the likely escape routes of any surviving runners and the fabled TaiGethen yet to make an appearance, The Raven were alone in the field and they were peerless tacticians.

"The question is, what are the enemy thinking?" said Darrick.

"Is it?" asked Denser. But The Unknown was already nodding, giving Darrick the confidence to carry on.

"We're making dangerous assumptions at the moment. Which is fine if the enemy either aren't here or not expecting anyone. But not helpful at all if there are either more of them than we think, or they've been contacted and are already dug in and prepared.

"Now we're able to see the terrain we have to deal with we can ask the questions that need asking. What we know is that the enemy have, or had, mage support. Should we assume they have contacted the reserve and, if so, at what point? And then, what information could they have passed on and what is the likely response of the reserve?"

"Right, assume this, then," said The Unknown. "They know the number of runners. They know how near they are and how fast they are. They also know the hunters are close behind and that they have to establish a safe perimeter beyond the open ground of the estuary itself. Any suggestions?"

"Narrowest defensible point," said Hirad. "But where open space for the runners to cross is limited or at least covered by archer and mage fire."

"Correct," said Darrick. "See where the outflow begins between the cliff edges?" He pointed to an area perhaps three hundred yards across. "It's the most secure but it's broken by the outflow and the larger channels. It can't be completely spanned and any force would have to fragment to hold it."

"So why would they set their line there?" asked Erienne.

"Because if they come any further forward, the forest takes over and they can be outflanked far more easily. They need the cliff edges to secure their flanks. And because there can't possibly be enough of them to hold a longer line. And to defend further seaward is pointless. The defenders will have their view of the swamp and forest edge disabled because there'll be no flank view. And the flanks are where our runners are most likely to break cover.

"There's something else." Darrick smiled. "They might know a few TaiGethen are coming but there's no way they can be aware that fifty swords and a few mages have come downstream. No way."

"So what?" said Denser, looking around at the huge arc of forest that ten times fifty couldn't hope to cover effectively.

"So it gives me an idea."

It was not long before the Al-Arynaar reported back that enemy forces were in place bordering the swamp area, so dispelling the vague anxiety that the runners had already been and gone. Without confirmation from TaiGethen or ClawBound about the position of any of the hunted, The Raven had to assume they could appear at any time.

After a great deal of debate, Darrick's plan was put in place, though the former general had advised Rebraal to present it to the elves as his own. The Al-Arynaar scouts had been within thirty feet of the forward enemy positions and reported seventy swordsmen spread across the outlet to the estuary, backed by fifteen archers and what were assumed to be six mages. The elves were also confident that more strangers were positioned in deeper cover, less than Darrick had assumed but a threat nevertheless. The strangers were positioned much as expected, with good immediate fields of fire or open spaces to strike into, but Darrick had no intention of facing them on their own terms.

With the arrival of the TaiGethen imminent, Darrick had advised that to be sure of seeing and then stopping any of the runners, they should not spread their line too thin in an attempt to cover the impossible. So the Al-Arynaar and Raven were gathered in four groups—their boat groups—in an arc around the open area of the swamp looking both in and out.

The Raven and Rebraal were out on the left flank, as close as they dared to the enemy but in a position where none could circle them unseen. Al-Arynaar elves took up a similar position opposite them on the east bank with the other two groups closer to the Shorth, one on either bank. Darrick considered that the two flanking groups would be able to cut off runners from anywhere, while the central groups could take down any that came too close but, more importantly, would engage the reserve in the event of them being drawn out.

Tucked into position with nothing to do but wait, Hirad crouched at the end of The Raven line slightly apart from the rest to give him a view of the edge of the cliffs where they soared into the darkening sky and the ground between their position and the enemy line. Looking right, he could just about see Darrick, eyes everywhere, assessing whether he'd set everyone right and searching his mind for anything he'd missed. He was relying on the speed of response and the skill of the TaiGethen, and his lack of knowledge of them clearly worried him.

Behind Hirad, Thraun was looking back into the forest, his keen eyes as good as any elf's, his ears tuned to the sounds around him, listening for any approach. The barbarian smiled. With his sword in his hand and The Raven poised around him, Hirad felt good.

He felt a prick in the side of his neck, sharp and deliberate. He moved his head, his eyes straining round. The blade of a dagger entered his vision. He raised a hand and began to turn his body slowly. His eyes moved up the hilt of the dagger, along the dark-garbed arm and up into a face painted in deep greens and browns. The elf behind the paint stared back with undisguised hatred, his whispered words conveying his intent though Hirad understood none of them.

He should have been scared, he knew, but instead he was impressed at the stealth that had brought the elf so close without any of them knowing. To cry out would probably be to die. He and half The Raven. The TaiGethen, and he assumed this was one, worked in threes, so Rebraal had said.

But they were not invincible. Hirad smiled.

"I don't know what you're saying, my friend, but one thing you should know is that no Raven is ever alone."

Thraun's sword rested against the elf's neck in turn. He stiffened and hissed, his eyes narrowing but never moving from Hirad. Sudden commotion from two sides and harsh whispered words stopped the situation developing any further. Two more elves came in from Hirad's right as he sat, Rebraal and The Unknown from the left. Hirad pushed the blade of the dagger away.

"Sheath it unless you intend to use it."

The elf didn't understand him either but he and Rebraal spoke quickly and urgently, the elf still with his gaze locked on Hirad.

"These your famous TaiGethen, are they?" asked Hirad.

"Not now," warned The Unknown.

Ilkar had joined them and got Thraun to move his blade. At last the painted elf looked away and up at Rebraal. He snorted contemptuously and bent back toward Hirad, whispering something meaningful before moving silently away, taking his two colleagues with him.

"Clever," said Thraun.

"You're lucky you're not dead," said Ilkar.

"So's he," said Hirad. "Who is he?"

"That's Auum, leader of the TaiGethen. You don't want to know what he was saying to you."

Hirad shrugged. "No, I don't. What I do want to know is, where are the runners?"

Ilkar put the question to Rebraal.

"They've caught and killed another two groups of warriors further into the forest. That's eleven men down altogether. There are others apparently on both banks but they haven't a bead on any of them. This side, Auum says the strangers are travelling under magical obscurement of some kind. On the other, there's someone he apparently respects for his forest skill but wants to skin for killing a ClawBound pair. Their guess is that both sets of men are close. More TaiGethen are crossing the river now. We shouldn't have to wait too long."

But they did. All the rest of that day and on into the night. It was a very uncomfortable vigil. They had no relief, they had no time to eat anything other than dried meat and they had to ignore the inevitable host of insects as best they could. In the heat, humidity and rain it was a test of stamina and endurance. The TaiGethen and ClawBound were combing the forest but had so far found nothing.

Leaving Thraun, Ren, Aeb and Rebraal watching in all directions as the light faded to nothing, The Raven talked.

"It'll happen under cover of darkness," said Darrick.

"No reason why," said Ilkar. "They'll know elves see just as well now as in daylight."

Darrick tapped his head. "The reasons are all up here. Remember, they're scared and tired. They want every advantage, real or perceived."

"Think they're in contact with this lot ahead?" asked Hirad.

"Impossible to say," said Darrick.

"I doubt it," said Denser. "Communion's a spell their mages can't afford.

It's draining at the best of times. And thinking about how we were all beginning to feel just coping with the insect bites . . ." He shrugged.

"He's right," said Ilkar. "And don't forget, we've got one group apparently under some kind of moving illusion that's good enough to confuse elves and panthers. That's going to be one impressive spell."

"Why don't they just come straight in?" asked Erienne. "I mean, if that spell is so good, why are they worrying? Just wander up to the line and be safe."

"Good point, but I suspect it's the terrain," said Darrick. "Splashing through that swamp will be like ringing warning bells, hidden by illusion or not."

"Right," said The Unknown. "Here's what I suggest now."

But he didn't have time to impart his idea because, a hundred yards to their right, the swamp exploded into life. Footsteps rushed headlong through water, plumes of spray scattering in all directions. There was the deeper splash of thigh-deep water and, from the lines ahead, the odd voice raised in encouragement.

"Raven!" roared Hirad. "Raven with me!"

Hirad led The Raven out of cover, heading for their holding position on the left flank.

"HardShield up," said Ilkar.

"SpellShield active," said Erienne.

"Keep watching that left flank," warned The Unknown.

"On it," said Darrick.

"Denser, we need that illusion pierced," said Hirad.

"Way ahead of you," said the Xeteskian.

The Raven plunged into the swamp shallows, keeping their arc line as best they could in the heavy vegetation at its edge. Behind the hidden runners, the Al-Arynaar and TaiGethen were coming. The moon broke through the clouds, giving the swamp and forest an eerie luminescence; a multiple wailing pierced the air and Hirad saw the glint of metal in the sky. A panther roared, its voice taken up by a dozen more.

Denser came to a sudden stop, uttered a command word and shoved his arms out sharply. His ForceCone hammered away into the night, slapping into the roiling area of swamp where the runners had to be. Suddenly, men were visible, sprawling in the water, dragging themselves back to their feet. It hadn't been an illusion. Some sort of multiple target CloakedWalk. But now it was gone and that was all the TaiGethen needed. With extraordinary speed, three of them cut through the swamp almost as if they were skating across the surface of the water. Blades glittered in the moonlight.

The shouts from the estuary entrance became louder and more urgent. The thrum of bowstrings was plain. Arrows arced across the sky, falling behind the runners, slicing into the swamp waters. After them came FlameOrbs, four pairs, their orange glows like dying suns, throwing shadows into sharp relief and lighting up the faces of the TaiGethen, who scattered instantly.

"Ward!" shouted Denser.

The Raven stilled. FlameOrbs spattered down on them, fizzing and crackling over Ilkar's shield. It held. It always did.

In the afterglow of the spells, the runners saw their plight all too plainly. One threw a bag to another, the mage. He stood stock-still, desperately trying to cast. His three companions gathered in front of him as the TaiGethen tore into them. The first leapt high, left leg snapping out, taking his opponent in the chest. The man staggered back, sword swiping at empty air. The TaiGethen drove through his unbalanced guard, piercing his neck. The second and third elves flung jaqrui. They were knocked aside but their targets were distracted. With incredible swiftness, the TaiGethen blades whipped in. The expanding slick of blood was black in the moonlight.

ShadowWings sprouted at the mage's back. He shot skyward, a laugh of relief on his lips. Jaqrui wailed after him, none finding its target. He turned in the air, flying for the enemy line.

"Damn!" yelled Hirad.

Behind him, a bowstring twanged. The arrow speared the mage between his shoulder blades. He juddered forward and shouted briefly, arms clawing reflexively at his back. His wings vanished and he fell, momentum taking him just beyond the swamp edge. No-man's-land.

Hirad turned. "Good shooting."

The smile was back on Ren's face but there was no time for self-congratulation.

"We must have that bag," said Rebraal in halting Balaian.

He set off, TaiGethen and Al-Arynaar two hundred yards behind him but sprinting through the swamp and gaining quickly. "Leave the water," he said over his shoulder. "Piranha."

But The Raven were already chasing after him. Hirad saw more arrows arc toward them and the elves from the estuary defenders. HotRain fell from the sky. Here was where it would happen. The sides closed on each other, the mage's body marking where the lines would clash.

"Watch that left flank!" he shouted as he raced on, sword raised high, running for the enemy.

Erys hadn't the stamina to cast Communion again but ClearSight was far more simple. He'd related to Yron everything he could see through the darkness. TaiGethen and Al-Arynaar were on both sides of the Shorth, some closing in behind them now. As Yron had hoped, their reserve force was spread across the entrance to the estuary, unfortunately split by the Shorth and its channels, but so were the elves.

Yron, Erys and the miraculously still living Ben-Foran were an agonising three hundred yards from safety in the hands of the reserve. But Yron smelled a trap and he'd been alive too long to ignore his instincts. He put a hand on Erys's shoulder, staying the mage, who was preparing to run in.

"Wait," he said.

"But . . ."

"Wait," he repeated. "This isn't the stroll it seems. Trust me."

Almost at once he was proved right. A commotion on the other side of the Shorth shattered the relative peace of the rain forest. They could hear footsteps splashing through water and the shouts of men and elves. Arrows and spells flew, the TaiGethen pounced, panthers sounded from every angle. The ClawBound were near.

Erys grabbed Yron's shoulder and pointed into the sky.

"Stenys," he breathed.

Yron followed his arm and saw the mage climbing into the sky.

"Go on." Yron clenched a fist. "Go on."

Stenys wheeled and moved toward the estuary, getting higher all the time. Jaqrui wailed but missed. Yron's heart beat harder.

"Nearly there," he whispered. "Shit!"

He saw the arrow plunge into Stenys's back. Saw him fall from the sky and saw the elves move toward his body. Erys's grip on his shoulder slackened.

"Sorry, Erys."

Erys shook his head. "So close."

"And we'll get closer still. Our chance is very soon."

Yron focussed on the coming battle. He knew there were Al-Arynaar very close but in the confusion they might just get enough of a head start. If their luck held. He smiled grimly. This would not be a good time for it to falter.

The reserve waited, just as they should. Hidden from view. Arrows and spells arced into the moonlit night. He saw flaring as shields took the brunt of the magic and explosions on the ground where the Orbs fell directly to earth. Behind him he thought he could sense something but he couldn't see any movement. Perhaps the elves this side of the Shorth were distracted. He had to hope so.

With a clash of steel, the two forces met. It had to be now or never.

"Ready, Ben?" Ben-Foran was propped against a tree. He looked dog-tired but nodded anyway.

"Erys, you're flying."

"No, sir. I'm carrying. I don't have the stamina or the nerve for wings anyway."

Yron nodded. "If we falter, run on. Don't hesitate. We need those writings safe."

The two men lifted Ben between them, balanced his weight and stood, breathing hard, pulses tripping fast, every nerve alive. In front of them, three hundred yards of forest, swamp, water and then safety. It looked a terribly long way.

"Don't look back, don't cry out, don't even blink," Yron said. "As soon as we break cover, run like you've never run before."

They manoeuvred Ben to the very edge of the forest. Right in front of them, the swamp waters glimmered darkly. Yron prayed the piranha were too busy feasting on the bodies of the others by now. And the crocodiles. He shivered.

"All right, you two bastards," he whispered, then almost laughed as he said words he never thought he'd hear himself utter. "Run for your lives."

Chapter 32

Denser ran behind Hirad and The Unknown Warrior in what was surely the safest place on the battlefield. Beside him Ilkar and Erienne, minds deep in concentration, ran steadily, their consciousnesses divided using a skill only the finest truly mastered.

The Raven kept hard to the left flank, leaving the fight for the mage's body and the bag he carried to the elves in the left centre. The mage had fallen close to the bank. While The Raven held the flank and pressured the centre, the elves would have to contend with the enemy in front of them and possible fire from across the river. So far, the elves on the right bank hadn't moved to attack. Instead they continued moving up slowly, trying to flush out anyone that might be hidden there.

As he ran, Denser prepared again, this time the same spell as Erienne would choose once The Raven were engaged and she could drop the Hard-Shield in safety. They would cast together so, for now, he fine-tuned his mana shape and scanned the enemy no more than twenty yards ahead as they splashed out of the swamp. More arrows came in, rattling uselessly on the HardShield, spots of HotRain fizzing over Ilkar's rock-steady casting.

The scene had a distinctly surreal quality to it. The afterglow of spells burned a halo in the air above, the moon ebbed and strengthened as cloud passed across it, and the forest animals were silent under the sudden barrage of violence unleashed in their midst.

In the curious half-light, Denser saw the faces of those they were about to fight. Men who had been hiding for a pace too long, believing they would have the element of surprise but now having to charge at their enemy. And as they came Denser could see they recognised who they were about to fight. Mouths spoke The Raven's name and more than one faltered in his stride while grips shifted on weapons and eyes betrayed growing fear.

They shouted orders and encouragement as they came, closing with Hirad Coldheart and The Unknown Warrior, The Raven's heart for fifteen years. With Ry Darrick, Balaia's most famous soldier and now deserter. With Thraun, the shapechanger. And with a blank-faced Protector. Men who gave you an edge even before a blow was struck.

Hirad roared to clear his mind, energise The Raven and inspire more fear, his sword crashing down right to left across his chest, his legs already moving to balance him for his defence and next strike. He sheared his enemy's blade, sending the man stumbling back, then reversed his sword up into the unprotected chin, hurling his corpse back into his faltering comrades.

"HardShield down," said Erienne. "Preparing offence."

Next to Hirad, The Unknown caught a strike on the guard of his dagger, twisted the enemy weapon aside and swept his sword into the ribs of his opponent. Not waiting for him to drop, he stormed forward, headbutting the man behind and punching his dagger into his temple.

Beside him, Aeb slashed a path, his wide-bladed axe scything through helmet and bone, his sword stabbing forward like a rapier. He made no sound, just exuded control and destruction. And at his side, Darrick ducked and twisted, his blade held in two hands, now in one, never letting a sharp edge get close to him, death and injury in every strike he dealt out. At the opposite end of the line, with Ren behind him firing shaft after shaft into the defending mages, Thraun powered his way into the line, his howls like those of the wolves he had left behind, his animal side allowed free rein.

"Ready, Denser?" asked Erienne.

"I am," he replied. "On your command."

"Hirad, Unknown, Aeb," she shouted. "On my word."

Denser saw each of them nod his understanding, never breaking the rhythm of their blows.

"Down!"

The trio dropped as Denser and Erienne took a half pace and cast. IceWind savaged over their heads and scourged into the line ahead. The strangers' SpellShields screamed as the cold hit, those under the Shields shrinking back, mist and gale filling the air in front of them. In the background a mage cried out in pain. Someone shrieked at him to hold firm. Still the IceWind raged, its edges reaching out and chilling everything it touched.

Ren's bow sang, the screaming mage crumpled, the shield collapsed and the awful spell ripped into the helpless enemy, freezing flesh and bone, blinding, cracking and breaking. Cries cut off as mouths were paralysed. Metal shattered, men fell, the line fractured and The Raven ploughed on.

"Come on!" yelled Hirad, and Denser knew it was as much for the elves on their right as The Raven themselves. The barbarian hurdled a frozen body, chased into the vegetation and began the fight again, his friends left, right and behind as he knew they would be.

Denser glanced along the line, saw the TaiGethen weaving their swift death, the Al-Arynaar providing mage and blade support. More FlameOrbs soared out, casting their ghastly light. Across the river, he could see more of the enemy, looking on helplessly as their companions were taken apart. And there, splashing through the swamp and caught in the moonlight, were the other runners.

Almost straight away, Ben's legs had given way. Erys and Yron scooped him into a chair lift, the lad gasping in agony as rough hands and leather scraped at his raw infected wounds. Yron had his arm high up around Ben's chest, Erys supporting his lower back, as they splashed into the shallows of the swamp.

Yron tried to hear everything around him above the sound of his own breathing, of his feet hitting the water over and over. He strained for the sounds of pursuit, of the wail of jaqrui and the whistle of arrows. But with every pace he took he heard none of it. He began to dare to believe they might actually make it.

A hundred and fifty yards to go and he saw men standing up, beckoning them on, urging and encouraging. Others of the reserve ran to join them, some carrying bows. Shouts went up, increasing in their urgency as Yron and Erys pounded across the swamp, dragging their calves through the deepening water.

"Keep going," gasped Yron.

"I hadn't thought of stopping," replied Erys.

Ben's breathing was ragged and tortured.

"Nor had I," he managed.

Arrows started to fly. The shouts of encouragement became a clamour for more pace and men ran toward them. Faces looked desperate now, exhorting them to greater effort. FlameOrbs soared high over their heads, heading for the pursuing pack. And now Yron could hear them. A flurry of feet rushing through the swamp. Not far behind. Perhaps not far enough.

More arrows arced over them. The elves replied in kind, shafts fired on the run hissing past, slapping into the water around them. Jaqrui wailed and whistled. Yron ducked reflexively.

"Faster," he said. "We've got to go faster."

Erys responded and the two men upped their pace. Yron felt the water become shallow again and relief flooded through him. He looked forward, seeing naked fear on the faces of those only seventy yards in front of them now and he thanked the Gods he had no time to look round. He didn't need to. He knew how fast an elf could run.

"Stay with us, Ben, we're so nearly there," he said.

Ben's words were little more than grunts of pain. "If our luck holds."

"It's holding," said Erys. "Keep going."

On they ran. More arrows splashed around them, others flew past seeking elven targets. Jaqrui fizzed and keened. A panther roared.

"Oh dear Gods," muttered Yron.

He could hear his men now. Yelling at him, pleading. The second roar was close, so very close. Some of his men moved further forward and began to form a line. Thirty yards to go. Twenty.

A huge impact sent them all sprawling. Ben screamed. Yron felt his left arm torn half out of its socket. He rolled over and came to his haunches.

"No!" he bellowed. "No!"

The panther had leapt on Ben's back and taken him down. Yron ran forward, hitching out his axe; the animal looked up, yellow eyes boring into him. It made to spring again.

Erys was shouting. "Yron, no!"

Very deliberately, the panther bit down, snapping the boy's neck.

"Bastard!" Yron made to move but felt arms around his shoulders, forcing him back.

"We've got to go, now!" Erys's face was right in his.

Yron could see the elves closing in just a few yards away. He saw his reserve running in to block their path. He saw more arrows and spells, Flame-Orbs lighting up the sky giving him a last look at Ben-Foran. His strength abruptly went and his men dragged him away, his gaze locked on the body.

"I'm sorry, Ben," he said, the tears misting his vision. "I'm so sorry."

Rebraal had seen the action on the right bank of the river and came running up from the elven line, which was driving the enemy inexorably back. The Raven were trading blows with more competent soldiers now, progress slow but still sure.

"Runners are through," he shouted.

Denser turned, losing the shape he'd been creating. In front of him, Hirad blocked a strike to his chest, shoved his attacker back with a grunt and rained down blow after overhead blow, swearing as he bludgeoned.

"We'll push hard," said Denser.

"You must get to the estuary. We must catch them."

"Hirad!" shouted Denser. "Runners broken through right."

Hirad nodded. He crashed his blade down a final time, smashing the weakened defence aside and crushing his opponent's skull, blood and brain spraying into the air.

"Raven! Pushing right. Go!"

Darrick and Aeb responded immediately, arcing in, driving the defenders back toward the river. Aeb upped the rate of his strikes, delivering overhead with his axe and sweeping horizontally with his sword. Around the back of them TaiGethen came running, forcing themselves into the gap, sprinting away behind the strangers' lines, dealing mayhem and death.

"Let's give them space!" shouted Hirad. "Denser, the archers!"

"Got you. Erienne, ForceCone. I'll carry you."

Denser uttered a short incantation. ShadowWings appeared at his back. Erienne nodded and he swept her into his arms and straight up into the night sky. He could see a group of half a dozen archers kneeling in a circle, loosing off shots at the TaiGethen elves.

"Ready," said Erienne.

Denser angled his body horizontal to the ground and tightened his grip on Erienne, who hung below him, his arms clasped under her breasts, her legs locked around his. He heard her mutter and drag at the air with her fingers as she finished the preparation. He flew over the archers, just thirty feet above their heads. One looked up instinctively, shouted and angled his bow. Too late.

Erienne jerked her arms downward. The ForceCone flared out, battering the archers to the earth. Bows and limbs snapped as the pressure of the spell beat relentlessly down, compressing everything beneath it into a six-inch-deep indentation in the soft ground, perfectly circular and ten yards across.

Denser circled while Erienne maintained the Cone until the pleading and crying out had stopped. She thrust her arms again, hard. Denser imagined, only too easily, the rib cages crumpling. He wheeled back toward The Raven before any fire could be brought to bear on them, magical or otherwise.

"Angry about something?" he asked.

"You could say," she said. "My head is killing me."

Denser cruised in low over the left flank. Below them The Raven and Al-Arynaar were breaking the last of the resistance. With TaiGethen in behind them, the enemy were cut off and frightened. And while the Al-Arynaar, unused to in-line battle, were able to make little headway, The Raven had no such trouble and corpses littered the ground in their wake. One massive strike from Aeb finished it. His axe smashed through an unprotected skull, top to bottom, the force of the strike taking the weapon through the man's shoulder and shearing off his right arm. The survivors turned and ran.

"Go, go!" shouted Hirad, and The Raven charged after the fleeing enemy as they sought to dodge the TaiGethen, pursuing them through the gap in the cliffs, along a sandy beach and out into the flat, silt-filled estuary.

"Stay up," said Erienne. "Assuming your arms are up to it. I'll prepare again."

"Anything in particular?"

"I thought HotRain."

"It'll do the job."

Denser swooped low. "Hirad, we're going forward, see if we can't disrupt the runners or the defence."

"Be careful."

The mage pair headed up once more. Denser could see panthers in among the elves, joining the push forward, their enigmatic partners sprinting close behind, unarmed and unconcerned. The defenders on the other bank were falling back, trying to maintain an orderly retreat with the Al-Arynaar and the awesome TaiGethen pressing forward with increasing ferocity, though they were outnumbered almost three to one.

Denser flew on over the heads of the defenders and out into the estuary. A small knot of men was running toward one of ten or more rowing boats. Out in the bay, three ships were moored, flags fluttering atop mainmasts. One unfurled lazily as he watched, caught in a wash of pallid moonlight. It was unmistakable.

"I don't fucking believe it." He dived for the knot of men. "Let's get those runners."

"Suits me."

Denser flew in fast and low, keeping tight control of his concentration as his fury threatened to boil over. Erienne released the spell, sending a focussed cloud of HotRain spearing down, flaring in the sky as it fell, each drop of magical fire the size of her thumb.

Sudden blue light mixed with the orange of the spell as the HotRain crackled uselessly over the shield covering the runners.

"Dammit," snapped Erienne.

Denser growled his frustration and wheeled once more, looking down on the faces that craned to see who it was that attacked them. Arrows came from the night, flicking close but harmlessly by. And from somewhere DeathHail sheeted up at them, forcing him into a desperate climb and turn. Too close. Gripping Erienne tighter still, he took a last look down, meeting the eyes of a man he recognised.

"We'll hunt you!" he called, as he rushed skyward beyond sight and arrow range. "Don't you realise what you've done?"

"Calm down, Denser," said Erienne. "What's got into you all of a sudden?"

"Tell you when we land."

The Raven were being left behind, refusing to sacrifice their discipline for a headlong charge. Not that it mattered. The TaiGethen and Al-Arynaar were outpacing everyone else.

Denser saw a TaiGethen come alongside a fleeing warrior, snap out an elbow and send him crashing to the ground, hands over his nose and mouth. The elf stopped and spun gracefully like a dancer, then stepped in to finish the man off, skewering his brain through an eye.

But they weren't quite fast enough. Boats were already being pushed out into the bay, desperate oarsmen pulling hard, arrows fired at them sending the blue of HardShields flaring into the night. The Raven could see it all and slowed as one. Denser landed behind them and let Erienne out of his arms. Hirad, feet ankle deep in estuary water, threw his sword down into the silt.

"What did they think we were doing, fighting for the good of our health?" he said, and directed a contemptuous gesture at the elves on the right bank.

All the boats were away now and the fugitives who hadn't made it into one were plunging into the water and swimming out after them. Only a couple of bodies could be seen floating with arrows protruding from back or neck.

"They aren't used to fighting like this," said Ilkar. "It isn't their way. SpellShield down."

"No? Well they'd better learn fast if they want their precious thumb and writings back," said Hirad.

"Assuming those who escaped had anything."

"I don't care about bits of parchment," said Ilkar. "I just want one of those we've killed to have the thumb in some inside pocket."

Hirad nodded. "Me too, Ilks, me too."

"What now?" asked Darrick.

The Raven began to walk back toward the Al-Arynaar, searching for Rebraal. Behind them, they could hear the cheers of the enemy as their boats neared their ships and safety.

"Let's see what my brother has to say," said Ilkar.

Denser felt weary. He followed behind his friends in silence, hand in hand with Erienne. She wanted to know the cause of his anger but he ignored the questioning look on her face. All of them had to hear it together.

They found Rebraal in conversation with Auum, his fierce expression telling them all they needed to know about the results of the fight. They were standing by the bodies of the four strangers who had been running cloaked. Hooked from the swamp before the piranhas could do much damage, they'd been stripped and every stitch of clothing searched and torn to shreds before being scattered on the ground around them. Ilkar asked the question before reporting back to The Raven.

"Parchment and texts only, I'm afraid," he said. "The thumb is on one of those ships."

"How can we be sure?" asked Erienne. "Any of them could have dropped it anywhere between here and the temple."

"Pray that's not so," said Ilkar.

"Put it this way," said The Unknown. "The men that escaped are the only clues we've got. Whether they have the thumb or not, we have to catch them."

"So we need our ship very fast," said Darrick.

Ilkar nodded. "And the elves are coming with us. The message will be sent. Every elf with a sword or bow is going to be heading north to Balaia."

"They're going to invade?" asked Hirad.

"What choice do they have?" Ilkar shrugged. "They don't want to die. We don't want to die."

"Right," said Denser, coming to a decision. "I'm flying back to Ysundeneth. Starting tonight. Jevin can sail round here, it'll be quicker that way."

"Done," said Ilkar. "But I'm coming with you. You might just need a friendly elf."

Denser smiled rather sadly and felt the blood pounding in his throat. "Friendly, eh? Well here's a new test of our friendship, Ilkar. You want to know who it was attacked the temple?

"It was Xetesk."

CHAPTER 33

Jevin had confined his crew to the ship for the last three days and had paid two mages very well to travel with the *Calaian Sun* back to Balaia, whenever that day came. Like all elves Jevin wasn't given to rushed action but the situation overtaking Ysundeneth was quite without precedent. For eight days he'd watched as first unease, then anxiety and finally panic had engulfed the city.

At the first signs of the plague being anything more than a localised infection, he had sent his crew out to hire the mages and to provision the ship. Water, cured meat, rice, grain, biscuit and root crops were the order, as well as apples and unripe grapefruit and lemons; anything that would keep longer than a few days.

Below deck, his cargo holds had already been converted to accommodate passengers. Conditions were cramped and public but neither Protectors nor Xeteskian mages had made any complaint. He wasn't sure exactly how many mages Ilkar expected to make the trip. Over a hundred if he could get them, and Jevin had provisioned for that number.

But as he watched the disaster unfold in Ysundeneth and heard rumours of similar events in other cities, he wondered if Ilkar and The Raven would be back at all. It was unutterably depressing having to watch helplessly as the elves of Calaius's largest port turned from calm private individuals into an angry mob in so short a time. Not altogether surprising, though.

The plague, and such it had to be, had gorged itself on the population, but at random. There were no patterns of contagion, just as there was no cure. It struck at eight members of a family and left a sole survivor with nothing but grief as a companion. No areas were immune, but in the middle of a street one house would be free, while in the next street it would be the opposite: one household annihilated, the rest untouched. The randomness inspired hope and hatred in equal measure but far more destructive to Ysundeneth society was the latter. Survivors in devastated areas had been persecuted as carriers of the plague, some beaten, some even killed for the crime of living.

But elsewhere those free of the disease pooled their eroding strength and demanded help from city authorities quite unable to provide it. Food had been looted and hoarded, rubbish had started to pile up in the streets. And so, latterly, had corpses. Businesses, inns and shops were closed and boarded up. Markets were empty.

Jevin, like all the skippers at the dockside, had moved to anchor offshore. It wasn't just disease that concerned him; it was the mobs roaming the docks wanting out of the city by the quickest means possible. Already Ysundeneth was empty of every nonelf. They had been the first targets of suspicion but, being primarily merchants and seamen, they had simply hauled anchor and sailed back to Balaia, not that the Northern Continent was exactly stable. But a dozen ships had no cargo and therefore no financial means to sail.

And for elves to leave would be desperate, even futile. The plague was not contagious; it did not spread through the air or in food or water. It was something far deeper than that and it attacked elves at their core. There was no escape.

At a meeting on board the *Calaian Sun*, the remaining twelve skippers had agreed to monitor the situation and play the waiting game for as long as they could. Eventually, someone would have to sail north and beg for help. Jevin had said that he would go, but only when The Raven reappeared. Until then, the dozen ships would remain anchored in a defensive formation, protect themselves from attack by boat and magic and wait for the inevitable. For if one thing was certain, it was that one day, probably very soon, they themselves would begin to die.

Jevin stood with one of the mages at the port rail, gazing out at Ysundeneth on a perfect sunlit morning with the mist dispersing and the first clouds rolling across the mountains far to the south. From where he stood, the city was a tiny interloper in the mass of lush verdancy that was the rain forest. But his keen eyes could penetrate the quiet streets and see the catastrophe that had overcome it.

"How many do you think have it now?" he asked the mage.

Vituul was a young elf of average height, his dark blue eyes set in a classically angular face. His long black ponytail fell down the back of his light brown leather cloak. He had no family in the plague city and to be offered—with his equally poor friend, Eilaan—a good wage and a way out was a prayer answered. People were increasingly demanding that elven mages produce a miracle cure. The miracle wasn't going to happen.

"It's almost impossible to say," he said. "The total is probably in the region of a third of the population, but as people start to die in large numbers so the actual number of live cases, if you'll excuse the term, will decrease also."

"But there are a hundred thousand people there," breathed Jevin.

"Not any more," said Vituul. "Thirty thousand are already dying."

"And no word on a cure," said Jevin.

It hit him then like it hadn't before. He'd managed to ignore the ramifications of what was going on in front of his eyes but Vituul's numbers scared him to the bone. If those numbers were right, in fifty days there'd be less than twelve thousand people left alive in Ysundeneth, and four thousand of them would be dying. And with that level of mortality possibly affecting the whole continent, Jevin wasn't just witnessing a devastating plague, he was witnessing the death of the elven race. He shivered.

"How can there be a cure?" Vituul looked at him matter of factly. "No one is going to be alive long enough to do the research. And there's no spell that can even slow its course. We don't even have a lead yet."

"What can we do then?" Jevin felt helpless. "There must be something."

Vituul smiled but there was no humour in his face. "Wait for it to pass."

"And if it doesn't?"

"Pray that Yniss forgives whatever sin we've committed, because the way it looks now, we're all going to die, sooner rather than later."

Jevin leant on the rail. He should be *doing* something. Every elf should. To his knowledge no one had survived having the plague so far, but then not many were in the final stages yet. Just one survivor could give them some hope. But what could he do? This wasn't a question of tending the sick or supplying the herbologists with raw materials. There was no battle to be won. Not yet. Elf catches plague; elf dies.

Jevin's own family lived deep in the rain forest and he preferred not to think about them. It kept his hopes alive.

"So why have none of the crews gone down yet?" asked Jevin. "Odd, don't you think? Surely that's a lead?"

"It's a point, I suppose. No stranger catches it. No travelling elf catches it. Yet."

"Surely it means something?"

"We are still Tual's creatures. Perhaps the curse of being away from the forest also carries a blessing. Perhaps your sin isn't as great as ours."

Jevin had been looking for something less theological. But this mage, at least, had no answers.

"You see what I'm getting at?"

"There is no biological reason why any particular elf catches the plague," said Vituul with a shrug. "It must be something else. I don't believe you, I or any of the crew have greater immunity than the poor souls on shore."

Jevin was considering his reply when his eye was caught by movement on the dockside. There was activity on the approach roads to the east and the odd shout echoed out across the water. The tone was of surprise, even astonishment, but not fear. People were congregating on the dock. Not a mob. Not the hundreds, even thousands, they'd seen a couple of days ago, but a slowly growing crowd.

It continued to grow over the course of most of the morning. Jevin thought at first that it was city folk gathering for a demonstration, but every time he looked up from his duties there were more of them. Just standing there like they were waiting for a ship to dock. Then Jevin realised what he was looking at. These weren't Ysundeneth elves; the city folk's clothes were so much brighter than the greens and browns he could see.

Around midday he rejoined Vituul, who had barely left the rail all morning. Despite his life taking him from the land of his birth and his Gods, Jevin prided himself on having enough of the Calaian elf in him still to understand his people. But not this. Left and right, the rails of other ships were crowded with crew and it seemed a quiet had descended across the city and the sea.

"They are who I think they are, aren't they?" he asked.

Vituul nodded. "TaiGethen," he said, pointing vaguely, but his voice was edged with excitement. "Al-Arynaar. And ClawBound. I see the panthers. I see them."

It was something most elves had never expected to see in the forest, let alone on the dockside at Ysundeneth.

"What are they doing?" Jevin implored anyone who might hear and answer him.

These people never, but never, came out of the rain forest. Never stepped on the worked stone of the streets. They thought them evil. Necessary but evil. A sin Yniss allowed because civilisation had to flourish. To them a city was an alien landscape. An imbalance in the harmony of the forest, its air, magic and denizens. Yet here they were, gathered and waiting, and quite suddenly, the disaster that faced the elves became so much more real.

"What do they want?" This time the question was directed at Vituul alone.

"Whatever it is, it isn't good."

"We should launch a boat," said Jevin. "Ask them."

But answers came far more quickly than that. Up in the crow's nest, the lookout shouted and pointed east. Two dots were flying in from the forest, low and erratic. They swept over the docks, stopped momentarily and spiralled into the sky again, before moving out to sea and the ships moored there.

Jevin followed them, half knowing who it was, seeing them change direction twice before heading straight for the *Calaian Sun*. One of them dipped very low, called out, rose and then fell into the water a hundred yards from the ship. The other didn't pause but flew over the deck, landed and collapsed in a flurry of limbs. When Jevin reached him, Ilkar had managed to turn onto his back and was gasping in air.

"Ilkar?"

"Jevin," Ilkar gasped. "Better . . . better get a boat over the side. Don't think Denser can float for too long."

The order was given. "Where have you come from?"

"Shorth Estuary. Flew all night." He struggled to a sitting position. "Explanations later."

He stopped to gasp in more air. His hair was plastered to his skull and his face was drawn and exhausted.

"Xeteskians have desecrated Aryndeneth. They've destroyed the harmony. But we can stop them. Tell all the ships. They've got to take the elves to Balaia. A stranger is holding part of Yniss's statue. And we've got to get it back before the plague takes us all."

"And me?"

"You're coming with us. Got some friends to pick up at the Shorth."

Jevin nodded. Answers were before him and his desire to help was satisfied.

"Bosun!" he called. "Signal the ships. I need to see the skippers and it has to be now." Turning back to Ilkar, he grasped the elf's shoulder. "Let's get your wet colleague on board safely, then you can both tell me over a goblet of wine just exactly what is going on."

The trio of Xeteskian vessels was under full sail, moving well across a swell of six to eight feet. The wind was strong and constant beneath thin rolling cloud and the acres of canvas billowed dirty grey.

Captain Yron sat beneath the mainmast of the lead vessel on some netted crates, turning the fragment of the statue's thumb over and over. No one had dared come near him all morning. He must have looked a frightening sight with his hands and face covered in balms and bandages, but it wasn't that which kept them away.

Throughout the night he had prowled the deck, unable to sleep despite his fatigue. Healing spells had been cast on him as he moved and the bandages were only there because Erys had made him stop for long enough. After the eighth or tenth man had congratulated him on the success of the mission he had exploded with vehemence enough to wake the slumbering on all three half-empty ships. It needed saying. As if any bounty could justify this loss, let alone the pathetic collection of parchments and texts Erys had brought out.

One hundred and fifty men had journeyed into the Calaian rain forest, wreathed in mirror illusions of enormous complexity to obscure their progress from TaiGethen and ClawBound. And until they had reached the forward camp, it had worked. Now only two of those one hundred and fifty were alive to tell the tale and a further forty had perished in the defence of the estuary.

Success? He had failed. Xetesk could go hang. The Circle Seven would greet his return with broad smiles and grasping hands. He had no doubt Erys's assessment of the importance of the documents he had retrieved was accurate.

No. It was Ben-Foran. Ben, who had trusted him so completely and believed in him utterly. And Ben who lay dead because right at the last, he, Yron, had believed they were safe and had failed to take into account how fast a panther could run.

Yron had never had a son, a family. He had never married. He was the classic soldier, too engrossed in his career to realise the swift passage of years. But in Ben he had seen a way to release the regret and frustration he felt. To take the boy and make him the man Yron knew he could be. To give himself something of which he could be truly proud.

But he had failed. And the boy who could have rivalled the Lysternan, Darrick, as Balaia's most talented soldier . . . all that potential would remain tragically unfulfilled. The only thing that could possibly give meaning to his death was the stolen writings. Otherwise it would all have been a waste. And Yron hated waste.

The netting shifted to his right and he looked across. Erys had sat down next to him. He sat in silence, the only companion Yron would tolerate, the only one who could possibly understand. And he waited for Yron to speak, if he wished. After a time that was exactly what Yron wished.

"It's not over, Erys. Not by a long way."

"The guilt will pass," said Erys.

Yron shook his head. "That's not what I meant and no, I don't think it will. Not completely."

"Oh." Erys was silent for a moment. "Don't worry about The Raven, Captain," he said, getting it at the second attempt. "We'll be safe inside Xetesk before they've even set sail. Where's their ship? Ysundeneth at best."

"How old are you, Erys?"

"Twenty-five, sir."

Yron chuckled. "Thought so. Still at the young-and-talking-bollocks-at-every-turn stage, then."

"Eh?"

"Don't look hurt, boy; we've all been through it." Yron turned to face the young mage. "Thing is, when The Raven got going you were only ten. I know you'll have heard a few stories but, locked away in the college like you were, you missed the reality."

"So explain it to me then, Captain."

Yron paused and looked at the mage to make sure he wasn't being made fun of.

"First thing you should have asked yourself is, why in God's name are they here? And, more unbelievable, why did they show up at the Shorth Estuary fighting for the elves? I mean, you're sitting there saying, 'Oh look, it's The Raven but we've escaped them.' You've got to think harder than that."

"I'll concede it was a big coincidence, but the point remains that we got away, so it doesn't matter."

"And that's what I mean by missing the reality. It *always* matters what The Raven are doing. Everywhere they've gone and everything they've done in the last decade has changed things. Not always world shaping but significant. Always significant. And they aren't used to failing."

"Didn't stop the Nightchild dying though, did they?" Erys was still plainly sceptical.

"Yes, but she died; she wasn't killed by Dordovans. There's a difference."

Erys shrugged. "If you say so, Captain."

"You're young, Erys. And you think old warriors like The Raven can't hurt you. But you're wrong. Ask the people who faced them yesterday. They are awesome. And they aren't on our side. Mark my words, boy, it will worry the Circle Seven. When you report to Dystran, he will want to know what they were doing on Calaius. Because they sure as hell weren't taking a holiday. You got an answer to that?"

Erys shook his head. "None of us have. But then none of us should lose sleep over it either. I'm not going to be barring my bedroom window."

Yron sighed and pushed himself off the crates, feeling a growing sense of irritation. He'd thought more of Erys but he was just as blind as the rest.

"So leave your window open. But I for one am worried because Denser knows me and The Raven are after us. And I want to know why he said what he said. And before you smirk, think on this. The Raven don't fight for money anymore; they don't need to. They fight only when they believe they have to. And they never give up until they've completed their task. Never. It tells me that what we've started is bigger than Dystran would have us believe. If I'm going to be a target, I want to find out why and I strongly advise you to do the same."

"You're scared of them, aren't you?" said Erys, apparently surprised by his own statement.

"Bloody right I am. But I'm also worried about the elves. We don't know why The Raven went to Calaius but they've ended up allies with the elves.

Think about it, Erys. The Circle Seven will. Don't make yourself look a fool in front of them. Not after what you've achieved here."

Erys nodded but said nothing, his expression thoughtful. Yron walked away toward the bow of the ship, his anxiety growing now he had given it voice. He looked over the rail down into the frothing bow wave. Thirty yards off the beam, dolphins tracked their progress, sleek bodies sliding effortlessly through the waves.

He understood Erys's scepticism. The Raven were after all only a tiny band. But, as had been remarked upon countless times and even noted by students of warfare, The Raven alone or as part of something larger made things happen the way they wanted them to. Erys hadn't seen them in action but Yron had. And he knew what would happen if he ever faced them, sword in hand. He'd die.

CHAPTER 34

By the time The Raven left the Shorth Estuary and put to sea they were three full days behind the Xeteskians. The *Calaian Sun* would make up some of that time but, with the best will in the world, they would reach Balaia at least a day and a half adrift.

However, the enforced inactivity was not without its benefits and The Raven had time to rest, heal, train and talk. But any thoughts that the elves travelling with them would thaw in their attitude were consigned quickly to the desert of dreams.

True, they sparred with the Al-Arynaar on deck, but their opponents were reluctant and there only because Rebraal had told them to be. But the six ClawBound pairs and ten TaiGethen cells who had come tentatively aboard with the thirty-eight fully fit Al-Arynaar were not so much aloof as invisible. They exercised at night, ate in their bunks and refused The Raven's offers of discussions on tactics. Hirad was minded to let them stew and was insulted at their lack of gratitude. The Unknown, however, was more circumspect and ensured Rebraal was present early one morning when The Raven spoke about the days to come, knowing he would report back.

"We've got to do this right," said The Unknown. "From mooring to travelling, to negotiating, to—"

"Negotiating?" said Hirad, as if he'd just popped rotten fruit in his mouth.

"Yes, Hirad, negotiating," repeated The Unknown. "You may be happy taking on the considerable might of Xetesk but I'm certainly not."

The Raven and Rebraal were in the Captain's room, sitting round a table covered with plates and goblets. A steaming jug of herb tea rested against the raised lip by Denser's right hand. Aeb was in a room forward, bathing his face and talking to his brothers in the Soul Tank.

"So, your plan is for us to walk up to the gates of Xetesk and ask for the thumb back."

"In a nutshell, yes," said The Unknown. "You have an alternative?"

"Not necessarily, Unknown," said Hirad, "but I think you're being misty eyed about Xetesk's motives for wanting all the stuff they stole. It's hardly going to be so they can enhance their relations with the elven nation, is it? They are at war and they want all the advantages they can get."

"I understand that but I can't believe they knew what they'd be unleashing by taking the thumb. Surely they'll just hand it straight back. Even if they do want to dominate Balaia, there's no reason to exterminate the elven race."

"But look what they did to get it," said Ilkar. "We have to ask the question, could they have known? And so was the theft deliberate?"

They all looked at Rebraal. Ilkar repeated the question in elvish and waited for the reply, his brother not yet confident enough to always express his thoughts in Balaian.

"He says it was impossible for a stranger to know the effects of desecrating the statue. Most elves don't, and that includes me. But then he'd also have said the same about the location of the temple. He and all the servants of Yniss think it a deliberate act designed to harm the elven race; they are just finding it hard to believe anyone would do such a thing to them."

"We gathered that," said Darrick. "But that means Xetesk actually intends to destroy the elven nation, or at least deal it a catastrophic blow. I'm not sure I believe that."

"I'd like not to," said Denser. "I really would. And Xetesk may not have known the effect the theft of the statue fragment would have. But I'm afraid that things are rather falling into place." His voice was leaden and low. Hirad stared at him, feeling for his sense of betrayal.

"Would you care to expand on that?" asked Ilkar quietly.

"Whatever Xetesk wants to learn from the writings and the artefact won't be for anyone's benefit other than Xetesk. They'll be looking to gain an advantage over the elves, some knowledge of their inherent magical ability and makeup. Something like that.

"They're on Herendeneth too. I know we had to bring them there to have any chance of learning enough to release the Protectors and repatriate the Kaan but they have shown their true colours now. What we wanted was a by-product. What they want is access to their dimensional magic again. Don't forget, Dystran is a specialist in inter-dimensional theory.

"And, if all we hear is true, then Xetesk do want to rule magic on Balaia. Let's face it, they haven't offered any help to Julatsa, have they?"

Denser stopped for a moment, his frown deepening and his shoulders slumping even more.

"What I'm trying to say is that although they might not know what they've caused by their theft, I don't think Dystran will stand in the way of a plague wiping out the elves, should he discover that's what the theft has caused. After all, no elves, no Julatsa."

Hirad saw Ilkar's jaw drop as he took it all in.

"And dimensional magics will make them almost unstoppable," said Erienne.

"Particularly if they continue to neglect to free the Protectors," added The Unknown.

"Still want to get the thumb by asking for it?" asked Hirad.

The Unknown shook his head. "I really hadn't seen all these possibilities. Even if Denser's wrong, we can't afford to take the risk. No, this changes everything."

"You really think Xetesk would willingly preside over racial genocide?" asked Ilkar.

"Not Xetesk," said Denser. "Dystran. He's thirsty for power and wants to see Xetesk the dominant magical force, perhaps even the only magical force, no matter what he says to the contrary. And he won't even have to see or acknowledge the destruction his actions have caused. All he has to do is not listen to the truth. Something he finds very easy, believe me."

The door to the Captain's room opened and Aeb walked in. Behind his mask his eyes sought Denser and The Unknown. He walked round the table to sit between them. Denser poured him a mug of tea.

"Thank you." He sipped.

"What's up?" asked Hirad, seeing the tension in the Protector's shoulders.

"I am uneasy," admitted Aeb. "I need guidance."

He looked square at Denser, who nodded. "I understand you may have conflict in the Soul Tank. But remember you have done nothing bar protect me as you are directed and The Unknown Warrior as you desire. And while I remain your Given I will ensure you have all the latitude available to you."

"I am humbled," said Aeb.

"Don't be," said Denser. "We understand you, The Raven that is. We know something of the bond you share and the pain that you suffer every day."

Aeb inclined his head and took another sip.

"My brothers know I travel with you. Soon they will know we fought Xeteskian forces on Calaius. They will not reveal what they don't have to, but at any time a mage might ask the question of my part in The Raven's actions."

"Your unease is clear," said Denser. "We will have to keep you from direct conflict with Xeteskian forces on Balaia. But remember they cannot invoke punishment through the DemonChain unless the Act of Giving is rescinded from me. You are safe at the moment. We'll talk later."

"All right," said The Unknown. "The central point to it all is this. We cannot risk Dystran finding out just how important the thumb is to the elves because if he is intent on damaging them, he'll simply keep it. Rebraal, you've got to impress that on your people. If they must fight, let it be for the writings. That means we have to get the piece back by some other means, the best bet being to capture this Yron that Denser recognised and hope he has the information that can help us.

"Bear in mind that once Yron reaches Balaia, or maybe before, he will be able to tell Xetesk that we are involved in some way and that will make us targets. Aeb is right to be concerned for himself and we will all have to tread very carefully. I suggest that we land near Blackthorne because at least we'll get a friendly reception there. I'd expect to know by then where Yron made landfall, although I believe we can assume he is heading for Xetesk via Arlen.

"The TaiGethen will help us by their actions whether they want to or not. Again, remember we're all on the same side here. Hirad, that means don't antagonise them, whatever the provocation. Anyone with any ideas, we'll talk again at dinner. We know what we're after, we know what the man we want to catch looks like and we know where he's going. That at least is good news. I— Erienne, are you all right?"

Hirad looked to Erienne, as did they all, and it was clear that she wasn't. Her face was sheet white and she was rocking in her seat. Denser hastened to her side.

"What is it, love?" he said, as she half collapsed into his arms.

"I feel awful," she mumbled.

"Your head?"

She nodded. "Sorry to spoil the meeting."

"Don't think about it," said The Unknown. "Denser, you know what to do." The Xeteskian nodded and helped Erienne from the room. "Look, I think we've done all we can here. Hirad, can you contact Sha-Kaan? I'm anxious for news. My family could become hostages in all this and I want to know if the Al-Drechar are still strong enough. Darrick, I want to ask you a few questions. Ren, Thraun, Aeb, hang on here. When we're done we need to go out on deck and work on our moves to get Ren into the line to fight. All right?"

Hirad nodded and stood up, catching Thraun's eye. He smiled. "How much of that did you get, I wonder?" he asked.

"All," said Thraun. "Erienne has too much pain."

It was a comment that took Hirad by surprise. "What do you mean?"

"She must open to those she hates. It is hard."

Hirad frowned. "I don't—"

"It's to do with the One," explained The Unknown. "I think she's going to have to let the Al-Drechar help her now, and so does our quiet but very perceptive shapechanger."

Thraun growled in his throat at the term, his eyes flashing brief anger. There was much of the wolf still left inside him.

"Sorry, Thraun, but it's what you are," said The Unknown. "I meant no offence."

Thraun shook his head. "I am Raven."

"You got that right," said Hirad.

It was the most Thraun had said at any one time, and as Hirad left the Captain's room to go to his cabin he felt hope that the lost man wasn't too far from home.

Erienne lay down on the small cot with her head pounding like never before. It had come on so suddenly, though she'd been feeling rather elsewhere all day. She'd found it hard to concentrate, almost as if she'd drunk too much and was viewing events from a distance. And when, quite without warning, the pain had hit her like repeated and heavy blows to the back of her head, she'd struggled to remain conscious, too confused even to ask for help.

"This can't go on, love," said Denser gently, his face near hers, hand stroking her thudding head, a cloth held to her nose, which had begun to bleed.

"But what if it's them causing the pain to make me need them?" she asked, fighting to think straight and glad of the gloom in the curtained cabin. She had her eyes closed and had managed to relax sufficiently to stop feeling nauseous.

"How else will you find out?" asked Denser. "But you can't live with this pain. It was bad enough before."

"I know," said Erienne. "But—"

"It's not like admitting defeat," said Denser. "Don't you think you've made your point?"

Erienne sighed. She knew he was right. But she hadn't won; rather just not lost by not acknowledging what she carried for so long. She'd repressed it so easily when all she could think of was her grief over Lyanna. But now that had eased slightly, now her mind was more open and her mood that bit more positive, it was as if the One was trying to assert itself.

"Will you stay with me? Help me?" she asked, opening her eyes and clutching his arm.

"Where else would I be but by your side?"

She felt a rush of love that swamped the pain for a moment. "All right. If you think I should."

"I do," he said, still stroking her hair. "But you must think so too."

She nodded. It had to be now. The pain smashed around her head and she knew there was only one source of help. She closed her eyes again and spoke to them with her mind, hoping it would be enough.

Are you there? she asked, knowing her tone was unfriendly but with no desire for it to be otherwise. They should know from the outset that this was not forgiveness for what they had done but acceptance of what she carried. *Myriell? Cleress? Are you there?*

Erienne, we have been waiting. Always near but never within your mind. Cleress's voice was like honey over a sore throat. *It is a joy to hear you.*

It is not a joy to be speaking to you but I must, said Erienne.

We understand that you still harbour anger and hatred, said Myriell. *But please believe us that we just want to help you accept what you hold in your mind before it destroys you. And destroy you it will.*

Don't threaten me like that, said Erienne, the pounding in her head excruciating. *I am not some child you can control with scare stories.*

I am simply informing you of reality and nothing more, said Myriell. *You are in pain, I take it?*

I have never experienced anything like it, conceded Erienne. *It has been with me for days but it is suddenly so intense I can barely see or stand. It had better not be inspired by you.*

Oh, Erienne, how could you think that? We have never sought to cause you harm, admonished Cleress gently.

Erienne all but laughed as the bitterness showered through her. *You killed my daughter. How much more harm do you think you can possibly do?*

We so wanted Lyanna to live. But the One was killing her; I wish you would believe that.

And now I have the One whether I like it or not, don't I? said Erienne, fighting back the throbbing agony a little longer. *You didn't feel the need to give me a choice. Your arrogance is that great.*

Erienne, your daughter couldn't contain the power because Dordover awoke it too early, said Cleress. *You, being her mother and a Dordovan, were the only host capable of keeping it alive. Of keeping that part of Lyanna alive. And there was a battle going on. We had no time to discuss this and anyway you would have refused.*

There was no hint of guilt in Cleress's voice. No real regret. Just an assumption of necessity. Erienne knew she should have been enraged by them. But though she hated what they had done, at least she could feel that the One magic that resided in her mind had been nurtured and grown by Lyanna. Beautiful Lyanna. She felt tears on her face and Denser's soothing hand on her brow and across her hair. He said nothing.

You have to take the pain away, she said. *You have to.*

We can, but for that you must let us into your mind all the way and you must accept that one of us will be with you always to guide you, said Cleress. *We will be silent unless you ask something of us or if we believe your mind to be at risk. But you must know that once the process is started it cannot be stopped.*

I don't want any process to start. I just want the pain to go.

That is the beginning of the process, said Myriell.

So be it. But don't push me where I don't want to go. Don't presume to control me or anything about me or I will fight you. Do nothing without my express agreement.

Both Al-Drechar laughed. *Erienne, we know you well enough not to presume anything ever again.*

It is no laughing matter, snapped Erienne.

No, it isn't, said Myriell. *Now, are you ready? Just relax your mind.*

Begin, said Erienne.

And, with the most gentle of probing feelings, her pain vanished and she saw for the first time the well of power that was the One magic, hers to control if she had the strength. It was a force for good or evil far more comprehensive than any single college's magic. It drew on the energies of land, sky, mana and sea. Its scope was endless. With it at her beck and call, there was so much she could do.

The ship had sailed in under cover of darkness, and before dawn much of the loading had been done. Sha-Kaan had woken to the sounds of Xeteskians preparing to leave on the next tide and he took to the air, anger surging within him, powering his tired wings.

Stay and rest, Nos-Kaan, he pulsed, as he swooped down on the house from which Sytkan, the lead Xeteskian mage, was emerging. *I will call should I need you.*

The mage knew he was coming. The boughs of nearby trees bent under the downdraught, dust, and sand were whipped into the air and the noise of each beat of his wings drowned out any speech on the ground. To his credit the Xeteskian faced him squarely, having picked himself up and dusted himself down. Others of his order were not so calm, haring off down the path to the landing beach.

Sha-Kaan glowered down at Sytkan, choosing to sit up on his hind legs and angle his neck down, noting the ten Protectors who stood in a defensive circle around him.

"Was I to be privy to your decision to leave these shores or were you hoping we would sleep until your ship was out of sight?"

"Our work is done here, Sha-Kaan. Aside from the defence force we will leave to guard the Al-Drechar and their people, we must all return to Xetesk to validate our research."

Sha-Kaan bent his neck further, moving his mouth close to Sytkan and sighting along his snout at the mage, whose eyes widened. Protectors drew weapons.

"Tell them to sheathe those things. They cannot harm me."

Sytkan gestured and blades were lowered.

"What is it you want of me?" asked Sytkan, a superior and rather bored tone to his voice.

"Finish what you started," said Sha-Kaan. "You need go nowhere to validate your research. Indeed, I forbid it. You will free us to return to our own dimension before I free you to return to your petty squabbles on Balaia."

"You are in no position to forbid anything, Great Kaan," said Sytkan, clearly unaware of his own vulnerability. "We are in charge here, and I suggest that if you do want to return to Beshara, you let us set the timetable. That means we leave to employ our research in a practical fashion before turning to lesser matters."

Sha-Kaan almost swatted him then and there but refrained, Hirad's caution echoing in his mind.

"You tread delicate ground, frail human," he said. "The timetable as you call it states that we do not have the luxury of waiting on your whim. And, as you will discover if you choose otherwise, there are no greater matters than completing your work to send us home."

"Don't threaten me, Sha-Kaan," said Sytkan. "We have foreseen your reaction and taken appropriate steps. Without your fire you are much weakened, as the Dordovans discovered. Don't think we will hesitate to defend ourselves. Together, we are very strong."

"But individually, very weak," said Sha-Kaan.

His head snapped forward and he scooped Sytkan into his jaws, wings unfurling to project him into the sky and away from danger.

Nos-Kaan, take to the air. The Xeteskians have to be stopped.

In his jaws, Sytkan struggled. Sha-Kaan brought his head to a foreclaw and deposited the mage in it, bringing it in line with an eye.

"You have very little time," growled Sha-Kaan "Remove your work from your ship before we sink it."

"And lose everything for which we have worked and that could benefit you?" shouted Sytkan into the wind. "It stays there. You don't dare touch it. Set me down."

"You think me a foolish reptile, I am sure. Ignorant. But I hear much and am told more. I know the exactitude of a Xeteskian mage. All your papers are in watertight containers, are they not? And I am a very good swimmer."

He watched Sytkan's fragile confidence disappear and proper fear replace it. But the mage was not done.

"Release me or Nos-Kaan dies now."

Sha-Kaan swept round to face the hillside. Nos-Kaan was hovering, waiting for him. Below, hidden by the curve of the slope, a dozen mages. Nos hadn't seen them and they were casting.

Sha-Kaan bellowed in rage and arrowed down toward them, pulsing alarm at his Brood brother.

Fly! They are below you. Fly!

Nos-Kaan moved as the mages cast their spell. An orb of fire thirty feet across raced from their position, catching Nos-Kaan's left wing on the down-beat and rolling along its length to scour his back. Flame ate at his scales and burned the wing membrane. Nos roared pain and, smoke trailing from his savaged wing, spiralled into the sky, heading for the quenching ocean.

Sha-Kaan powered on, Sytkan forgotten in his claw. The Xeteskian mages could not react fast enough. The huge dragon landed just upslope and slid down on them, his great hind claws tearing up the ground as he came, his wings beating again, his weight shuddering the earth. His head launched forward, his fangs slicing through human flesh, jaws snapping open and shut to crush puny bodies. His claws scythed through torso and limb, dug up stones and dirt and flung them down.

With the next beat of his wings he took to the air again, banking sharply to check for any survivors. One was running, the rest either dead or dying. He powered in again and seized the running mage in his other foreclaw before chasing out to sea after Nos-Kaan.

The dragon's entry point was clear and the smell of burning scale and membrane hung in the air. Sha-Kaan put Sytkan to his eye once again, seeing the mage shaken but still just conscious.

"Weak am I? Pray to your false gods that Nos is still alive. Pray that your lungs can hold and your body does not break."

With that he dived into the ocean, tucking his foreclaws in to protect the mages from the impact. He might have need of them. His eyes pierced the clear blue waters easily and he didn't have to swim deep before he saw Nos-Kaan struggling to the surface, his left wing dragging him back, his tail stroking weakly.

Nos-Kaan, I am here.

Sink the ship, Great Kaan. I will survive. But his thoughts were feeble. *They must not escape.*

They cannot outpace me. I will be back.

Sha-Kaan stormed back to the surface and broke into the air. In his claw Sytkan gasped a lungful of air. The other mage hung limp. Sha-Kaan discarded him. He flew toward the ship, which still lay at anchor, keeping high to avoid the spells. On deck he saw two groups of mages crouching together, spells no doubt on their lips.

"So anxious to get on board," he said, Sytkan once again large in his vision. "Let me help you."

He threw the mage down, watching him cartwheel as he fell. The human prayed he hit the water. His Gods did not hear him. Sha-Kaan turned from the splayed mess far below on the deck and dived back after Nos-Kaan.

The wounded dragon was close to the surface now. Sha-Kaan swam under him and pushed him from below, moving him fast toward a nearby island with a beach on which he could rest. He could feel the pain through Nos-Kaan's mind. The dragon, who had never fully recovered from attack by Dordovan mages out in the Southern Ocean two seasons before, was dreadfully injured.

He heaved Nos-Kaan from the waves. The stricken Kaan laid his neck out on the sand, leaving his tortured burned body in the salty water.

Tell me, Nos. Your injuries, can they heal?

But he already knew the answer. Nos-Kaan's wing lay on the surface of the sea, outstretched, membrane ruined in so many places. And the scales along his back were puckered and oozing.

It has been a great adventure, Great Kaan. And I would have loved to rest back in our Brood lands, but it was ever a dream I feared I would never realise.

Then rest now, my brother. Rest now. You will be avenged.

But Nos-Kaan couldn't hear him.

Sha-Kaan rose up on his hind legs, beat his wings and bellowed grief, rage and torment. Birds took flight and lizards scattered on the beach. Back at anchor, the Xeteskian ship lay waiting. He decided not to keep them any longer.

But even as he rushed into the air to revenge himself upon them, a voice sounded in his mind. It spoke reason and sympathy and it took the edge from his rage. It told him that he must live. That the Brood Kaan would wane without him, that there were other places to fight the battle. It told him it loved him and that it would see the research into the hands that would help.

The voice was that of Hirad Coldheart, his Dragonene, and it surely saved his life.

CHAPTER 35

D ystran, Lord of the Mount of Xetesk, was in excellent spirits. He had enjoyed his lunch enormously and took the remains of his wine out of the dining room he had shared with the rest of the Circle Seven into the Corridor of the Ancients. Looking along the impressive line of portraits in the brightly lit corridor, he reminded himself to organise his own. Every other master on the walls was very old. A dash of youth would be just the job.

He heard footsteps behind him and turned. Ranyl was walking slowly toward him, pain obvious on his face but defiantly upright despite the natural desire to stoop to try and relax the pain from the cancer in his stomach. He smiled as he approached.

"My Lord Dystran, I have more news," he said, "concerning the search on Calaius."

"Really?" Dystran's pulse quickened slightly. "Good I hope?"

"I would welcome a seat and a glass of whatever it is you have." Ranyl smiled.

Dystran raised a hand. "I'm sorry, my manners."

He led the old and dying master back to the dining room, where they sat at the end of the cavernous chamber away from the inquisitive ears of the rest of the Seven. Servants were clearing plates and glasses from the long rectangular table on which seven candelabra supported strong white flames. In the wood-panelled room, voices echoed loud so Dystran lowered his voice as he poured wine and sat down with his adviser.

"You'll be glad to hear, old friend, that our key researchers are even now returning to Balaia from Herendeneth. There was trouble with the Kaan dragons but they escaped intact. They'll land in approximately nine days and be in the college inside twenty. Fifty Protectors are with them. The answers are close, Ranyl. Very, very close. If we can hold our borders for just that little bit longer."

"Well, Heryst's caution still plays into our hands though Rusau's unfortunate demise was regrettable. Intelligence indicates he is mobilising his forces. His strength could yet be pivotal. We should consider talks of some kind," said Ranyl. He smiled as he drank from his glass.

"About what?"

"It hardly matters," said Ranyl. "As long as it stops any concerted invasion for long enough. Why not discuss the dispersal of the Herendeneth research? It won't stop Vuldaroq but it might give Heryst pause, and that is all we need to see our people home."

"The timing will be important," said Dystran, a warm feeling creeping into his bones as he saw the sense of Ranyl's plan.

"Indeed. We should act as soon as possible. You might try personal Communion with Heryst. Soothe his pain, so to speak."

"My dear Ranyl, I will never find another to replace you," Dystran said, and squeezed the old man's free hand. "But this isn't what you wanted to tell me about. Calaius."

"Ah, my Lord, the Gods are organising everything to speed your ascension," rumbled Ranyl through a cough. "I have had Communion from our fleet. They are on their way back from Calaius. They have the writings we need."

"Are you sure?" said Dystran. He felt elation rush through his body.

"It was a difficult operation. We lost many lives but both Erys and Yron survived. Erys is as sure as he can be that what they have is the text you had in mind."

"How difficult?"

"We lost almost one hundred and ninety people," said Ranyl quietly.

"What!" Dystran's voice echoed across the dining room and stilled the hum of conversation from the remainder of the Seven. His next words were an angry whisper. "What in all the hells happened? Did they run into a storm or something?"

"Elves," said Ranyl. "TaiGethen, Al-Arynaar. They are apparently far more deadly than the myths suggested they were."

Dystran sighed. "Yes, but even so, we had a complex enough illusion pattern. What happened to that?"

"It was fine until the mages started to get sick or exhausted," said Ranyl. "They couldn't keep it up. By the time they reached the forward campsite, it was unsustainable. Yron was surprised at the tenacity of the temple defence and from then on the elves were closing in. We were lucky anyone got away."

Dystran drained his glass and refilled it, his earlier good humour ebbing away. He was still buoyed by the thought of the elven text he craved—the key to their longevity—but the scale of the disaster that had befallen his raiders would leave a bitter taste.

"What about the elders? When can we expect the demands?"

"I've no idea," said Ranyl. "But we can replicate the text quickly enough. We'll have the time. I'll word a particularly compelling apology."

"Do that." The Lord of the Mount stared at Ranyl, whose eyes were sagging, drawn with fatigue and pain. He'd be taking the loss of life personally. "I'm sorry. You'll have lost friends."

Ranyl shrugged. "It's not so much that. There's something else you should know."

"Someone drop the writings in the sea, did they?"

"The Raven were there. Fighting with the elves."

Dystran was about to dismiss this final item of information with a wave of his hand but stopped in mid gesture, cold trickling across his mind. He almost shouted again but checked himself.

"How the hell did they get involved? Why?" He was blustering and he knew it, but their presence raised so many questions. "How did they know what we were trying to do? And why, Gods burning, was I not told they'd left Herendeneth?"

Ranyl waited until he was sure Dystran had stopped asking questions.

"It's impossible for them to have known our mission to Calaius. I feel it was a coincidence, though admittedly a very unfortunate one."

"I'll say it is."

"Please, my Lord. Yes, it is unfortunate, but I think we should turn our minds to why they were in the middle of the rain forest at all. They're up to something. As to why you weren't told they'd left Herendeneth, it's because it wasn't a question that was ordered asked of the Protectors."

The smile reappeared on Dystran's face. "Well, we can soon put that right, can't we? Denser's still Aeb's Given mage, I take it?"

"Yes, my Lord."

"Well, get to finding out exactly what The Raven were doing there. Find out what they know. Aeb can't refuse to answer a direct question."

"Should we not rescind the Act of Giving for this Protector?"

"What? And give up our spy in the camp? I think not, Ranyl. He may be powerful muscle but he's only one man."

"You should know that Denser swore to hunt Yron down," said Ranyl.

"Did he? Well, that may answer some of our questions about what they know now, if not why they were there in the first place." Dystran thought a moment. This was an unexpected and potentially serious irritation. "They mustn't be allowed to get their information, whatever it is, into the hands of anyone friendly toward the elves. And that means Heryst and Lystern. Presumably they're after Yron.

"Come up with a plan. We need safe passage for Yron, Erys and the research team from Herendeneth. It may be necessary to clear a path. But that's not all. The Raven are a risk I'm not prepared to take. I want them caught or killed."

A black cat trotted smoothly into the dining room and leapt onto Ranyl's shoulder, where it turned to face Dystran before morphing into the demon form of the old man's Familiar. Dystran screwed up his face.

"I can't understand why you are determined to keep that thing," he said. "How long have you had it now? Must be decades."

"Friend," corrected the Familiar, stroking Ranyl's face.

The old man smiled. "He's right. And, more than ever, I need companionship. Dying is a lonely business."

Dystran shuddered. "Not me. Think I'll stick to women. Gods, why do they have to be so ugly?"

He took in the monkey-sized winged and hairless body, the pulsating veined head and the tongue which hung from its fanged mouth, dribbling spit onto Ranyl's collar.

"It can prove useful for the uninitiated victim," said Ranyl.

"I'd keep it as a cat if I were you," said the Lord of the Mount.

"But the cat can't talk. And the cat can't fly."

"They are of little real use though, talking pet apart."

"Not so, my Lord," protested Ranyl. "Indeed, I am encouraging more of our mages to adopt them now we have some limited linkage back with the demon dimension. They are useful as spies, and unless you know how are particularly difficult to kill."

"Perhaps you should send them after The Raven then, prove to me they are worth the revolting body and endless drool."

"Perhaps I will."

It was early evening seven days after Selik's brief and predictable meeting with Blackthorne and Gresse. He had brought his men to a stop half an hour's walk from the garrison at Understone. He wanted them to rest because in the early hours of the morning they had to be at their ruthless best.

They lit a fire in a shaded copse, knowing the light would not be seen in Understone, and ate very well from a deer one of his archers brought down with an astonishing shot as they rode into their temporary campsite. As he watched them eat and talk, even share the odd snatch of song, Selik knew they felt it. This was the march of the righteous. No one could stand before the Gods and stand in their way.

"Rest!" ordered Selik, once the carcass was stripped. "Sleep if you can; we have justice to serve."

There was no complaint. They knew he was right. Come the end of the night some of them would be dead but a blow would have been struck. The first of many. While they slept, Selik watched and reflected. He had little need for rest these days, his mind churning endlessly with thoughts of duty and destiny.

When it was time to wake his men, Selik did so feeling like a father waking reluctant children. He served them hot tea himself, feeling closer to them than at any time and starkly responsible for what he was about to begin.

For a moment these twenty men with dreams of their own—who wanted life, had wives and children—were more than just pawns to him. They were people he should nurture and protect. Just for a moment.

The walk was made in total silence. All the talking had been done. In the blank dark of early morning, deepened further by the looming shapes of the Blackthorne Mountains at their backs, the Black Wings took up their positions. It had been relatively simple. Anders, the garrison commander, posted no guards outside the compound, having long since abandoned the ghost town to its ethereal residents. This mistake allowed the Black Wings to lay their trap and, when they were ready, to spring it.

Across the quiet of the night came the sound of a lone horse, galloping hard. Its rider could be heard urging it on, begging it for more speed. The animal tore up the last twists and turns of the southern path before bursting into view in the dark cloudy early morning, sprinting for the only puddle of light it could see. Understone barracks.

Voices were raised inside. Feet could be heard running on earth and wood and the odd lantern was hung outside the walls, augmenting the firelight within and the braziers ranged along the top of the stockade.

The rider swung into the street and slowed to a halt in front of the gates in a cloud of dust, horse steaming and sweating, froth oozing from under the saddle and dripping from its bit. The rider all but fell from his mount, staggering to the gates and hammering on them, pleading with those watching from above to let him in, fear threatening to overwhelm him.

"Please! Please let me in. Dear Gods, they're right behind me. Please!"

"Who are?" demanded a voice. "Calm down, man."

"Black Wings," gasped the rider. "Can you not hear them?"

And there it was. The unmistakable sound of multiple hoof beats echoing across the town.

"You're a mage?"

"What else?" shouted the man, desperation edging his voice. "Don't leave me out here to die, I beg you. Please."

A brief conversation was ended by an order barked down from the parapet. A heavy plank slid back from its mountings and one of the braced stockade gates began to creak open.

"Now!" shouted a voice slurred by paralysis.

A dozen pairs of hands shoved at the gates as men ran from the shadows either side. Simultaneously, a quartet of arrows whipped up to the parapet, punching two men from their feet to thump lifeless onto the earth below. More followed, volley after volley, while the Black Wings drove the doors back.

Shouts ricocheted across the compound as the Black Wings pushed through. Selik headed them, moving left to slash his sword into the back of one of the men trying to keep the gates shut. His men piled in behind him, laughing as they came, slapping the gates back the last few feet and trapping one hapless college soldier against the stockade wall.

"Split!" yelled Selik. "Gain the ramparts. Loose groups. Watch for spells. Go!"

He sped on, breath wheezing into his part-paralysed chest. He ran straight across the compound, stables to his left, barrack buildings ahead. Devun was at his shoulder, others either side, and he felt energy flood through him.

The door to the wide low barracks building opened and men spilled out, half dressed, half asleep, still buckling leather as they came. Anders led them. It was too perfect. Selik swept back his hood and struck hard, right to left. Anders, distracted, missed the blow, which sheared into his left arm and on into his unarmoured ribs. The garrison commander went down in a welter of blood, not even having the breath to scream as the blade sliced through his lung and heart.

The fight against magic had truly begun, and as Selik blocked a disheartened sword thrust and the first spell bloomed behind him, he still had time to remind himself to praise Devun for his superb acting performance before the compound gates.

Chapter 36

A eb lay alone. The *Calaian Sun* was three days from Balaia and sailing well, easing through the water and eating up the distance. Above him, on the sun-swept deck, The Raven trained. He could hear Hirad shouting orders and The Unknown urging better cohesion. He could hear the occasional ring of steel, the creaking of the ship's timbers and the snap of the sails on the masts.

But he couldn't be with them because, like Erienne, who spent so much of her time lying still under the tutelage of the Al-Drechar, he had been called to commune with the Soul Tank. He felt the unease as soon as he opened himself fully. It was uncomfortable, drowning for a moment, the intense feelings of brotherhood he had with every Protector, near or far. It was what kept him sane and focussed; it was his life. His soul mingling with those of the other three hundred and twelve now left, still mourning those lost, still joyful in their own union. Still so powerful.

To be called to commune was a seldom-used level of psyche in the Soul Tank. It was as close to an interrogation as the Protectors ever got, not that the voices were ever silent. Aeb could always hear the voice of every soul. He would hate the emptiness if they were taken from him and that was what he feared most about being freed.

My brothers, it is joy to share my mind and soul with you, pulsed Aeb.

He could sense them all near him, feel the warmth shot through with anxiety as they responded in kind to his greeting. The Tank was agitated.

We must know where you are, Aeb, said Myx, one of the Lord of the Mount's honour guard. *The Master worries.*

It was what Aeb had been fearing. Thus far, he had kept the details of his mission from the Circle Seven but now his complex loyalties were set at odds. He was sworn to protect Xetesk but above that, he was given to Denser and stood by Sol. Sol, the beacon of hope, Sol the brother who had regained his soul. He felt a helplessness. Betrayal was coming. He knew it, his brothers knew it. All they could do was mitigate the scale.

Ask as you are ordered, said Aeb. *I will respond as I must.*

They could not refuse to ask a question they had been given and Aeb could not refuse to answer. To do so could invoke punishment from the demons who channelled the paths between their bodies and their souls. Nothing scared them but that.

Aeb listened and answered, and when the Communion was done, went to find Denser. There were things his Given had to know.

The *Calaian Sun* sailed into the Bay of Gyernath three days later, still at least a day and a half behind the Xeteskian force but with the advantage of a stop-off at Blackthorne to get a firsthand and trustworthy account of the current situation from the Baron.

Aeb had been as careful as he could during his questioning in the Soul Tank. He had been forced to admit that The Raven had joined elves seeking revenge for the desecration of the temple and the return of the stolen texts. The Raven's original mission was also now known to the Xeteskians but Dystran would assume it had failed as The Raven hadn't persuaded a single mage to come with them. The fact that a dozen were on board and plenty more were assembled at Ysundeneth was not something Aeb had been required to reveal. After all, no one had asked him.

For his part, having been given complete licence by Denser to ask whatever he felt he could, Aeb had gleaned some useful information. More than just the Xeteskian task force had landed at Arlen. The ship carrying the surviving researchers and Protectors from Herendeneth had arrived two days later and both groups were travelling north under guard.

Potentially more worrying from The Raven's point of view was that Xetesk was effectively surrounded—by Dordovan forces to the south and by Dordovan and Lysternan forces north. Lystern had not yet struck a blow against Xetesk but Dordover was attacking at every opportunity, trying to disrupt the precarious link between Xetesk and its forces in Arlen. The fluid situation would make The Raven's job of catching Yron all the more difficult and gave them much to ponder during their lengthy walk from the bay to Blackthorne.

Anchoring in midchannel, they'd landed at a deserted jetty surrounded by squat warehouses. Nothing looked particularly permanent.

"Just a stopgap till Gyernath gets back open, I expect," The Unknown said.

"Certainly isn't up to Blackthorne's usual standard," agreed Hirad.

He scanned the horizon, took in the Blackthorne Mountains at the head of the bay and the mist-covered peaks of the Balan Mountains to the east. He felt a pang when he saw them. The Balans had been his home for almost five years when the Kaan dragons began their exile on Balaia. Anger invaded his thoughts. Only one Kaan dragon left here now thanks to Xetesk, and he living on borrowed time.

"Good to be back though, isn't it?" said Denser, coming to Hirad's shoulder. "Feel that fresh cool air and the lack of a million mosquitoes."

"And snakes, rats, spiders and ants," said Erienne.

They were right. It smelled different here. It smelled good. It was home. Hirad chuckled and looked across at Erienne. She looked pale and tired despite almost constant rest. A frown creased her brow and in her eyes there was a depth that he found a little unsettling, like she was focussed on something elsewhere.

"You all right?" he asked.

"I don't know," she admitted. "I've slept most of the voyage but my mind is full, like I've been studying nonstop. There's so much to take in. I can't really explain it."

"Just as long as they aren't hurting you," said Hirad.

Erienne smiled and placed a hand on his arm. "No, Hirad, but thank you."

Behind Erienne, Thraun was standing on the edge of the jetty sniffing the air. Darrick was by him, looking about, before shouldering his pack and wandering off toward the warehouses. Aeb, as always, stood silent and close to Denser and The Unknown, his axe and sword crossed over his back in their snap fastenings.

Another boat nudged against the jetty. Al-Arynaar and TaiGethen jumped out and jogged away to join their brothers and the ClawBound where they were gathering on a rise. Ilkar and Rebraal were with them, the two brothers deep in yet another heated conversation. Hirad watched as one of the Al-Arynaar mages spoke to them briefly, nodded curtly and moved away as if being near Ilkar upset her somehow. More words were exchanged before Ilkar clutched Rebraal in a half-hearted embrace and Ilkar strode over to The Raven, shaking his head.

"Another happy family discussion?" asked Hirad.

"Oh, it's not him," said Ilkar. "Not this time. Come on, let's go."

He cast about for his pack and picked it up off the jetty, throwing Hirad's to him at the same time.

"And are they coming with us?" Hirad jerked a thumb at the elves.

"No," said Ilkar. "Come on." He set off along the rutted wagon trail that cut into the soft earth. "I presume this is the quickest way to Blackthorne."

"What's got into him?" asked Denser.

Hirad shrugged. "Them, I expect."

The elves were all knelt in prayer, a low murmuring drifting across on the wind. It was going to be a fine if cool afternoon. Hirad felt a smile tugging at the corners of his mouth. He'd forgotten what it was to see open land and not be hemmed in by impenetrable forest.

Out in the bay, the *Calaian Sun*'s sails billowed. Jevin was heading for

Arlen, hoping to pick up a cargo and news of Xeteskian strength. He'd be returning to the bay in twenty days.

The Raven set off after Ilkar. Simultaneously, the elves stood and headed away north and east, splitting as they went. ClawBound pairs ran alone, TaiGethen trios likewise, with the main body of the Al-Arynaar following.

"Trouble for someone," said Hirad.

"You're not wrong," said Darrick. "Glad we're not in the firing line."

They caught up with Ilkar quickly and walked in a loose knot around the Julatsan mage, who explained as he pushed on.

"They don't feel they can wait," he said. "Not for information from Blackthorne and certainly not for us. I'm just worried they'll run into more trouble than they can cope with."

"So what were you talking to Rebraal about?" asked Denser.

"I was warning him about the power of Xeteskian magic and what a Protector army can do. Not that he really wanted to listen. I mean they all saw Aeb in action but they don't understand what two hundred at once really means. They've never seen a true college battle line—you know, properly organised cavalry, foot soldiers, mages. They won't know how to handle it."

"But they're confident all the same?" said Darrick.

Ilkar shrugged. "It's more the pressure of time. Three TaiGethen died on the voyage. So did four Al-Arynaar, along with a couple of Jevin's crew. You can understand it."

"But there's a problem," said The Unknown. "Or you wouldn't have been so irritated."

"They still don't think we can help," said Ilkar. "They don't understand this place—the politics, the factions, who they can trust—though they think they do. They just assume people will be sympathetic or stand aside because we have a common enemy. I only just managed to persuade one of them to give me her Communion signature."

"And do you expect to hear from her?" asked Denser.

"No, but she'll be hearing from me. Us. They may not care what they're getting themselves into but I care about the effect it has on what we're trying to do."

"So what are they planning?" asked The Unknown.

"Well, remember Rebraal and all the Al-Arynaar mages know something of Balaia. They've all spent a lot of time here. ClawBound are going to scout the likely route from Arlen to Xetesk. TaiGethen will be close and will gather any information they can.

"If the Xeteskian force is too big to attack when they first find it, they'll wait for the rest of the elven army and then attack. That's it. No talking, no discussion."

"Bloody hell," said Hirad. "This is going to get messy."

"Quite," said Ilkar. "So we need to get hold of the thumb before the elves launch a war on Xetesk."

"How?" said Erienne.

"Right now I don't know, but we'd better come up with a plan quickly. I'm rather hoping Blackthorne will be able to provide some good intelligence."

"May I speak, Master Denser?" Aeb's voice, deep and powerful, rolled over them.

"Of course," said Denser.

"I am a risk to everything you do," said Aeb. "You should dismiss me immediately."

His voice was neutral but Hirad knew what dismissal meant; the Unknown had been very clear about it. Though not under punishment, Aeb would be bereft of his link to a mage. The demons in the chain linking his body to his soul would torment him until he made it back to Xetesk. If he made it back.

"I can't do that," said Denser. "You know why."

"Recovery of the statue fragment is more important than my discomfort," said Aeb. "Xetesk can track all of us through me."

"Discomfort is an understatement," said Denser. "But there's more than that. You're one of us. You're my bodyguard and The Unknown's left-hand defence. The Raven do not send their people away because it's more convenient that way."

"I could bring about your deaths," said Aeb. "This is bigger than The Raven."

"Nothing is that big." Hirad locked eyes with the huge Protector. "Nothing."

Aeb said nothing in reply, merely switched his gaze back to Denser.

"Master?"

"Subject's closed, Aeb," said Denser. "You stay."

"I understand," said Aeb, and there was no disguising the relief in his voice.

"What ties us together isn't dissimilar to what binds the Protectors," said The Unknown. "If Denser dismisses you it is a betrayal of us. You do understand that?"

"Yes," replied Aeb. "But I also understand the Elfsorrow and what it will do if not checked. I risk that."

"We'll have a better chance of reclaiming the thumb and returning it to Calaius if you're with us," said The Unknown. "The only thing that worries me is Dystran rescinding the Act of Giving."

"Unlikely at the moment," said Denser. "While he thinks he can track us and keep us at a distance, he'll see Aeb as an advantage."

"What happens if he does rescind it, though?" asked Hirad.

"Well, Aeb would no longer be under my control. He could be assigned to another mage or returned to Xetesk."

"But I will never fight against The Raven," said Aeb. "No Protector will bear arms against Sol."

"Still, Aeb, you're only a risk if you know exactly what it is we're planning to do, right?" said Denser, a twinkle in his eye.

"Yes," agreed Aeb.

"I mean it's all very well knowing where we are in Balaia but quite another thing knowing where we're headed, would you agree?"

"Yes."

"Well, you may not be able to lie but I intend to exercise my imagination to its fullest," said Denser. "And clearly you'll have no choice but to report it as the truth."

"Yes," said Aeb a third time, and there was the faintest trace of humour in his normally impassive voice.

"Excellent," said Denser. "Could be fun, this."

"Fun, he calls it," grumbled Ilkar, but there was a smile on his face. "The whole elven race is under threat and he's about to engage in a game of bluff with the Lord of the Mount of Xetesk."

The Raven reached Blackthorne late in the afternoon, under escort from a pair of mounted militiamen. Leaving an area of woodland, they were greeted by the sight of a busy vibrant town. Hammering echoed into the sky, the sound of children laughing floated above that of hooves on packed earth, and everywhere columns of smoke spiralled into the cloudy sky from furnaces and cook fires.

Blackthorne had a population of eight to ten thousand, though that number had been significantly swollen by refugees, and there were tented camps on three sides of the town. The rebuilt Blackthorne Castle presided benevolently over the southern end of the town, pennants flying white and blue in the breeze, its pale grey stone washed clean.

Walking through the town behind Blackthorne's horsemen, The Raven's reception was mixed. There was awed recognition, curiosity and shouts of welcome to Hirad as an old friend of the town, but concern because walking with them was a Xeteskian Protector.

Baron Blackthorne had no reservations and welcomed them in his private dining room with flagons of excellent red and white wine, plates of vegetables, bread and cheese. There was some meat but it was obviously in short supply.

His eyes sparkling under his stern dark-haired brow, Blackthorne greeted each one of them in turn, remarking on the return of Darrick, kissing Ren'erei's hand on meeting her for the first time and shaking that of Aeb, though the Protector looked uncomfortable at the touch. Hugging Hirad to him, he ordered wine poured for all his guests and sat them down around his table. Aeb stood behind Denser but accepted a drink.

"Gods, but it's good to see you alive and well," he said. "We need some sanity in this country and I can only bring that to a small corner."

"We've heard plenty of stories about conditions here," said The Unknown. "You seem to be bearing up well."

"Only because I have enough men to defend my resources and the support of my people," said Blackthorne. "Elsewhere, it's wild. Gresse and I have been touring but there's little we can do and he's back at Taranspike Castle. It's down to the colleges now and the war is worsening by the day. So what brings you back from your tropical paradise?"

There was a pained silence. Blackthorne sighed and clapped a hand to his forehead. "Curse my stupid mouth. Erienne, I am sorry. I heard about your daughter."

"Seems like the whole world has," said Erienne, voice trembling slightly.

"That's about the size of it," said Blackthorne. "And I will say this because you need to know the mood of people outside my lands. The news of her death and the end of the elemental destruction was greeted with joy, not tears. She is not spoken of well, my lady, and neither are you, your husband or much of the mage community."

"I can see their point," said Erienne. She pulled out a handkerchief and dabbed at her eye.

"I, on the other hand, am aware of the full story. It's just a shame that the colleges have determined to compound their stupidity by going to war."

Denser raised a hand. "Before you tell us what you know, and we tell you why we're here, Aeb, you should leave. Go beyond earshot. I can hardly lie to you effectively if you've heard everything already, now can I?"

"Master." Aeb bowed and left, placing his glass on the table.

Blackthorne was frowning.

"It will all become clear, Baron," said Hirad. "I think you should recharge your glass. If you think the situation's bad now, just wait till you hear this."

Into an increasingly stunned atmosphere, first Hirad, then Denser and Ilkar outlined the events on Calaius and Herendeneth and their suspicions and certainties concerning Xeteskian involvement and motivations. Blackthorne didn't touch his wine or food, just stared back at whoever was talking to him. He asked no questions, merely nodded his head to indicate he'd understood. And despite the fire in the grate Hirad fancied he felt the room chill. Not just due to Blackthorne's shock, but because to hear it all again brought the enormity of the situation home to The Raven.

"You've got to get word to Heryst and Vuldaroq," said Blackthorne into the yawning silence that followed, his voice oddly quiet. "Xetesk must not be allowed to take possession of either research or artefact."

"That's why we need your help," said The Unknown. "Our clear priority is to recover the thumb fragment. Going to Lystern or Dordover is days out of our way. You're a respected statesman and a supporter of magic. This sort of news might be better coming from you. We're not exactly friends of Vuldaroq's these days."

Blackthorne rubbed his hands over his face and drained his glass in one long swallow, refilling it himself having dismissed all his servants.

"The situation is very tense. Lystern has formed an alliance of sorts with Dordover, but Dordover, or more specifically Vuldaroq, is the more active partner. As far as I know, Heryst still has a diplomatic team in Xetesk but details are sketchy. He's a man of reason as you know but he's not in a strong position. He's gone the only way he can, blockading lands and defending Julatsa, but it's put him in thrall to Vuldaroq whether he likes it or not. There's no doubt that knowing what you've just told me about Calaius and the elves would be enough to bring Lystern firmly into the war on Dordover's side. But I'm not sure that'll help you, considering in all probability you'll need to get inside Xetesk."

"On the other hand, as soon as the elves encounter Dordovan or Lysternan forces, the story will be out and we'll have had no chance to mitigate the message," said The Unknown.

"Indeed," said Blackthorne. "Well there's really only one course of action we can take as far as I can see. I reckon it's time I sent a trade delegation to Lystern. Quickly." He smiled. "I might even go myself, perhaps try and find time to have an informal talk with Heryst. You lot, on the other hand, need to get toward Xetesk as quietly and as quickly as you can. I think I can spare some horses and trail food though having an elven archer might help you down something a little more appetising."

"My Lord, I hadn't considered you travelling there yourself," said The Unknown. "You're powerful enough to request Heryst communes with your senior mage."

"Face to face is the only way," said Blackthorne. "This is too important for third-party communication."

"Just make sure you take a mage we can contact," urged Ilkar. "If events overtake us, you need to know before you get too close to it all."

"I'll do that," said Blackthorne. "We'll discuss the finer points of travel later but there is something else I need to apprise you of if you're travelling direct to Xetesk."

"Wouldn't have anything to do with Selik, would it?" asked Hirad.

"Your friend and mine," said Blackthorne, nodding. "He paid me an unexpected visit a few days ago. Unexpected and odious. He's getting cocky. Very cocky. And with some reason. He's got considerable support. Desperation does that to people and he's a master at playing on people's fears."

"But they'll be old men, young boys and farmers," said Hirad. "Not exactly battle-hardened."

"But there will be lots of them. Thousands," said Blackthorne. He leaned forward. "This is a warning, Hirad. Don't underestimate him. He's powerful now and most of the mages are too scared to come outside their college walls. He's someone else that needs stopping."

"Well you're talking to the right man," said Hirad.

"Later, Hirad, all right?" said The Unknown. "Let's get this thumb back to the elves first."

Blackthorne pushed himself to his feet. "Right. Raven, I'm going to organise you some beds and horses, then we are going to talk further. If we want Balaia back, we've got to do this right."

CHAPTER 37

Erienne couldn't sleep. The state room she shared with Denser was airy and large, the bed beautifully comfortable. Denser lay quietly beside her but she was unsettled from having spent so much of her time over the last few days exhausted from the continuous training the Al-Drechar had given her.

It had gone on day and night during the sea journey but they'd left her alone for the walk to Blackthorne. They'd known she needed her energy and said they'd be back to help her sleep, but she'd heard nothing and now she felt fearful because without the touch of those she despised to keep her safe she wasn't sure she could control the power that had awakened within her.

She felt gorged with energy and thought of waking Denser before she realised she couldn't channel it physically. It was there in her mind. So instead she lay quietly, trying to still her thoughts as Cleress had taught her, and visualised her mind as a plug that fitted precisely over the well of energy surging in the One entity. But every time she tried to force the plug into place, flares of deep brown mana energy escaped. Not dangerous but very uncomfortable, the mana energy sniped at her consciousness and fed on her doubt. She felt as if she were alone with a wild animal, trapped in the cage of her own skull. And then fear swept her. How could she hope to control what she couldn't even understand? The pain grew again, thudding and reverberating.

"Oh, Lyanna," she whispered, seeing for the first time the edges of the torment that must have gripped her innocent little child.

Yet saying her name brought Erienne renewed determination. Fail now and fail Lyanna. She repeated the words as she fought to calm herself, to see through the fear, and in doing so realised her mistake. She had been seeing the One as a force wholly like mana, the random fuel of magic. But it was something much greater. It drew on everything around it, on the air and the earth as well as mana itself, like it was an integral part of the world, bound into its fabric.

She would have to adjust the way she thought, for while the One could be moulded as mana could, it could not be contained in the same way. It was not inert until channelled, like mana; it was already focussed because it reflected the land and elemental forces around it. That meant its focus would shift wherever she went so her mind would have to do the same to retain control. It would be like continually starting from scratch.

Deciding sleep would be a long time coming, Erienne settled back and tried to examine the One magic that already seethed within her, barely checked but not yet even fully awakened. Tuning her eyes further into the mana spectrum to give her a clearer view, she could see the deep brown of the One, delicate strands upsetting the random flow of the mana around it. Where mana normally flowed through everything, it was repelled by the One yet drawn to it at the same time. Unchecked, she could well imagine the devastation a full awakening of the One would wreak on a defenceless mind and in the world around because as it drew and expelled the mana it gained in intensity.

Watching the gossamer strands gradually thickening gave her an idea. She traced them down to their source within her consciousness, to the dark pulsating entity she thought of as the heart of the One. Forcing the strands back with her mind as she had been trying wouldn't work, she could see that now. Instead, Erienne wove a pattern with the mana around them, using the attractive and repulsive elements to funnel the strands back on themselves, making loops that fed back directly into the pulsing core.

Almost at once its energy lessened as it was forced into relative dormancy, feeding only on itself. At the same time Erienne felt a wave of tiredness travel through her. She could partition her mind to maintain the simple mana shape that blocked the One strands but it would drain her slowly.

She snuggled up to Denser, feeling the comfort of his gently moving body as he slept. He stirred a little at her touch, then stilled.

It is a lesson consummately learned. You are a very talented mage. Cleress's voice, soothing and quiet, stole into her mind.

Erienne's instant irritation at the intrusion was replaced by relief that the Al-Drechar were still with her.

I wondered if you'd be watching, she replied. *But don't push your luck.*

You must learn to control the One without us as soon as you can. Tonight you understood a tiny part of that control.

Meaning?

That what you felt were the merest tendrils of the potential of the One magic. Myriell was holding back the tide with you.

Erienne blanked for a moment. *How small a force was I being exposed to just then?*

Perhaps a thousandth, said Cleress. *Minuscule.*

Erienne gasped. And she had felt that energy easily enough and seen it feed and strengthen.

How could I ever hope to control or use the whole?

You cannot. No one can, not even us. We will teach you to keep the mass dormant so that it becomes second nature, and to use only that which you need. It is a tightrope but you have the ability. Now do you begin to understand?

What? But Erienne knew exactly what the old elf meant.

Lyanna could never hope to contain it. She was too young even to weave the simple mana shape you just employed. Erienne, the One returned to rest when it transferred to you. In Lyanna, it was fully awakened. By the time we met her it was already too late. The Dordovans had set something in motion that was unstoppable.

You still let her die, said Erienne, but her hatred was fading.

We really did have no choice, Cleress's voice pleaded inside her. *As a host for the One, Lyanna was doomed, Erienne. And she would have killed us all before she died in torment had we not effected the transfer.*

By "us" you mean the Al-Drechar.

Initially, said Cleress. *But you've seen how the One feeds on the elements around it. And you know what the uncontrolled power can do hundreds of miles distant. Before it killed her, the One would have gorged itself further, making the destruction you witnessed seem as nothing.*

All right! snapped Erienne.

Transferring the One to you was the only way to stop it but keep it alive.

Yes, I— Erienne broke off, considering for a moment. *And what if I hadn't been there to host it?*

We would have had to extinguish it, said Cleress, her tone leaden. *And we couldn't afford to do that.*

Erienne froze, all thought of sleep gone. She opened her eyes and looked down on Denser, still sleeping beside her.

There's something I have to know, she said, fearing the answer. *Could you have extinguished the One and kept my daughter alive?* Her heart thudded in the silence inside her mind. *Could you?*

Cleress sighed. *It was possible*, she said eventually.

Thank you for your honesty, said Erienne, feeling her strength collapse. *Now get the fuck out of my head.*

Erienne, no—

And take your senile witch sister with you.

Erienne, please—

Get out. Now.

I'm afraid we can't do that, Erienne. It was Myriell, voice strong, with no hint of sympathy.

Erienne felt her mind filling with a fury she had no desire to quell, her grief washing over her again as if Lyanna had died just there and then.

Go. Your touch sickens me. She could barely get her thoughts in order.

It had to be that way, said Myriell.

You let her die for an experiment. She could still be alive. The tears were falling down Erienne's cheeks and her body was rocking where she sat in the bed. *She could still be alive.*

And countless numbers would now be consigned to death with no one and nothing to save them. This was no experiment.

Don't give me that. You're lying.

First it would have been all the elves, next everyone on Balaia, said Myriell, like she was listing goods on a cart. *And we mean everyone.*

Go.

We will not.

You're lying. Lyanna died two seasons before the Elfsorrow took its first victim. Erienne couldn't believe what she was hearing. *Just what exactly am I supposed to be able to do with this curse inside me? March to Xetesk and take back what they stole with my overwhelming power? Think I'm stupid? You want the One for yourselves. To perpetuate what you have. I'm your legacy and that's all. Don't try and make me into a saviour.*

Erienne, you have to listen to me, said Myriell. *Will you do that?*

I don't appear to have much choice.

Erienne felt used. More like a mere receptacle for the One than a saviour of nations. And helpless with it. Because the One was awakening, and though she wanted the Al-Drechar out of her head she knew she couldn't survive without them. For now, at least.

Please don't think of it like that, urged Cleress, her tone so much softer than her sister's.

How the hell else do you expect me to think? Talk if you must. I'm listening.

Myriell's voice filled her mind once more.

The One opens pathways. Lets you see outlines of possible futures if you know what to look for and if you study for long enough. And we have had all the time in the world to study. There was a sadness to Myriell's voice now, its stridency gone. *Before we were even aware of Lyanna, we feared for Balaia. The stress in the mana over the colleges was critical. So much mistrust, so much risk of destructive power being unleashed. And then Lyanna came along as an answer to our prayers. A girl strong in the One can do so much good.*

And as we watched the world through the flow of the mana and harmony, we saw more danger signs, more potential for darkness. It was already apparent a crisis of huge proportions was coming. We could almost taste it. But even we were surprised at its scale and swiftness.

Yes, we could possibly have saved Lyanna but the risk in losing the new birth of the One magic was too great. And though we are distraught at the loss of your daughter, we have been proved right. What we see is never certain at the outset but there is always a sense of good or evil, and what we had sensed was so terribly bleak.

Erienne, you must remain strong, you must accept more power and you must remain alive. When the statue of Yniss was bound into the harmony of the elves thou-

sands of years ago, it was done using the One magic. When the fragment is returned, the process must be repeated. We cannot travel to Calaius so you must be our channel. No one else can do that.

I am sorry for the burden this places on you.

Myriell had stopped speaking for some time before the roaring in Erienne's ears died away.

And if you'd chosen to save Lyanna?

Nothing could have saved the elves and finding the thumb would have been futile.

What do I need to learn? said Erienne.

Later. Sleep now. We will withdraw from your conscious mind for a while, let you think in peace.

You're too kind.

I really am sorry, Erienne, said Cleress.

Don't bother, either of you. We'll do what we have to do together but I would advise you never to assume any of my grief. Whatever your reasons, you let her die. You had better be proved right as you claim.

Erienne felt the Al-Drechar fade in the form of a quietness enveloping her mind. They were still there, keeping control of the One entity, but Erienne felt no comfort in that. She felt none of the enormity of what the Al-Drechar had told her. Maybe that would come when she had time to consider it. One thing she did know was that it wouldn't change the way she acted with The Raven. And the first thing she had to do was tell them.

She looked down at Denser, wondering whether to wake him but finding she didn't have to. He was lying there looking up at her, a frown creasing his forehead. He reached out a hand and rubbed her lower back.

"What is it, love?"

Erienne opened her mouth to speak but instead a wave of sorrow broke over her. It was a long time before she was able to tell him what was wrong.

Auum sniffed the air of his first dawn on Balaia and didn't care for it much. It was dry and chill, without the mists he was used to, the growing heat or the ever-present threat of rain followed by the glorious cleansing downpour. He felt exposed without the closeness of the trees, and though the landscape he looked at was green and healthy, to Auum it looked blasted. His sharp eyes recoiled at the brightness of the dawn in which he could see rolling plains, a range of mountains far smaller than those now behind them, and a collection of dwellings, fenced and still.

A wind blew above the Tai where they sat, backs to a low rise, a fire in front of them, rabbits roasting on spits above the flames. They'd travelled quickly the afternoon before, Rebraal's descriptions and the position of the sun providing the information they needed. They knew what they were looking for. Their path was to travel north and east, past the Balan Mountains they currently faced, track to the west of a forest known as Thornewood, and then head northeast to pick up the trail which connected the port of Arlen in the far south with the college cities in the north.

There were signs that all was not well on Balaia. Rebraal had told them the land was fertile if bleak and open, with great swathes of evergreen and deciduous forest punctuating the rolling landscape. However, all they had seen so far were stunted boughs and some new growth as if, years before, a great hand had swatted the trees flat. They had also passed a hamlet late the evening before. It had been deserted, the buildings wrecked and stripped of timbers.

Auum turned to his Tai. They, like him, had their light cloaks tight around their bodies but could still feel the cold away from the fire.

"It will warm," said Auum.

"Small wonder their Gods have forsaken this place and none worship the ancients," said Duele, warming his hands over the flames.

"You are fit to run?" asked Auum. Both elves nodded. "And run we will, if only to warm our bodies. But first prayer and food."

Auum led them in prayers to Yniss and Gyal to keep them safe in the wilderness of Balaia, and to Tual to keep their senses sharp though the rain forest was far away. They did not paint their faces. They did not anticipate combat yet, not for days, and in this land they had to be careful not to waste their paints. Where would they find the materials for more?

"Are we covered for the route?" asked Evunn, biting into a scrawny roasted rabbit.

"Other Tai and ClawBound will track to the south of Greythorne and as far west and north as Understone and the pass beneath the mountains there. Our meet point with the southern trackers is the northern tip of Thornewood. There we can assess enemy strength and plan accordingly. Opportunities to kill are to be taken by any of us. The Al-Arynaar will also meet us there. And, if it is so decided, we will wait for the others. They're three days behind us at present but will travel directly to the meet."

"And have the ClawBound recovered, do you think?" asked Duele.

Auum blew out his cheeks. "We pray to Tual to calm their minds but the sea journey was least kind of all to them. But, like us, the feel of the land, whatever land, is like the touch of menispere leaves on a fevered brow."

They all smiled at that. For a race born to forests and sluggish rivers, the days on the gently rolling ship, lost in the vast openness of the sea, had been purgatory. Below they felt sick, on deck nothing short of scared. And though this land was alien and unpleasant, for the first hours at least it had felt good simply because it was not the sea. Only now, in a new dawn, did they really begin to see where they were.

Auum bade them hurry to ready themselves and the Tai set off at a trot, bows slung on backs, swords and jaqrui sheathed. They moved quickly as the sun gained in strength, repeatedly looking up at its majesty in a blue sky unhindered by the endless but comforting canopy.

With the foothills of the Balan Mountains just ahead and the sun approaching its zenith, Auum slowed suddenly, his Tai responding. They were running through a scrub-filled shallow valley at the base of which a river burbled southward. Trees flung their branches out across the valley floor and for a few precious moments they could have been back in the forest.

Ahead, through the trees, the valley flattened out and a handful of dwellings were grouped on the level ground. They were poorly constructed as if built in a rush or by those with no skill. Auum could see three people just away from the buildings, kneeling over the body of a fourth.

He nodded left and right and his Tai moved off soundlessly, Auum taking the centre. He had instructed minimal contact with Balaians. Elves could be approached but only because they might understand what was asked of them. Auum could smell fear ahead, and the tone of the voices backed up his instinct.

He crept to the edge of the cover, Duele and Evunn ten yards to either side, and looked out. About twenty yards away, on the bank of the river that now gushed shallow over rocks, the strangers huddled. From the houses he could see bows pointed and at the end of the ramshackle hamlet three men stood with swords drawn, looking away north. Auum concentrated on the scene in front of him, seeing one of the people, a woman, take a bloody cloth to the river and rinse it. On the ground, the injured man lay quite still as the cloth was reapplied to the side of his face.

Auum looked left and right, the nods he received telling him they had seen everything they needed to. He gestured a gentle push with both arms, stood and walked from cover, his hands loose by his sides and clearly visible. They were spotted at once, an urgent shout causing heads to turn and the swordsmen to come running. To his right, Duele was covering the archers. Auum didn't believe they would fire, and given the shaking of the bows in their hands, they were likely to miss if they did.

Auum let the swordsmen come to him and Evunn, who closed in on his left. They grouped ahead loosely, unsure what to do. One of them held up a hand and shouted. Auum stopped and pointed at the stricken man by the water's edge.

"I would help this man," he said in the hope that one of these strangers understood common elvish. Their blank expressions told him they did not.

The three swordsmen spanned as many generations. Their blades were dull with neglect, their clothing shabby and patched cloth and fur. Auum could see hardship in their eyes and the effects of starvation in the slackness of their stances, their bony hands and hollow cheeks. He moved again and the swords were raised. He thought hard, fighting for the word in Balaian. He had heard one of the strangers on ship say it.

Auum pointed again. "*Help.*" His mouth twisted as he pronounced.

The face of one of the men darkened, he mouthed a stream of gibberish and gestured threateningly with his sword. To Auum's right, Duele tensed but immediately relaxed as his leader made a minute movement with his hand. Auum knew he should back away but his decision was made, and unless he was very much mistaken he knew how the injured man had become so. And he was unused to being baulked.

He pointed a third time. "*I, help.*" And he made to take a pace left.

Immediately, one of the swordsmen stood in his way. His blade moved too close. Auum stepped inside his guard, blocked the sword arm away and smashed the base of his palm into the man's chest, knocking him from his feet. Another of the men moved but Auum's gaze stayed his action.

"Keep an eye," said Auum to Duele. "I will see if we were right."

He walked over to the group around the injured man, ignoring the threatening raised voices.

The instinctive bunching around their fallen comrade loosened as Auum approached the two women and a man. He waved them aside, speaking the word again. Whether they understood him or not was unclear but he certainly scared them enough even though he was still unarmed.

He ignored their worried, angry stares and knelt by the man's head, moving the bloody cloth to reveal a trio of deep gashes torn down the left side of his head. Another set had flashed across his chest but these were not as deep and the bleeding not bad. ClawBound.

He turned to Duele, who stood easily in front of the uncertain swordsmen; the one Auum had knocked down had regained his feet and was rubbing at his chest. Nothing would be broken, he hadn't hit him hard enough.

"The ClawBound's minds are not yet clear," said Auum. "The panther has hurt this man but they aren't killing blows, just warnings."

"These are not from Xetesk, then?"

Auum shook his head. "They have no magic. Look around. They're barely alive. And scared. You can see how this could happen."

The TaiGethen had no feelings whatever for these strangers but it was important to sense the mindset of the ClawBound. It gave them a problem. If this was typical, then the peerless trackers would be unpredictable, even a little careless, as had been the case here.

Auum unslung his sack and took out his herb pouches. He broke off some legumia bark, stood and walked away to the fire that burned in the centre of the settlement. Water in a pan bubbled on it and he scooped out a mugful, dropping the legumia into it to soften and infuse. He knew they were all looking at him. They amused him, these strangers who presumed themselves superior to forest-dwelling elves but knew nothing about how to bathe a wound and stop infection at its source. A bloody cloth rinsed in a stream would do more harm than good.

Walking back to the man, he cast around for some clean material, in the end pointing at a scarf around one of the women's necks until she shakily handed it to him. He dipped a corner in the hot water and wiped away the blood from the man's face and chest to expose the edges of the wounds. They would scar badly but he was lucky. He was alive. Then he took out the bark, tore it into fine strips and laid it over the wounds, hushing the fledgling protests. He beckoned one of the women to him, took her hand and pressed it against the bark, pointing up at the sky with his other and indicating one passage of the sun. She nodded.

"Let's go," said Auum, rising and shouldering his sack. "The ClawBound isn't far ahead. Perhaps we can stop any more of this until we find our enemies."

He led his Tai from the settlement, the stunned stares of the strangers on their backs, their silence breaking into a confused babble and fading with the distance.

CHAPTER 38

Heryst had just finished another long and difficult Communion with Vuldaroq and had woken shivering with exertion. Heryst thought he had made it clear to Vuldaroq that his position remained one of defence and negotiation unless he was attacked but the Dordovan would not listen. He was annoyed Heryst had refused to sign a full alliance and he meant to drag Lystern into the war regardless of her wishes. For that he had to tempt Xetesk into Lysternan or Julatsan lands.

Heryst had been particularly explicit concerning engagement. Commander Izack was to defend Lysternan land and to block any attempted hostile incursions by Xetesk into Julatsan territory. Nothing else. Heryst was aware of the rising tensions and had recently ridden out to reassure his own men and warn the Dordovan field command. But every day Dystran refused to speak to him, war came closer. Vuldaroq would ultimately get his way. A mistake would be made. For Heryst, it was like waiting for the death of a mortally wounded friend. This time the friend was peace for Balaia.

He barely had time to gather his thoughts and take in the spring shower rattling against the windows of his chambers when there was the sound of footsteps outside, a sharp rap on the door and someone, it had to be Kayvel, entered. He was red in the face and breathless.

"My Lord, I have a report from Xetesk."

Heryst's heart was suddenly thumping in his chest. His thoughts became instantly clear.

"Never mind the niceties of reporting, Kayvel. Tell me the outcome."

"Dystran," he said. "Dystran wants to talk to you about sharing research. Apparently his people are on their way home."

"Yes!" Heryst slapped the arms of his chair and surged to his feet to grip Kayvel's shoulders. "I knew it. Dammit, I knew it! When?"

Relief cascaded through Heryst and the fatigue of the last dozen days melted like ice in a flame. Now there was hope, genuine hope. And Vuldaroq could be made to listen.

"As soon as you are able," said Kayvel.

"For this I am able right now." Heryst sat back in his chair. "Signal our delegation that Dystran can commune immediately he is ready. He has my signature and I am waiting. Likewise the Dordovan delegation. Tell them what is happening. Vuldaroq must be informed immediately.

"Oh, and Kayvel. Have my aides monitor the mana spectrum and my MindShield. I do not trust Dystran as far as I can throw him."

Dystran's voice entered Heryst's mind gently and expertly, with due deference and respect.

"My Lord Heryst, there has been silence between us for too long."

"Not at my behest, Lord Dystran, but I welcome your decision to contact me at this most difficult time."

"Before we begin, may I offer my heartfelt sympathy for the loss of the Lysternan negotiator, Rusau. A most unfortunate incident."

Heryst bridled but bit down on his response. "Though you are not personally to blame, your forces killed him. He was an innocent man."

"Indeed it was a Xeteskian pike but you must see it was an accident. We had no axe to grind with Lystern, so to speak. And we still do not."

"Even though we have made informal alliance with Dordover?" Heryst was prepared to let the matter of Rusau's death drop for now. Blame could be correctly apportioned at a safer time.

"It was a decision we regretted," said Dystran carefully, and drew a deep breath, knowing it would boom and echo. It was a curious acoustic anomaly of Communion. "And it has been one reason for my continued silence though you are aware that we have not detained any Lysternan or indeed any other college official inside Xetesk."

"It has been noted."

"But, after taking considerable counsel, I understand the reasons for your action: we are nominally stronger, we have been blamed for the death of a neutral in battle and Vuldaroq is a very persuasive man. Very. For a man who only three seasons ago made an alliance with the Black Wings."

"I am aware of Vuldaroq's past misdemeanours. As I am of Xetesk's," said Heryst. "It was a despicable and unseemly act for any mage, born out of desperation, but the destruction caused by the Nightchild speaks in defence of his actions."

"Your General Darrick did not agree," said Dystran smoothly.

"Neither did I," said Heryst. "And our cool relations since then testify to my unhappiness. I, however, prefer to look forward as, I hope, do you."

"I apologise, Lord Heryst; this was not the reason for my contact."

Heryst chuckled, forcing himself to relax. "I should hope not."

"Our research on Herendeneth has revealed some fascinating possibilities which I am very happy to share with all other colleges."

Heryst was taken aback. "Your actions in Arlen, which I abhor, do not support such a statement," he said. "You have ignored the rules of engagement and that cannot be forgotten. But that can be left for another time when the threat of wider conflict is gone. What are your conditions for sharing the information?"

"They are few and simple. I require the immediate cessation of hostilities toward Xeteskian forces and the withdrawal of Lysternan and Dordovan forces from our borders."

"Anything else?"

"I would like leave to call a Triverne Lake meeting at a time of my choosing when we have had a chance to evaluate the research of our mages."

Heryst paused before replying. "Vuldaroq will refuse. He will not withdraw on a promise from you, a man he is unable to trust."

"In that case you can guarantee my mages' passage to Xetesk yourself. You do not need Dordover."

"I am looking to reduce threat to Lystern, not increase it. I cannot do this without Dordover's consent. I'm sure you understand. And I can't agree to Xetesk having exclusive first sight of the research."

"And what is your alternative?"

"That your mages prepare and present to a four-college delegation at Triverne Lake at the earliest opportunity and before they come to Xetesk. And my forces must travel with your researchers as a sign to Dordover that you are genuine. That might mollify Vuldaroq. If your ambition is to share all that the Al-Drechar have revealed, surely that is a reasonable request?"

"At first sight, yes," said Dystran. "But I believe there are issues with some of the information. Potentialities not necessarily being realities, work that needs more translation from ancient magics . . . I could go on."

"We are all capable of aiding in such an analysis," said Heryst.

"Even so, I am advised that a few days' examination by key experts in Xetesk will be of great benefit to us all."

"Meaning you personally?" Heryst could well imagine the smug expression on Dystran's face.

"I flatter myself that I have more detailed expertise on the subject of dimensional magic than most," said Dystran.

"And is it your understanding that what is coming will help repatriate the Kaan dragons?"

"Signs are most encouraging," evaded Dystran. "But, as I say, some expert analysis is still required before we can present effectively."

"Right," said Heryst, drawing in breath expansively. "I will discuss your offer with Vuldaroq. He will refuse it and we will be back to square one. My offer of secure passage to Triverne Lake is one you must take more seriously. Otherwise the war will go on."

"Thank you for hearing me," said Dystran. "I will confer further with the Circle Seven."

"We can resolve this, Dystran. As long as we are all prepared to give a little. The question really is, do you want to see an end to this war?"

"It is my dearest wish."

"Keep it so," said Heryst, and carefully but firmly, he broke the Communion.

Lystern's Lord Elder mage sat with his eyes closed for a time, mulling over everything he had heard and considering how he would broach Dystran's offer to Vuldaroq. When he opened his eyes, Kayvel was standing waiting.

"He's wavering," said Heryst. "Or he's lying. Either way, we may have room to move peace a tiny step forward. But I have to make both him and Vuldaroq concede ground. But I suppose it's progress of a sort. At least there is discourse. And now I must confess to a little tiredness. Wake me for supper and I'll brief the council."

The Raven rode from Blackthorne on a sunny morning with cloud far to the north. Hirad had not slept well. Beside him rode Ilkar, an elf and one of his oldest friends, under a sentence of death.

"Can I ask you something, Ilks?"

Ilkar turned to him, his sombre face lifting a little. "Would it make any difference if I said no?"

Hirad shook his head. "How does it feel to be you? Your next heartbeat could bring on the Elfsorrow without warning. Not sure I'd deal with that too well."

"Thanks for reminding me," said Ilkar.

"I'm sorry, Ilkar. I—"

"I'm joking. Not a moment goes by when I don't think about it. The point is, I have to live with it and being scared isn't going to help. Best I can do is everything I can to repair the statue and stop this thing. And meanwhile I live every day as if it was my last."

"I think the whole of Blackthorne heard you and Ren treating last night as if it was your last."

"Hirad, do you mind?" It was Ren from just behind them.

"Those corridors didn't half echo, you know," said the barbarian, revelling in Ilkar's deep blush.

"Hirad, stop it," said Ilkar.

"Tried to get a good night's sleep—"

"Ah, Hirad, but many of us were with our loved ones last night, weren't we?" said Ilkar. "For me it was Ren, then there's Denser and Erienne and I understand The Unknown had contact with Diera through Aeb. And you talked sweet nothings with Sha-Kaan."

"Now who's lucky, eh, Hirad?" said Denser.

"Is it my fault if I am called by a higher intellect?"

"Wouldn't want to sleep with it though, would you?" said The Unknown.

"Too much chafing," agreed Ilkar.

The Raven dissolved into laughter, Ilkar bent double over his saddle, Hirad taking both hands off the reins to wipe his eyes.

Fifty yards ahead, Aeb had stopped and turned in his saddle, his blank mask asking the question more eloquently than any words. It served to sober them up a little. The Unknown waved him on.

"How is Sha-Kaan, anyway?" he asked.

"Angry," said Hirad. "And now alone. We have a lot to hate Xetesk for, don't we? No offence, Denser."

"None taken. I agree with you."

"Good," said The Unknown. "Then let's keep focussed. We've got a job to do. If the TaiGethen can't get the thumb from the Xeteskians before they reach the city it'll be down to us to go in and get it for them. Remember who we're doing this for and remember not to speak loosely around Aeb."

Hirad leaned over and punched Ilkar lightly on the shoulder. "I'll take it as a personal affront if you die before we succeed in this, all right?"

"I'll see what I can do," replied the elf.

The Raven upped the pace. Xetesk was at least seven days away.

Selik stood on the ramparts inside the Understone stockade feeling deeply satisfied. Since the massacre of Anders and his pathetic garrison of frightened boys, the twelve surviving Black Wings had been busy making as much of the town as habitable as they could. Water butts were full all down the main street, boards had been removed from buildings and firewood was stacked next to the butts. The bodies of the garrison had been burned long ago and their ash blown away by the wind.

Selik saw this town as the birthplace of his new order, and though it was rotten now it would one day be the centre of his power. The foundations were already there, they just needed renewing. Perhaps it should be renamed. After him would be good, or maybe after his mentor, Travers.

But first they would have to fight, and under cloudy afternoon skies he saw his army begin to assemble. From the east came a line of men from Pontois, some riding, most walking or hitching rides on the dozens of supply wagons rattling along behind them. Later, he knew militia from Orytte, farmers from the devastated lands around Corin and Rache and refugees displaced from Korina and Gyernath would all come. He had no idea how many there would be or what sort of men he could expect, but with every person who walked into Understone he saw his power grow.

He was under no illusions. Though his captains would drill and he would speak, the thousands who marched on Xetesk would be little more than an ordered mob. They would not have the skill of those they faced but if, as he expected, battle had worn down the colleges, his numbers could surprise and overwhelm.

Hundreds upon hundreds would die, but such was the price of freedom and righteousness. Selik nodded to himself and went down to meet his recruits.

Thraun cantered along at the back of The Raven formation, feeling a sense of distress invade him. His recollections of Balaia were occasionally very sharp and the scents all around him fed his lupine side. Along with the thrill of the grass and the trees they passed, the sounds of birds and animals and the fresh smells of spring life, came memories of fire and tortured howls. He saw again the betrayal in the eyes of his pack and their helpless bodies burning under mage fire, cut off from the embrace of the forest.

And in the laughter of The Raven and their close companionship were more images of death and fear. Of his best friend Will lying still beneath the sheets of an infirmary bed in Julatsa. Of his chest falling never to rise again. Blame. He was to blame. And there was nothing he could do to right the wrongs.

He had been in the body of a wolf when Will's fatal wound had been received and had eventually fled in that body to escape his grief, only to be found wanting again. And so here he was. Back in a man's body but feeling like an intruder in the world of men yet unable to face the prospect of life as a wolf. Nothing he could do would be right.

"Thraun, are you all right?"

Thraun looked up. The Unknown Warrior was dropping back to ride beside him. He didn't answer.

"You had a bit of a wobble in the saddle just then. I wondered if you were feeling all right?"

Thraun shook his head. "No."

"Can you tell me what's wrong?"

He could understand everything they said, everything they asked him, but just couldn't find the words to explain the hopeless divide within him. The frustration threatened to overwhelm him at times like this and it was made all the more acute because he could remember being able to speak so freely. He had chosen silence until now rather than anger himself by failing to make himself understood.

"The words won't . . ." He waved a hand uselessly. How could it be this way? He could think it all but he just couldn't say it. Something was missing.

"Then let us help you," said The Unknown. "Don't be silent because there's a block in that head of yours."

"I . . . I can't." He sighed and punched the pommel of his saddle.

"Take it easy. Why don't you let me ask the questions? Just say yes, no or whatever you can. Repeat what you hear, if it'll help."

Thraun could see the sense but couldn't tell The Unknown that it made him feel like a child. Worse, an idiot.

"I'm not trying to patronise you, Thraun. You do understand that, don't you?"

Perfectly, he thought. But it doesn't make any difference. So instead he nodded and bit down on his shame.

"Is there anything we say you don't understand?"

"No."

"Do you think in the words you want to speak, then?"

"Yes."

"Do you remember all that happened to you?"

Thraun shrugged. "Yes?"

"Or you think so at least. Sorry, stupid question. How can you know what you haven't remembered?"

Thraun smiled. "Yes."

"You have memories as man and wolf?"

"Yes."

"Bad?"

"Bad," agreed Thraun. "Bad."

"You feel guilt?"

"Guilt."

"Responsible?"

"Yes."

"You aren't to blame, Thraun."

"Yes, I am."

"And there's nothing you can do, is there? Nothing to make it better."

"No, there isn't!" he stormed. "They're all dead because of me and there's not a fucking thing I can do about it. I ended so many lives because I can't be man or animal so what do you expect me to say? Sorry? I'm in torment here in my head and no one understands because I don't have the words."

He broke off, aware that they were all looking at him. Yet despite his sudden fury, he felt massively relieved. He relaxed his bunched shoulders.

"Thank you, I think," he said.

"Any time, Thraun. I think you're trying too hard sometimes. Don't think. React. Let it happen."

"I'll try," said Thraun, but he could feel the veil falling again.

"And I'll be there to provoke you, don't you worry."

Thraun nodded, unsure whether to laugh or cry.

CHAPTER 39

There was far more to the situation than Auum had appreciated and for the first time he wished he had listened more closely to The Raven. This was no simple two-way fight. At least two other factions were involved and that made decisions complex. However, the outcome was still not in doubt.

The ClawBound had discovered the party of Xeteskians on the third day of searching, moving steadily along the trail Rebraal had indicated. Their communications had spoken of a sizeable force. It had been another day before Auum and his Tai had found the pair. Although sympathising with how unsettled they were, he had rebuked the ClawBound for attacking an innocent. He had then personally tracked the Xeteskians for another day before moving quickly to the meeting point.

He reached it half a day ahead of the enemy and immediately began to plan, gathering other Tais to him and assessing information from the northern scouting. Troops in battle lines had been found a further three days north, their purpose unclear because they faced both north and south. There was no knowing if they were Xeteskian but the fact that they could be enemies added further weight to the argument for attacking the travelling force at the first opportunity.

"The enemy strength is not considerable in numbers but the warrior and mage quality is high," said Merke, leader of the second Tai tracking the travelling Xeteskians.

"Agreed," said Auum.

And it was so. The mounted forces numbered fifteen mages and thirty cavalry. On foot were twenty foot soldiers and fifty of the masked warriors. It was these last about whom Auum was most concerned. He had seen the one who fought with The Raven and his speed and raw power were beyond question. Rebraal had been at pains to emphasise that the more of them there were in one fight, the better they became. So fifty were to be rightly feared.

Given their strength and the focussed magic they could bring to bear, to attack them with the numbers that had landed from the *Calaian Sun* would be foolhardy. But the main elven force was now on land and travelling north. If they kept up their pace, there would be a chance to attack the Xeteskians south of the battle lines. Assuming the troops in the line were also Xeteskian, it was vital to attack the marching force as soon as possible.

Auum called Rebraal to him.

"What are the numbers we can expect here?"

"A further fifteen TaiGethen cells, four ClawBound pairs and a hundred and seventy Al-Arynaar. But every day more fall prey to the Elfsorrow."

"The Tai have been mercifully free of the Elfsorrow since we left Calaius but it won't last," said Auum. "We have an opportunity but I need to combine our forces quickly. Hold Communion. Have the main force move more quickly northward and be prepared for battle a day after they join us. We must strike before the enemy reach the college lines to the north."

"And if we don't secure the fragment?" asked Rebraal.

"Alert The Raven," said Auum. "They say they can help. If we fail, we'll see what they can do, won't we?"

"You are sceptical, Auum?"

Auum shrugged. "It is the way of an elf. You have listened too closely to your brother. Rebraal, one more thing. We are going to track the strangers from a distance. They must have no idea we are following them. If they increase their pace, we are lost. Be sure your people understand."

"Don't worry. None of the Al-Arynaar will travel forward of the TaiGethen or ClawBound."

"We are in an alien land," said Auum, "People talk and messages cross long distances by magic. Unless you have no option, keep clear of Balaians. This must be the greatest victory since the unification of the elves. Our lives are all at stake. Be sure they are mindful of that, too."

"We understand, Auum," said Rebraal.

Auum nodded. "Pray with me."

"It will be my honour."

Ilkar came out of his Communion with the Al-Arynaar mage and outlined the elves' plans.

"Where do they report seeing the college lines?" asked The Unknown.

"Three plus days north of Thornewood."

"That's the southern border of the Xeteskian mage lands," said Darrick. "When you talk to her next, tell her the troops they can see are going to be Dordovan; the lines they can't see a couple of miles further north will be the Xeteskians."

"And they're planning on attacking where, exactly?" asked The Unknown.

"Rebraal's brief is a little sketchy but it'll be close to the lines. Perhaps not in sight but not far off. It's all a question of getting the main force that followed us into the Bay of Gyernath north quickly enough. With the best will in the world, they can't catch Yron and the researchers much south of the Xeteskian lines. They're all on foot after all."

"But fast," said Ren. "And resolute."

Ilkar nodded. "So where does that leave us?"

"Simple," said Hirad. "We can get north of Yron's force and perhaps even contact the Dordovan lines. Let them know what's coming. What do you say?"

"It's good enough for me," said Ilkar.

The Unknown looked at Darrick, who nodded his agreement. "Let's do it."

Yron had never been able to shake off the idea that they were being watched. For practically every mile of the ten-day journey since they had left Arlen with the researchers, he'd had a nag at the back of his mind. He knew they drew glances from everyone they passed but that wasn't it. Hollow-cheeked men and women trying to work the land or with bow in hand on the hunt, traders wary of attack giving them a wide berth on the trail and refugees in any number just drifting; they weren't the problem.

Nor were the Dordovans. He'd been given clear assurances that their path to Xetesk was clear of enemy college forces until close to the mage lands. And he had no reason to disbelieve the army command. The devastation in Arlen, shocking as it was, served as ample proof of Xetesk's intent to see them safely home. There were parts of the town where nothing would grow again, the magic had caused so much damage to the core of the earth. Like a smaller version of the Torn Wastes far to the west.

But something wouldn't let him relax, and it wasn't the vague threat of Black Wings and misguided nonmages. Riding in the midst of fifty Protectors he would hardly fear those. It was the elves. He had no evidence whatever that they had followed him across the ocean as The Raven would have done. And he had no evidence they were being trailed or watched but he just knew it was so.

And because of this feeling he ordered them to follow a path away from the cover of valley, crag and forest. He would even have avoided long plains grass if he could, but to do that they'd all have had to fly. So instead he drilled his guards and kept half of his mages awake and shielding them day and night. He was aware they thought he was mad, but they hadn't been in the rain forest. They didn't understand these elves' capabilities.

The Protectors of course said nothing, and he was grateful for their reassuring presence. The rest of them would be welcome to laugh in his face the moment the gates of Xetesk closed behind them. In fact, he decided, he'd be the one to start the laughter. Only Erys understood, but all his words with the researchers, foot soldiers and cavalry served to do was make him seem as ridiculous as the Captain.

Yron had spent several nervous days riding between the ruins of Grethern Forest and Thornewood but with no incident. They had stopped off in Erskan to find themselves unwelcome and the gates of the castle closed against them. And they had skirted the earthquake rubble of Denebre over which the birds would not fly. Nothing. Not a hint of trouble.

They were less than half a day from the Dordovan blockade of the Xeteskian mage lands as late afternoon began to give way to dusk, but still Yron refused to relax. One word from him and the Protectors that ran with him would pass the message to their brothers in the battle lines and the way would be cleared, but still he could not stop fidgeting.

His eyes flicked over everything. There was forest to their left but it was a mile away and to their right a long rolling hillside ambled up to a sheer cliff twice as distant as the forest. They rode through a plain of waving grass that barely brushed his feet.

"See anything, Erys?" he said.

"No, Captain," said Erys a little wearily. "But I am still watching, believe me."

"Don't humour me, boy," said Yron. Never mind weary, he felt absolutely exhausted. He'd hardly slept a wink since they'd left Arlen. "Just do what I ask. Point and laugh later."

"I won't be doing that," said Erys. "I've seen too much of you to take your hunches lightly."

"Good, because I'm still sure."

But inside he *wasn't* sure. Was he simply being paranoid? Dystran had assured him that The Raven were being monitored through the Protector, Aeb, and presented no immediate danger. And he hadn't seen a single elf. But he couldn't afford to be complacent. Because in complacency lay death.

The Xeteskian force rode and ran on easily, eating up the distance. Yron reacted to every bird call, every whinny of a horse, the rattle of tack, the chink of metal and the breeze playing over the grass. He shivered constantly, just waiting for the awful keening sound of a jaqrui crescent scything through the air.

Six miles from the lines he ordered the lead Protector to him.

"We will be nearing the Dordovan supply lines or rear scouts," he said. "They know what we're attempting and will be ready. Assume they know our position."

"Yes, sir," said Esk.

"I want a clear run. I don't want a single sword, arrow or spell coming within a hundred yards of me, do you understand?"

"Yes, sir."

"Then I leave the timing to you and your brothers across the lines. Strike as required."

"It will be done."

Immediately, Esk ran off, twenty-five Protectors moving seamlessly to join him. The remainder closed ranks around Yron and Erys, the cavalry forming a wedge ahead, the mages scattered through the foot soldiers and cavalry, half holding their HardShields as they rode, the others with offensive spells part formed for quick casting. It was a drain but it wouldn't be for much longer.

Yron nodded, watching the Protectors sprint away to assault the rear of the Dordovan lines. It was oddly comforting to see them and he knew without any question that they'd achieve their aim. Still he carried on watching until long after they were completely out of sight. He turned his head to speak to Erys and the plain came alive all around them.

Shadows surged from the grass on both sides and crossed the path in front of them. An instant later, bows hummed and jaqrui howled through the darkening dusk. HardShields flared to deflect the incoming missiles, Flame-Orbs arced into the sky, HotRain began to fall.

"Oh dear Gods," muttered Yron, then shouted, "I told you, I told you!"

The cavalry charged, riding down the elves ahead, swords thumping into the Al-Arynaar, who had no experience of fighting mounted swordsmen. At the end of the charge, the cavalry turned and split to sweep back along the flanks. The Protectors unsnapped weapons and stormed away to meet their attackers, the foot soldiers trailing in their wake. Yron dragged his sword from its scabbard, kicked his horse to escape the HotRain that poured from the sky and headed for the mêlée.

"No!" shouted Erys. "No!"

"What?" Yron turned and saw Erys leaning out of his saddle, grabbing at his reins to pull him round. FlameOrbs splashed down close by, smearing across helpless foot soldiers.

"We've got to go!" yelled Erys.

"I will not run, boy."

"Leave the Protectors. We have to get our cargo to Xetesk. Now."

Yron knew he was right but recoiled from running and leaving others to die. TaiGethen and Al-Arynaar were closing in, hundreds of them streaming across the grass. How had they got here so quickly? More arrows bounced from the HardShield covering Yron. Somewhere nearby a panther roared, its voice picked up by others all around him.

"ClawBound too," he whispered.

What in hell was going on? Surely this was a totally disproportionate response to the theft of a few crumbling parchments? But even as his blood chilled at the numbers suddenly against them, his horse moving nervously, skittish at the sound of the big cat, he could only marvel at how these elves had got so close.

"Now!" screamed Erys, as more HotRain appeared above them.

Yron nodded, put his heels to his horse's flanks, called the research mages and his cavalry guard to him and forged ahead, the sounds of death echoing in his ears.

Auum made a quick analysis as he ran in, blade in his right hand, jaqrui in his left. The spells had served to scatter the foot soldiers and the tight knot of horsemen at the centre of the enemy but now answering spells were coming. Five elves at least were ablaze and dying, their bodies torches to light the gloom, their cries invitations to Shorth to take them.

To his left, well-ordered horsemen had carved through the ambush and were circling round to sweep along their flanks. Ahead, a line of Protectors spread in perfect order to wield the dual weapons they all carried and moved toward them. Behind them, spearmen moved nervously and, at the hub of it all, were the strangers he wanted, unsure and scared.

With Duele left and Evunn right, he sprinted in on a slight arc, other TaiGethen running counter arcs designed to confuse the enemy. Panthers roared and growled. He saw black shapes next to tall bound-elves running in from at least six points, one pair very close to him.

Auum flicked out his jaqrui. It flew straight and fast, wailing in the air. As he ran into the fight, he tracked it. The masked man hadn't seen it. Auum had mentally noted the kill when the man's blade came from nowhere to block it away in a shower of sparks. His gaze settled on Auum an instant later.

The TaiGethen joined battle, the enemy spacing allowing them two to a target. Auum flicked in a slash to the stomach which was blocked away, Duele carving toward the mask only to see the flat blade of an axe clatter against his sword, the sheer force knocking him momentarily off balance. Auum leapt, drop-kicking the enemy in the chest with both legs, forcing him to step back, but already the heavy axe was up and ready, the sword crashing down. Auum swayed right, deflecting the heavy blow, then skipped back a pace, narrowly avoiding a blow from the next Protector right. Duele mimicked Auum's movement, an axe grazing his arm, tearing the leather.

Next to them, Evunn had the help of a ClawBound pair. He ducked a cross swing from an axe, his blade licking up into his opponent's body. Simultaneously, the panther leapt, clamping onto the sword arm in midswing and bearing it backward. The Clawbound elf went for the man's face, hardened nails clawing at the mask's sides and teeth ripping at the eye slits. The Protector fell back, trying to push the elf away. His defence compromised, Evunn pierced his chest.

Auum checked in again, rolling under a sword thrust and whipping his blade up into the enemy's thigh as he rose, his head crashing into the point of the man's chin, snapping his head back. Duele saw his opportunity and roundhoused a kick to the Protector's head. Auum slashed his throat, turning as the body dropped.

Across the line it was slow going. He saw one of the masked men decapitate an elf in front of him, and with the follow-up with his sword, thrash it through the chest of another. The Protector moved forward, another beside him deflecting a blow he had no right to reach, allowing him to carve his axe into the body of a third Al-Arynaar. There was no sound from them and they worked closely in concert, just like Rebraal had said. They would be overwhelmed but it would take time.

In the centre of the enemy, their key targets kicked at their horses and sprang away. Auum heard shouts and some of the horsemen broke off, turned and followed.

Auum called his Tai and raced off, gathering others to him. He whipped out another jaqrui, this one finding a gap in the shield net and thudding into the back of one of the rider's heads. The cavalryman pitched from his horse.

"Get the runners! Get the runners!"

Ahead of him arrows flew and elves sprinted on the chase. ClawBound joined them, the panthers snapping at the heels of cavalry horses, one cat leaping to snatch a trooper from his saddle and bear him screaming to the ground. But the key men were getting away.

The surviving Protectors curved in more sharply, blocking the elves' route to the escaping Xeteskians, and around their flanks came the remains of the cavalry, swords held high, yelling war cries, their mounts thundering across the plain.

"Arrows!" yelled Auum, and he pulled another jaqrui from his belt pouch and flung it, seeing it miss its target as the rider ducked reflexively at the sound, hunching close over his saddle. "Tai, be sure."

The horses were on them, eight riders crashing into the line of TaiGethen, the elves dodging, waiting for an opportunity to strike. From the sides, arrows came in, thudding into three of the horses, which grunted in pain but ran on. One rider was downed, tumbling forward and under the hooves of his mount.

Auum could all but feel the breath of the animal on him when he skipped right and slashed his sword high, taking his opponent in the leg. He turned to watch them halt and turn. Auum took off at a sprint, racing past battling elves and men and hearing the scream of a dying TaiGethen cut off abruptly. The rider had pointed his horse and was kicking it back into motion, holding his sword low this time and to his left, defending his wounded leg.

But Auum wasn't interested in dodging this time. Going full tilt at the horse, he gauged the closing distance, leapt high, rolled in the air and arrowed in straight legged, his feet catching the rider on the top of his head and catapulting him from the saddle. Auum landed rolling, coming up fast to finish the job, but there was no need. The broken angle of the still body told him everything.

He swung back to begin the chase after their main targets but could see immediately he was too late. Yelling in frustration, he turned to look for his Tai in the closing moments of the battle only to see a Protector impossibly close to him. He caught a glimpse of slashed mask and bloodied face behind it and an axe blade flashing toward him. He dived reflexively right, looking up to see the weapon coming at him again, head height. He raised his blade to block but knew it wouldn't be enough.

A black shadow crossed his vision and a panther took the Protector at the neck. The axe came through, catching the animal's hindquarters, shearing off a leg. It dropped to the ground dead, its ClawBound partner howling anguish. The bound-elf dived onto the prone enemy and stabbed straight fingered again and again into his throat until it was nothing but bloody gore.

Auum placed a hand on the elf's shoulder. Elsewhere, the fight was done, the Xeteskians disengaging and running; some escaping, others being cut down as they went, victims of sword, spell and arrow. The ClawBound's howls split the air, his cries taken up by his brothers and their animals. The elf hugged his panther to him, smoothing its bloodied fur as ClawBound ran in from across the plain to mourn his loss.

"I am sorry," said Auum. "That blade was meant for me."

The elf looked up at him, paint streaked with his tears, eyes red and glistening. "It was vital you lived," he said, then he let his head drop in prayer. He would be buried with his panther.

Auum backed away and rejoined his Tai. The war was not yet won.

Tendjorn had been moved to command the Dordovan forces south of Xetesk and took it as a rebuke for his failure to lure the Xeteskians into an incursion across the River Dord. It had been a one-sided affair, he had lost far too many men and perhaps he was right to be shamed. The thought, though, did not improve his mood.

It was early evening, and in the camp between the south and north lines he was debating what to have for supper. He was bored with thick soups and stews and wondered if he could persuade some of the men to go out hunting deer. It was against regulations to leave the front but a forest two miles to the east was said to be home to a few. It could hardly hurt.

He was in charge of two hundred foot soldiers and mages spread thinly against an attack he didn't believe would come; not now Lystern had joined the blockade. And they had been effective in reducing supply to Xetesk to a trickle at best. The Lysternan leader, Heryst, was engaged in diplomacy which Vuldaroq was determined would fail. And though part of Tendjorn wanted it to fail too, so he could avenge his earlier poor showing, most of him wanted to go home, put his feet up and continue his research.

Tendjorn ambled out of his command tent and wandered over to one of the perimeter guards to the south of the camp. The majority of his men were north, well dug in against a Protector force he knew was out there. But he had stationed as many as he could spare in his south-facing line because command said Xeteskian researchers were heading home and would try to break the blockade. He didn't believe that either.

"Anything to report?"

The guard saluted then smiled and shook his head. "Still nothing, sir."

"Have they checked in?"

"A couple of hours ago, nothing to—"

FlameOrbs appeared in the sky perhaps three miles south, maybe less, quickly followed by the unmistakable sparkle of HotRain.

"What on earth?" he said. "Have we got anyone that far south?"

"No, sir."

"The Lysternans?"

"Not as far as I'm aware, sir," said the guard.

They watched for a while, seeing spell after spell crack across the sky, getting no nearer.

"Get out to the first watcher," ordered Tendjorn. "Get me some information."

"No need," said the guard, pointing.

Someone was running toward them, arms flailing for balance, legs pumping hard at the coarse scrub-covered ground. He was shouting something unintelligible and seemed to be waving them away. Tendjorn stood where he was, a hand cupped to his ear.

"I can't hear you!" he shouted, and beckoned him on. "Get closer."

The man was screaming his words out. Tendjorn frowned. Someone else was shouting too, but from behind. The watcher got within earshot.

"Protectors!" he gasped. "Twenty-five, running this way. Bring in the defence."

Tendjorn nodded and turned, running back toward the centre of the camp.

"Captain, I need a defence south. Protector force coming this way. Twenty-five. Mages, FlameOrbs and DeathHail. Now move!"

But there was something else. While some ran to do the Captain's bidding, more were running the other way, grabbing weapons from stands, other officers screaming orders, faces white with fear.

"Gods, what is happening?"

Tendjorn hurried up to his north line, cresting a rise that looked out across a long plain. They had chosen this position as an ideal battlefield. Coming across it were more Protectors. A hundred more at least. They would have their battle.

"Shit," he rasped. "Keep them back as long as you can. Beware our south! More coming from the south."

He turned and ran back toward his tent. From the south line, the ring of steel and the crump of spells had begun. Tendjorn slipped inside the tent and lay back on his cot, trying desperately to calm himself enough for a Communion. Vuldaroq had better be receptive. Tendjorn didn't have long to live.

CHAPTER 40

Hirad saw the bloom of spells above the tree line back to his right and urged his horse to greater speed, The Raven hard in his wake. Echoes of voices rose above the sporadic detonations, the battle itself hidden by forest and hill.

"Running out of time, Raven!" he called over his shoulder.

But they'd travelled as fast as they could. Keeping away from settlements of any size had been difficult enough and the route they'd taken had been made even less direct by their need to keep Aeb in the dark about their direction for as long as possible. Xetesk now knew their destination—that was a given—but in the lattice of valleys, crag formations and plains that made up the lands to the immediate east of the Blackthorne Mountains, it was easy enough to lose yourself if, like The Unknown and Darrick, you knew how.

It had worked thus far but now the hiding was over. Riding at the rear of the party, Aeb could sense Protectors close by. The Unknown and Darrick were at Hirad's shoulders with Erienne, Ilkar and Denser in a line behind. Ren and Thraun rode just in front of Aeb.

The light was fading fast, the haloes of spells bright in the sky for a long time. Hirad felt a thrill as he hunched over his horse's neck, The Raven with him, travelling fast over Balaian ground, heading for the fight. This was why he was alive.

They galloped up a very shallow slope, rounding a stand of trees that had somehow survived the elemental devastation of two seasons before, and saw it all mapped out before them. To the right, the elven army was tackling a Protector force augmented by mages and cavalry. The elves had been halted by the positioning of the experienced Xeteskian forces, which had allowed a group of over twenty-five to get away; they were charging north at a hard gallop.

Hirad swung north to give chase, The Raven following. They were perhaps a hundred yards behind and closing quickly enough to catch them before they hit the Dordovan lines. With any luck, they would be enough to stop them.

With a mile to go, spells flared into the night directly ahead and the distant roar of voices followed soon after. Hirad pushed harder still, eating up the distance. It didn't take much to work out was what going on ahead but The Unknown confirmed it anyway.

"Protectors backed by mage support," he shouted across to Hirad as they galloped. "I can feel them. So can Aeb."

"We've got to catch them fast." Hirad turned. "Ready, Ilkar?"

The Julatsan nodded, the SpellShield already formed, just waiting to be cast. Either side of him, Denser and Erienne prepared in time-honoured fashion. Hirad looked forward. They'd been seen.

"It's got to be now! Go Raven!"

Ilkar deployed the shield as weapons were hauled from scabbards and The Raven spread to a line, charging at the rear of the fleeing Xeteskians. Wings sprouted at Denser's back and he left his saddle, plucking Erienne from hers, the two of them shooting forward, climbing high into the dusk sky, their horses following the chase, stirrups bouncing.

Ahead a group of cavalry swung back to face them. Denser tore down for Erienne to release FlameOrbs before arcing high toward the main body. The Xeteskian cavalry scattered from the approaching spell. It splashed onto a single rider, who died instantly with his horse in a deluge of flame.

Before they could re-form, The Raven were on them. Hirad veered hard left and lashed out his sword, slicing into the chest of a cavalryman. The impact slowed him and he pulled back on the reins of his horse to keep from falling, dragging his blade back and hacking down through the man's shoulder to finish the job. He pulled his horse round. Ren was trading blows but winning her battle, her quick strikes too much for the horseman who leaned away as he defended.

Further away, Aeb's axe took the head from a horse and the rider plunged to the ground as the animal collapsed. Thraun was riding a wide circle, followed by a pair of riders. Hirad set off after them, roaring a call. He jumped a fallen horse, saw The Unknown with Ilkar, defending the mage easily from a clumsy attack, and drove into the flanks of the pair chasing Thraun. Letting go his reins, he leaned out and smashed his fist into an enemy face, feeling the cheek crack under the force of the blow, then raised his sword. The rider saw it coming, recovered to block but fell from his horse nonetheless.

Thraun had turned. He rode in hard, blond hair flowing behind him. Raven coming from either side, the Xeteskian turned and fled.

"Let him go!" shouted Hirad. "Raven! Raven with me!"

The regrouped Raven galloped away to resume the chase. Hirad could see Denser coming in from a great height, diving incredibly fast at the knot of Xeteskians who were now two hundred yards distant. Behind the group, three horses and riders wheeled to a stop. Mages.

Erienne released a blanket of HotRain to force a change of direction in the main group. Denser soared back into the sky. Hirad watched them go, saw Denser veer sharply right, dip suddenly as if hit, right himself temporarily then crash in a heap from a height of ten feet or more.

"Thraun, Darrick! Defend them."

The two men broke from the group and charged away to the fallen Raven mages as enemies closed in around them. Hirad erased unbidden thoughts from his mind and carried on north, finding himself riding through the evidence of a very recent massacre. Tents burned, fires were scattered everywhere, the bodies of men lay twisted and broken, their brutal wounds the type only Protectors could inflict.

With The Unknown and Aeb right beside him and Ilkar behind, the shield still holding, he charged up a short rise, plunged down the other side to continue the chase and found a wall of Protectors blocking their path.

He hauled hard on the reins, his horse slowing to a stop with an angry grunt as the bit sawed at its jaws. Beyond the Protectors, their quarry galloped on into safety. He stared at the blank faces in front of him, sensing The Unknown and Aeb riding to his sides, Ilkar and Ren behind.

There had to be close on a hundred of them. Hirad felt the sweep of reverence like a breeze across his face. The Protectors were facing Sol, who had almost God-like status among them. And there with him, Aeb, the Protector who was about as close to a rebel as any of the calling could get.

Hirad knew they weren't going to be attacked. He laid his bloodspattered blade across his saddle and turned to The Unknown.

"Can't you make them move?" He eyed the crescent line. They were not going to be able to simply ride around.

"No," said The Unknown flatly. "They should be killing us but they won't bear arms against me or Aeb. They will stop us following though."

"Damn, but we were so close to them," said Hirad. The sound of hoof beats had faded and a curious silence had fallen. Hirad was at a loss. "So what do we do?"

"I don't know," said The Unknown. "But their support mages must be close. We shouldn't delay here too long."

And then Aeb spoke.

"We do not seek to harm Xetesk's sons," he said, addressing the Protectors aloud presumably for The Raven's benefit.

There was a ripple in the line but none spoke, the masks staring back impassive. Aeb continued.

"We seek a fragment of a statue taken by Captain Yron. The elves will die without it."

"Aeb, enough," said The Unknown, and to the Protectors: "Xetesk is wrong to have taken it. Please. If there is anything you can do, help us recover it. A whole race depends upon it, not a few hundred lives. And do not speak Aeb's words in the Soul Tank. You know where it might lead. They were my words. Let it be so. We are one."

"We are one," murmured the rank of Protectors, and Hirad felt the completeness of their union.

He looked left toward the sounds of shouting and horses. Four men, cloaks flying, were riding their way.

"Time to go," he said. "We need to find the others."

"Incoming," said Ilkar distantly.

Fire flared over the SpellShield, venting harmlessly across its surface and into the ground.

"Our Given mages are close," said a Protector from the middle of the line.

"Too close," said The Unknown. "We wait."

"What?"

"Trust me. They'll need some administrative guidance, as Ilkar calls it."

The quartet of mages cantered up, riding between The Raven and the Protectors.

"Why aren't you attacking them?" one of them screamed at the Protectors. "Why aren't they dead?"

"Because I am here," said The Unknown. His voice was quiet but carried total authority. Hirad felt a shiver along his spine. "And they will not strike me."

"Ah, The Unknown Warrior," said one, turning to them. "They can protect you but you cannot protect them."

"That is true," said The Unknown evenly, taking the quartet in with his slow stare, a slight and dangerous smile on his face. "But if a single one of these men is subjected to punishment for his actions today, I will know. And then your lives, all of them, will be forfeit."

It was why Hirad loved him. He didn't have to shout or posture. He just had to speak and people listened and, more important, they believed.

"They have prevented us catching those we want," said The Unknown. "Their task is therefore successfully completed and that is enough. Are we clear?"

Almost as one, the mages nodded. Hirad almost laughed.

"We've done what is required," said one. "We can leave it at that, I think."

"Good answer," said Hirad.

They watched while the Xeteskians wheeled and trotted away, the Protectors following them in close guard.

"It's what the Master wants," said Aeb suddenly.

"I beg your pardon?" asked The Unknown.

"For the elves to die," explained Aeb. "It is more than he dreamed of."

"How do you know that?" asked Hirad.

"The Soul Tank knows it," said Aeb.

"Think we've got a good deal to talk about tonight," said Hirad. "Come on, let's go and find the others."

The Raven rode into the dusk.

Heryst was surprised at Vuldaroq's calm as he joined Communion.

"Vuldaroq, I'm sorry," began Heryst.

"What did I tell you?" Vuldaroq said. "Gods burning, I warned you. He lies to us all. He played you for time, pure and simple. Kept you off your guard and from formal military alliance. It is I who should be sorry. Sorry that your ideals, naive though they are, are misguided. The research is through and on its way to Xetesk and there is nothing we can do about it. Now will you join me and save our country?"

"What do you intend to do?" Heryst felt so weary. He'd clung to hope and yet Vuldaroq was right. He had been taken for the fool he was.

"We have to strengthen our defences south of Lystern, we have to block any route to Julatsa and we have to abandon the southern blockade to do it. And when we are assembled, we will march on Xetesk."

It was a nightmare, pure and simple. Everything that Heryst had sought to avoid was coming to pass. Everything he feared for Balaia would happen. The war would engulf them all. He had failed. Dystran wanted dominion; he had to be stopped and war was the only way.

"I will issue the orders to Izack and my field commanders immediately."

"We have battle plans," said Vuldaroq. "You must fight to our design. You must let Dordover run this war as we have been for a season now."

Heryst would have said no but Darrick wasn't here to improve Dordover's plans. And Heryst was not a student of the military.

"I will grant you overall field command but I will not have my forces committed to suicide. There will be discussion on the ground at every front."

"Of course," said Vuldaroq.

"One thing I want to make very clear, Vuldaroq. This war must not go so far as to destroy Xetesk. This country needs magical balance and so it needs the Dark College. This war removes Dystran and the current Circle Seven and nothing more. Do I make myself clear?"

"I had planned for nothing more," said Vuldaroq. "You won't regret this."

"I don't doubt that I will," said Heryst.

He broke Communion and put his head in his hands. Lystern was at war with Xetesk.

Selik stood on the ramparts of the Understone garrison and looked down over the army assembled before him. The sun was warming the earth from a clear blue sky and a gentle breeze ruffled his cloak. Men, women and youths from two dozen towns and villages were standing looking up at him. Refugees scattered across the land had come to his side to avenge what had been done to them.

Most of them were tradesmen or farmers. There was a scattering of militia and soldiers but the vast bulk of the estimated two thousand seven hundred would be holding swords in anger for the very first time. Some would run, others would be heroes and many would die. That was the way of war. He scanned the pinched and hungry faces, the eyes looking to him for leadership, for a way out of their darkness. They had come to the right man.

"My friends," he said, his voice loud, carrying across the silence. "You are all standing here because the time has come to right a great wrong. The time has come to win back the land of Balaia for its God-given people. To take it from the mages who destroy it so casually. To make it pure again.

"Because make no mistake, our land is riddled with the disease of magic and only the righteous can purge that disease. And I am looking at the righteous here and now."

A great roar erupted from the crowd below, fists and weapons punched the air. Selik held up his hands for quiet.

"You have all seen the war spread. It has torn down our peaceful towns and is destroying our beloved land. And now it is our turn to strike. Last night Lystern joined the war, as we knew they would. Even those who preach peace have betrayed us now. What more evidence do we need that, if we let it, magic will kill us all? So we will join the war. We will fight on one front only and that front will be Xetesk."

A murmur ran through the crowd.

"They are the dark heart of magic and they must be thrown down. And once the surviving colleges see our power and the righteousness of our fight, they too will fall before us. We are on a march to victory. Nothing can stop us."

Another roar.

"My friends, this is a great day to be a Balaian. Return to your commanders, strap on your swords and prepare to march!"

Selik turned to face Devun, a smile broad across his ruined features.

"It's finally happening, my friend. What Travers began a decade and more ago, I will finish. When will you reach your positions south of Xetesk?"

"Three days, Captain."

"Excellent. I will join you in the field as soon as I can. There are more reserves coming in and I need to be here for a while yet. Meanwhile, you know the plans and the people trust you. It's beautiful isn't it?"

"Sir?"

"Light will dawn on a new order, an order not dominated by the evils of magic. We will all live outside the veil of fear. We are the righteous."

"So what happened to you last night?" said Hirad to Denser as they rode from their camp the following morning, heading to the west of Xetesk, aiming to throw any pursuit off the scent.

"Some of their mages were sharp. As we flew in to drop the HotRain, I could see them casting. I veered away when Erienne cast but got clipped by the edge of a ForceCone. The jolt knocked my concentration all to pot and it was all I could do to hang on to the shape until a few feet from the ground. We were lucky."

"That's what you call luck, is it?"

"Could have been DeathHail. Then we wouldn't be riding with you at all. As it was, I managed to get my legs under me as we landed but I was going way too fast."

"Bad moment," said Hirad. "How's Erienne?"

"Well the arm's not broken but it's sore. It's a good job we're a couple of days from more action or she'd have trouble casting."

Hirad was silent for a moment. He didn't feel in control of the situation and that made him uneasy. There were too many variables. Too much to go wrong.

"Are you happy with this hare-brained scheme we cooked up last night?" he asked.

Denser shrugged. "I don't really see any alternative. If we're going to try and snatch Yron, then we have to have accurate information on his location in the college or we'll fail before we start."

"But Aeb . . ."

"I know," said Denser. "It's just a matter of time before he's found out and he knows that. But he's the only one who can talk to the Soul Tank and get us what we need. Other Protectors are going to risk themselves too. Funny, isn't it? All these years and then you find Protectors have a collective conscience."

"Yeah, and all these years and we find they're actually so vulnerable."

"I suppose, but none of them have ever gone against Xetesk before, so a punishment for that crime has never even been considered." Denser paused and looked across at Aeb, who rode between him and The Unknown. "We could still get away with it though. With the war escalating every day, rescinding the Act of Giving for one Protector isn't going to be top of anyone's agenda."

"I hope you're right."

"Xetesk have more important things to worry about. Lystern have been forced into the war alongside Dordover and that changes the balance against them. Blackthorne will be in Lystern in a couple of days to effectively pledge baronial support. Rebraal is going there too and the elves will be fighting alongside the other colleges. It's nasty out there."

"I can't quite believe Dystran wants what Aeb says he does," said Hirad. "It doesn't make any sense."

"Like I said, no elves, no Julatsa," said Denser. "But we've got to be focussed, not get caught up in the war. For us, saving Ilkar and Ren is all that matters."

Hirad chuckled. "So strange. Remember when we first met?"

"You wanted to kill me."

"Sorry about that."

"No offence taken," said Denser, smiling.

"I hated you. So did we all. But now, a few years down the line, you'll attack your own college to save Ilkar."

Another shrug. "He's Raven. That's all there is to it."

CHAPTER 41

Yron strode through the halls of Xetesk toward his meeting with Dystran, Erys scurrying to keep up, an escort of four mages and two Protectors around them. His anger had sharpened throughout the ride across Xetesk's mage lands to the city of his birth, and the immediate summons to Dystran's audience chambers at the base of the Tower had done nothing to calm him.

Filthy from the road, he swept through the doors as they were opened for him by a servant. The audience chamber was small but welcoming. Fires were lit on opposite walls and the sun shone in through a large arched window in front of him. Chairs were spaced around the room, all unoccupied. Leaning on the mantel to the left was Dystran, and standing next to him, supported by a stick, Ranyl, gaunt and sick.

Dystran came forward, his face alight with a smile.

"My dear Captain Yron and the excellent Erys, may I welcome you at the end of your fantastic journey."

"Too many men are dead for any celebration, my Lord Dystran," said Yron. "And only by luck am I here at all."

"Yes, I heard you had trouble with elves," said Dystran.

"Trouble? My Lord, there is an army of them out there. They are well trained fighters. Their mages are skilled and all are utterly determined. Don't underestimate them. They are fearless and can take on Protectors because they are quick enough to beat them. And they will be coming here, though why the theft of some parchments, however holy, should inspire such a reaction, I'm not sure." Yron could see Dystran was barely interested. He bit his tongue to be silent.

"Indeed," said Dystran. "But please, don't worry about it. We have the situation well in hand."

"In the same way you have The Raven well in hand?" Yron said sharply. "I am sorry, my Lord, but they came within twenty yards of catching me and I was assured they would be taken care of. Never even found them, did you? I say again, why are they and the elves so desperate to recover these texts?"

Dystran's smile thinned. "Captain, Captain, Captain. Please calm yourself." Had he not been the Lord of the Mount, his patronising tone would have earned him a punch in the face. "It is true some of the efforts made to track The Raven have been less than effective but you have my personal assurance that they will shortly be dealt with decisively. Meanwhile, you are a returning hero. You have suffered terrible loss but all those who died have done so for the greater glory of Xetesk. And you have been on the trail too long. Look at you; clothes torn, axe blunted. I must apologise for dragging you here now but I would have sight of your treasures."

Yron nodded, managing to relax a muscle or two. He turned to Erys, who passed over the leather satchel. Yron unclasped it and drew out the four texts that had made the trip. So many men dead, so little to show. He handed them to Dystran, who laid them immediately on a table near him and spread them out.

"The one in the middle there, my Lord," said Erys, pointing at a bound volume with intricate embossing on the cover and gilt-edged pages. "That is the Aryn Hiil unless I am sadly mistaken. In there are the secrets of elven longevity."

Dystran brushed his hand across the cover reverentially and looked up. "No mistake, Erys," he breathed. "If there was one text I needed, this was it. You two have no idea of the rewards Xetesk will heap on you for what you have done. This will bring us what we desire."

"My Lord, we live to serve," said Erys, bowing.

Yron looked at the young mage and shook his head.

"And you have the healthy cynicism of experience," said Dystran, noticing the gesture. "Captain, all I can offer you now are my thanks, the respect of the Circle Seven and a place to bathe and change. I have had chambers readied for you both just a little way down the hall. I have had clothing laid out for you and while you bathe, Captain, your axe will be polished and placed in a new holster. I trust you like it. And that is only the very beginning.

"But before you go, I would see the statue fragment you have." Dystran held out his hand.

Yron looked at Erys again. "Thanks a lot."

"I'm sorry, Captain, I . . ." At least he had the good grace to look embarrassed.

"My only memento of this whole mess and my only solid memory of Ben-Foran. You owe me, boy."

He dug into his trouser pocket and pulled out the thumb, handing it across to Dystran, who clutched it greedily.

"Oh, don't worry, Captain; it will be returned to you. But it needs to be researched and studied." He looked up and smiled again. "Rest assured, it remains your property. Now, please, both of you, wash, rest and dress. We are hosting a dinner in your honour in the rooms adjacent to this one. There we can discuss what is to be done to appease the elves while we have to. Thank you, Captain Yron, Erys. You have done Xetesk a service greater than you know."

But as Yron left the chamber, he wasn't so sure he had. Not so sure at all.

It had been a long and, if Yron was absolutely honest with himself, very pleasurable evening when the war outside the gates seemed distant. He'd spent the day relaxing in sumptuous chambers, he'd taken two baths and he'd slept in a bed for the first time in so long he'd forgotten what a luxury a mattress and sheets were.

And dressing in the fine dark silk shirt and stitched leather trousers Dystran's tailors had so expertly made from the template of old clothes taken from his barracks room, he began to feel that perhaps his earlier misgivings were, well, misplaced. His only regret was that Ben was not here to enjoy the fruits of their success.

He'd left the gold- and silver-veined holster, in which his old axe sat like a pig's trotter in a velvet glove, on his bed, feeling the need to be free of the accoutrements of battle for the evening, and had gone to join the dinner. It had been everything Dystran had intimated. He and Erys had been toasted repeatedly, fêted by the most powerful men in Xetesk and urged to describe ever more freely their exploits on Calaius.

Yron, cautious and close at first, had found his lips eased by the vintage red wine in his seemingly ever-full goblet and had relaxed into the celebration with growing enthusiasm. For once in his life, he was truly ahead.

As the evening wore on, and feeling more light-headed from the wine than he was used to, Yron had gone to relieve himself and then wandered back along the lantern-lit picture-hung corridor to the huge vaulted dining chamber. Bright light spilled from the open doors and the sound of laughter and the chink of glasses and cutlery echoed out to him in welcome.

He paused just to the side of the doors to let a servant laden with dishes hurry out and became aware of Dystran's voice inside but very close. It never hurt to hear the unguarded thoughts of the mighty so he checked the corridor was empty. Barring the Protectors flanking the doors, it was, so he listened.

"The Aryn Hiil will provide great insight, I am sure," Dystran was saying.

"My scholars are working on the translation even now," said Ranyl's cracked voice.

"Well, you must keep me apprised." The disinterest in his tone was obvious. "But now we have this outwardly insignificant item, we have a far less troublesome solution to our problem."

"It is a severe course of action, my Lord."

"Innocents die in every conflict, Ranyl," said Dystran. "But with this small piece of admittedly very well-carved marble, we don't have to lose a single man or mage in fulfilling this part of our plan. Julatsa will cease to exist as a magical power. All we have to do is hang on to it and watch the elves die. As many as we want. What a treasure."

"Assuming we can keep the allied colleges from our gates," said Ranyl.

"That I entrust to our commanders and they assure me we will prevail."

Yron's head swayed and he placed a hand on the wall to steady himself. His mouth was dry and nausea galloped through his stomach. All the glory was gone, and in its place the betrayal and murder of an entire race. That couldn't be allowed to happen.

Straightening his clothing and forcing a smile back onto his face, Yron walked back into the banqueting chamber and straight over to Dystran.

"Ah, one of our heroes. How does it feel to be going down in history, Captain?" asked Dystran.

"Difficult to put into words, my Lord," said Yron, wishing to God he had his axe, though murdering Dystran wouldn't right any wrongs. "I wondered if I might be excused for the night. The wine and my exhaustion have conspired against me."

"Of course, Captain. You have graced us for longer than we should have allowed. Erys has already retired, feeling a little sick, I think."

"I know how he feels," said Yron.

"I trust you have a quiet and restful night," said Dystran.

"Well done, Captain," said Ranyl. "I knew you would repay my faith."

"I've certainly done that," said Yron. He bowed stiffly. "Good night, my Lords."

He spun on his heel and left the banqueting hall, walking quickly to his chambers. He listened at the doors of Erys's room and could hear nothing. At least the boy was not being sick. Good, because he had a great deal of work to do. He turned and almost walked straight into the Protector standing directly behind him. His heart fell. Dystran must have known he'd been overheard. His hand fell to his waist but his axe was behind a closed door. He waited for the end.

"We will not stand in your way," said the Protector. "We understand."

"Eh?"

"You will do what you must." And the Protector moved away silently.

Yron put a shaking hand on his door handle and pushed down. He would have to do it tonight or it would be too late. He might never get another chance like this. What was going on? Protectors turning against their masters? It could only be down to one group of people. People who rode with an ex-Protector.

He closed the door behind him, walked over to his wash bowl and made himself sick.

It was the early hours of the morning. Darrick was on watch and sat by the cook fire, letting it die slowly. It wasn't a cold night. The Raven were in a sheltered hollow surrounded by undulating plains, the lowering presence of the Blackthorne Mountains on the western horizon. Cloud had come across the sky toward the end of their ride, locking in the warmth of the day.

They were deep in Xeteskian mage lands, to the northwest of the city and within a day's ride of both it and Triverne Lake. Darrick was worried. The plan, though well laid, smacked of desperation. The Raven were famous for pulling off the seemingly impossible but this had to be beyond even them. A raid on the Dark College. It revolved around Denser and Ilkar carrying people over the walls to drop them in the college, snatching Yron from the rooms they knew him to be in and flying out again.

One bonus was that Aeb, being a Protector, was capable of maintaining ShadowWings and could fetch and carry too. But for Darrick there were going to be too many times when The Raven were split and when warriors were marooned inside the college with no magical support nor realistic means of escape.

Trouble was, he couldn't think of another way. The coming battle at the walls of Xetesk would take too long. With the mortality rate from Elfsorrow, the elven army, such as it was, would literally die on its feet before the war was won. And back on Calaius the consequences were already almost too awful to comprehend. Dystran was not going to give up the thumb so it would have to be stolen, and only The Raven were capable of taking such enormous risks and living to tell the tale.

His eye was caught by movement high up in the sky. Outlined against the moonlit cloud, three birds were circling. They were big, about the size of vultures, but with stubby wings, narrow bodies and extended tail feathers. Actually, looking at them, they resembled winged lizards more than birds. Darrick frowned. It was hard to make out anything more at this distance but he'd not seen the like before.

He watched them making lazy turns and playing in the air, diving and climbing. He saw them come together in a line, hover for a second and then power down. Darrick shifted where he sat on a heavy log they'd dragged to the fire, his frown deepening. They were heading directly for the camp.

"Dear Gods falling," he whispered, and stormed to his feet, sword already coming from its scabbard where it rested against the log. "Raven! We're attacked!"

Those weren't birds, they were Xeteskian Familiars, demons melded to and controlled by mage minds, and as the camp came to abrupt wakefulness around him, Darrick could hear them chittering and laughing as they drove in, promising death.

"Ilkar, we need a shield; they won't be alone," called Darrick, not looking round, knowing The Raven would be forming to defend. "Erienne, Denser, offensive spells at the Familiars, and let's defend behind the fire."

Aeb was at his shoulder first. "I sensed them," he said. "There are just three."

They were hideous even to those like Denser who were well used to them. Completely hairless, their small bodies had long powerful limbs ending in vicious talons. Mouths were crammed with long fangs and their skulls pulsed, veins throbbing, eyes wild and black in the firelight. Darrick shuddered, had to breathe deep to drag his courage to him and squared up.

The Familiars attacked, taloned hands and feet outstretched, wings braking their descents, dripping mouths gaping, fangs catching the firelight. Aeb, axe in one hand, snapped out his free hand and grabbed one around the throat as it came at him, ignoring the raking of the talons on his forearm. He bore it to the ground in front of him, dropped his axe, picked up one end of the log and dropped it on the creature's chest, pinning its arms and leaving it helpless; spitting, cursing and promising death. A second landed on the back of his neck.

Beside him, Darrick traced a defensive pattern with his blade, the third Familiar snapping at his sword but driven back into the air to circle behind, not able to find a way through. Darrick knew he couldn't damage the demon with his blade but he could keep it at bay until spells were ready.

The Unknown ran into the firelight, grabbing at the Familiar on Aeb's back, ripping it away and throwing it down into the embers of the fire. It skidded through the red-hot ashes squealing as it landed and thrashing its wings to take off, vitriol spilling from its mouth. The sky lit up as Flame-Orbs soared from left, right and behind in concert, targeting the camp.

"Ilkar, we need that shield now," said Darrick.

"It's there," said Ilkar, voice quiet. "Shield up."

"Raven, we're surrounded," said Hirad. "Unknown numbers. Let's circle, keep your spacing. Ren and the mages inside. Just as we practised."

They formed up fast as the two free Familiars flew in again, darting close, lashing out claw or tail and rising again. Aeb, The Unknown and Thraun faced away from the fire, Darrick and Hirad into and beyond it, covering the angles. Ren, bow tensed, looked for targets among the shapes racing in, Ilkar stood behind Hirad like he always did and Erienne and Denser occupied the rest of the defended space, spells forming in their minds.

"Keep eyes to the sky," warned Hirad. "We can't let those bastards too close."

As if to make his point, the demons streaked in again. Hirad slashed over his head, sword connecting with a leathery body. The demon yelped and fled back skyward. The other raked a cut into Darrick's face and chittered in triumph as it corkscrewed back into the night, preparing to dive once more.

"If we can take the Familiars, we can cripple their mages," muttered Denser. "Two birds, one stone, so to speak."

"Sure?" asked Darrick.

"Trust me on this. Focussed Orbs, Erienne. It's the best way."

"With you," said Erienne.

Hirad watched the enemy come in, remembering he'd seen the advance pattern before. Two ahead of a third, six of the trios, well spaced and running.

"Mage defenders," he said. "But not with Protectors. Just swordsmen."

"Ren, look for the mages. We can handle the blades," said The Unknown.

The FlameOrbs splashed down, fizzing over the shield and scorching into the ground around them. Simultaneously, DeathHail pattered against its edge, the razor-sharp mana ice shards bouncing and shattering as they struck.

"Holding," said Ilkar. "No problem."

And, thought Hirad, their own spells were keeping their Familiars away. He could see them wheeling above, looking for the next opening.

The Xeteskian swordsmen attacked, running in from all angles, spread well, shouting orders and confident. The Unknown tapped the ground at his feet and Hirad cleared his head with a roar. He raised his blade and swept down to knock aside the first blow, kicking the man back. Another came in, Hirad blocking him away too, his eyes adjusting to the shadows. He squared up, waiting. They came again, both at the same time, standard formation. Beatable.

The first thrust came in low, Hirad sweeping his sword left to right to knock it away. He ducked as the second whipped by above his head but he was ready, thrashing his blade up as he stood, catching the man on the hinge of his jaws and shearing into his face. He screamed and fell, Hirad swinging quickly to face his second attacker. He was quick, his blade already cocked to strike. But as he stepped in to deliver, Aeb's axe split his skull wide open.

"Talking, Raven!" shouted Hirad, looking out.

"Orbs away."

Balls of mana flame the size of apples shot out in lines from the centre of the Raven group. They fired into the sky and Hirad heard a screech as at least one found its target. The screech was accompanied by a howl from ahead of him and a mage crumpled to the ground, holding his head.

"One surviving," shouted Denser over the clash of steel and the grunts of the fight.

Next to Hirad, Aeb had pulled his axe out of the Xeteskian he'd killed and used it to bat away a tentative strike. His sword came through straight afterward, a massive strike taking the head clean off the same man. The body crumpled.

Around the other side, Darrick was trading blows with a pair of good swordsmen, blade and dagger in his hands. He had a cut on one arm but was holding his own. An arrow whipped out and took one of them from the game. Darrick muttered his thanks, pressed his attack, caught a blow on the hilt of his dagger and stabbed forward into the throat of his opponent.

"Go Raven, we're taking them!"

And then the third Familiar came in from nowhere. Dropping straight onto Denser's head, it jammed its claws through his skullcap and bit down on his shoulder. Denser cried out, tripped and fell into Ilkar who, taken completely by surprise, stumbled into Hirad's back.

"Shield down! Shield down!"

And more spells were coming in. FlameOrbs.

"Scatter Raven!" roared Hirad, picking Ilkar up and moving dead ahead at speed, heaving his sword into the legs of an attacker.

Order dissolved into chaos. Aeb turned and dived for Denser and Erienne, scooping them and the Familiar up and diving headlong away from the fire as the FlameOrbs seared in. The Unknown rolled left, coming up quickly and slicing his dagger into the arm of a Xeteskian swordsman who hadn't been quick enough to adapt. Thraun and Darrick simply charged into the enemy, looking to confuse and spread mayhem. Ren loosed off another shaft and ran into the night.

The Orbs splashed down just beyond the fire. Denser, the Familiar shouting curses into his ear and dragging its talons down his face, was covered by the body of Aeb. Erienne was crushed beneath them both but safe from the flame that spattered across the campsite. It smeared over Aeb's back, eating into his leather, burning the skin where it touched. He rolled away, grunting in pain, tearing at his jerkin straps while the fire ate through to sear the flesh beneath.

Denser grabbed at the Familiar, rolling aside to let Erienne free, punching upward blind and feeling his fist meet the demon's head again and again. It yowled but didn't stop, its tail raking down his arm, a fury of thrashing limbs and scything talons and teeth as the pair rolled on the scorched earth.

And then, incredibly, Aeb was there. Bare chested, his axe in one burned hand, his other reached down to grab the Familiar at the back of the head and wrench it clear. Denser felt the talons gouging at him as it was torn free and heard Erienne's voice close to him.

"Aeb, hold it still, keep it still."

Denser looked round, wiped a film of blood from his eyes and saw Aeb holding the Familiar at arm's length while it boiled and heaved in its desperation, calling for its master.

"Too late, you little shit," said Erienne, and she clamped both hands over its skull. FlamePalms erupted from them and blazed through its head, killing it instantly.

Aeb threw the body away, helped Denser to his feet and ran back into the battle, the Raven mages right behind him.

The Unknown saw a mage crumple ahead of him in the act of casting another spell and breathed a sigh of relief. He charged into the swordsmen defending him, delivering his sword overhead and through the shoulder of an unprepared man, rotating on his weaker left leg and kicking into the stomach of the other.

Pain from the old injury flared briefly and he landed unbalanced, barely getting his sword up to block. The Xeteskian was good and quick, moving to The Unknown's left, seeing it was his weaker side and forcing the attack. The Unknown fielded blows on dagger and sword, looking for an opportunity, but didn't need it. An arrow took the man clean through the neck as he backed off to compose himself and Ren ran past, nocking another.

The Unknown turned, searching through the dark for The Raven. Hirad and Darrick were together, Ilkar behind them, casting again. They were facing three swordsmen and a mage. The Unknown watched as Darrick disarmed one of them, disembowelling him with the return strike. Hirad leaned in and head-butted his nearest opponent, following up with a punch to the nose and his sword across the man's chest. He turned far more quickly than the third man was expecting, switched his sword to his left hand and jabbed it forward, slicing through his neck. The two Raven men advanced on the doomed mage.

The Unknown ran back toward the fire and Aeb. The Protector, with Denser and Erienne in his wake, his axe in both arms and his back covered in burns, savaged into the two men attacking Thraun. The shapechanger was only just keeping them at bay but Aeb changed all that, unleashing a blow of shocking power that divided one of the enemy in two from left shoulder down to right hip. He hung together a split second, eyes wide, and fell in a mass of gore. The other disengaged and ran. He didn't get far. Thraun was far quicker, clattering his blade through the enemy's lower back.

It was over. Hirad and Darrick quartered the field checking the bodies of the Xeteskians, quick thrusts killing those that still breathed. Aeb, at Denser's instructions, came back to the fire. The Unknown followed them, as did Ren and Thraun.

They had been lucky. Very lucky. The Unknown wanted to know how they had been found and attacked so easily and there, still trapped beneath a log by the fire, was the route to the answers. Damaged by FlameOrbs but still spitting and cursing was the surviving Familiar.

The Raven gathered around it.

"See to Aeb, will you?" said The Unknown to Denser. "I'll ask this some questions."

"His master is dead," said Denser. "He's fading but still dangerous. Don't let him up."

The Unknown nodded and knelt by the creature. It stopped its squealing stream of abuse and fixed its gaze on the big shaven-headed warrior.

"Sol," it hissed, dragging out the word.

"Yes, Sol," confirmed The Unknown. "And you are dying."

"Soon," said the Familiar, its voice like a rake over gravel. "Let me up."

"I don't think so," said The Unknown. "But maybe I will if you answer me truthfully."

The Familiar's hairless head pulsated, veins throbbing. It spat into The Unknown's face. "Traitor."

The Unknown wiped the fetid spittle from his cheek. "No. We did not start this."

"We will finish it. Raven will die."

"How did you find us?"

The Familiar chuckled. "You know already. Your allegiance is your weakness."

"Aeb," he said, and the Familiar smiled, its fangs revealed, slicked in blood. Its tongue licked out. "Why do you want to kill us?"

The Familiar coughed. It was fading quickly and its voice was weaker now. "You would stop us. Take what we need. . . . Not allowed." It was struggling for words. "There will be more."

The Unknown watched the fury in its eyes dim as its heart failed. "You will not beat us."

"We hold the power." Its head fell to the side and it breathed its last.

The Unknown stood and looked at The Raven, Darrick, Denser and Aeb all with wounds. Aeb's looked bad. Denser had blood running from his face and Erienne was seeing to him while Ilkar moved his hands slowly over Aeb's burned back. The elf's hands were shaking.

"Are you all right, Ilkar?"

He nodded through his concentration but didn't look round. "I'm just tired. I don't like losing spells suddenly. It drags at the reserves. I'll be all right."

"We've got to get on. We need to find secure rest and we have to get into Xetesk tomorrow night. Something tells me we've run out of time."

From the corner of his eye, he saw Ilkar nod.

CHAPTER 42

Yron waited and waited. He threw the windows of his chambers wide to let in the fresh air, he paced the room, he ate from the fruit bowl on a side table, he plunged his head into the cold water of his wash bowl. He played word games in his mind, he fenced against the full-length mirror, polished his already gleaming axe and holster. Anything to focus his mind, sober up and stay awake.

He waited while the college quietened and the last of the revellers staggered to their chambers. He waited while the servants cleaned the banqueting chamber, cleaned the table and mopped the floors. He waited until the deepest depths of the night. And only then did he slip from his room, rough travel cloak covering his new clothes, cleaned leather and glittering axe holster, and into Erys's room.

The mage was lost to sleep, flat on his back and snoring gently. A smile played on his face and his arms were flung wide across the luxurious bed. Yron placed one hand over Erys's mouth and shook him hard awake. The mage's eyes flew open and his hands scrabbled at Yron's in sudden panic, only relaxing when he saw the captain's smile. Yron removed his hand.

"Don't worry. Just me," he whispered. "Get up."

"What the hell is going on?" Erys hissed. "It's the middle of the bloody night!"

"I'll explain while you dress. We've got to do something. Now."

Erys frowned and passed a hand over his head, breathing out heavily. "Is this your idea of a hilarious joke?"

"No," said Yron sharply, dragging the covers from Erys. "Now get up. And you'd better be able to cast."

"I'll see what I can do. Never tried it after so much wine." He sighed and heaved himself from the bed, heading for the wash bowl. He poured a jug of water over his head. "So what's it all about, Captain?"

Yron told him, and by the time he had dressed Erys looked both awake and stone cold sober.

"You are with me, aren't you?" asked Yron as he walked to Erys's door.

"I can't be a party to genocide, unwitting or not," said Erys.

"I thought not. Now, Dystran will have taken the thumb to his chambers."

"You'd better hope not. Have you any idea how many Protectors guard him up there?" Erys jerked a thumb upward.

"Don't worry about it," said Yron.

"Don't worry about it? Are you crazy? It only takes one, unless you've got an even better axe arm than I think you have."

"Just show me the way."

Erys closed his eyes for a heartbeat and led the way from his chambers into the silence of the Tower. The two men walked back past the banqueting and audience chambers, down the darkened corridors that made up the wide base of the Tower and back toward the main doors.

Before they got there, Erys directed them down a left turn, through a curtained entrance and around another sharp bend and into a small oval chamber. The walls were lined with benches and hung with portraits of Lords of the Mount long dead. Directly ahead of them, in front of an intricately carved heavy wooden door, stood a pair of Protectors, silent and unmoving.

"You'd better be right about this," said Erys.

"Have faith, boy," said Yron.

He walked forward, feeling none of the confidence he hoped he was exuding, and stood before the Protectors. For one hideous moment he felt their hostile eyes sizing him up and thought he'd got it all horribly wrong.

"You will not harm him," said one, and the pair turned away, their backs forming a passage to the now unguarded door.

Yron turned the handle and opened the door inward, its travel silent on oiled hinges. He beckoned the open-mouthed Erys on and began to climb the spiral stair in front of him. It was carved from a pillar of marble and set on the western side of the Tower's central shaft. Above, six levels ending in Dystran's private chambers. Below, entrance to the catacombs and labs and the passages that crisscrossed under the college.

"How did you organise that?" said Erys.

"I didn't," said Yron. "I'll explain later."

Taking every step gently, his boots ghosting the surface, Yron climbed, refusing to let himself think about where he was or what he was doing. His heart thudded in his chest, his palms were damp and his breathing was shallow and rushed. His limbs were shaking and his muscles felt weak. He forced himself to go on, one step at a time.

They passed level after level. At each one, a Protector stood on a tapestry-hung landing in front of a door to a set of offices, personal audience chambers or guest rooms. Each masked man stood silent, watching them pass and making no move to interfere.

"This is suicide," whispered Erys.

"And if we don't, it's genocide," said Yron, pleased at his clever response.

Finally, they stood at Dystran's door and it all came home to him. He, Captain Yron, was about to enter the most private chambers of the Lord of the Mount of Xetesk, Balaia's single most powerful man, and steal a prized treasure. He shuddered the length of his body as the pair of Protectors moved a pace aside to allow him entry.

"Just the thumb," he whispered. "Nothing else."

Centre stage of the big open room was Dystran's curtained bed. To the left, a screened-off washing area, to the right, wardrobe and dressing areas, and at the foot of the bed, the prize. Yron saw it immediately and held out an arm.

"Stay there," he said, voice barely audible. "Keep the door open."

Erys nodded and Yron stepped delicately into the room, his boots soundless on the thick rugs that covered the stone floor. On a table flanked by tall candle stands, on a silk-covered dish, rested the thumb of Yniss.

Sweat ran into Yron's eyes and he wiped it away, smearing his palm against his cloak. He leaned over the table and reached out a quivering hand. He swallowed hard and picked up the fragment, finding its touch cool and comfortable. He took in a grateful breath and slipped it into his pocket. He turned to smile at Erys but the look on the mage's face froze him where he stood.

He was looking to Yron's right. The captain twisted his head as far as he could and peered out of the corner of his eye. The curtains around the bed were moving. A long slender leg appeared, followed by the rest of a naked woman. For two glorious paces, she moved directly toward the screened-off area and then, as if feeling their eyes upon her, she stopped and turned gracefully toward them.

"Oh shit," breathed Yron, and he moved, fast.

She was going to scream. Reflexively, she covered herself with her hands and arms, drew in breath and opened her mouth wide. Yron's punch took her square on the jaw and she staggered back, falling dazed to thump against the floor, head bouncing on the rugs. She yelped once and lay still.

A groggy voice sounded from inside the curtains and they moved again. Dystran's head appeared. He took in the woman sprawled on the ground and Yron standing over her and very close to him.

"Oh, no," said Yron.

"What the fu—"

Yron's fist swung again, swiping into the side of Dystran's head. The Lord of the Mount grunted and sprawled but remained conscious.

"Erys, get in here. He needs to sleep very deeply."

Dystran dragged the curtains aside.

"Guards!" he barked, before Yron got a hand over his mouth.

Erys was casting as he came, Protectors only a couple of paces behind him. A touch from the mage and Dystran stopped struggling and slumped. Yron laid him down gently and faced the two masked warriors, both of whom had axes ready.

"He's not hurt. Just sleeping. Please."

"Your time is short," said one. "Run."

"See me go," said Yron. "Erys."

Yron sprinted from the chamber, Erys a beat behind him, and clattered down the stairs.

"Erys, which way at the base?"

"Dystran'll have a pulse out. The college will be waking," said Erys.

"Don't tell me how bad it is; tell me how we get out."

"Straight through the front of the Tower and head right to the long rooms. Let's go for the west gate."

Yron nodded. It made sense. They could lose themselves in the artisans' quarter of the city more easily than anywhere else. He leaped the last step, slid by the Protectors in the oval room and kept on going, rounding the bend, tearing the curtain aside and racing toward the front door of the Tower.

As he headed across the marble entrance hall to the door, it opened and a pair of mages strode in. Yron ran straight at them while they dithered, shouldering one aside hard, sending him crashing into a wall. There was a crack behind him as Erys straight armed the other.

They burst into the night, seeing torches and lanterns waving all over the college grounds as their holders ran toward the Tower. Going right, they raced round the base of the Tower, Erys dragging Yron right again and down the side of the first long room. Erys now leading, they turned behind a lecture theatre, along the side of the refectory and into the press of narrow passageways around the barracks and stables. Beneath a stone stairway to a hayloft, they stopped to catch their breath.

All around them, sounds of pursuit echoed in the dark. Harsh voices organised search parties and doors banged open near them, feet clattering down stairs and across cobbles.

"No one's going to open a gate for us," said Yron. "Any ideas?"

"The postern door by the west gate," said Erys, breathing hard. "It's small enough. I can focus a ForceCone, probably crack it."

"Probably?"

"Definitely," said Erys. "It may not burst but a kick should finish it."

"You'd better be right," said Yron.

"Your turn to trust me."

Yron waited while Erys gathered himself and formed the shape of a ForceCone in his mind. His eyes moved under closed lids, his hands teasing at the mana Yron would never see. The captain was in awe of mages; they were blessed with a vision he couldn't imagine and an ability at which he could only guess. Erys opened his eyes.

"Let's go," he said, voice elsewhere as he concentrated hard.

Yron led off, pacing evenly down the passage, keeping himself hidden in deep shadow. Twenty yards ahead, a team of soldiers ran across their path. Yron slowed further, approaching the crossway. Beyond it a short run and then the open space by the west gate. It might be full of men and mages. There was only one way to find out. He listened at the crossway. All was quiet in the immediate surroundings. Offering a short prayer, he hurried across the space, Erys behind him. His ears strained for the shout that would tell them they had been seen but he heard nothing.

He began to hope. Dangerous, he knew, but he did it anyway. At the end of the passage he could see flickering lights and hear more voices. He crept up to the corner; the walls to left and right were the mana bowl and the infirmary. Three paces from the end and a figure strode into the passage, tall and masked. Yron's heart sank and he drew his sword.

"Keep behind me, Erys," he said.

The Protector marched toward them, axe and sword ready. He stopped in front of Yron, looked at him briefly, and walked on.

"Now or never," said Erys over Yron's relief.

The postern gate was a forty-yard run directly across the marshalling area for the Xeteskian cavalry. Only a few soldiers were there and all were moving to join the search.

"When you start, keep running, Captain. I have to stop to cast then I'll be right behind you."

Yron nodded. He didn't want to leave Erys but there was no choice. "Don't get caught," he said. "Ready? Let's go."

The two men sprinted into the yard and had covered ten yards before the shouts went up. Left and right, soldiers ran in to cut them off. Yron pushed harder. Crossbow bolts skipped off the ground at his feet. He heard Erys slide to a stop.

"Good luck," he breathed and, giving Erys clear sight of the door, ran on.

The air was full of torchlight and shouts for him to stop. Behind him, he heard Erys's command word, felt the shadow of the spell rush past him and saw the postern gate buckle outward, hearing timbers creak and snap. He glanced over his shoulder, saw the mage surge to his feet and chase after him.

Left and right, his former colleagues closed in, yelling warnings, urging him to give himself up. Fresher and mostly younger, they were gaining fast, and he knew if he stopped at the gate he'd be caught. Already feeling the pain he was about to experience, he ate up the last few yards and shoulder-charged the spell-weakened iron-bound oak gate.

As he struck he didn't think it would give, but, with the crack of splitting timber, the gate gave way and he sprawled out into the streets of Xetesk. His shoulder shrieked in pain as he dragged himself to his feet, sparing a glance back inside.

"Come on, Erys!" he shouted.

The mage was running hard, head down, legs and arms pumping. Framed in the gate arch he seemed so close to freedom. But from the side, a soldier rushed in, swung his sword and caught Erys a glancing blow across the shoulder. Yron saw the blood spray and Erys tumble heavily onto the cobbles before an arrow whipping past his head brought him back to himself and he tore off into the maze of roads, alleys and passages that made up Xetesk's artisans' quarter, cursing all the way.

Merke and her Tai were deep inside Xetesk. They and seven other TaiGethen cells were scouting the city at night, looking for information, looking for weaknesses but above all looking for a way into the Dark College itself. For all the Xeteskian soldiers and mages marching to battle the other colleges, the walls, the Protectors and their watchers, the TaiGethen had pierced the city defences easily enough, scaling the walls in four places and scattering into the night.

Three cells were combing residential areas, two were around the markets and three studied the college itself, including Auum's. But for once he had not chosen the right place. From where Merke, Inell and Vaart were hidden, overlooking one of the gates of the college, they had seen an extraordinary sight.

Right before them, a side gate had buckled. Heartbeats later, a man had crashed through, rolling over, dragging himself to his feet and running from the college, heading down an alley not twenty yards from them. They waited for the pursuit and it duly came: men with swords and the masked Protectors, splitting into groups of three, four and five, scattering into the blank shadows of the warehouses and stinking foundries. Some ran straight past them, others took the alley their quarry had used.

Merke looked at her Tai. Vaart shrugged.

"The one running is more likely an ally than an enemy."

"It'll do as a reason for now," said Merke.

The Tai moved, ghosts over the ground, unslinging bows, unsnapping jaqrui pouches and scabbard covers. Merke was ahead, Inell and Vaart left and right, emerging from the alley where they'd watched it all unfold, across the front of a warehouse and down its far side.

The blank walls of its neighbour were no more than fifteen feet away, sheer sides rising up better than thirty feet to angled tiled roofs. They hemmed in the TaiGethen like no rain forest ever could, the smells of city life mixing with the drab buildings to produce a place Merke couldn't believe any sane man would want to live. But live here they did. And die.

Merke whispered over the ground, sword and jaqrui ready, bows flanking her. Ahead, she could make out the figures of four men hurrying down the alley. They turned left and disappeared. She heard calls and shouts and upped her pace, rounding the corner. It led to a dead end and a man trapped against a high stone wall.

He was facing the quartet like a warrior, upright, with his axe ready as they approached him, two of them in masks, one weaponless, the other with a crossbow. They were speaking to him and he was shaking his head.

"Left and right," she whispered.

Arrows flew, punching through the necks of the masked men, who fell without a sound. Her jaqrui wailed away, its keening sound setting roosting birds to flight. The weaponless man, a mage, turned in time to see it flash into the bridge of his nose. He screamed and fell.

Taking his chance, the hunted man leaped forward, one arm hanging limp, the other holding his axe effectively enough. Panicked, the crossbowman fired, taking him in the thigh, but he came on, blade smashing into the man's face around his mouth, splitting the base of his skull and sending him crashing against a wall to slide dead to the ground.

He ignored the corpse and sized up the Tai, Merke a little confused at his reaction. There seemed to be no relief that he had been saved, only a sort of weary resignation. He stooped, wiped his blade clean and resheathed the weapon in a gaudy impractical-looking holster and held out his hands in a gesture of peace.

Merke walked forward, her Tai with bows ready and tensed.

"Please," he said in serviceable elvish. "I have what you need. Let me help you."

"Then we will take it from you," said Merke. "Give me the thumb. No stranger should carry a shard of Yniss. You cannot help us."

The man nodded and dug in a pocket, producing the statue fragment. Beside her, Vaart and Inell dropped to their knees in prayer. The stranger held out the piece reverently. Merke took it, kissed it and offered prayers that it had been returned.

"It is ours once more," she said. "Harmony will be restored."

She turned and gestured her Tai to rise, catching Vaart's eye. He nodded minutely and she looked back over her shoulder.

"You are hunted here," she said to the man.

"Yes," he said. "I am . . ." He struggled for the word. "Unpopular."

Merke smiled briefly. "You have done us a great service. We will take you out of here."

"Thank you," he said.

She shrugged. "Auum will want to know why. Follow. Do not tire. We will not wait."

CHAPTER 43

"My Lord, please calm down," said Ranyl.

"I can't think of a single reason why." Dystran nursed his cheek, feeling the tender bruising that covered it for the most part.

"He will be found," said Ranyl. "But you have other matters to attend to urgently."

"Excuse me, dear friend," said Dystran, "but I do not. In case it escaped your attention, that bastard marched right into my bedroom and all the while my Protectors, whom I mistakenly assumed had no option but to *protect* me, were staring at their boots."

"My Lord, it isn't—"

"I could have been killed!" Dystran heaved himself from his chair by the study fire, walked past the nervously fidgeting Ranyl and went to the windows to look out at dawn breaking over Xetesk. "Gods burning, I know Lords of the Mount have been assassinated in the past but never in the central Tower bedroom. That is not the sort of history I was planning on making."

"My Lord, you were in no danger of death," said Ranyl.

"Oh, I am so relieved. Just a beating, then," said Dystran, turning back into the room. "And how did you come by that knowledge? The Protectors tell you?"

Ranyl nodded. "We are undertaking a thorough investigation."

"Hold on. Are you telling me that Xeteskian Protectors were complicit in the theft?" Dystran frowned. "Is that possible? How did Yron gain such influence?"

"Not Yron. He was merely the beneficiary of arrangements made for others."

"Then who . . . ?" But he knew. He bloody knew. And Ranyl's nod merely confirmed it for him. "The Raven. Is there something else you want to tell me about last night's events?"

"Our strike team was unsuccessful."

Dystran shook his head slowly and kneaded his forehead. He was still slightly muddled from the spell Erys had cast but it was clearing fast.

"Please entertain me with the details."

"As you know, my Lord, you yourself only authorised three Familiars, six mages and twelve swordsmen due to the war situation we find ourselves in. We have heard nothing from them. Word from the Soul Tank is that The Raven killed them all."

"Dear Gods, I am defended by incompetents and cretins. It was the middle of the night. They should all have been asleep bar a guard."

Ranyl made an apologetic gesture. "The Raven are an exceptional group of people."

"I just don't understand it," said Dystran, feeling the rage build inside him. "I do not understand it! I am supposed to be the most powerful man in Balaia yet some bunch of ageing mercenaries thirty miles away is managing to screw up all my plans. They turn Protectors into pussycats at will and it's probably them that sent the elves in to snatch Yron from under our noses. This is a bloody walled city. How the fuck did they get in and out so easily? How is all this possible? Please tell me, Ranyl. I'd be really interested to know."

Dystran watched for Ranyl's reaction. He'd suffered these outbursts before and like the previous times his calm was commendable.

"We will have answers to all your questions in due course. However, I think you will find that the elves are acting quite independently. And remember, we have the Aryn Hiil and a wealth of Al-Drechar research. Your original plans are still achievable."

"That makes me feel so much better," said Dystran caustically. "And how many years do we have to keep Dordover and the elven nation from our gates until we're ready to use our new knowledge, eh? Let me tell you what's going to happen. We are going to find Yron and the statue fragment and both are to be brought back to me undamaged. Commit as many men as you can without compromising our city defence and our main battle fronts. That is all that matters."

"And The Raven and Aeb?"

"Use them. Track them and you'll track the thumb; we know it's what they're after. As for Aeb, we'll take him back when the time is right, but for now he's more useful where he is. Now then, these more pressing matters?"

"The war outside our gates, which has taken a turn for the worse," said Ranyl.

"Oh yes, how could I forget?"

Dystran closed his eyes and listened.

The Raven woke to a misty, dew-heavy morning. Having left their last camp in the middle of the night to find a safer spot, sleep had been in short supply. They had eventually decided to rest with their backs to a low crag overlooking a sweeping hillside above a wooded valley. The mages had laid alarm and trap wards a hundred and fifty yards away on the open ground and, with Denser, Darrick and particularly Aeb needing healing spells, mana stamina was low.

The prevailing mood had not been improved by Thraun and Ren's lack of success on the predawn hunt, making breakfast a thin stew of root vegetables cooked over the fire they'd only dared light as dawn edged the sky.

More than all that, their plans had been rendered useless by the news Aeb had heard from the Soul Tank.

"And what did they say, exactly?" asked Denser.

"My brothers did not impede Captain Yron or the mage, Erys. Captain Yron escaped the college. Erys was killed."

"So where is he? Yron, I mean." Hirad took a spoonful of the stew and grimaced.

"He was chased," said Aeb. "He escaped but he had help. Two of my brothers were killed. We believe the TaiGethen have him."

"Well, that's excellent," said Hirad. "Just make sure they don't leave without us because of what Erienne has to do. Why are you looking like that, Unknown?"

"There are other issues this raises," he replied. "Ilkar, can you commune with your Al-Arynaar contact? Make sure we link up."

"I can. Just don't ask me to cast anything else today."

"I'll do my best," said The Unknown. "Aeb, tell me about the college reaction."

Aeb was standing near the fire. He had been lent a white undershirt by The Unknown. It covered the burned skin on his back but looked incongruous. Protectors only ever wore black.

"They are searching for him," said Aeb. "Mages, soldiers and Protectors all left the college before dawn when the city sweep was complete."

"That isn't what I was asking."

Aeb's stare signalled he knew that. "There is suspicion. The brothers of Dystran's personal guard are under investigation. There could be difficulties."

"For you?"

"My name has been mentioned."

"Then we have to get to Dystran," said Hirad. "Stop him recalling Aeb and invoking punishment."

"No," said the Protector. "There is no time."

"Aeb, the implications for you . . ." Denser trailed off.

"Master Denser, I acted by choice. So did my brothers who looked away. It is a freedom we had almost forgotten. What comes after is understood. Delay will kill more elves." He indicated Ilkar, deep in concentration, and Ren, who sat stroking his hair.

There was a moment's silence before Hirad spoke. "That's a Raven speaking."

"Nothing is certain," said Aeb.

"Don't hide the risk you're taking," said The Unknown. "Styliann is long dead and the current Lord of the Mount is clearly capable of any atrocity. But whatever happens I'm going to make it my business to see your sacrifice, if it comes to that, is the last."

"It'll be The Raven's business," said Hirad. "Anyway, those researchers could have brought back key information. About releasing the Protectors, I mean."

"You can't really think that's likely," said Denser. "I mean, look about you. There's a war on. Think he's interested in releasing his most potent warrior force? Think it's even on his mind that he promised to send the Kaan home?"

"That'll have to wait." It was Ilkar, propping himself up on his elbows, his expression one of deep concern. "She's gone. My contact. She's just not there."

"Dead?"

Ilkar nodded. "Gods falling, Hirad, this is terrifying. Every moment that passes, more die. We've got to stop it."

"We'll do it, Ilks," said Hirad. "I swear. We'll have to ride to find Rebraal. It's the only choice we've got, isn't it?"

"Where are the Al-Arynaar based?" asked Darrick.

"Southeast of Xetesk," said Ilkar. "We'll have to ride across the lines to get to them."

"Well, no time like now," said Hirad, getting up and tipping the rest of his stew onto the fire. "At least I can avoid eating that dung disguised as vegetables."

Beside The Unknown, Aeb had already strapped his weapons over his back and was donning the riding cloak Darrick had given him.

"All right to ride?" asked the big warrior.

"Yes," said Aeb. "Fighting will be sore but not impossible."

The Unknown nodded. "Thank you, Aeb. For everything."

"It is my calling to protect," he said simply. "Saving Ilkar and Ren protects you."

"Look!" said Thraun suddenly.

The Unknown turned. The shapechanger, his sharp eyes focussed east, was pointing into the distance. Though the mist still clung to the bottom of the valley, further off it had burned away to a beautiful clear sunlit morning. Far away, where they knew Xetesk to be, they could see the faint lights of hundreds of spells in the sky. A pall of smoke was rising and they could imagine all too easily the suffering beneath.

The assault on the Dark College had begun.

The ease with which the TaiGethen and he escaped Xetesk would have worried the old Yron. They simply scaled the western walls of the city and dropped into open ground, hurrying away under the shroud of night. Once clear of immediate pursuit, Merke had stopped to attend to his crossbow wound, removing the bolt, applying a dried herb pack and tying it down with a tough bandage. It served to ease the pain of the puncture in the muscle at the front of his thigh but didn't do a great deal to staunch the blood as he trotted along behind the Tai cell.

They were heading southeast as dawn touched the sky, looking to clear the college lines before joining up with the rest of the elven army. Yron had very mixed feelings about it all. While he was glad to have returned the thumb to its rightful owners, it was abundantly clear that neither Merke nor her largely silent companions had any idea who he was. This Auum, whoever he turned out to be, might have a much better idea. And if that was so, he could look forward to nothing but death, which by turn he felt he deserved and was equally sure he didn't. Funny old world.

Moving across open ground and making for one of the few surviving forest areas five miles south of Xetesk, they were seen by a group of twenty riders galloping across the tufted muddy plain crossed by a lattice of narrow streams. The horsemen had been heading north but turned when they saw the TaiGethen, moving to intercept. Immediately, the Tai unslung bows.

"Leave it to me," said Yron. "They could be friends."

"They could be Xeteskians," said Merke evenly.

"They don't have the look," said Yron.

"We will be ready."

"I don't doubt it."

Yron faced the riders, the elves standing behind him in a loose group, bows pointing to the ground. The horsemen came to an orderly halt, one man trotting a little further forward. He took in Yron and the elven trio. Their faces were still covered in deep brown and green paint, having had no chance to clean them under prayer.

"Hunting?" said the rider abruptly.

"Escaping," said Yron, knowing immediately they were not Xeteskians. "Xetesk is an unpleasant place."

"We are in accord there," said the rider. He was a black-haired man, youngish, with heavy brows and a hard face. Yron didn't like him. "Tell me your purpose."

"It isn't my way to state my business to total strangers," said Yron. "Perhaps you'd like to tell me who I am addressing."

"My name is Devun and these are men from the army of the righteous. We are the vanguard of thousands."

Yron cursed under his breath. Black Wings. Not promising.

"Pleased to make your acquaintance, Devun. Now I would ask you to move aside and let us continue. My friends and I have pressing matters away from your battles with the colleges."

"Not so fast, one of only four," said Devun, and there was threat in his voice and posture. "The only innocents fleeing the colleges now are refugees, hungry from seasons of deprivation. None of you have that look."

He was looking past Yron again at the TaiGethen.

"And these are neither refugees nor college representatives," said Yron, and he walked a little closer to Devun. "My friend, you are among those who hate Xetesk with the same passion as you do. Let's not cause trouble here. These elves are not used to people standing in their way. It makes them nervous."

"Well, since we are friends, there is no harm in you telling me both your name and your business."

Devun had no interest in letting them go. Yron could see his posturing impressing those with whom he rode. But there was no harm in the truth; it might just do the trick. He drew himself tall, ignoring the blood running down his leg and the dull ache of the wound.

"I am Captain Yron, late of the Xeteskian college guard, now on the run for desertion and treachery. These are members of the TaiGethen from Calaius. Take me if you must but don't get in their way. You'll live to regret it. Or rather, you won't." He spread his arms. "Your move."

Devun didn't even pause to think. "Commander Selik will want to talk to you all." He signalled to his men. "Hold them."

Yron sighed and ducked to the ground, rolling over and out of immediate trouble. Riders heeled their horses, moving to surround them, others began to slide from their mounts, drawing swords. The TaiGethen exploded into action.

All three elven bows drew and released, knocking three men from their saddles. The cell split. Merke threw a jaqrui ahead of her, drawing her sword, running and leaping in a blur of movement. She caught a rider feet first in the stomach, knocking him from his horse to hang by one stirrup. She landed smartly, rose and slashed out his throat. More jaqrui wailed, more men died.

Vaart was surrounded by four. He feinted and ducked a straight blow, punching his sword clean through the eye of his attacker and following him as he went down, rolling over the corpse and dragging his blade clear. The other three came at him. He lashed a kick out front, winding one, caught a blow on his sword from another and swayed away from a reckless swing.

He rolled right, coming up and stabbing into the thigh of the nearest man, whose sword lashed out and caught him a glancing blow on his left shoulder, biting deep before swinging clear. Vaart rolled again with the blow, fending off the two who still came at him. He stood, drop kicked one in the windpipe, a killing twist of his foot as he landed atop the Black Wing. He spun on his heel, hurled a jaqrui into the face of the man with the thigh wound but the last was just quick enough to bury his sword in Vaart's chest. The elf died silently.

Yron pushed himself to his feet, running to Merke's aid. To his left, Inell was backing away from three bowmen, eyeing up which to take first, the bodies of two in front of his dripping blade. Yron ignored him, drawing his axe and thrashing it into the back of a man attempting to flank the cell leader. At the same time, Merke thrust her sword up into the belly of a swordsman still on his horse, spun and almost tore Yron's throat out, just pulling her blow. She nodded and half turned but then stumbled forward, falling into Yron and bringing him down, an arrow deep in her back, puncturing her heart.

Yron fell flat, winded, his head thrown back, his gaze passing across Inell, two arrows in his chest, punching flat-palmed into the nose of the man who stood over him, driving bone into his brain. The man fell twitching to the ground, Inell following him, a blade driven through his lower back.

On top of him, Merke moved, her hand pressing on one of his. He opened it and the thumb was pushed into his palm.

"You know what to do," she said, drawing a final ragged bubbling breath.

Rough hands pulled Yron from beneath her body, he making a play at struggling in order to slip the fragment into his pocket. His axe was taken from him and cast aside. Devun was in front of him, looking open mouthed at the scene of carnage. More than a dozen men lay dead or dying.

"I told you," said Yron thickly.

Devun swung round, his fist connecting with Yron's front teeth. He felt them give and pain flared in his head as blood started to flow from his mouth and down his throat. He spat to clear his breathing.

"Don't you say another word, Xeteskian. The only reason you're still alive is that Selik will not thank me for killing you before he's interrogated you."

"I'm already looking forward to it."

"But I'm damned if I'm going to listen to your filthy college tongue all the way to Understone."

He nodded. Yron felt a sharp blow to the base of his skull. It didn't hurt for long.

CHAPTER 44

The Raven rode hard throughout the day, aware that Aeb's injuries and the lack of casting power of all three mages made them vulnerable. Denser would be sporting new scars on his face and neck from the Familiar's attack but was otherwise not physically damaged. Ilkar had drained himself completely through healing, shielding and Communion, while Erienne was struggling with her concentration as the Al-Drechar fed her power from the One magic and asked her to cope with its increasing ferocity.

All the way across the south of Xetesk, Dordovan forces had pulled out, leaving Xetesk's search for Yron and the TaiGethen cell unmolested. Their threat had forced The Raven further south than they had anticipated and, toward the southwest, they saw the disturbing sight of clouds of dust hanging in the air, the unmistakeable sign of an army on the march.

The smart money was on the Black Wings but it wasn't something they could worry about unduly as they sought the allied college lines and information on the whereabouts of the elves and, most particularly, Rebraal and Auum.

They pushed their horses as far as they dared, hearing the battle very clearly long before they got close enough to begin identifying the forces engaged in heavy fighting to the southeast of the city. From their initial positions on the borders of the Xeteskian mage lands, Hirad estimated the Dordovan and Lysternan forces had driven in over thirty miles and were encountering Xeteskian resistance some five miles from the walls.

The Raven encountered several perimeter patrols, mainly Lysternan cavalry. These meetings gained them crucial information but the rumour mill would start too and its outcome was not necessarily positive. Although The Raven were a sight most allied forces could only dream of seeing, one of their number was the former commander of Lystern's army and wanted for desertion. Another was a Protector.

There were two hours of light left when The Raven rode into the forward camp of Lystern and Dordover's joint command. They were only a mile behind the battle lines, on a rise that gave a good view of the whole front. The Unknown and Darrick led The Raven to an observation point and they looked down on the extraordinary spectacle of college warfare.

The fighting was concentrated in an arc around a quarter of a mile across though other fronts were evidenced by smoke and light further to the east and northeast.

Below The Raven, the main allied force pressed a sword and spear attack.

Behind both lines, ranks of archers fired at each other and the knots of offensive and defensive mages, while the flanks were protected by pikemen and the more mobile cavalry.

Izack was here, so they were told, directing battle and rotating his cavalry to keep them as fresh as he could. They harried the flanks of the Xeteskians, engaged their cavalry, feinted charges deep behind the enemy and rode hard in defence of any weakening areas of their own line.

The roar of battle was deafening, even from here. The desultory thud of spells punctuated the yell of orders, the cries of panic and pain, the whinnies of horses and the constant clash of metal.

Reinforcements ran in from both sides, groups of fighters moving under questionable mage protection. Shields flared under the bombardment, those that cracked leaving their charges helpless to the merciless mana power. And older men, women and youths were everywhere—supplying arrows, water and food where they could and carrying the injured and dying from the battlefield.

All around The Raven the air smelled of blood, sweat and fire. HotRain sluiced out of the sky over the support and reinforcements, ForceCones smashed out, DeathHail sliced away at groups of cavalry. Across the lines, ruptured earth and heaved stone were the residue of EarthHammers.

The Unknown turned to Darrick. "How do you see it?" he shouted over the din.

"Xetesk can't outflank." Darrick pointed away west. "They must be fully committed on all fronts. We need to get down there onto the field. Speak to Izack."

"Got a couple of ideas for him?"

Darrick nodded, smiling, and The Unknown could see him yearning to be there in the midst of the confusion, a snorting horse under him, blood-slick sword in hand.

"We'll also get the best intelligence on the elven positions."

"I don't see any Protectors here," mentioned The Unknown.

"No, interesting, isn't it?"

"Raven!" The Unknown turned. "We are leaving."

The big warrior led them back to their horses, the animals tethered in a group fifty yards from the observation point. They looked tired and forlorn, eyeing their riders with weary resignation.

"Hirad, Thraun, flank positions," said The Unknown as they mounted, the noise of battle diminishing just enough for normal speech. "Mages, inside the arc, and if you have enough for a SpellShield, now's the time. Darrick, centre with me. Ren, Aeb, you've got the rear."

The Raven kicked away, drawing cheers from some they passed. The Unknown took them quickly down the slope and into the maelstrom. Among the fighting, the untutored eye saw nothing but a storm of blood, mud, men and steel. Immediately to their left, a pair burst from the mass, Xeteskian tumbling over Dordovan in the mud, punches flying, each man desperate to get a blade round for a killing blow. But the Xeteskian was lost in the midst of the enemy. He was hauled up by Dordovan hands, stabbed half a dozen times and dropped face down.

Far out on the right flank, The Unknown saw a man who had trained under the best. Izack was leading a charge into a confused area of fighting. Xeteskian spells had crashed through one too many SpellShields and allied reinforcements had died before they reached the line. Archer support was weak and it was all the remaining mages could do to shield those who still stood.

As the Lysternan cavalry galloped in, Izack's booming voice could be heard across the battlefield. Foot soldiers pushed away and disengaged, giving the horsemen maximum space to move through.

"Tight!" roared Izack. "Tight!"

The cavalry kept close form, dodging their own men as best they could, angling in steeply to avoid the worst of pike and spear to thump into the Xeteskian lines, driving men back, trampling those who failed to react, using their swords to fend off and scatter.

Behind them, the allies regrouped as arrows peppered the momentarily disordered Xeteskians. Izack's cavalry withdrew and both sides ran in again, marshalled by the calls of field captains and lieutenants. Izack was now clear, cantering past the next section of Lysternan horsemen who took orders, wheeled and rode hard on a flanking manoeuvre.

The Unknown led The Raven across the back of the fighting line, cloaks flowing, arrows falling around them but bouncing off the HardShield lattice covering much of the allied rear.

"Izack!" bellowed Darrick as they approached.

The cavalry commander hauled his horse around, his face splitting into a broad smile in recognition of the voice of his erstwhile general. He leaned out of his saddle and clasped hands with Darrick. The Raven stopped and surrounded him, well out of spell and missile range.

"Dear Gods, General, it lightens my heart to see you!"

"And I you, though I'd wished for kinder circumstances."

Izack nodded, glancing quickly over The Raven, his eyes never straying too far from the battle.

"What brings you here?" he asked. "I'd heard The Raven were near.

Blackthorne told us as much but I thought you'd be headed back south again by now."

"So did we," agreed Darrick. "But we need to find the elves. We believe one of the TaiGethen cells has recovered something vital to them."

"I've heard nothing," said Izack. "The elves are all fighting further east. They're with a Dordovan force trying to reach Xetesk's east gate. They're incredible fighters, so they say. The painted ones particularly."

"You'd better believe it," said The Unknown. "One to one as good as Protectors, in my opinion."

"And in Xetesk's too," said Izack. "The Protectors are heavily committed against them."

"Are you in contact?" asked Darrick.

"Only by riders. Can't spare mages for Communion."

Darrick nodded. "We have to get to them. How's the land in between?"

"Safe enough," said Izack. "Don't stray too far west, Xeteskian cavalry is moving out there." He smiled. "Go on, tell me what I'm doing wrong."

"Nothing," said Darrick. "But weight your left. Keep cavalry out there. We've seen an army on the march north. Don't get caught."

"Know about it already," said Izack. "Black Wings. They're here to attack Xetesk, I think. They might even help us."

"Not by choice," said The Unknown. "Don't underestimate them."

"One other thing," said Darrick. "Their cavalry commander here isn't confident. He sees things too late. Next time you see a breach, you might try riding through it, but take half of your men with you."

The two Lysternans shook hands again.

"You know I'm supposed to arrest you," said Izack. "Pity I didn't recognise you."

"Another day," said Darrick. "I'll come back, answer for my actions."

"Raven!" Hirad took up his reins. "Raven with me!"

Taking The Unknown's place at the head of the arc, he galloped away toward the east gate of Xetesk.

The dusk was deepening when The Raven finally rode into the allies' forward camp on the eastern battle front. With the coming of night fighting had ceased, and the echoing memories of the battle clashed with the enforced calm of the aftermath.

The Raven had been forced to move slowly. Their horses' exhaustion, marauding bands of Xeteskian cavalry and the deep suspicion of Dordovan patrols had all made for a circuitous and difficult passage. But a sympathetic finger had pointed them the way to the mess tents and the elven encampment. And although they drew glances that ranged from awe to open hostility, they had eaten and their horses were picketed, rubbed down and fed.

With Ilkar leading, they walked into the quiet of the elven camp. Most were already asleep, stretched out under the cloudy sky, but those still awake displayed the signs of people who had experienced their first day on the battlefield: shock, deep weariness, disbelief.

Hirad sympathised. They would have feared for their lives every heartbeat, and finished the day bruised, deafened, exhausted and guilty that they lived when their friends had died. And worse was to come. It would have to be faced all over again as dawn broke, but with every muscle screaming for rest and the risks as great, if not greater. But for these elves, there was also the fact that they would never have seen such a mass of humanity in one place all trying to kill each other. Never mind their willingness to fight and die for their cause and never mind their skill and mental strength. Nothing prepared you for that first day of mass battle. Nothing.

They found Rebraal and Auum together, cuts bathed and bound, sitting cross-legged near a fire discussing the day gone and the day to come. As The Raven approached, Ilkar ushering tired elves out of the way to let them sit to talk, Auum looked up, his distaste undisguised and eyeing Hirad with what amounted to contempt. The Unknown put a calming hand on Hirad's shoulder and sat him next to Ilkar, who Rebraal had been plainly happy to see.

The conversation began, Ilkar translating the elven words.

"So what brings you here, little brother? We thought you were in the city by now."

Ilkar chuckled. "You know perfectly well why we're here and not in Xetesk. The TaiGethen have recovered the Yniss fragment and we're here to join you. Erienne has to travel with you to aid the binding, and where Erienne goes, The Raven go."

That got Auum's attention. His head snapped up and Hirad could see his eyes spearing Ilkar.

"Wrong," he said. "We are going back in tonight to attempt entry into the college itself."

"I don't understand," said Ilkar.

"What is there not to understand?" said Rebraal. "We don't have it. And patently neither do you despite your grand words about The Raven's skill. Why else do you think we're still here?"

"Aeb was in contact with the Soul Tank the day before we were due to raid the college. You remember I explained Protectors to you."

"And we fought them all day for very little gain," said Rebraal. There was a murmur around the fire.

"Not surprising, really," said Ilkar. "The point is, two souls departing the Tank reported they had been killed by TaiGethen who took Yron, the man who holds the thumb."

"Which Tai?" demanded Ilkar.

"I don't know. How could I?"

"Where was this incident?" Auum was sitting bolt upright now, an expression of anxiety across his face, his hands gripping his thighs.

"Just outside the west gate of the college, right by the artisans' quarter," said Ilkar.

Rebraal and Auum shared a glance. "Merke," said the TaiGethen. He looked back to Ilkar. "They have not reported back here. You are sure about this?"

Ilkar nodded. "Absolutely. Protectors are unable to lie."

"Then the Xeteskians must have retaken them," said Rebraal.

"Not possible," said Ilkar. "Aeb would know. They escaped the city early this morning."

"They have not returned," said Auum.

Ilkar sighed. "I don't believe it," he said, turning to The Unknown. "We've lost it again. Somewhere between here and the college. The Gods only know where it is."

"Well, we'll have to search," said the big warrior. "Find out where this Tai went in and work back from there."

Ilkar posed the question and didn't like the answer.

"Southwest corner," he relayed. "Right where the Black Wings are advancing."

"Any chance they ran into a patrol?" asked Hirad.

"It would have to be a big one to stop a TaiGethen cell," said Ren.

"How good is this Yron?" asked Rebraal, dropping back into elvish to speak to Auum.

The TaiGethen snorted, getting his meaning. "Not good enough."

"It doesn't matter anyway, he wanted to find them. It was Yron who stole the thumb from the college. The point is, they must be holed up somewhere, trapped maybe," said Ilkar. "Look, this is what we know. Merke's cell got out of the city with Yron and now Xetesk will be looking for them and they have a head start. But coming at them from the south is an army of farmers driven on by Black Wing witch hunters. They are caught in the middle of it somewhere and we have to get them out fast."

"We will sweep from here to the coast," said Auum. "We will see everything. But first we have to rest. We'll leave before dawn."

"You can't do that," said Ilkar. "You can't abandon this front entirely. Xetesk will know straight away what you're doing."

"Then perhaps these Dordovans we fought for can return us the favour," said Rebraal. "Or perhaps you and your Raven. After all, what have you done so far?"

"Got you here," said Ilkar. "And created the conditions for Yron to take the thumb and escape the college. And that's just for starters."

"You have some great and better idea, do you?" said Auum, his voice dismissive.

"Yes, I do," said Ilkar. "What you're suggesting is too slow and Xetesk will be able to track you all the way because the land is too open. All it'll lead to is more mass conflict with Xetesk and Black Wings and you'll get no nearer the prize. Do it The Raven's way. Trust me, it'll work."

"What do you have in mind?" Rebraal looked at Ilkar hard. "We're dropping like flies here. We need speed. We're losing more to the Sorrow than to the Protectors."

"Just be ready to leave when we come for you. You and Auum's Tai. And a ClawBound pair if you can get a message to one. Get some rest."

"What do you have that we have not?" sneered Auum.

"Horses, men who know the land and mages that can fly," said Ilkar shortly. "Any of those skills of yours?"

"Ilkar—"

"No, Rebraal, he has to hear this," said Ilkar, standing and looking down at Auum, who looked ready to strike, his face grey and angry in the firelight. "The Raven are doing this for me and for you. For all the elves. We're doing it because it is right and, believe me, there are other things we could be doing. Like saving our own land from destruction for a start.

"But we're doing this first because The Raven would do anything for me. That's what being one of us is all about and it is something you, Auum, should understand. So get your head out of the trees, respect those that deserve it and join in. Because we are your best hope of recovering the thumb. Believe it."

"Your confidence in your ability is remarkable," said Auum.

Ilkar leant in very close. "That is because we are the best. So watch and learn. This is our land."

He stalked away, The Raven getting up and following him. Hirad spared Auum an ingratiating smile and a wink. "Told you, eh?" he said, having not understood a word.

"Feel better for that, did you?" said Ren.

"Needed saying," said Ilkar. He turned and grinned at Hirad. "You'd have been proud of me."

"So what did you say, exactly?" asked Hirad.

Ilkar told him as they wandered back into the Dordovan area and kicked a dying and abandoned fire into new life.

"And what exactly is your plan?" Darrick poked at the new flame.

"None of the Al-Arynaar have learned ShadowWings. It's a pointless spell in the rain forest. We can all do it and that means we can scout a wide area very quickly. Look, I'm not talking about overflying Xeteskian or Black Wing positions, but there's a mass of open ground on the route they'd have taken trying to get back here. We'll find them, I can feel it. And if we leave a few hours before dawn, we can be beyond Izack's lines before sunrise and practically on top of where Yron and Merke's Tai came out."

"Then you'd better sleep," said The Unknown. "All of you. And if there's anything you can do to boost your stamina, use it. Because if I'm not mistaken, none of you could cast wings big enough to lift a mouse right now."

There was no argument but Darrick wasn't satisfied.

"Ren, can I borrow you to translate for me?"

"Sure," she said. "What?"

"Well, whatever we say, the elves are going to disengage and Ilkar is right about how the Xeteskians will react. So Ren and I are going to have a little meeting with Auum, Rebraal and the Dordovan command where I will explain how to conduct a phased withdrawal. Because if they don't do it right and get enough Dordovans in to fill the hole, Izack will have a new army to fight and I'm not having my people left exposed like that."

"Ever the general," said Hirad.

Darrick shook his head. "No, Hirad. Just feeling guilty."

CHAPTER 45

While he'd been unconscious, they'd blindfolded him and tied him across his saddle. He came to his senses at some point during the ride that followed, a ride that he thought would never end. They took him off his horse when they stopped for the night but didn't untie his hands, remove his blindfold or feed him. And they wouldn't speak to him, just gave him infrequent mouthfuls of stale water.

The crossbow wound in his thigh was excruciating. Periodically, he could feel the blood flow down his leg but he ignored it, such was his general discomfort and the racking jolts into his stomach which came with every stride of the fast-moving horse. He was certain he was being caused probably fatal internal damage and the blood he coughed into his mouth periodically was all the evidence he needed. It left him glad they'd starved him. He'd only have vomited anything solid up anyway.

When at last they stopped, after the dull thud of hooves had become an echo off buildings and he'd heard the sound of many voices, of hammering and harsh laughter, and he was pulled from his horse to lie flat on hard mud, he knew he'd travelled his last. Wherever they'd brought him to. Whatever town or village they were in, the Black Wings were in control and he wasn't going to be leaving.

All that kept him alive was the elven salvation he had in a pocket. And even that was taken from him when he was marched somewhere quiet that smelled of old ale, with timbered floors and a high ceiling. After the search that revealed so little, he was forced into a chair, his arms were untied and the blindfold pulled roughly over his head.

He didn't know what to do first so he tried to do it all. He blinked to get some focus into his gluey eyes, tried to move his arms and massage life back into his hands and fingers and felt at the wound that thudded with every weary beat of his heart. It all became confused so he stopped, took a breath and decided looking at his situation was the best start.

He forced one arm up to his face despite the protestations of his shoulder and elbow and used the stiffened fingers of the hand to gouge at his eyes. Slowly, painfully, he brought the room into bleary reality. He was sitting on a straight-backed chair across a table from a man. The man was flanked by two others. On the table were tankards, a jug and a plate of bread and dried meat. The look of the food repulsed him, his stomach turning over and sending renewed nausea swimming through his body.

He was in an inn—the shape, smell and remnants of a bar told him that—but it was an inn that had not seen custom for a long time. Heavy drapes covered window holes and he could now make out sounds from the outside. They were to his left and he got the impression he was as far into the building as he could get.

Focussing on the man's face in front of him in the dim light, it seemed distorted. One of his eyes was white and his mouth was downturned but just on one side. He had never met the man before but knew exactly who it was.

"Selik," he said through a mouthful of old blood.

"Captain Yron, Xeteskian soldier," replied Selik, his voice a little slurred as if he was drunk. "Quite a mess you made of my valuable patrol, so I'm led to believe."

Yron managed a dry chuckle though he had never felt less like laughing. "I tried to warn them."

Selik raised a hand. "Well, we'll get on to all that later. First, I'm sure you could do with water. I'd offer you wine but I'm afraid this place ran dry a long time ago."

"Where are we?"

Selik poured him a tankard of water and he gulped at it, feeling its chill freshness revitalise his throat. He spat on the ground.

"A place of legends," said Selik. "Hard to believe I know, but so much that has shaped us happened here in years gone by. And is doing so again. I'm surprised you don't recognise it even from this small sample. I'd have entertained you in my office but the compound is being used for drilling men and it's all very noisy at the moment. Much more peace here."

Yron had a better look round, took in the empty room scattered with broken wood and the dark of night through the door at the far end. There was only one place he knew as dead as this but still standing. He'd drunk here once.

"Understone."

"Very good," said Selik. "I see the ride hasn't jellied your brain though I see from your colour the same cannot be said of your gut. Shame. The bread is fresh."

Yron was tired. He wanted to sleep or die. Either would have done. But he could see that Selik wanted to toy with him. Well, he didn't want to play.

"What do you want, Selik? I've just about lost everything except my life and I'm none too keen on that, so don't go threatening death to get your answers. Giving me back to Xetesk holds much more fear."

"Hmmm." Selik tore off a corner of bread and fed it into the right side of his mouth, chewing carefully. "Yes, that was one of the things I wanted you to help me with. That and a few details about the layout of your beloved college. And, more out of curiosity than anything else, why you're carrying bits of carved marble in your pocket." Selik indicated the thumb which lay on the table next to Yron's empty holster.

"Is that all?"

"For now."

"Where do you want me to start?"

"How cooperative."

"You haven't heard me answer yet, boy."

"Just before we get on, I think I should make it clear that the only people who could ever call me 'boy' were my parents. You will address me as 'Selik,' or 'Captain.'"

Yron scoffed. "Selik it is, then. You're certainly no captain. That's a term reserved for soldiers of rank, not self-styled peacocks like you."

Selik smiled thinly, ignoring the barb. Yron wasn't sure if he was pleased at that or not. He didn't want to endure more pain unnecessarily but he had to know how far he could push.

"I should make a couple of other things clear. You are going to die here. And I will get my information. It is merely a question of how easy you want to make your last hours."

Selik sipped his water, looking at Yron over the rim for a reaction. Yron made sure he saw nothing but calm acceptance.

"I think your men have already helped me along that path," said Yron, feeling his gut. "Ask."

"I'm intrigued," said Selik, "why a Xeteskian soldier should be found running from his college in the company of elves and not as their prisoner. I have heard of these elves in the past days. Are they not fighting against Xetesk?"

"Xetesk has committed a great crime—unwittingly at first but now with full knowledge—and it has to be righted. The college would not do it so I took it upon myself. You stopped me. Us."

"I am sorry," said Selik. "Fortunately, I am the right man to talk to about righting college crimes."

Yron managed a smile. "You have no conception of the scale of what you have done by stopping me."

"Perhaps you'd care to enlighten me."

Yron shifted, wondering what he should say.

"How much do you want to damage Xetesk's ambitions?"

Selik frowned. "There is not enough time in a day to explain. Why?"

"And how much do you want to live?"

"There's much more work to be done," evaded Selik. "And I do hope there's a reason for these questions."

"Well, you have the tools to do both and neither right here," said Yron.

Selik cleared his throat. "The ice is thin beneath your feet, Captain."

"Oh really? I thought it had already cracked and you were merely holding me above the drop."

Selik waved a hand impatiently. "What is this?" He turned the thumb over in his hands.

"I had no idea you were interested in archaeology."

Selik sighed. "I can make this very painful for you," he said without looking up. "But I had hoped it wouldn't be necessary."

It was Selik's casual attitude that told Yron the Black Wing would torture the information from him. And if he was going to die, it might as well be on his terms. He was not afraid to die. Nor was he afraid of pain but he'd wanted to resist Selik and had tested his narrow limits. But as he sat there, aware of his own unpleasant smell mixing with the stale sweat and ale of the room and those around him, he asked himself what it was he was so desperate to keep from Selik.

And he couldn't think of a single thing. He relaxed.

"I'd talk easier over a hot drink," he said.

Selik shrugged and nodded at one of his men.

"And for me too."

"Thank you," said Yron.

"Now, Captain," said Selik. "Time for you to begin."

"Well, Selik, the summary is this. What you have in your hand there is part of the thumb from the statue of Yniss that stands in the Aryndeneth temple on Calaius. Its separation from the statue has unleashed a plague which threatens to wipe out the entire elven nation. I was taking it back. You must do the same. If you do you'll gain a very powerful ally. If you don't they'll kill you. All of you." He leaned back. "I can see you don't believe me but I assure you it's true, if a little difficult to grasp that something so small could cause something so awful. So, ask me what you want and I'll tell you all I can."

Selik asked and Yron told him. Everything.

Barely rested but driven by a desperate need, The Raven rode from their forward camp in the dead of night, allowing their horses to pick careful routes through the tussocks of grass, moss-covered rocks and bracken thickets of their route back to the southwest side of Xetesk. During their rest, another dozen Al-Arynaar had succumbed to the Elfsorrow, as had three TaiGethen, one of them Marack, who had already seen the rest of her Tai cell die. To her it had been a release from grief.

A Communion between Dordovan and Lysternan mages eased their passage between the two battle fronts and on toward the no-man's-land to the south and west, which was still nominally controlled by Xetesk but under pressure from the Black Wing force camped a few miles south.

The Raven, with their quartet of elven guests clinging unhappily to the saddles of their cantering horses, had made good progress through the latter half of the night, and as dawn brightened the sky, the three mages took to the air.

The decision had been made to cover the ground in a wide arc and track back along the most likely route Merke's cell would have taken on leaving Xetesk. There was some risk attached to the tactic as Xeteskian mage-defender trios were out looking for the same quarry. Ilkar was the southern-most, Denser nearest to the walls of Xetesk but a good four miles distant, with Erienne in between them, slightly ahead of both and with a brief to look as much into the sky ahead as at the ground below her.

They flew a mile ahead of The Raven, who split as necessary to check knots of trees, heavy bushes and areas of taller bracken. With the horses going at little more than a trot, Auum and his Tai had taken the chance to dismount and track. But for hour after hour there was no sign.

From where he flew some fifty feet from the ground, Denser could see the plains south of Xetesk stretched out before him. Several miles ahead—it was difficult to guess exactly how many—he could see the smoke from dozens of fires and the off-white of tent canvas that must be the Black Wing camp.

It was large and within half a day's march of the walls of Xetesk but Denser still didn't feel they presented a threat. With no magic in their ranks they were terribly vulnerable to spell attack, and that was what would pour from the city walls should they approach too close. No doubt the Black Wings had already been scouted from ground and air and Xetesk was happy they could be contained. All that would worry them would be the drain on their mage resources.

Xetesk itself was wreathed in a heavy mist. It was a still morning and the mist wouldn't lift too quickly. Behind them the battle had already been renewed, while ahead the Black Wings seemed in no particular hurry. Of the Xeteskian hunters, there was currently no sign.

He cruised over a dozen hues of green empty but for birds, a rabbit warren and a wandering fox on the trail of prey. Over pockets of mist in dips and shallow valleys. Nothing. Glancing behind, he saw the rest of The Raven trailing them and the specks that had to be the TaiGethen a little further in advance, tracing a cross pattern as they studied the ground.

A sudden rattle of wings and the harsh calls of birds as they took flight caught Denser's attention. Away to his right, crows and seagulls rose out of a misty hollow on the plain, spooked by something. Probably that fox. Denser watched as the crows flew back down in ones and twos while the seagulls circled, waiting their chance. Curious, Denser drifted across and closer to the ground, the birds around him paying little heed, their attention focussed on whatever carrion lay hidden by the mist.

He overflew the area, hearing the irritated bark of a fox or wild dog and a scuffling on the ground as he approached. Just a few feet above the ground and what lay beneath the calf-deep mist revealed itself. A glint of metal, hair waving in the wind, a broken bow standing half proud from the ground, an empty face with dead eyes pecked out.

Denser landed. This close, the mist was thin enough to see through. He checked the bodies quickly, saw Black Wing tattoos on the necks of every dead man and found the bodies of three elves. Auum was not going to be happy. Of Yron, though, there was no sign, but here is where the hunt would truly start.

He took off again, signalled The Raven and waited, hovering above the corpses, seeing his friends galloping and flying toward him, the TaiGethen sprinting at remarkable speed. With them all nearing, he landed again and dismissed the wings, anxious to maintain as much stamina as he could. He stepped away from the scene and let the experts come in to assess what had gone on. Thraun, Ren and the TaiGethen examined the bodies and the area around them, occasionally kneeling to check a print in the grass or standing to talk and point.

Quickly, with Ren translating, there was consensus.

"The Black Wing riders came in from the south. Twenty, judging by the density of prints and the tracks we've found," said Ren. "Can't tell why a fight started but the TaiGethen caused mayhem when you consider where the Black Wing bodies have fallen. The survivors rode off back the way they came. We have to presume they took Yron with them. None of these dead have the thumb."

"Well let's pray he still has it. How long ago did this happen?" asked The Unknown.

"A day, day and a half at the most. The Tai can track them."

Denser looked at the TaiGethen and Rebraal. They had moved their dead from the mist and laid them out beneath the warming sun. Auum was crouched at their heads, leading his Tai in prayer. The Raven fell silent out of respect, heads bowed as the mist gradually cleared, Auum's low voice in their ears, his tone reverential.

When he had finished his prayer, he touched each one of the elves on the forehead and stood up. His face was expressionless but his eyes betrayed his anger. He motioned to his Tai and they trotted away, following the trail left by the Black Wings.

"Well, aren't they going to bury them or something?" asked Hirad.

"No," replied Rebraal. "Nature will consume them."

"I just want everyone to know now that if I die I don't want to be consumed," said Hirad. "Burned or buried, all right?"

The Unknown clapped his hands together. "All right, Raven, let's get moving, I—" He broke off. "Ilkar, are you all right?"

Denser beat them to the Julatsan, who was on all fours, coughing violently at the ground and drawing in great heaving agonised breaths.

"Ilkar?" he said, crouching beside him. "Something wrong?"

Ilkar turned his head. His face was grey with pain, his eyes sunken and dull like he hadn't slept for days. "Yes, something's wrong." His mouth was covered in blood and where he had been coughing the grass was stained red.

"Relax," said Denser. "It'll pass. Probably something you ate last night." But Denser's heart was quailing. He could sense the others standing around them, no one able to utter a word.

Ilkar took them all in and managed a sad smile. "No, it won't, Denser. You know that. We all do."

Denser sat back on his haunches, feeling true helplessness sweep over him as it must be sweeping over them all. He could hear Ren begin to cry and saw her rush to Ilkar's other side and cradle his head against her chest. He looked around at them. The Raven. Strong people. But this was surely beyond any of their capacities.

Hirad was staring at Ilkar. Denser could see the barbarian's chest moving with his measured breathing and saw the refusal to believe in his eyes. When he spoke, his voice was husky, barely in control.

"Aeb, Ilkar will ride with you. There's been a change of plan."

CHAPTER 46

The Raven followed Hirad because they trusted him, because they would not let him do what he planned alone and because, if by some miracle they were to save Ilkar, there really was no other choice.

They reined in briefly by the TaiGethen. Auum looked up from the trail, took in Aeb holding Ilkar before him in the saddle, and for the first time Hirad saw a gentle emotion in his eyes. He nodded to Hirad in sympathy and looked questioningly at Rebraal.

"Tell him this," said Hirad. "Tell him that we don't have time for him to follow a trail. Tell him we have to know right now if those bastards have taken Yron and where. Tell him he's welcome to come with us if he can keep up but our friend is dying and it's become personal now."

And soon they were all galloping west. The TaiGethen's natural sense of balance just about made up for their lack of skill in the saddle but still none of them was able to hold the reins alone and all clutched saddle pommels as their horses sped along beneath them.

Hirad spared them a glance, glad that they were with him. His head was full of rage and a sense of injustice he hadn't felt since Sirendor Larn had died under an assassin's poisoned knife in the time before Denser cast Dawnthief.

He was furious at the Black Wings for stopping and killing the TaiGethen. He was furious at Yron for stealing the thumb and condemning so many elves, and maybe Ilkar, to death. But mostly he was furious with Xetesk for what it had so casually brought about. Revenge for that would come later. Right now he cared about one thing only.

They tore toward the Black Wing camp, Hirad not knowing what he'd do when they got there but sure he'd think of something. With people coming and going from the camp on foot and horseback, and with the slackness inherent in a nonmilitary organisation, The Raven rode right up to its edge before being so much as challenged.

Arriving at the mass of tents, weapon stands, wagons and fires, The Raven reined in. Three men walked toward them calling others as they came. Hirad slid from his horse and strode toward the three, seeing them falter as they recognised him and those behind.

"Aeb, stay with Ilkar," he heard The Unknown saying. "Denser, we need a HardShield. Erienne, ForceCone—something to hurt them, not kill them. Remember who most of these people are. Form up, Raven. Let's keep close."

Hirad knew he'd be protected so he carried on, not even bothering to draw his sword. He focussed on the guard in the centre. He was no soldier. A trader by the look of him. Soft hands. He had no stomach for trouble. The barbarian grabbed him under the chin.

"Where's Selik?" he demanded.

Another of the men grabbed at his arm. Hirad turned his head.

"Take your hand away or lose it."

"HardShield up," he heard Denser say.

The Raven closed in around him and the hand on his arm was gone, gripped and crushed by The Unknown.

"You heard him. Now get back."

The man whimpered in pain. Hirad turned back to his charge, seeing people running in from all sides.

"Speak. Selik. Where is he?"

"I don't know," stammered the former trader. "Not here."

"Gods burning." Hirad thrust the man away from him. "Get me a Black Wing." He raised his voice. "Any of you got the tattoo? Show yourself."

By now quite a crowd had gathered. Not too close but there were hundreds of them. Hirad knew they were on dangerous ground but guessed none of them would want to make the first move. Someone shouldered his way through the crowd, a confident man with a bushy beard and grey-flecked hair. He walked into the space between the crowd and The Raven, taking them in and looking behind to where Aeb sat with Ilkar.

"I am Edman," he said. "Your mages can consider themselves under arrest as can the monstrosity on the horse there. The rest of you are complicit in supporting magic. I suggest you lower your weapons."

Hirad waited for him to get to the point of no return before pacing out to meet him. But instead of facing him, he stepped in, grabbed Edman's lapel and swept his feet from under him, landing on top of him in the dirt. All around there was a concerted move forward but The Raven were in front of him in moments, the TaiGethen ready with bows to the sides.

"You've got about a heartbeat to live," said Hirad. "Some of your men took a Xeteskian soldier to the east of here. Got into trouble with some rather handy elves like the ones standing with us. Know anything about that?"

Edman struggled uselessly beneath him. Hirad fetched out a dagger and held it to his throat.

"I'm not going to ask you again," said Hirad.

"You're way too late," said Edman, forcing a smile onto his lips. "They took him to Understone. He'll be dead by now. The cleansing is coming, Raven man, and you will be washed away like all the rest."

"Not by you though," said Hirad. He snapped the dagger into Edman's throat, holding the thrashing soldier there while his blood pumped into the soil.

"You shouldn't have done that, Hirad," said The Unknown.

"Just wait till we get to Understone," he said.

He stood and picked up Edman by the front of his armour, dragging him through The Raven line and dumping his body in front of the swelling crowd, which fell silent.

"Anyone tries to stop us leaving, it's the same for them," he said. "Gods, what are you doing here? You're sensible people with your heads turned. You're farmers, bakers, merchants. Husbands and fathers. Why don't you just go home?"

"Because we don't have homes," said one. "Magic took them away."

"So build them again," said Hirad. "Why are you wasting your time here?"

He swung round and faced The Raven. An arrow whipped in, bouncing from the Shield. The answering shaft from Auum took the archer through the chest. There was a murmur in the crowd.

"I'm disappointed," said Hirad, turning to face them once again, his voice loud enough to carry over their heads. "We have no fight with you, just your Black Wing friends. You all know you could overwhelm us if you wanted to but how many of you are going to die first, eh?" He pointed at people in the crowd. "It'll certainly be you. And you." He shrugged and tapped his head. "Just think about it. And think of the hundreds waiting for you on the walls of Xetesk."

Slowly The Raven backed away to their horses, Denser keeping the Shield up, the TaiGethen and Ren with their bows trained on the crowd. Hirad had been right. None of them had been in a hurry to die. But as he spurred his horse away toward Understone, he wondered how many of them would waste their lives at the walls of Xetesk, helpless under a barrage of magic.

They rode until exhaustion and The Unknown forced them to stop and rest. Ilkar had recovered during the ride, and although weak was no longer in any pain and took food with them around their fire. Denser had set alarm wards around the campsite and Aeb had chosen to patrol, declining both food and rest.

Hirad couldn't take his eyes off Ilkar. He was tired to the bone but could barely sit still and his mind was buzzing. Sleep would be a long time coming. They would all be feeling the same.

"How're you feeling, Ilks?" asked Hirad.

"Since you last asked me just now, nothing has changed. I feel all right. I ache and I'm dying, but apart from that no problem."

Ren pulled him closer and he rested his head on her shoulder.

"You might be dying but you won't if we get the thumb back to the temple," said Hirad. "Right?"

"Hirad, even if we had the thumb now, it's eight days to Blackthorne, another seven across the ocean and another three upriver. As far as we know, this thing runs its course in as little as four days." Ilkar's eyes were glistening in the firelight. "You work it out."

"Let me worry about that. You just fight it. Don't give in."

Hirad felt an arm around his shoulders. It was Erienne. She squeezed and he felt better for it.

"My dear old friend, there are some things even you can't sort out," said Ilkar.

"But this isn't one of them," said Hirad. "If you don't stop believing, we can save you."

"Hirad—"

"I don't want to hear it. You aren't dying on me and that's final."

He was aware his hands were shaking. Erienne kissed his cheek.

"Keep on telling him," she whispered into his ear.

He nodded.

"So," said The Unknown. "Before we all turn in, what's your plan for Understone? Would I be wrong in thinking it included a good deal of riding through the town laying about us with swords and spells until we find what we're looking for?"

Hirad couldn't stop the chuckle though the Gods knew he didn't feel like laughing. "You forgot the bit about where I cut down Selik, but apart from that you're not far from the mark. You have something better in mind?"

"Well, actually, I do," said Darrick. "I know plenty about Understone, and with one small alteration and a slight detour, your plan might just work."

Darrick sketched out his idea quickly and accurately. Later, as Hirad felt sleep steal his thoughts from him, he felt they might just pull it off. They had no idea how many there were in Understone or where exactly they'd be but they didn't have to. After all, they weren't rescuing anybody, just one object. And eventually they'd find it, no matter how many were killed in the process.

Hirad turned over, his saddle a pillow for his head, the ground soft beneath him and his cloak covering him against the night's cool. Only Ilkar's coughs and his occasional gasp of pain kept him from easy rest.

Auum and his Tai sat by the fire long after The Raven had taken to their rest. They sat in silence, listening to the sounds of sleep and those of the night around them. The Protector, Aeb, was ill at ease as he walked the perimeter, sometimes stopping for an extended period in one place, his body quite still but his lips moving soundlessly. The ClawBound pair padded in some time after midnight, the elf sitting with his back to a tree stump, the panther curling up at his feet.

"The Al-Arynaar and TaiGethen should stay," said Auum. "We can return the fragment and the Raven mage will facilitate the binding. We still have sacred texts that must be reclaimed."

Duele raised his eyebrows. "Confident in their ability, are you?" he said, scepticism in his voice.

"They are certainly . . . determined," conceded Auum. "And they care, that much became apparent today."

Evunn nodded. "They move fast and are direct. We would have been a long way further back down the trail tonight."

"I am confident enough that we can succeed on our own with them. Moving the rest of the elves will bring trouble. Ilkar was right. We should stop the withdrawal." He turned to the ClawBound elf. "You are in contact range?"

A nod.

"The elves must fight on. I have asked for this. I'd rather the Sorrow took them while they fought than uselessly on board ship. We will recapture the thumb. Will you relay these messages?"

Another nod.

"Yniss will see us safe. He has given us these strangers to aid us," said Auum. "We should not be ungrateful."

The light of the next dawn was still faint when the panther began to growl and roar, the alien sounds of ClawBound communication echoing over Balaia for the first time.

Ilkar felt every stride of his horse through his body as if the hooves were trampling over him. He'd demanded he ride on his own, determined not be an invalid. Against all odds, he'd had a fairly comfortable night and it was not until the panther had set up its unearthly resonant calls that the pain had gripped him again and all but taken the breath from him.

He still remembered Ren's touch and he recalled her tears as they fell asleep. He was just thankful she was still free. But his own sudden falling had been a stark reminder that in the next breath it could be her turn.

The Raven rode hard or walked their horses at a march for the whole day, once stopping briefly for a meal. Their direction would take them close to but east of Understone on a route that would keep them hidden from the town, with Darrick assuring them that ideal cover and a base for their attack was only a mile or so the other side.

Ilkar hoped and prayed he was right. At times during the day the pain became all but unbearable but he refused to cast to dull it or ask them to slow to ease it. There was fire in his veins and venom in his muscles. His stomach felt like it was being eaten from the inside, there was a rattle every time he took a breath and his heart beat off rhythm, palpitating, slowing and pounding such that he felt it would crash through his ribs. His eyes played tricks on him while his ears heard sounds that couldn't be—his mother's voice calming him, his tutor at Julatsa chiding him for laziness, the sound of the wind in the sails.

Through it all he kept upright in the saddle and replied in the affirmative when any of them asked, and they asked so often it almost made him laugh, whether he was all right. Stupid question and they all knew it.

It was past dusk when they stopped in a river valley into which rocks had tumbled in ancient times, creating a maze of streams and a patchwork of green and grey. Darrick had been right. It was ideal cover. The ClawBound loped in an hour or so later. Ilkar only dimly heard what Hirad and The Unknown said to the pair before they settled down to rest. By the time he had eaten, his ears roared with a sound like thunder and his body shook with cold although the night was mild and cloudy.

"It's just us now," Hirad said, more for the benefit of Ren and Darrick than the more seasoned members of The Raven. "We have to work closely, move as one and keep on moving whatever we come up against. We faced down an army yesterday. Tomorrow we go to fight not talk. We all know why."

"We'll be moving just before dawn," said The Unknown. "Take the fight to them while they're still dull with sleep. We can't rely on Ilkar's defence because we won't know his condition one moment to the next but we're all right because they won't have spell attack. We'll be fighting without the TaiGethen or the ClawBound pair. They will attack as they must, all we've agreed are start points. Don't look to them. We're The Raven; we don't need anyone else. Not to defend, and not to help us." He watched them all for reaction. "Now, Aeb, you have something you need to say."

The Protector was standing at the periphery of the fire.

"You were wrong to bring me," he said. "The Act of Giving will soon be rescinded. It is just a matter of time."

"It was a risk we were all happy to take," said Denser.

"Xetesk know we are here," he said. "They know what we seek."

"And when will they get here?" asked Hirad.

"Tomorrow. Morning."

"Then," said Thraun, surprising them with speech after another lengthy silence, "we had better be quick."

CHAPTER 47

W hen The Raven camp stirred, a light drizzle was falling. Ilkar had not slept much and looked every inch the dying elf. It was awful to witness. Shivering, Erienne kissed Denser, rose to her feet and breathed in deep. She felt the cool air rush into her lungs, banishing the fog she always felt around the entity of the One at first waking and easing the thumping in her head.

The Al-Drechar hadn't spoken to her since that night in Blackthorne Castle and she was glad of it. They had opened the door a little further to power from the One and allowed her the freedom to handle it as best she could. And she had responded, working on partitioning her mind a third way to deal with the new power she alone on Balaia possessed. Further than that they had not offered questions or advice, leaving her and The Raven to do what they did best. And today was going to be a severe test of their belief. She wondered whether she dared employ what she had learned.

Windmilling her arms to smooth out the knots in her muscles, she looked at them all preparing. In so many ways like so many other preparations. While they honed the edges of their swords The Unknown, Hirad, Aeb and Darrick talked quietly, refining tactics and attack order, with Thraun standing near, taking in everything. Next to Erienne, Denser sat cross-legged in meditation, focussing his mana and examining his stamina levels. Ever since the casting of Dawnthief, he had come to a new understanding of mana. It had made him an exceptionally efficient caster.

Even Ilkar went through his routine, walking in tight circles, testing shapes and speed. Erienne wasn't sure if he was achieving anything in casting terms but it would keep his mind as far as possible from the dreadful fate toward which he marched.

Only Ren was apart from it. The bags under her eyes and the puffiness of her face told their own story and she was just sitting on the grass, her back to a rock, staring out into nowhere. Her gaze occasionally crossed them all and she would shake her head.

Erienne walked across and squatted down beside her. She had great respect for the quiet elven woman who had been such a source of strength to her in the long days that preceded Lyanna's death; when her desperation had been as keen as her grief subsequently became. Now the tables needed to be turned.

"Hey, anyone there?"

Ren'erei looked at her, a tear squeezing past her eye. "I don't think so."

"Time to get ready," said Erienne. "Have you checked your bow and blade?"

"Eh?" Ren frowned. "Oh, yes."

She waved her hand vaguely at her bow, which rested against the rock next to her.

"I'm no expert, Ren, but I always thought bows needed a string to work."

The elf crumbled and threw her arms around Erienne's neck, buried her head in her shoulder and cried hard. Erienne held her, looking around at The Raven and gesturing them to stay away. Even Ilkar stared on, his face creased with a guilt he had no right to be feeling.

"Sorry. I'm sorry," said Ren eventually, pulling away and wiping at her eyes.

"It's all right. You probably needed it."

"Seems like I've been needing it constantly just lately."

"I know, Ren, but you have to put it aside for now. String your bow and be ready to fight with us."

The elf nodded and grabbed her weapon from its resting place. "I don't know how you do it, any of you," she said, fishing in her sack for her leather-wrapped bow string. "He's dying and there's nothing we can do and yet you go on like nothing's happened."

"Don't ever talk that way," said Erienne sharply. "You have to believe. Ilkar's not dead yet and if Hirad believes we can save him, we all believe it and you must too. We've been here before. We've seen our friends die, and the best way we can honour them, if that's all it can be, is by doing the right thing. This time it's reclaiming the Yniss fragment and saving as many other elves as we can without losing any more of our people.

"That's why we look so calm. It's because if we thought for one moment we might fail and that Ilkar might die, we'd already have lost. And The Raven do not like to lose."

"So I've noticed," said Ren. "But you're not even with him, talking to him. It could be the last chance you get."

"Fate decides that, Ren. And, who knows, he could survive the trip to Calaius. Until he dies, we believe we can save him."

"But—"

"No buts, Ren. It's as simple as that." Erienne pushed herself upright. "It's the only way to think. Come on."

She held out a hand and Ren accepted it and pulled. The two walked back to the centre of the camp.

"We all ready?" asked Hirad.

"Yes," said Ren decisively.

"Good, then let's be on our way."

The Raven walked out of the camp. Hirad put an arm around Ren's shoulder.

"It's all right to feel like you do. We all do. But do it later. Right now, we have work to do and we need you."

"You do?"

Hirad shrugged. "Of course. You're Raven."

Behind them, Erienne smiled. Denser was beside her and they watched as Ilkar walked as easily as he could to Ren's other side and laid his arm across her shoulders too. She responded, wrapping an arm around each of their waists.

"A picture of the professional mercenary approaching battle," said Denser.

Erienne jabbed him. "Leave them be."

"How's the body this morning, Ilks?" asked Hirad.

"Agony," said Ilkar. "But I'm walking."

"Good. Can't spare anyone to carry you, anyway."

"Your sympathy overwhelms me."

"I do my best." Hirad looked across Ren to Ilkar, and Erienne could see his expression in profile, picked out in the vague predawn light. It was desperate, still disbelieving. "Anyway, the pain won't last forever. It's only twenty-odd days to the temple."

Ren tensed but Ilkar laughed. "I'll attempt to keep my insides from decomposing too much before we get there."

"Bloody right," said Hirad. "I'm not sharing a cabin with you if you smell."

Their chuckles echoed a little loud.

"Keep it down," said The Unknown.

It was only a mile to Understone.

Auum watched The Raven go, ambling away down the slope like they were out for an early morning stroll. He heard their talk and laughter and shook his head.

"Perhaps my assessment was premature," he said.

"It's their way," said Rebraal. "We pray to ease the tension and fear, they talk to keep their minds from it until the moment arrives."

"I will never understand strangers," said Auum.

The TaiGethen bowed their heads and prayed to Yniss to keep them strong for the fight to come. Auum murmured offerings to Tual while he painted Duele's face, and when all three were ready they stood with the ClawBound.

"Fight with us, Rebraal. You are our link to The Raven so keep close. This day we will start to right the crimes committed against us. This day I will hold the thumb of Yniss in my hand or I will be travelling to meet him to account for my failings in this life. This I swear."

The TaiGethen jogged from the camp, heading for the eastern edge of Understone, Rebraal with them. The ClawBound, swift and sure, were just ahead. Auum felt no thrill, just a sense that Yniss might once again be prepared to look their way.

And the god would be looking down when the desecrators and thieves and those who thought to kill his people paid.

The Raven looked down on Understone. It was quiet. Along the single street the ramshackle buildings still stood: the inn, the grain store, the boarded-up traders' offices, the whorehouses, a few homes. Elsewhere the ground was covered with tents and shelters, all dark and silent. There were over a hundred of them. The only life was in the stockade at the western end of the town. Fires burned around the rampart and lanterns shone from barracks windows. They could see figures walking the raised platform. After the end of the second Wesmen wars, the town had been rebuilt in the image of the old in the hope of renewed trade with the west and just as quickly abandoned again. Only the stockade had remained staffed.

"That'll be where Selik is," said Hirad.

"All in good time," said Darrick. "We'll do this in the right order and be the safer for it."

They moved quietly now, heading for the first tents. Spread panic, Darrick had said. Target the tattoos. Let them make the moves and see who is prepared to fight. Not many, guessed Hirad, but time would tell.

Fifty yards from the tents and all was according to Darrick's plan. The bulk of the Black Wings were looking after themselves in the stockade and the innocents, if you could truly call anyone that who had travelled here to fight with Selik, were unguarded in their tents. They didn't understand conflict. Didn't realise the vulnerability of masses of men to targeted magical attack. Why should they? They were tradesmen.

"He'll have paid mercenaries too," said The Unknown. "We'll know them when we see them."

"Paid," mused Hirad. "An unfamiliar idea for us these days."

"Erienne, Denser, ready?"

The pair nodded, preparing, melding their constructs for wider effect.

"A short sharp shower. When it's down, we go and we don't stop," said Darrick. "Is everyone clear?"

"Ilks?" asked Hirad.

"My ears are on the side of my head not in my gut, Hirad. Yes, I hear and understand."

"Just checking."

Hirad felt a touch on his back. "Thank you."

Hirad readied himself, checked his hilt for loose binding again and angled the blade to see the edge. The drizzle had stopped and the cloud was shifting. It would be a bright dawn. A few birds began to call. From somewhere the bleating of a sheep carried over to them. It was tranquil. Just for a moment.

"Casting," said Denser faintly.

HotRain filled the sky above the southernmost tents. For a while they watched it fall, tears of flame the size of thumbs. Thousands of them. People were going to die in terror. So be it. From the stockade the first shouts of alarm were raised. HotRain struck canvas and canvas burned. The screaming began.

"Raven!" yelled Hirad. "Raven with me!"

He ran toward the first tents, seeing movement bulging against the canvas. The HotRain shower was almost gone but it had done its job, deluging the acre of canvas in flame. Everywhere smoke was rising, fires agitated at rope and cover and the pitch of voices rose with every heartbeat.

He slashed at the guy ropes of the nearest tent and thumped his hilt against a shape inside, sending the victim sprawling.

"Run!" he shouted. "Run!"

A head emerged from a flap. Hirad smashed his fist into it and dragged the body out, his clothing smouldering. He pulled their faces close.

"Run. Don't look back. Take your friends."

The man jabbered as Hirad dropped him, then he wiped blood from his mouth and took to his heels away out of Understone.

The Raven roared through the burning campsite. Aeb laying about him with his axe, smashing ridge poles, splitting skulls and kicking burning canvas into the air. Thraun was howling like the wolf he had once been and, like Hirad, was shouting at men to run and not look back. The Unknown and Darrick strode in behind, the mages at their backs, preparing again.

Utter mayhem descended. Swords slashed, burning men flailed uselessly, cries crescendoed and the choking smoke thickened. Hirad turned on a pair of men standing with swords ready; neither was fully dressed, neither a soldier. He sprang at them, hacking downward as he landed, his blow striking the blade of one and jarring it from his hands.

"What are you waiting for? Fight or run, I'm happy either way."

He switched his grip three times, very fast. The men turned and ran to join those pouring into the main street and away. Most of them headed out of the town but a few went up toward the stockade in which activity must be starting in earnest.

"Raven!" called The Unknown. "Move on!"

The campsite was pitched next to the grain store. The Raven gathered by its rear doors, out of sight of the stockade, hauled them open and ran inside.

Auum saw the signal. The rain of fire from the sky. He sprinted into the town on the north side of the main street and headed for the second tent encampment. The elves would spread their fear in another way entirely. The Claw-Bound panther roared and leapt at the nearest tent, her bound-elf at her side, slicing through the bindings.

Auum and his Tai split. His blade carved open the side of a tent, revealing all those inside, five of them just coming to waking. Very slowly. Auum whipped his sword into the upturned face of one, stamped down on the head of the next and moved through the panicked tent, his blade flickering, his feet jabbing out. Taking a man through the eye, he leant in to the last survivor and used the word he had been taught.

"Run!"

He peeled away. Screams filled the air around him. The panther had torn the throat from a stranger and by her, the bound-elf faced a man carrying a sword he had no idea how to use. He swung it but the elf simply stepped inside the blow and rained straight-fingered blows into his exposed neck, blood spraying over his face. The man dropped. The ClawBound moved on.

Auum tracked them through the camp. Duele emerged from a tent right, a survivor racing in the opposite direction. Evunn had split the stomach of a stranger stupid enough to face him and was moving on toward the main street. The panther darted around the camp, roaring at every turn, growling deep, teeth and claws lashing out, scraping rents in tent sides.

The sound of voices was a babble of fear. Auum smiled mirthlessly, watching the strangers run, many only part clothed. Across the street, the other camp burned fiercely and through the tumult he could hear The Raven. Like causing a stampede of animals. The night, the fire, the smell of blood and the threat of steel. Too easy. But down on the street, up toward the end of the town where the stockade stood, it would be more difficult. Men were gathering.

It was time to move.

Lanterns were alight in the grain store, which had become a dormitory for three dozen and more. The Raven hauled the doors back to see men in the act of scrambling to put on clothes and belt weapons. Sleep was muddling minds and the storm that came at them stoked their confusion.

"Run or die!"

Hirad chased in, The Raven forming around him. The Unknown left, Darrick right.

"HardShield up," said Denser.

Already some of their opponents were running for the opposite door but others faced them, one with the Black Wing tattoo. Hirad swung his sword right to left, clashing against an enemy blade, driving the man back. He rebalanced, jabbed forward—the blow turned aside—easily blocked the riposte then swept his blade up in a left to right diagonal, catching the man in the base of the gut. He fell back, entrails boiling from his stomach.

Next to Hirad The Unknown wasn't wasting as much time. His first strike crushed the ribs of his opponent and he stepped forward across the falling corpse, deflecting a blow with his dagger and driving his sword into the exposed midriff of the next man. Simultaneously, Aeb delivered a massive flat-bladed axe blow, catapulting his enemy from his feet to crash into the man behind.

The survivors wavered but the Black Wing brought them on. He snapped out a command for order and came at Hirad. He whipped in a quick jab which Hirad blocked, followed up with high strikes to either side of Hirad's head which the barbarian ducked and deflected respectively before being cut at the top of his sword arm. He swore.

The Black Wing smiled and came again but found Hirad had changed his sword to his left hand. The expected block came from the other side, forcing him round and off balance. Hirad seized the opening, backhanding his blade into the Black Wing's lower spine. The man grunted and fell.

"Not smiling now, eh?" spat Hirad, and looked into the face of his next victim. The man was nervous. Hirad feinted to move and he sprang back like a frightened dog. "Had your chance."

Hirad struck out, the defending sword knocked aside, the tip of his blade slicing through cheek, nose and forehead. The man wailed and staggered. Hirad finished him with a thrust through the chest. Everyone else had run.

"Good work," said Darrick.

He hurried to the front entrance of the grain store and looked out, The Raven crowding behind him. Right, the scene was still chaotic; fires were burning fiercely, dozens of men running in every direction. They could see the TaiGethen moving toward the main street just by some boarded-up sheds.

To the left the picture was little different barring a group of swordsmen walking out of the stockade and moving up the street.

"There you go," said Darrick. "Told you they'd show themselves."

"We'll take the back route," said The Unknown. "Come at them from the side."

Nearby, the panther growled and then padded past, frightened people scattering in front of it. Her partner was close by. The TaiGethen had made the road and had obviously seen the organised group.

"Excellent," said Hirad. "Perfect decoy."

The Raven ran the length of the grain store and back out into the lightening dawn. They moved quickly along the back of the store, a private house of some substance and the remains of a brothel before turning back toward the street again.

"FlameOrbs ready," said Erienne.

"When we clear the buildings," said The Unknown.

Voices of authority were beginning to be heard over the chaotic shouts of the poorly prepared Balaian men. There was concerted running in the direction of the stockade. Time to snuff out the voices. Time to render the Black Wing army leaderless.

CHAPTER 48

A uum and his Tai sprinted down the main street, ignoring the white faces of fear they passed, heading for the heart of the army, such as it was. Rebraal was with them, sword bloodied, a gash on his thigh but grim belief on his face. In front of them, men were gathering about thirty yards in front of the stockade. Twelve men had formed a line across the street and others were behind them. Crossbowmen stood on the flanks.

The Tai unhitched bows and nocked arrows as they ran, releasing shaft after shaft at the crossbowmen. Auum's first arrow was wild but his second found an enemy arm. Duele, who was their best archer, saw his first shot rip into the mouth of his target and his second drive deep into a stomach. The bolts that came back were few and inaccurate.

Discarding his bow, Auum unsheathed one of his swords and snapped open his pouch of jaqrui. The enemy had begun moving toward them now but were still some forty yards distant. The ClawBound pair raced in along the left, inducing more panic in the strangers' ranks.

"At will," said Auum.

Jaqrui wailed and whispered across the open space, another sound to add to the cacophony and another killer unleashed against the milling Black Wings. Auum flicked out three jaqrui. They were his last. One cut into the back of a running man's neck, pitching him forward into the mud. The second bounced off a mail shirt and the third chopped into a sword hand, slicing away two fingers.

They were closing with the swordsmen when The Raven beat them to it. Rushing from between two buildings, they fell on the left-hand edge of the line, the barbarian hacking deep into the neck of the first man, kicking out into the stomach of the next and plunging his sword into the back of a third.

The enemy bunched and turned. The masked Protector exploded into a group of four, his twin weapons whistling through the air, burying themselves in flesh. The quiet powerful blond man with the animal eyes took the arm from one man and straight-punched his companion in the chin. Both victims dropped.

The Tai entered the fight. Auum backhanded his blade into the chest of one man, drove the heel of his palm into the same face to knock him from his feet and delivered a killing thrust to the chest. He rolled right, a blade thudding into the mud by him. Darting to his feet far too quickly for his opponent to follow, he stabbed straight through the man's groin. He screamed and fell, blood pulsing out and down his legs.

The ClawBound roared together, the panther clouting a hapless Black Wing across the jaw with one paw and landing on top of her victim and biting down hard on the neck. Weaponless but never helpless, the bound-elf jabbed straight fingered into the girth of his target, caught the sword arm in his other hand and bit forward himself, his teeth shearing through nose and tearing away. He spat out the flesh and flew in again.

Auum crashed a fist into his next enemy's chin, spun, and delivered a straight kick which caught the man on the point of his jaw. He stumbled back, bringing up his sword in defence, but Auum had dropped to his haunches. He swept away the Black Wing's legs and broke the man's neck as he fell, catching his head and twisting hard. He stepped away from the battle, knowing he was covered, and turned to see where they had positioned themselves. While a great number of the strangers had run, panicked way beyond organisation, the braver were on their way back. He could see weapons glinting in the early light and heard more orders bringing men into the street at their backs. It wouldn't be long before they were cut off and overwhelmed.

Fortunately, The Raven had seen the danger too and FlameOrbs soared out over his head.

"Press in!" shouted Darrick, slashing at the arm of a Black Wing, his sword biting deep. "We need to break them. Come on. Erienne, Orbs to the rear. They're massing."

Hirad hadn't noticed. He had cuts on both arms now and the edge of a blade had nicked his left ankle as its owner had fallen dead but he didn't care. This was what he lived for. Next to him, The Unknown hammered in blow after blow, his massive muscles delivering awesome power only matched by Aeb. The Black Wings were falling back before them, and with no escape right because the TaiGethen were there, were breaking toward the stockade.

The barbarian closed with a wiry old fighter, his tattoo dulled with age. Probably a man that had served with Travers. Their swords met high and Hirad pushed back hard but the man stood his ground, driving his heels into the mud for purchase. His fist whipped in. Hirad saw it and angled his head, the blow missing him left. He stepped back smartly, hauling his sword in front of him and striking out again. Slightly unbalanced, the Black Wing only just blocked. Hirad struck again, right to left. Another block. Jabbed straight. Blocked again. The man was good. But not that good.

Needing to change his point of attack, Hirad leapt to the left while his sword moved right, sweeping across his enemy's body, forcing him to block away. He saw his peril just too late, began to turn square, but Hirad sent in a haymaking punch with his left hand that caught him on the ear and sent him stumbling into the path of Aeb. The Protector split the fighter's skull with his axe, gore and brain spattering the ground and his mask.

Erienne's FlameOrbs lit up the sky, racing away to the right to splash down on undefended bodies. What small order existed in the forty or so gathered there dissolved in an instant and the air was filled again with the screams of the burning and dying.

"Raven!" called The Unknown. "Pushing left, let's go!"

The Black Wing resistance on the street was faltering; some had already made the run back toward the stockade and the remnants, just five, were staring full face at death. Thraun and Darrick went at them, the pair working like they'd fought together all their lives. The shapechanger's powerhouse blows rained down on the Black Wings, the sword in his hand wielded like a twig, while Darrick's fencing skills left little to chance, his quick feet making him so hard to track. They'd downed another three before the final pair turned tail and ran.

"Come on, Raven. They can't be allowed to shut the gates."

Hirad led The Raven down the street. He glanced at the stockade. Not a man moved on its parapet. They were close now, he could feel it. He ran as fast as he could but with ten yards to go the TaiGethen cruised past him, the ClawBound pair right behind them, Rebraal on their shoulders. They seemed to be making almost no effort and Hirad found himself wondering just how fast they could go.

"Keep inside the shield!" shouted Hirad. "There'll be archers in there."

Rebraal heard him and relayed the message, the elves all slowing. In a group, they chased the two survivors into the compound of the stockade. There were men ahead of them. Dozens of them. Hirad slowed. Behind him, the gates swung shut with a thud, the bolts thrown across. He looked quickly around him. Archers and crossbowmen now lined the ramparts. Swordsmen emerged from buildings to their left and the shadows on their right.

The Raven, a TaiGethen cell, a solitary Al-Arynaar warrior and a Claw-Bound pair. And they were surrounded by seventy at least. Too many.

"Any ideas?" asked Hirad.

The panther growled but was held in check by her partner. The enemy were waiting.

"We can't take all sides on at once," said Darrick. "What have we got spell-wise to disable one side? Somewhere we can back against."

"Denser's got to keep up the HardShield," said Erienne. "I can't deal with the area on my own."

"Keep thinking," said The Unknown.

A door ahead opened and a man walked out. Smeared face, one milky white eye. Selik.

"Welcome to Understone," said Selik.

"I could take him from here," said Ren quietly.

"Don't do it," said Darrick. "We need time to think."

"Now, as you can see, your valiant but doomed efforts to take what I have in my possession are at an end. Actually, I'm hurt you think that I wouldn't want to return the statue fragment myself."

"Anything that hurts you is fine by me," said Hirad. He was desperate to rush Selik but knew he'd never make it across the open space. "But we don't have to fight here. Just give the thumb to us and no more of your men will have to die."

"I fail to see that you are in any position to make demands, Hirad Cold-heart," said Selik. "And in case you hadn't noticed, you are harbouring mages. I am at war with mages."

He waved a hand and a dozen arrows and crossbow bolts hurtled down, all bouncing from the HardShield. Ren's answering shaft took one of the archers down.

"As we can see, you are shielded," said Selik.

"And you are not," said Hirad. "The next arrow is for you."

"Unwise," said Selik. "You would all be killed as a consequence. I am aware of your skills but even you will see this as a situation you have lost. Put your weapons down and I might spare your lives. Erienne, it would be delightful to remake your acquaintance."

Erienne ignored him though a shiver passed across her body.

"We don't have time for your games," said Hirad. "We have a sick elf here and you are holding the cure."

"Oh, I am sorry," said Selik. "Ilkar off colour, is he?"

"This is getting us nowhere," whispered Darrick. "Unknown, any thoughts?" The big man shook his head.

"I have," said Ilkar.

"Am I interrupting something?" asked Selik. "I think I made myself clear, did I not?"

"What exactly?" asked Darrick.

"A mage can reverse the flows from any spell or construct and in doing so draw mana in from a wider area."

"I said, put your weapons down. There's no room for debate," said Selik.

Hirad held up a hand. "Ren, put your bow on him. Don't shoot," he said before turning to Selik. "Actually, we're just debating whether to surrender or go down in a blaze of glory. You can attack now if you want but you're first to die, Selik, and we'll see fifty of your men go with us. Or you can wait and maybe we'll all stay alive."

And he turned his back on their captor, who just shook his head at the Black Wings' questioning glances. "Be quick about it. I am impatient for your surrender."

Erienne looked square at Selik and put a finger to her lips, feeling the voices of ancients in her head. Something flooded from her across the space to the Black Wing captain. She wasn't sure she was in control of it but she knew it had worked.

"Wait," she whispered. "Wait."

"Erienne?" asked Denser.

"Just buying us a few heartbeats. It'll wear off momentarily."

None of the Black Wing soldiers was moving. The sounds of the world about them had faded. It was as if they were standing in a painting, looking at still life.

Hirad hadn't noticed the change. "Are you helping us, Ilkar?"

"Look," replied Ilkar. "I'm dying already. But we needn't all go. I can make the difference you need."

"You're staying with us and we're getting you out of this," said Hirad. "We'll get the thumb and stop the plague."

"Hirad, you don't understand. There is no cure. I've got Elfsorrow and I will die of it. All you can do is stop more catching it. And I'd rather die trying to save my friends."

Hirad felt stunned. He'd assumed there was hope. He'd come charging in here because he could still save Ilkar. And now he found he couldn't.

"You didn't tell me," he said.

"Would it have made any difference?"

"Probably not."

"So I'm going to do this."

"What?" asked Hirad.

"Ilkar's suggesting a focussed backfire," said Erienne. "He can form the shape of a spell like FlameOrbs then detonate it within himself. And because the shape is within him, it will hold together for longer and draw in far more energy than it should."

"But how . . . ?" began Hirad.

"I'll have to be high up."

"No way," said Hirad. "No way. There has to be another answer."

"Hirad, there isn't." Ilkar clutched his arm. "Please let me do this. It's all I've got left."

The reality hit Hirad like a hammer. His grip on his blade weakened and he let it fall. The thump was unnaturally loud on the packed ground.

"That's better," said Selik from behind them.

The sudden resumption of reality made Erienne jump. She wanted to repeat the casting but realised immediately she didn't actually know how. There was so much she still had to learn.

"Shut the fuck up, Black Wing," grated Hirad, not turning. "You can't die, Ilkar. You were there at the start. We can't do this without you."

"You don't have any choice," said Ilkar. "I am dying and you can't save me."

Hirad fought to keep himself together. They were in a desperate situation already and Ilkar had just made it worse. He couldn't afford to lose control now. He set his jaw.

"Please, Ilkar, don't."

"I have to," said Ilkar. "Goodbye, Hirad."

"No." Hirad could feel his throat tighten.

"You have always been my closest friend," said the elf. "Don't forget me."

Hirad looked around at them all, their desperate faces. At the tears flowing down Ren's cheeks as she fought to keep her aim, not daring to turn round. He felt the briefest of kisses on his cheek, saw Ilkar caress Ren's head, heard an incantation and then he was gone, shooting up straight into the sky.

"Get back down here!" shouted Hirad. "Ilkar, no!"

Arrows followed Ilkar skyward, none of them even close to their target.

"What's this?" Selik's voice was laden with sarcasm. "The Raven flying away, are they, Hirad? Those that can. Some bond." He laughed.

Hirad would have pitched after him then but The Unknown had a strong hand on his shoulder.

"Wait," he said. "Soon."

Hirad craned his head high. Everyone in the compound was doing the same. He watched as the elf manoeuvred himself above a parapet and ten archers, underneath which upward of fifteen soldiers stood ready.

"Ilkar!" called Hirad. "Fly away. Please fly away."

But the words caught in his throat. He leaned into The Unknown, felt the big man's hand tighten and waited.

Above the compound Ilkar hovered, the pain in his stomach excruciating and threatening his concentration.

"Just one more time," he said to himself. "Just one more time."

He clung on to the ShadowWings, his body poised a hundred feet from the rampart, aiming to remove the archer threat in one go. It was the shortest side of the stockade, the one closest to The Raven and the easiest flank for them to defend. Partitioning his consciousness, he pulled the shape of Flame-Orbs together, saw the lattice shape closing, felt the flows moving as they should, coursing around and over the shape, the excess filtering away into nothing.

He was ready. He began to descend, picking up speed. He sealed the shape, refusing to let the excess bleed away. The spell reacted, pulsing larger and larger as it dragged in, the flows becoming stronger and stronger. Thirty feet from the parapet, with arrows flicking past him, he lost the wings and plummeted. He opened the spell out, reversing the flows in an instant, feeling the pressure build and the shape decay as he had been cautioned against ever since his training began. The sphere flattened, became an unravelling cylinder, sucking in mana energy to accelerate its demise. There was no way he could contain it, his mind was not strong enough. No one's would have been.

He heard Selik's laughter choke in his throat and Hirad shouting words to him that he hoped he could take with him to the afterlife. They made him smile.

He opened his eyes, saw the stockade rush toward him and the men on it trying scramble clear. Too late. Much too late.

He struck.

CHAPTER 49

"Down!" roared The Unknown, and The Raven hit the dirt.

Hirad saw Ilkar plunge into the rampart just left of centre, the spell he'd kept within him detonating just before he connected. The explosion drove out and down with incredible force. Mana fire gouged out, destroying archers on the parapet, a great sheet of flame washing across the stockade, blasting away timbers, tearing men apart and hurling their bodies high into the air.

Below Ilkar's body, the parapet gave way, bringing timbers and planks crashing down in front of a wall of flame. The flame speared out into the compound, the swordsmen in its path vaporised. A great whoosh of hot air surged over The Raven where they lay. Timbers bounced end over end in all directions, the explosions rang in Hirad's ears and the agonised cries of the dying sounded in his head.

"Shield down," said Denser.

Hirad heard The Raven begin to move but couldn't take his eyes from the fires. In the centre of them, Ilkar's body lay, consumed by flames of his own making. Dead. After all they had survived together.

He heard a concerted roar and the sound of running feet. The dirt by his head sang, an arrow skipping off a stone inches away. He could hear the Black Wings coming but he felt weak inside, unable to react.

But into his confusion came a voice.

"Hirad, move!"

The Unknown stooped and grabbed his collar, jerking him from the ground. His face was too close to focus on.

"Hirad, don't let this be a waste. We have to move. Get in line."

Hirad's vision cleared. He couldn't allow Ilkar to have thrown his life away.

"I'm with you."

He grabbed at his sword and moved. The Raven had backed up as close to the fires as they dared but there were gaps in the line where he and The Unknown should be standing.

He started to run, heard The Unknown clash swords right behind him and saw Denser spread his arms wide.

"Down!" shouted Erienne. "Down!"

Hirad dived straight forward, feeling a thump as The Unknown dropped beside him. The freezing chill of an IceWind washed over their heads into the approaching Black Wings. The screams began but Hirad didn't stop to look, already scrabbling up and racing for the Raven line, the enemy closing fast to his left.

The Unknown was right by him again and they slithered and turned together. The Black Wing charge had been literally shattered. More than ten had been caught in the blast, their flesh solidifying, the blood freezing in their veins, hearts stopping as the ice rushed through their chests. Bodies had fallen to break into shards, and where the spell had caught a trailing arm or leg the victim writhed, shivered stumps clutched in disbelief, the sounds they made awful.

The Unknown tapped his blade on the packed earth, waiting. A surge of anger enveloped Hirad and he roared into the faces of the Black Wings.

From the right, the Black Wings ran in. Hirad snapped his blade to ready, blocked up and swept back low, the keen edge of his blade slicing through ribs and gut. He wrenched it clear and checked his next target.

"Ren, seek the archers," said The Unknown. "Denser, Erienne, offence. We can't afford a shield. Cast whenever you're ready."

Behind them weakened timbers continued to fall, and now the Black Wings came in from three sides.

On The Raven's left the TaiGethen and Rebraal launched a stinging attack. All four had dual short blades drawn and used them to devastating effect, forcing the Black Wings back. Beside The Unknown warrior, Aeb, his axe and longsword whirling, practically struck the head from his first enemy and crashed his sword again and again on the weakening upper defence of the next, eventually breaking through to carve the blade through shoulder and deep into chest.

The Unknown himself fought silently and powerfully, his dagger flicking everywhere, defence that could attack at will. He slashed it across the face of one man, who reacted by bringing his blade up to block the return blow only to catch the Raven warrior's sword in his waist. The Unknown turned it, pulled it clear and kicked the body away.

Hirad had no such pretensions to silence. Looking for a way through to Selik, he bellowed into the faces of those against him, using his sword two-handed, driving his arms to work it through again and again, his muscles beginning to protest. He ignored the pain, leaning in and butting the nose of his nearest enemy before heaving his sword through close to his own body and into the man's ribs. He forced the blade clear, raising it to block the next Black Wing's strike and sweeping immediately down to hack into his leg. The man fell on his dead companion and Hirad chopped down on his neck to finish the job.

Ren's bow thrummed with metronomic regularity, her arrows taking the remaining two archers from the platforms above the gates before getting to work on the men in the middle of the compound.

But, for all their killing, The Raven were being pushed back by sheer weight of numbers. Hirad took a cut across his chest as he leapt away from a clever reverse strike, the blow slicing his armour and drawing blood. He blocked the next away, Darrick next to him taking the man out with a downward stab through the collarbone into the heart.

"We need more effort!" called Hirad. "Where are those spells?"

"Right here," said Denser. "On my signal."

Hirad changed to a one-handed grip, punched into the mouth of the man standing in front of him and kicked him clear.

"Now."

Hirad ducked. The DeathHail surged out, dealing awful damage. Needle- and razor-sharp flecks of ice fired into the faces of the Black Wings, flaying skin from bone, goring into eyes and ripping holes in hands and clothing. In front of Hirad the attack momentarily collapsed. At the same time Erienne dumped more FlameOrbs at the back of the press, and from the far left the ClawBound pair broke free and panic engulfed the edge of the attack.

"Push Raven, now!"

Hirad stormed back into the fight, sensing The Unknown and Darrick on either side. He opened up a huge wound in the side of a man whose face was covered in blood, levered him down and raced on, hacking into the top of a skull, kicking out right and connecting sharply with a groin and ripping his sword clear to bury it in the chest of the next.

He looked left. A blade was coming at him. He raised his guard but there was no need. The Unknown turned the blow aside easily and plunged his dagger into the eye of the Black Wing, where it stuck as the man fell. Aeb thundered on, bleeding from his waist and thigh. His sword sheared that of his opponent, his axe bit through backbone.

"Come on!" shouted Hirad.

Almost too late, he saw a sword flash his way. He swayed instinctively left but it caught him in the side. He felt the edge come through his leather and cut his side, deep but not debilitating. He cried out, clearing his head of the sudden pain, and clamped his right hand on the hilt of his opponent's blade, pushing it clear as he crashed his own down, chopping deep, very deep, into the Black Wing's hip.

Next to him, Darrick slipped two amateur thrusts with embarrassing ease and shuddered his own blade into the neck of his enemy. The Black Wings were down to their last men and it showed. The battle swung conclusively The Raven's way.

Out on the left, the ClawBound pair sank fangs, claws and fingers into exposed flesh. The TaiGethen, movements blurring, rolled, kicked, stabbed and slashed out, driving men in front of them. Hirad took on a raw recruit, saw the fear in his eyes and batted the boy's axe blade aside before skewering his right lung. He coughed blood in a spray and fell back and aside. Hirad's path was clear.

"Selik!" he shouted.

The Black Wing turned and ran back toward the barracks.

"Raven leaving the line!" said Hirad.

"Covered," said The Unknown.

It was all Hirad needed to hear. He tore off after Selik, the cuts to his arms, leg and side pulling and bleeding. He gasped at the sudden pain but didn't let up, leaping up the stairs into the barrack block and kicking the door in.

"Nowhere to run, Selik!"

A door banged up ahead, Hirad shouldered his way through it and saw Selik at the opposite side of the small room, working at a lock and stiff bolt.

"Turn round, Selik," said Hirad.

Selik did so, drawing his sword. They were in an office. A desk and chair were to one side and a bookshelf held various papers. A window let out on to the compound where The Raven and TaiGethen were mopping up the remnants of the Black Wings.

"Brave move, that," said Hirad.

"I felt I couldn't take you all on," replied Selik.

"Well, now it's just me."

Hirad beckoned him on, keeping his blade in his left hand. Selik rushed at him, overarming his sword. Hirad stepped smartly aside. Selik's motion brought him on, his sword cut thin air and Hirad helped him through, shoving him hard in the back and sending him careering into the bookshelf. Selik turned.

"Oops," said Hirad. "Fancy another go?"

Selik was fast, Hirad gave him that. This time he moved in and whipped out a strike left to right at waist height. Hirad stepped back, his sword cracking across Selik's, driving it down to thump into the floor. The barbarian saw his opening, slashing in an upward arc, but Selik saw it coming and swayed back, the breeze of the sword ruffling his hair. Hirad came on again, jabbing straight forward and moving right to dodge the counter-thrust and steady for the next. Selik obliged, a wild swing Hirad took on the up, knocking it aside hard.

Losing control for a heartbeat, Selik reversed half a pace, his sword in no position to defend himself. He tried to bring his defence back in front of him, but overcompensated and Hirad, waiting his moment, struck down two-handed and took Selik's sword hand off just above the wrist. Selik howled in agony and staggered back against the bookshelf, papers cascading over him. He stared down at the bloody stump in disbelief and up into Hirad's eyes.

Hirad's heart was beating so hard he thought Selik must be able to hear it. He stood over the hated man for what seemed like an age.

"I have waited for this for a very long time," he said.

"We will still prevail," managed Selik. "You can't beat us. No one beats the righteous."

"But you won't be there to see it."

With every ounce of strength in him, Hirad swung his sword, severing Selik's neck. The head cartwheeled off, bouncing onto the floor and rolling to rest by the door the Black Wing had been trying to escape through.

"Still no way out," said Hirad.

He turned and ran back through the barracks, bursting into the sunlight, a grim smile on his lips. Their leader was down, the Black Wings were beaten and The Raven and TaiGethen were mopping up the stragglers.

Close to him, Auum dispatched a pair of frightened youths, moving impossibly fast. His left elbow crunched into one's throat, the dagger in his right hand thudding into the other's temple. Hardly pausing, he led his Tai up the steps and past Hirad into the barracks to search for their prize.

Back in the compound, Aeb delivered the final blow, weapons crossed in front of him, axe carving unprotected flesh, sword swiping into helmet, crushing metal into skull. His victim dropped, blood dribbling down his forehead.

It was over.

Hirad leaned heavily on his blade, feeling the exertions of the morning. His body was slick with sweat, he sawed huge breaths into his lungs, the cuts in his sword arm and side stung very badly and every muscle ached.

He looked at The Raven, experiencing none of the elation he was used to after winning a fight. None of them did. Erienne was comforting Ren by Ilkar's charred body while Rebraal looked on, head half bowed. Denser and Darrick shook hands as if they'd played chess not won a game of life and death.

Thraun stood alone, blood dripping from his sword, just staring around him. The ground was stained deep red-brown and here and there severed limbs still clutched swords and axes. Already the birds were circling.

Of The Raven, only Aeb and The Unknown moved, checking bodies. They released the dying from their pain and searched for any without tattoos who could possibly be saved. Hirad pushed himself straight, circled his shoulders and walked toward them.

"I got him," he said, satisfaction crawling through him. "I got that bastard."

The Unknown wiped a hand across his bloodied face, wiping clean a cut across his brow. He nodded.

"He was always going to be yours," he said, and opened his mouth to speak again but shock cascaded across his features.

Both he and Aeb snapped their heads round toward the gates and began backing away.

"Oh dear Gods," said The Unknown. He hefted his sword. "Raven! Raven form up. We've got company!"

"Oh, no," said Hirad, not sure he could swing his sword again. "Who is it?"

They continued backing away toward the barracks, Aeb, The Unknown and Hirad already in the chevron, Darrick limping over to join Hirad and Thraun loping up the other side. The Unknown turned to Hirad.

"Protectors, mages, swordsmen," he said, voice bleak and scared. "Too many of them. And up in the sky, those aren't birds."

Hirad looked up. Now he could hear the chittering, see the shapes. And down they came. Simultaneously, the stockade gates rattled, The Raven twenty yards away from them now.

"Spells coming," said Denser from close behind. "Be ready."

The gates rattled again, bowed toward them and burst inward in a hail of splintered timbers and sheared bolts. Hirad put his arms across his face, feeling the blast hit, wood whip by, dust ripple across him and a sizeable piece of timber thump into the palm of one hand. Daring to open his eyes, he saw dust beginning to settle and the Xeteskians walking calmly in.

"Steady, Raven," he said.

"SpellShield up," said Erienne.

Hirad glanced left and right. Ren and Rebraal both held bows. It would have to do.

Ten Protectors, five on each side, flanked the same number of mages while behind them a dozen soldiers fanned out, three with crossbows aimed and ready. And low over the compound now, Familiars. Laughing and spitting, promising revenge, they circled The Raven.

"Well, what have we here?" said one of the mages, stepping forward. "Balaia's greatest mercenaries, I presume."

"It's all over here, Whytharn," said Denser. "Leave us alone."

"Don't be stupid, Denser," snapped Whytharn, a mage in his mid thirties, tall and powerful, a deep purple skullcap pressed down over his head, leather armour covering his neck and chest. "You know why we're here." He looked around him. "Some mess you made in here."

"And there'll be another one if you don't leave now," grated Hirad. "We're not in the mood."

"Your posturing is ridiculous," said Whytharn. "You are in no position to fight us. I am not under orders to kill, but I am to bring back the statue fragment. Give it to me."

"I'm afraid we can't do that," said The Unknown quietly. "You know why."

Whytharn studied the ground for a moment. "And how are you going to stop me, Sol? I am well aware the Protectors won't fight you but they will protect us. And flying above your heads is plenty enough to kill you all. Don't make this difficult." He clicked his fingers. "Oh, and I almost forgot." He pointed at Aeb, mouthed words in a language Hirad did not understand and dropped his arm to his side.

Denser cursed and clapped his hands to his head.

"Come, Aeb," said Whytharn. "Your place is with me. Step away."

Aeb took a pace from The Raven line. Hirad went cold all over. Beside him, The Unknown seethed, his hands tightening on his sword, his jaws grinding together, his muscles bunching.

"Don't you hurt him," he said.

"I am his Given. My judgement will prevail."

The whole Raven line took the pace that brought them back level with Aeb.

"Don't even think about it," said The Unknown.

Aeb took another step and before they could stop her Ren ran from the edge of the line, took cover behind Aeb's huge frame and drew back her bow string.

"He takes one more step, Xeteskian, and you die."

Everyone started shouting at once.

CHAPTER 50

"Tell her to stand down!"

"Get back, Ren."

"I'm not moving. Hear me, Xeteskian?"

"My men will fire, now get back."

"Keep down, Ren. Keep down."

"Last warning."

"Yours too, mage. He's Raven. You leave him and us alone."

"Aeb. Come."

Even the chittering above them ceased. Silence pressed. Hirad watched, they all did. Whytharn beckoned with a finger, The Unknown leaned forward.

In front of them, Aeb took a long deep breath. He moved.

"No, Ren, no!" shouted Thraun.

Arrows and bolts filled the air. Ren fired, missing Whytharn, the arrow smacking into the mage at his side, clear through the chest. A Familiar dropped from the sky wailing, already dying. A split heartbeat later, Rebraal's arrow punctured the side of a crossbowman's skull, spearing his brain. His bolt flew high and wasted, another thudded into timbers behind The Raven line but the third found its target. Ren was punched from her feet, sprawling backward by Hirad's feet. Her eyes were open but she was fighting for breath, the bolt protruding from her chest just above her sternum.

"They're casting," warned Denser. "Keep that shield."

The barbarian saw red. He growled, his gaze moving quickly up and catching Aeb's. The Protector's eyes narrowed behind his mask, the pair of them looked again at Ren, back to each other and nodded almost imperceptibly.

"Raven!" he screamed. "Take them down!"

In front of him, Aeb put one hand behind his head and ripped the mask from his face.

"Want me, you bastards? Then take me!" He hefted his axe and ran, huge strides eating up the ground.

Chaos.

The Raven surged after him, Hirad at their head, The Unknown by him and Thraun tearing up the ground, an animal bellow on his lips. Aeb swung down, his axe hammering through Whytharn's stunned body, dead before he could begin to loose a spell. Hirad drove in beside him, taking a casting mage apart at the shoulder, the arm flying into the air, spraying blood into the barbarian's face, his own pain and exhaustion a dim memory as he piled in.

Soldiers fought to get through their own line of mages to protect them, the Protectors standing confused until their minds were made up for them. At the back of the group a mage invoked soul punishment and Aeb crashed to the ground, the sounds from his mouth alien as he gibbered for mercy, his hands clamped to the side of his face.

"Get that mage!" yelled The Unknown, delivering a blow that took the sword and face of a soldier with it, his other hand punching and shoving his way through the mêlée. "Release that punishment. Now!"

A bow thrummed, Rebraal's next arrow another killing shot, and, with Aeb still crawling in agony in the dust, the Protectors turned on their masters. In a single move they spun and struck, axes hacking great splits in skulls, rising to spread gore and falling again. The Xeteskians fell back immediately, but there was no escape.

A Familiar landed hard on the back of Hirad's head, clawed hands raking across his scalp. The barbarian reached round and grabbed the creature while he fended off a soldier in front who looked to gain from his distraction. He slapped the blade aside, clouted his hilt into the soldier's nose and knocked him cold. Finding purchase on the Familiar's neck, he tore it from his head and brought it in front of him, clumps of his hair in its hands, its slathering mouth snapping at his face. He tightened his grip, the Familiar's tail whipping round and stabbing into his arm. He grunted in pain and looked for the Familiar's mage.

"This yours, Xetesk man?"

The Unknown had cleared a path, beating his sword into the back of a soldier, and Hirad pushed ahead, keeping his grip on the Familiar and dashing its skull again and again into the mage's face, the man trying to fend him off, the Familiar screeching its hate.

"Is it?" he said as he piled the demon in again. "Is it?"

The mage went down, face a mask of blood, Thraun's sword crushing his ribs. The Familiar went limp, its strength disappearing.

"Good guess," said Hirad, and dropped its dying body to the ground.

He looked left. Thraun was a man possessed. He caught the sword arm of a soldier, forced it back and stepped forward, jamming his blade into the man's stomach. Trampling over him, he overheaded his weapon into a mage's collarbone, slicing through into his chest, pushed the dead man away and went searching for more.

All around the Protectors fought silently, never once giving an opening, showing no mercy to their Given. Axes rose and fell, masks were smeared with blood, brain and dust. Eyes stared brooding through eye slits and mouths moved wordlessly.

But still Aeb cried out. The Unknown smashed his blade across the legs of the last defending soldier and bore down on the mage holding the punishment.

"Release him," he grated, pommel of his sword raised to crush. "Do it now."

"Too late, Unknown. Or didn't they tell you? Once invoked, it can't be stopped. There is only death."

"Right," said The Unknown. He brought the pommel down and dashed open the mage's skull, swinging round immediately to run to the heaving Aeb.

Foam flecked his mouth, his legs thrashed, his back arched and his fists beat the sides of his chest. His eyes were bulging and wild, the demons ripping his mind to shreds from inside, his soul in torment in the Tank. But even in the hell of his consciousness he locked gaze with The Unknown and Hirad heard one word gasped out.

"Please."

The Unknown nodded, drew a dagger from his belt and stabbed quickly into Aeb's temple. The Protector, at peace, lay still.

Quiet reined again.

Hirad sat down among the corpses, his hands draped over his knees, his body spent. He could feel blood oozing through his hair and dripping from his right hand to the ground but he ignored it.

The Unknown threw the dagger down by Aeb's body, stood, grabbed his sword from the ground and walked away toward the barracks. Hirad followed him with his eyes, hearing a soft sobbing. Erienne was kneeling over Ren, her body crushed in Denser's embrace, her shoulders hunched and jerking as she cried. Standing by them was Darrick, the bodies of three Xeteskian soldiers at his feet. Hirad hadn't even realised they'd broken through. Thank the Gods for the General or they might have lost all their mages in a day.

Hirad sighed and looked up. Thraun held out a hand. Hirad took it and pulled himself to his feet. With his sword dragging over the compound dirt, he forced himself after The Unknown, who was walking slowly toward Ilkar's body.

"This is a black day for The Raven," said Hirad.

"But we have the thumb," said Thraun. He pointed to the barracks. Auum was walking through the doorway, the prize in his grateful hands. Duele and Evunn came after him, pushing a man in front of them.

Yron.

Hirad started to move more quickly, a new target for his hate right before him. The Unknown stepped in his way.

"Leave it," he said, his face full of sorrow, his voice shorn of its usual power.

"He killed Ilkar," said Hirad.

Thraun growled deep in his throat.

"Yes," said The Unknown. "But Auum will deal with him. He can dispense elven justice on Yron."

The Raven trio walked toward him nonetheless. Yron focussed on them, his eyes still adjusting to the brightness.

"Sorry the TaiGethen didn't join you in the fight," he said. "What they had was more important than risking themselves against Xetesk."

The Unknown nodded. "Why did you do it?"

"I didn't know," said Yron. "If I'd realised that . . . souvenir would have caused so much death, I'd never have done it."

"Ilkar is dead because of you," said Hirad. "Ilkar."

Yron sighed. "Nothing I can say will help. But believe me I had no knowledge this would happen. That's why I was trying to return it."

"You should die for this."

"I am going to, Hirad. That's why I'm out here."

The elves gathered to offer prayers. The ClawBound pair padded out of the barracks and Auum opened his eyes and waved The Raven away from Yron. The Xeteskian mouthed an apology then knelt on the ground, Auum's hand pushing him down.

The TaiGethen spoke a few words, stepped aside and bowed his head. The panther padded up to Yron's back, placed her paws on his shoulders and bit down into his neck, breaking it and killing him instantly.

"We have our own rituals to observe," said The Unknown.

He, Hirad and Thraun joined Rebraal at Ilkar's body.

There was precious little left of him. His clothes were burned away and his body twisted and scorched. But when Rebraal turned him over they could see his features, saved because he had landed facedown in the slightly damp mud under the parapet. He looked peaceful enough; his oval eyes were closed and his cheekbones still carried a hint of redness though his lips were drained of colour.

"Oh, Ilkar," said Hirad, reaching out to stroke his face. "Saved us, didn't he? I just wish he knew it. What am I going to do without you?"

Hirad tried to picture Ilkar alive and a startling vision of the elf's beaming face as they talked entered his mind. He started and sucked in a quick breath.

"We should prepare for the Vigil," he said. "There must be a shovel here somewhere. We'll bury him out in the countryside somewhere. I'm not having him left where Selik has been." He took another look at his friend. "Goodbye, Ilks. Oh, no."

And he started to cry. He couldn't help himself. He shook his head as the tears came and he backed away, standing and facing The Unknown.

"What are we going to do, Unknown?"

"All the things we promised. Raise the Heart of Julatsa, free the Protectors, send the Kaan home. He wanted that as much as any of us." The Unknown put his bloodstained hands on Hirad's shoulders. "Come on, stop the tears. You know he'd only have laughed at you for it."

Hirad spluttered and rubbed a bloodied hand across his eyes. "Yeah, he would at that. Tell you what, Unknown, I'm absolutely knackered. And I could do with a bandage."

"That's more like it."

Avesh couldn't move anything. Every breath was shallow, his mouth blowing bloodied bubbles. He lay on his back, life pumping from the wound in his side to puddle beneath him. He'd been staring at the sky while they fought around him, watching the billows of smoke blow across the dawning blue. It was going to be a very pleasant day. He'd so love to have shared it with Ellin.

Two of them were near him. He couldn't see but he could hear them.

"This is all so wrong, Unknown," said one. Avesh had recognised him. Hirad Coldheart. A man he admired as he did all of The Raven. He had been so disappointed to see them ranged against the Black Wings. He thought they'd have seen the light. The righteous path, Selik had called it. But then one of them had borne the child who started it all so perhaps he shouldn't have been surprised. It was so confusing. He couldn't get his mind to work properly.

"I know," replied the other, The Unknown Warrior, a giant in folklore and no less in reality.

"Look at them. All these dead farmers. Our fight was never with them. What happened to them all?"

"Selik is a very persuasive man," said The Unknown.

"Was," replied Hirad. "His head bouncing off the floor is the only good memory I'll take from here."

Avesh coughed and the pain surged through his body. He convulsed.

"Gods, there's one still alive here!" Hirad again.

Avesh heard quick paces and the barbarian himself leaned over him. He felt a hand tracing down the side of his neck.

"He's no Black Wing," said Hirad. "Can we save him?"

Hope quickened Avesh's heart and his severed nerves howled in protest.

"No," said The Unknown, moving through the periphery of his vision. "Look at that wound. I'm amazed he's still alive."

Hirad knelt by his head and Avesh felt a hand gently smooth down his hair. He tried to speak but all he succeeded in doing was coughing more blood onto the soaked earth on which he lay.

"Shh," said Hirad. "Don't talk. Lie still."

"C'mon, Hirad," said The Unknown Warrior.

"No," said Hirad. "The least we can do is be with him. It won't be long." The barbarian appeared in his vision again, a frown on his weathered face, eyes betraying grief barely held in check. "Why did you do it?" he said. "You were fighting the people trying to help you. If magic dies, this land dies. Didn't you understand? All we want is Balaia returned to peace with its magic a force for the good of all. Has so much really changed in so few years? How was your memory so short?"

Avesh opened his mouth but the words wouldn't come.

"I'm sorry for your pain but I couldn't let you get in my way," said Hirad. "You're a fool, you know that? Blinded from the truth by a madman."

Avesh felt tears in his eyes. He nodded. At the last he understood. It was all so simple. If only The Raven had ridden into the camp and not the Black Wings he'd be with Ellin still. Ellin. I'm so sorry. Please forgive me.

"You're a good man," said Hirad. "It's in your eyes. I hope you have people waiting for you."

Avesh smiled and nodded again. Atyo. He'd be seeing Atyo. In fact, he thought he could hear his son calling him.

Hirad let The Unknown drag him to his feet and the two men stood over the dead man for a moment.

"That was good of you, Hirad."

"I killed him, Unknown. He never stood a chance. He was just a farmer."

Hirad let his gaze rove over the compound again. The elves stood in silent respect; Denser, Erienne and Darrick were sharing a water skin and the Protectors had picked up Aeb's mask and were mustered near the door.

"What about them, Unknown?"

"I'll speak to them before they go but what they'll face I just don't know. They're so vulnerable but the scale of their rebellion might even save them for now. Dystran can't afford to kill them all. He'd lose the war."

War. Hirad raised his eyebrows. He'd forgotten there was one. And just now he didn't care who won. All he knew was that The Raven had lost too much for one day. For any day.

"I'll see you back at the campsite," he said to The Unknown. "Come on, Thraun, there's Raven we need to carry to the Vigil."

It was night and the TaiGethen had begun their walk back to Blackthorne and the *Calaian Sun*. Rebraal had stayed with The Raven. They'd found candles in Understone and four stood about the freshly turned earth of each grave, representing the points of the compass. It was time for the Vigil, one that Hirad had never thought he'd face.

The Unknown stood by Aeb, Erienne by Ren and Hirad by Ilkar. The barbarian nodded to the big man and he spoke for all of them.

"By north, by east, by south, by west. Though you are gone, you will always be Raven and we shall always remember. The Gods will smile on your souls. Farewell in whatever faces you now and ever. The Raven will ride together again one day."

As he spoke each point, candles were snuffed until darkness covered them all.

The Raven did not move from the graves until dawn cracked the sky, but after the silence they talked, though Darrick and Thraun contributed little. They recalled battles and arguments. They cried and laughed together, they speculated on who would be next. It lightened their hearts and their spirits just a little.

"You never really got on with Ren, did you, Hirad?" said Erienne.

"Ilkar loved her and that was enough for me," said Hirad. "Let's face it, we'd none of us ever seen him so happy."

"Evasion, surely?" accused Denser. "You can do better than that."

"All right, all right." Hirad held up his hands. "I'll admit she had her faults as far as The Raven was concerned. She was a brilliant archer, the best we ever had, but she was so impetuous. Look what she did at the temple." He paused. "And look what she did yesterday."

The Unknown nodded. "But we'd have taught her. And what she did was extraordinary. Proved she was Raven. Prepared to give her life for one of us without question. That's why I honour her."

"I'll drink to that," said Hirad. "As soon as we get to Blackthorne, anyway."

"I'll miss the arguments, you know," said Denser. "I loved listening to you two."

"You're not so bad at it yourself," said Hirad. "And don't worry, I'll switch to you now. Got to have someone to poke fun at."

"You mean you haven't started yet?" asked Denser.

"Oh, my dear Denser," said The Unknown. "There were ten years before you even joined. You don't know the half of it. He hasn't even begun to scratch the surface."

The sky was lightening. The new day was coming. It would be a day without Ilkar, and for Hirad that was something awful to contemplate. But in his death he'd given hope to every living elf, and that was something that burned in Hirad's heart with an intensity that would never wane.

He stood up, brushed himself down and turned to The Raven.

"Come on, it's getting light. Time to leave our friends to rest a while."

He knelt and patted the earth of Ilkar's grave. "See you, Ilks, but got to go.

"It's a long way to Calaius and we've got work to do."

EPILOGUE

Erienne knelt before the statue of Yniss and its shattered hand that the Al-Arynaar had reattached but did not have the magic to bind.

Are you there? she asked.

Yes, Erienne, said Cleress. *Before we start, tell us how you felt in the stockade at Understone. You used the One.*

Were you with me?

Of course, but only to help you should you falter. We cannot afford to lose you. But you learned the essence of it all. Casting reflects desire. You wanted The Raven to have time to talk, and you gave it to them. You will be able to achieve almost anything but this strength is also the curse. Go further than the power of your mind and the One will swamp you, kill you. This is the limitation you must understand before we can withdraw from you.

I didn't feel in control.

You were not, said Myriell. *Not entirely. It will become more natural as you begin to understand how it feels.*

Erienne shook her head. *No more now. Elves die as we speak. What must I do?*

We will guide you, said Cleress. *You must open yourself to the One, let us feel what you feel.*

I'm just a conduit, right?

You are far more than that, said Myriell, her voice weak and distant. *But for this binding, yes, you can put it that way.*

What should I do?

Just place both hands on the statue. One on the thumb and one on the fracture at the wrist. Then delve down into the entity and feel us there with you.

Erienne placed her hands where she was asked and closed her eyes, tuning her mind to the mana spectrum. She dived deep within herself, down to the hated pulsating mass in her mind that was the One. She hovered above it for a moment, then plunged in.

The energy that stormed through her body was as overwhelming as it was beautiful. It took her breath away, stopped her heart and stole the strength from her limbs. But still she lived, still the blood raced through her veins and her grip on the statue was secure.

She felt uplifted and everything around her was so clear and pure. The water in the pool next to her, Auum and Rebraal standing near her, their bodies taut with tension, their minds so complex, so dark and yet so fundamentally good. She pushed outward and everything was in focus. She could feel the beating heart of a bird in a nearby tree, she could feel the roots of the tree itself, growing down as they sought nourishment. She could feel a panther and its partner outside the temple, their bond closer than mother and unborn child, and she could feel The Raven, strong but bowed by grief, waiting for her. Waiting and hoping she could do what she was asked.

This may be painful for you, said Myriell. *I am sorry if it is so.*

Do what you must. I am ready.

Very well.

The sound of their voices grew in her mind and at once the tendrils of the One started to move together. The language was ancient and elvish but power reverberated in every syllable. They were forging a shape like a cast. It was huge and rotated, dragging the essence of the One from the entity inside her, melding it to what they had already built.

And then came the pain. From the tips of her toes to the top of her scalp, every nerve came alive and shrieked. The raw spirit of the One was surging through her, only kept in check by the strength of the Al-Drechar's minds. The tendrils fattened to great twining ropes feeding into the structure that blossomed as it grew.

She knew she was juddering with the force of it all; her eyes and mouth flew open, spittle rolled over her chin and she heard a low wail that she didn't realise at first was coming from her. The voices grew so loud in her head she feared she would pass out but the One kept her upright; it wouldn't let her go.

The marble of the wrist, hand and thumb was moving, moulding and shaping. Like ants crawling on the forest floor, it shifted over itself, knitting together, the movement seething upward, the stone feeling alive beneath her fingers. It pulsed and writhed, every shard moved to its place, every nick was covered and every crack smoothed away.

Her eyesight began to fade as the sound of the Al-Drechar's voices dropped to a low bass. The floor under her began to vibrate, water in the pool splashed, dust filtered down from above, settling on her arms and head. She saw the sheath of mana pass over the hand, up the arm and then across Yniss's body. And as it did, her body quivered, every muscle in minute spasm, her nerves still alive and open, her pain quite without peer.

Yet beneath the agony she felt the purity of the force, the completeness of the One. She caught a glimpse of the world with the One as its keeper. It was the harmony. It was Yniss on earth. It was wonderful.

Outside, The Raven waited nervously. The Al-Arynaar had closed the temple door, and even when Erienne began to wail they would not move. All Denser could do was pace.

Hirad stood with The Unknown as time dragged on, still feeling the bitter taste of fresh grief in his mind.

"All this death and we achieved none of the things we left Herendeneth to do."

"Wouldn't have been anywhere else though, would you?" said The Unknown.

"No, I suppose not." Hirad scuffed at the ground with his feet. "You know, I'm starting to believe in destiny. For The Raven, that is."

"How do you figure that?"

Hirad shrugged. "Just look at the facts. Everything major that's happened has involved us right at its core. It's like we were supposed to be there when Denser found Dawnthief. Supposed to be there when the rip was torn in the sky. And the rebirth of the One magic? Could have happened to any two mages, potentially, but it didn't. It happened to Erienne and Denser. And now this. If we'd come here ten days earlier, we'd have known nothing about Elfsorrow until Ilkar caught it. But we were here. And we could help."

"Up to a point," said The Unknown grimly. "So what's next? Not a quiet retirement."

"No," said Hirad. "Aside from finishing what Ilkar started by coming here, there's the little matter of a college war going on. Reckon you're up for that? See, if it goes the wrong way before we're ready, there are things won't get done."

"Ah. Well, I reckon I could stir myself," said The Unknown. "For a good cause or two."

The door of the temple opened and Erienne emerged. Auum and Rebraal supporting her on either side, they led her over to Denser, kissing her cheeks before draping her in his arms. Across the stone apron, elves were offering prayers of thanks, their faces uplifted, light in their eyes, the haunting fear of imminent death removed.

"I take it this was a success."

Rebraal nodded. "Yniss is rebound. He will bless us once again. Can you not feel it? The harmony is growing again. It embraces us all."

"And how do you feel, Erienne?" asked Denser, crushing his wife to him and stroking her back with his hands. "How does it feel to have saved the elven race?"

"Tiring," said Erienne. "I think I need to lie down."

Auum moved in front of Hirad and bowed his head, speaking a few words.

"He is thanking you for all you have done. He salutes you and grieves for your loss. Among the TaiGethen and Al-Arynaar, you will always be welcome."

"It's what we do," said Hirad.

"I'm sorry we mistrusted you," said Rebraal. "I hope you will let us travel back to Balaia with you, to carry on the fight."

"I was counting on it."

Rebraal smiled.

"I'd give it all up to have him standing here," said Hirad.

"Would it help if I told you that in death he saved all of this majesty for every elf ever born from now on?"

It was a different take to his own but a good one. Ilkar, father of the elves. Hirad smiled. He rather liked the sound of that.

ABOUT THE AUTHOR

JAMES BARCLAY is in his forties and lives in Teddington in the UK with his wife and son. He is a full-time writer. Visit him online at www.james barclay.com.